About

Beverley enjoys life to the full and spends time improving her home and garden. She has numerous hobbies and loves animals, wishing she could do more to care for those mistreated and unloved. She also cares about charities which support women trapped in abusive relationships or are the victims of rape. During her life she has taught at Kindergarten level and lectured to Sixth-form students. She has worked for solicitors and in the haulage industry at an administration and clerical level, meeting a wide range of people from all walks of life. She enjoys travel especially to Greece. She has always enjoyed writing. This is her first novel.

Bed Of Roses

Beverley Cooper

Published by Cordelia Publishing Ltd in 2015

Copyright © Beverley Cooper 2015

Second Edition

The author asserts the moral right under the Copyright, Design and Patents Act 1988 to be identified as the author of this work.

All names, characters, businesses, events and incidents are the product of the author's imagination. Real places are used in a fictitious manner. Any resemblance whatsoever to actual persons, living or dead, is purely coincidental.

All rights reserved. No part of this publication may be reproduced, stored in a retrieval system or transmitted in any form or by any means without the prior consent of the author, not be otherwise circulated in any form of binding or cover other than that in which it is published and without a similar condition being imposed on a subsequent purchaser.

www.cordeliapublishing.co.uk

Cordelia Publishing Ltd

And he repents in thorns that sleeps in beds of roses
Francis Quarles, Poet 1592 – 1644

A mighty pain to love it is
And 'tis a pain that pain to miss
But of all pains, the greatest pain
It is to love, but love in vain.
Abraham Cowley
English Poet
1618 – 1667

Seduce: verb **1** entice into sexual activity. **2** beguile into a desired state or position. **3** persuade to do something unwise. From the Mediaeval Latin: seducere – to lead astray…

'You wanted to do it. This is work, Rose. And what they do.'

Prologue

London 1959

When they (Elizabeth, George, Valerie and he) had left the Balmoy Hotel quite merry, Valerie was completely soused as usual.

Once home and after two coffees, he'd brought out the chilled champagne, the tacit signal for their foreplay.

She was abandoned and beautiful, wild and desirable when under the influence, he thought. Drink didn't make her raddled or irritable – she wanted sex: sex, sex and more sex and was hungry just for him. It certainly wasn't new, so he wasn't bothered when she'd requested the cling film treatment – he had fetched the roll kept for the purpose, while she'd stripped and lain down on the sitting-room floor, sipping the ice-cold sparkling wine and shivering in anticipation.

Slowly, unravelling the tube, he'd progressed up her body, rolling her over as necessary, until reaching the tops of her shoulders he'd prepared to stop.

She'd insisted then he continued – taking it up and over her head until she was as a shiny female chrysalis. She'd lain there trusting him as with a pointed, sharp knife he carefully made a slit above her lips so she could breathe. Making two more little incisions above her nipples, he surveyed her approvingly as they stood out, dark and erect. That had done it for him. Tearing his clothes off and dropping them on the floor, he'd begun carefully cutting away an area at the tops of her legs with nail scissors. She'd called, indicating as best she could that she wanted him in her mouth.

This was innovation and he was all for that. It was incredibly stimulating, both visually and physically, her eyes wide and encouraging. He lurched forward, covering her face and crying out, the sensation was incredible. She moaned, moving her head from side to side, which felt wonderful and he hoped she was reaching a climax too. Then suddenly her teeth clamped painfully. Instinctively he grabbed her jaws which released as she choked violently. Her face was red, her eyes wide and watering. Quickly extracting himself and ignoring the searing pain he stared in horror, but then there wasn't anything, no movement at all.

'Valerie, *Valerie!*' He cried stupidly, 'come on darling, wake up, wake up!' Quickly, he peeled away at the messy, torn strips of cling film, wiped her chin and felt for a pulse. It was there, very weak, then stopped. A string of film had somehow become twisted tightly around her neck. Scouring the room for something to cut it with, he spotted the pair of nail scissors. Carefully slipping one little pointed blade underneath, he snipped. There was no red mark, it hadn't been tight enough to strangle her, but her breathing had stopped. He began the kiss of life, counting and repeating – nothing: all over in one evening.

His watch showed half past two in the morning. In six hours' time he was due at his practice in Harley Street. Serena Montague-Gower was arriving at nine with a cyst. Rhoda would make some coffee and offer a magazine, make small-talk for a while, but he'd *have* to get there.

He picked up the phone; it rang twice before a slurred and irritable voice answered.

'Hello? Rhoda here, who is it?'

He was quiet but urgent.

'Rhoda, I'm sorry, it's Douglas. There's been an accident and Valerie's dead.' He bit his lip, hardly believing it. 'I've killed her, but it was an *accident!*' Panic was escalating inside him, despite efforts to remain calm and in control. 'It needs to appear she died from too much alcohol, can you get here,' his voice rising, '*please?*'

Rhoda peered blearily at her bedside clock. It was nearly three. What the hell had they been up to and what a time to call!

Prodding around for her glasses, she replied, 'I'll be there as soon as I can. Leave calling the ambulance 'till I'm there, don't fiddle with *anything* until I get there.'

The line went dead. He slumped back in relief and waited.

Grumbling, she dragged herself out of bed and pulled on some clothes. It was warm outside. She shut the front door quietly and started the car.

* * *

Douglas owed her a lot: she was only twenty (to his thirty-two) but had overseen the whole thing from beginning to end – the police, the coroner, the pestering, nosy press and anyone else who'd tried to unravel the scandal to get to the bottom of it all. Hardest to deal with were the patients with whom he'd been conducting affairs, who were familiar with his sexual predilections. Being a gynaecologist had suited him down to the ground and he knew his patients: those he could trust and those he couldn't.

Jealousy was a wild card though and the stakes were high – some might have felt they had an axe to grind. He had a lot to lose. He'd provided an abortion service where necessary – and it *had* been on more than a few occasions. He'd provided also, with the not inconsiderable aid of Rhoda, women for gentlemen who desired a bit of upper-class skirt. Sex as a purely male preserve was a myth. Plenty of women were more than happy to be 'serviced' discreetly by men who were more exciting than their pedantic, boring, but rich husbands. It was a lucrative little sideline in an already well-paid profession, but now Rhoda had, as she let him know in no uncertain manner, acted far beyond the call of duty, which wasn't going to come cheap.

It didn't, so now they had a little 'arrangement,' which had saved his career and reputation and Rhoda was happy. A club was opening in Soho, a private club catering for the more adventurous-minded people, tentatively surfacing in the early dawn of a new and liberated sexual era. It was small and discreet, in a basement premises off Brewer Street. Douglas had a vision. He could sense which way the wind was blowing. The mores of the 'Balmoy set' would fast become outmoded and a sexual revolution (the like of which even he couldn't have envisaged completely) would engulf society and change its attitude forever.

Jed Zeitermann, at twenty-two, was a rich, innovative high-flyer, with an eye to a fortune, and keen to take the club on. His wife Ivana had told Douglas all about his enthusiasm and ideas while he'd been examining her and they'd all met up soon after and talked business. Douglas's reputation as a gynaecologist was good; he needed to keep his nose clean, but was very keen to keep his vision alive. Rhoda now kept him abreast of developments and became a paid go-between, slipping discreetly into a clerical position there, whilst maintaining her 'day job'. It involved a tidy sum, but secured Douglas against the true facts behind Valerie's death emerging in all their murky glory, plus he had a channel to a club which served his sexual preferences to perfection. Just as long as Rhoda stayed on board (and if that meant sleeping with her occasionally too, he would do it) everything would be fine.

1

'Try telling it as a story then, Stella, if that might help. You mentioned a Rose; can you pretend she's a character? Where did it all start; how did it begin?'

Looking at her counsellor she thought for a minute before hesitantly, she began...

Spring 1994
Little Denton, Dreightonshire.

Douglas felt for the telephone ringing beside his bed. 'Hello?'

'Hello Douglas, it's me. Did you get my card? I hope you're feeling better.'

It was Stella! He shot up from his slouching position, pushed back his lanky hair and felt his face – he needed a shave and a wash, he felt hot and sticky.

'It's hanging on a bit, I can't seem to shake it off,' he said, 'I got your card, thanks very much. That was very sweet of you!' he added. It was in a pile of papers somewhere on his desk downstairs: two little birds and 'Thinking of you.' He'd been surprised by it and quite touched.

'I thought you might like it,' she chirped, 'but anyway, the reason I'm calling is to ask if whether when you *do* feel better, you'd like to come round here for dinner. I've asked Clive and Martha,' she added carefully, in case he thought the invitation was for him alone, 'I thought it might be something to look forward to, you know, when you feel a bit more like yourself again.' She felt bold. This was the crunch. 'Would you like to?'

This was getting better! He still felt like death, but definitely fancied the sound of that.

'Well that's very kind of you, what date did you pro*pose?*'

Stella listened, she hadn't noticed it before, he emphasised the end of a sentence. It was un*ique*. Flicking through the pages in her diary, she found the spot.

'Tuesday the fourth of May was acceptable to the others,' she offered hopefully, 'if that's all right with you?'

'Right, I'll have a look, just a minute.' He rested the receiver and stretched across to open the drawer in his bedside table, ferreting for his month-at-a-glance for May. Tuesday the fourth was blank. Good.

'Hello? Yes, that looks all right. I'd be delighted to come. So…' he asked quietly, 'what time would you *like* me?'

Did he *know* he was doing it, she wondered? It was fascinating – she wondered where he'd got it from. It was a cultured voice but unlike any she'd heard before. She quite liked it.

'Oh, say seven thirty for eight o'clock? Would that suit you?' *Be casual and nonchalant. Ignore the emphasis. It's something you have to get used to…*

'That would be *fine!*' He smiled. 'Would you like me to bring some wine along, red, white?' No inflection.

'Oh that would be nice, thanks. We're having beef, so some red perhaps? I'll leave it to you. I'll look forward to seeing you on the fourth then. I hope you'll feel better soon. Wake up one morning and feel completely recovered.'

He grinned, things *were* looking up.

'I can't wait for that! Well *thank* you Stella, I'll look forward to it *very* much. *Bye!*'

Did anyone *else* notice it? She'd better be careful; she could imitate very well and had better guard against it. Anyway, *that* was done, now for Clive. She suspected what he'd think. Clive was sitting patiently in his car in the car park of the Royal Oak hotel, waiting for Martha to finish her Pilates class. The windows of the exercise studio were frosted glass. Indistinct forms were moving around, one of which was Martha. She fancied herself in Lycra and he had to admit that for her age, she didn't look as bad as some of them did with their great bulging behinds. Stella hadn't got a bulging behind, she was absolutely perfect. Speaking of angels, his mobile vibrated in his pocket – he answered, keeping one eye on the hotel.

'Hello? Stella?'

'Clive, the supper on May the fourth,' she began, 'I've invited you and Martha?'

'You have; yes?'

She was upbeat, brisk. 'Well, I've just rung Douglas and he's coming as well now, so there'll be four of us. It's better like that, don't you think?' *No he won't think.*

He didn't.

'*Stella*, I can't *stand* him!' he moaned, 'He's a total prat, a stuck-up, pompous prat. If you've *got* to make a four,' he reasoned, 'why don't you ask one of your girlfriends?' He was irritated.

She paused, in a quandary. He was right, so why hadn't she?

'Look, it's too late now and I know how you feel, but the reason I *did* it,' her tone coaxing, 'was so it wouldn't appear to Martha that the meal was so you and I could be together. Don't you see?' (A bit of quick thinking, *but whom was she trying to kid? Wasn't it a little because she wanted the other man there?*)

He understood, but was Martha *really* going to think that? Why should she?

'Well I don't like the idea, but you never know.' He turned his head and watched from the window as Martha honed in view, chatting to someone, a man, while flinging her jersey over her shoulders and looking quite animated. He wondered who he was. 'You never know,' he continued hopefully, 'she might even *like* him then we could pair them off!'

She was still nattering away cheerfully.

'I can just see her with him, just her type, more than can be said for me!' He gave a rueful snort.

'Anyway, she's coming now, so better go. Chat to you later?'

He scrambled out of the car, juggling the phone, taking Martha's sports bag and slinging it on the back seat while she climbed into the front. The man had wandered off.

Stella frowned. Too much was going round in her head. She didn't want to be tied down to further conversations later.

'If I'm around I will, 'bye.'

Ending the call, she sat pondering why she *had* invited Douglas, she'd noticed him around and had chatted to him at an official lunch a while ago but apart from that she hardly knew him. He was the sort of man, she'd decided, who would seek the services of an escort. There was something faintly sleazy about him, but in a sophisticated, man-of-the-world sort of way.

He had charisma. Not the eau-de-toilette version – if there was such a thing – but the concentrate. He was 'aware' of himself in the way that *she* was. To see him was to recognize something potentially addictive: a drug, casually enough imbibed to begin with maybe, but with the kick and inevitable dependency of cocaine.

It wasn't as if she didn't *try* when lovemaking with Clive, but the chemistry just wasn't there – no violins and the earth refusing to tremble let alone actually move, but he was 'kind' and that was rare enough these days; kind and considerate. She could honestly say she *liked* him, making it plain she did. It was the best there was on offer at the moment. He was a 'bird in the hand'.

* * *

During the week Stella usually worked in her shop, 'Nothing to Wear'. The name originated because in reality, she possessed *so much* to wear it was daft, yet whenever a new event or function presented itself, the invariable cry went up: 'I've nothing to wear'!

Noticing one or two dress agencies popping up in the vicinity (there was one in Wellingborough) Stella rented old Co-op premises in Great Denton, near to where she lived. With a loan from the bank, she and her best friend Cindy, who shared her interest – or obsession – with clothes, began business.

They'd decorated, set up shelves, found mannequins for the double fronted window displays and it was now thriving, with two part-time assistants. This Tuesday however, the fourth of May, Stella took the day off to prepare for that evening's supper, Cindy providing cover as long as she heard all about it the next day.

'Hi, is there anyone at home? Is that you Stella?'

Arriving to clean at nine o'clock, Cathy was surprised she was still there.

'Hi Cathy…it's okay, I've invited Clive and Martha and Douglas Spencer to supper tonight, I'm taking the day off to get ready.'

She heard her bustling around upstairs, '…prepare the pudding, find some flowers, get out the garden furniture and then try to relax!' she laughed.

'Okay we'll work round each other and chat at the same time. It's nice to see you anyway, makes a change. Oops, look out!'

A scrabble and a bark announced Jeeves, Stella's terrier mongrel, 'Come here you!'

Cathy picked up a mop and dangled the end, encouraging him to tug until at the sound of Stella rattling his lead, he dropped it and sat still.

'I'll let you get on with it while I take him for a walk and fetch a bit of shopping. Do you think you could start with the dining room? Then I can set the table when I come back. I shan't be too long. And help yourself to a coffee,' she added breezily.

Cathy donned an apron and got stuck in. 'It's quite warm out, should be a lovely evening for you!' she called. 'I'll see you later, bye Jeeves!'

Emerging from Morrison's, there was a text from Clive: 'Do NOT ask Douglas to stay after the meal. I shall be watching you like a hawk. I mean it. He must leave when we do, OK!'

Her immediate reaction was *no*, this was definitely *not* 'OK'! She'd ask him to stay on now however tired she felt. This wasn't on. So she barely *knew* Douglas, well here was an opportunity to get to know him. Clive was about to learn she wasn't in his pocket. She'd do as she wished.

She pressed 'delete', then dropping it back into her bag, whisked Jeeves back to the car, determined.

'I'm off now, Stella!' Cathy had finished, calling upstairs. 'Good luck with the meal tonight as well,' she added.

'Thanks Cathy! Everywhere looks lovely!' she called distractedly. 'But just before you go –' She descended the stairs and walked through to the kitchen. 'What do you think of this?' holding up an embroidered green evening outfit.

Cathy had no doubts. 'I love it. Great colour and really unusual; I think maybe you could just fix your hair up a bit perhaps, like this?' She lifted her hair to demonstrate. 'Just casually I think, with bits hanging down – very sexy. Tell me all about it next week!' She continued down the steps then hovered uneasily. 'Did you say you'd asked Douglas Spencer as well?'

Stella hugged the clothes to her.

'Yes; do you know him then? Why do you ask?'

'Well I think I know who you *mean*,' she answered cautiously. 'I've seen him at that market they have over at Great Denton where my friend's got a stall. He goes there most weeks I think. She thinks he's a bit on the creepy side, he's got a large black Aston Martin, did you know that?' Her eyes widened. 'He can't be poor!' She frowned, levelling with her now, curious. 'Do you *fancy* him then Stella? Does *Clive* know?'

Leaning against the door frame, Stella tucked a stray strand of hair behind her ear (a nervous gesture Cathy recognised) and considered.

'I think I *could* fancy him y'know,' she glanced down, avoiding Cathy's inquisitive eye, 'although he's a *bit* older than other men I've been out with.'

She fiddled with her nails. 'Something about him attracted me, I suppose,' continuing airily, 'I told Clive he was coming because I wanted it to be a four, to even it up for Martha's sake.' She looked up, blushing.

Cathy looked at her, not quite believing this either.

'Yeah *right*, for *Martha*! *Sure* you did, Stella!'

'I *did*!' She was irked by this remark. 'But then I had a text to say I wasn't to invite him, Douglas, he meant, to stay on after the meal, after he and Martha had gone.'

'Well he *could* have a point, he does like you himself, doesn't he?' she said quietly.

A twinge of guilt made her defensive. 'Well whatever! I'll invite him to stay and offer a…oh I don't know.' She shot her hands up, '…a brandy or something!'

She peered at a hook on the opposite wall.

'After all, it's up to *me* what I do and who I invite. But the silly thing is,' She now looked straight at Cathy, 'that if he hadn't said anything at all, I'd have probably left it. It was that text – that he'd be "watching me like a hawk." I *will* now!'

'Clive really *loves* you though, Stella!' Cathy persisted. 'Martha's horrible to him, uses him like a taxi service. She's always picking on him for something. I don't know.' She rubbed her neck. 'Don't be mean to him or hurt him, *I* think he's sweet really. I don't think I'd trust Spencer though.' She screwed a grimaced, altering her tone. 'I don't know what it is, but I haven't got a good feeling about him.'

Looking up, she caught Stella's pout.

'Yes I *know* it's up to you, but mind what you're doing. It's just a little warning!'

She went over to the bucket she'd filled and re-arranged the cellophane tubes. 'Your flowers will look lovely. They're down here in water when you want them. I'll be in next week.' She paused. What else was there to say? She'd warned her. 'Have a great time!' She let herself out.

* * *

The doorbell rang as she glanced at the clock. It was just after seven-thirty. Pushing the oven door up on the mouth-watering beef, she wiped her hands on a tea-towel, smoothed her best apron nervously, took a breath and went to answer it. Martha was waiting, Clive strolling up the drive behind her, having parked in the road.

'Hello Martha, please come in! It's lovely to see you.' She dithered over whether to air-kiss, deciding against it. 'Come straight through to the garden,' she invited, 'I've put out snacks and drinks. Douglas should be here in a minute then you can sit and chat while I continue 'stoving over a hot slave' as they say!'

Martha didn't smile, perhaps she didn't get it. It was one of Stella's mother's favourite expressions; she hoped this wouldn't set the tone for the evening. Clive loped in then, looking equally gloomy. Raising her eyebrows in silent query, he rolled his eyes in response and passed her a bottle of un-chilled white wine, which she stood on the sideboard.

Sensing tension already, she lightly touched his arm.

'I've sent Martha through to the garden. I'm just waiting for Douglas now. Then we can have some drinks and snacky things!' she added, more brightly than she felt.

Clive, strained and edgy, with his hands shoved in his pockets ignoring her touch, confirmed dryly,

'Oh she won't eat those, never touches nibbles or canapés, that sort of thing. She says it ruins her figure.'

He looked at Stella then – his eyes scanning her from top to toe in a second. If she'd been wearing a bar code she would have beeped.

'Do you approve?' She gave a quick twirl.

His reply was grudging. 'Very nice; haven't seen it before, I don't think. I'm glad you're wearing a bra.' His eyes were sharp. 'It's still a bit see-through though, isn't it?'

'Not really!' she returned, feeling equally on edge, 'The skirt's lined and the pattern covers over where I suppose my nipples would show if I *wasn't* wearing one! Look, you'd better go out to Martha and get her a drink…Oh, here's Douglas I think!'

She sprang to the open front door to greet him.

Clive watched as the Aston Martin swung off the road and up Stella's driveway, glinting and sparkling in the evening sun. The faint sound of classical music continued for some seconds after the engine had stopped. Continuing to stare, he saw Douglas release his seatbelt, straighten his tie and reach over to the passenger seat, collecting a bottle of red before opening the door and climbing out.

He gestured two fingers down his throat towards Stella before asking, 'Did you tell me it was beef tonight?' observing his bottle of German white.

'Yes; beef and orange, why? Isn't that all right then?'

Douglas strode up towards the front door looking like a distinguished Hollywood film star and for a moment it seemed completely surreal – he was walking up *her* drive.

'Oh it's *all right*,' he continued irritably, 'except *he's* brought red, which'll go with the beef. So which one will you open?'

Already het-up, if this was a book, he thought, I'd be 'bristling.' She's going to open the red – I know she will. He rammed his fists further into his trouser pockets. He'd got to greet the man, but he didn't want to.

In contrast and breezing in, Douglas was completely at ease.

'Stella how *lovely* you look!' Kissing both her cheeks, he looked round brightly. 'What a wonderful evening it is now, aren't we lucky? I've brought your *red*.'

He passed it with a flourish, his other hand grazing her arm and squeezing it. He rubbed his hands together and tweaked his tie again.

Spying Clive, he greeted him. 'Hello Clive, how are you?' He scanned the room impishly, his lips twitching. 'Martha not here?'

This barely concealed irony gnawed. 'She's outside,' he replied, his tone careful and precise. 'Stella's set up some drinks for us I think, haven't you dear? Shall we go through?'

Dear?! He'd never called her 'dear.'

'Yes I have, so come this way....' Now she was chattering amiably. 'We've got some red *and* white wine now! Will you have a glass of one of them? Open one now and the other later?

What would you like? Or I've got some sherry if anyone would prefer it?'

I'm the perfect hostess, she thought. *I've solved the wine problem and a bit of alcohol might cheer Martha up.* Martha was wandering round the garden, examining the late spring plants which were poking up; the Camellia in full luscious pink bloom. 'Would you like a drink, Martha?' she called cheerfully.

Martha turned and smiled.

'Thank you, yes please. I'll have a glass of white, I think.'

Clive retrieved the bottle and tore off the seal before opening it. 'Anyone else for white?' He waved it around.

Douglas purred. 'I wouldn't mind a sherry I think, if that's still on offer?'

He was poised by the French doors, one hand in his pocket, still wearing the coat of his suit. He looked refined and elegant. Clive, having abandoned his sport jacket in the sitting room on arrival, was happy in shirtsleeves.

Leaving Clive pouring the wine, she skimmed past Douglas to fetch a glass and received the faintest hint of after-shave: astringent, potent and very expensive. Imagining his eyes following her towards the kitchen she turned, but he was looking towards the others and advancing down the steps into the garden. She found a glass and bent to give Jeeves his supper. A hand directly on her bottom made her jump.

'I'm watching you, remember!' he snarled. 'I saw you gazing at him and how you brushed past him. Don't forget what I said…'

Stella was cross. 'Oh *pack* it in, Clive! I wasn't *gazing* at him as you put it and I *will* ask him to stay if you carry on like this. He's my guest and waiting for a sherry, so if you *don't* mind?'

She swept out of the kitchen and back to the garden. Clive felt helpless. His brief touch had told him she was without pants. Was that for *him* or...? He didn't want to think about it, wishing he hadn't had to bring Martha, resenting the fact that Douglas was, or appeared to be at any rate, fancy free. He'd better return to them.

Martha was admiring Stella's hostess apron.

'It's a very attractive pattern, very unusual. Where did you get it? I never see anything like that round here.'

Stella looked round for her glass of water and replied, 'Thanks Martha! I bought it up in Scotland actually, on a trip round the Royal Yacht Britannia. The pattern's from the decoration in the Queen's bedroom.'

Spotting Clive's return, Douglas joined in this polite conversation...

'It's *very* attractive Stella, it really *suits* you!'

She smiled cheekily and half curtsied.

'Why *thank* you, Douglas!'

Clive fought the irresistible urge to shove past him.

'Can you all just chat amongst yourselves a while?' she called, 'I'll fetch you when it's ready.'

Dinner progressed then without a hitch except for the orange sauce, which somehow in its preparation had evolved in to an orange blancmange, everyone being much too polite to comment. The beef was roasted to perfection. Stella relaxed. It would be all right.

Douglas, appearing to be in his element, attracted Stella – he responded to her efforts at polite conversation and filled her glass when it needed replenishing. Watching his hand surreptitiously as it tipped the water jug, she noted he held it firmly and poured expertly, a slice of lemon balanced at the spout. He didn't dither or faff around with his napkin either, every movement was polished. She felt gauche in comparison, cursing the sauce which he'd spooned politely in dollops over the meat.

Sensing Clive watching her, she beamed at both him and Martha, including them in the conversation too. Stella possessed an easy, conversational grasp of current affairs as long as the questions weren't *too* complex. Douglas however, was an experienced raconteur. He wasn't unconfident or unintelligent. Conscious of an ache between her legs, she crossed them. The very tops slid together, unimpeded as they were by underwear, signalling arousal. She shuffled in her seat and looked at Clive, who was addressing Martha, then rested her elbows on the table and smiled.

After the ice-cream which was a huge success, they took coffee in a summerhouse strewn with tiny fairy lights, creating a romantic glow in the dusk. Clive got up and strode around the garden in a semi-proprietary fashion, sub-consciously marking out his territory in the face of Douglas, who, observing this with quiet amusement, thought how pointless it was. He'd recognised the curiosity in Stella, it stuck out a mile – she was wanton, and his only rival this evening was encumbered by a partner. He was willing to bet she would ask him to stay on when they'd gone and if she *did*…well: all's fair in love and war.

Later, congregated the kitchen, Clive took his place at the sink. Martha looked round for a tea towel, then handed things to Stella who knew where they went, leaving Douglas in a supervisory role. He stood ramrod straight and authoritative, enjoying watching Clive in a position he was so obviously used to.

Once this was over, there was an uncomfortable pause. Martha excused herself to the bathroom, leaving Clive, hands dripping with suds, searching for a dry cloth. Douglas, nonchalant, watched Stella acutely, smiling wickedly. Ready, Clive glanced anxiously, because now he was stuck. She seemed intent only on ushering him and Martha out. He remembered what she'd said, but hoped she hadn't meant it. He was in no position to query this and they both knew it. The atmosphere was electric. The loo flushing and Martha's emergence, looking for her coat, cut through the undercurrent like a knife through butter. She proffered her thanks for a wonderful evening; unaware of the fact her escort was now hamstrung and lurching from foot to foot.

'Douglas, will you stay for a brandy?'

It was out. Stella watched Clive watching her and read his expression as Martha preceded him to the front door.

He mouthed something, but effectively was unable to do anything. Douglas agreed he would, waiting as the other two departed.

She opened a glass fronted cabinet. 'I've got an Armagnac here if you'd like it?'

Douglas was thrilled with that. 'That would be wonderful, Stella. I usually have one at home after my meal, how lovely.'

An uneasy twinge assailed her now that she'd actually asked him to stay – she could hardly retract this and ask him to leave, but why had she *done* it? She would *do* these headstrong things! Clive was suddenly safe and dependable. She felt tense and stressed, her stomach knotted with indigestion.

Composed, Douglas was taking everything in his stride.

'Shall I fetch a couple of glasses for you?'

Stella jumped and turned. He was balanced against the sideboard, leaning slightly. Her eyes travelled down to his crotch, drawn there – and he ***saw***. It was over in a moment as he continued waiting politely.

She bustled around now, grateful he'd spared her blushes. 'I'll fetch the glasses if you can take this,' passing him the bottle, 'shall we sit outside again? It's a pleasant evening!'

'It's de*lightful*, let's wander through then, shall we?'

Seated once more on the terrace, she was forced to engage him in further conversation. *Oh why had she done this? His emphasis now felt slightly menacing.*

'I'm on a local committee here in the village, as you know from seeing me at that lunch before you were ill,' she began. 'I have a shop in Great Denton, and found myself roped in when they wanted someone to help with fundraising.'

His look was unsettling, gently tipping the brandy round the glass cupped in both hands. She took a small sip from the minute amount in her own. It burned down her throat, making her eyes water.

'Do you know about it, the committee I mean…possibly?' She was floundering now.

Douglas raised an eyebrow; this was like cat and mouse, only more fun. 'I've heard of it, yes.' He changed the subject. 'I thought you looked lovely this evening.' His voice was like honey on a sore throat. 'And I love that colour green, it suits you.' He took a sip, savouring its warmth. 'I think it's very important to dress for an occasion, don't you?'

He'd found the right topic. Stella breathed relief.

'Very, yes I do, very important,' she chattered, 'I think grooming as a whole is very important. I like to look after myself….'

'Oh I can see that, Stella,' he murmured. 'One *very* well cared-for woman, I'd say!'

Taking another sip, she was cavalier almost.

'I'm going to get my teeth whitened soon actually. I thought I'd treat myself to it, you know…' She trailed off as he was twinkling amusement. *Now I've really made a fool of myself.* She peered into her glass and fiddled with it.

'I'm sure it'll all be worth it,' he chuckled smoothly, 'I shall look forward to seeing the result, wear my dark glasses just in case.' He was gently mocking her. He finished his glass and stood up. 'Well now, Stella, it's been a wonderful evening.'

He was leaving. She'd done it. No harm done after all. She led him back through the house to the door where he kissed her cheek briefly.

'Thank you *so* much for a lovely evening and a wonderful meal. I hope you have a good night.'

He waved as he walked back to the car and climbed in.

He was amused and ever so slightly excited by her spontaneous gesture with the brandy. Was this by way of an invitation, this little tête-à-tête, he wondered, and resolved that it was. However, *his* way of operating, his 'M.O.', was to take things very, very slowly. Eroticism was something to be anticipated and relished thoroughly, antagonisingly slowly. This woman declared her erotic aura, it was palpable in every movement she made and every word she spoke. He would drink this cup completely dry.

* * *

Stella was entertaining a friend Lydia for coffee the following Wednesday; whilst not as close as Cindy, and considerably older, Lydia was interesting company. Her family had come from Ireland; they were mentioned in Burke's Landed Gentry and Stella never tired of listening to anecdotes of days gone by, of a family life that was totally different from her own. There were stories about servants, chauffeurs and of life above and below stairs. She was just making some fresh coffee when the phone rang.

'Excuse me,' she apologised, picking it up. Lydia was happy to leave, but Stella shook her head, returning to sit with her.

'Hello?'

'Oh hello Stella, Douglas here; is it convenient to talk?'

She mouthed 'Douglas'. Lydia studied the opposite wall tactfully.

He continued. 'I was wondering if I could reciprocate your hospitality and invite you over to me for some lunch; if you were free and would like to?'

She felt alert, on edge, watching Lydia from the corner of her eye; waiting, listening presumably,

'Thank you Douglas that would be *lovely*, I'd *love* to.'

Would she? For some inexplicable reason, she was putting on a sort of show for her friend. That's what it felt like, she wasn't relaxed or her normal self, so what was she trying to prove? He was having an effect on her already. He was business-like.

'I wondered if it could be as soon as possible, depending on how you're fixed, how about this *Friday?*'

There he went again with that strangely compelling emphasis. Stella's throat was dry. *She* wasn't in control of events at all: *he* was. He'd entered the room somehow – by some strange act of osmosis he'd been transported down the telephone line. The hair on her arms stood up and she struggled to concentrate. Her voice was stilted and unnatural, too high.

'I'll just fetch my diary. Hang on a moment, it's right here.'

She scrabbled to open it and find May.

'Well, next Friday the fourteenth I'm out, the following one I'm away, but the last one, the twenty-eighth, that looks clear for me if it's all right with you?'

'The twenty-eighth, yes that's *fine*. Pity there's nothing sooner, but the twenty-eighth it is then.'

Stella was poised with her pen. 'What time would you like me to come?'

He chuckled, she was wonderful.

'Well my *dear!* Twelve-thirty shall we say?'

She felt hot, the pen slipped in her fingers as she entered the time.

'Thank you, I'll look forward to it.'

'Twelve thirty for lunch, then I'm sure we can then find *something* to do in the afternoon?'

A furtive glance confirmed Lydia was still staring straight ahead. '…discuss the meaning of *life* perhaps, and then you could have some *tea.*'

He made it sound vaguely obscene, but it wasn't a suggestion. Douglas didn't make suggestions, he was precise. Feeling that the conversation had gone on long enough and more than a little stimulated, she wound it up.

'I'll see you on the twenty-eighth then, at twelve thirty, thank you. Bye!'

Douglas smiled. His anticipation could now build and his mind enter seduction mode.

Stella replaced the handset and to dispel the slight air of awkwardness, went back to the kitchen to fetch some more coffee.

'That was Douglas as you gathered.' She called unnecessarily. 'He's invited me to lunch in a couple of weeks or so, on the twenty-eighth.'

She couldn't see Lydia's expression, but she caught her comment. '"Come into my parlour, said the spider to the fly". A lamb to the slaughter, my dear, I think.'

Her hands shook a bit as she poured the boiling water from the kettle. She tried to subdue a feeling of anxiety at the ready acceptance she'd made of his offer. Lydia, she decided, silly though it was, had lent her a dangerous feeling of abandonment towards his invitation: would she have accepted it so readily had she not been present? Too late now; once again, the die was cast.

2

It wasn't that Stella had set out to find someone like Clive, but her current relationship, after fifteen years, was beginning to pall.

She wanted to set higher sights, while there was time left to do it. She still possessed a slim and unblemished body – fast approaching the end of its shelf-life, but *not* its sell-by-date! Each new decade was a new beginning; a rejuvenation process, not an ageing process. Was your cup half full or half empty? Hers was half full, she decided, with space enough before the rim to fill it up with something worth having.

Her newly purchased personal computer was playing up. Bumping into Clive at a petrol station one afternoon, she'd asked him if he could come and have a look at it. Checking his diary he'd discovered the following Wednesday was free, if that was all right and possibly, he'd suggested with a cheeky grin, he could have a cup of tea?

Stella agreed, relaying all this to Cindy at the shop when she'd got back, telling her that in fact she was a little bit scared of him and his blustery manner, never smiling very much except if something tickled his fancy, when he'd laugh hysterically. It was all rather alarming.

He was tall, of heavy build but not fat, with rugged features, a mop of wavy dark hair and well spoken. She assumed he was married to Martha, with whom he lived, but he'd never referred to her as his wife and when she'd tackled him on the subject he'd replied rather vaguely it was something he didn't wish to discuss.

On the day of his visit, Stella was feeling low. She'd just had a bath and put on some fake-tan in readiness for whatever weather was going to pass for summer that year. Debating whether to dress or not, she'd slipped a white towelling bathrobe on and tied it round her waist. On arrival he'd sped towards her for a hug. Dodging him, she'd gone through to the sitting room where her computer sat on a desk. The air was buzzing. She perched next to him on the arm of an easy chair, wondering whether to let the robe fall open just a little or keep it firmly pulled across her chest. She'd let it fall open slightly, naturally.

Clive, intent on the PC, was staring at the screen and plugging away at the keys, chatting amiably all the while. He was different to the one she was used to when he was in his own home; more approachable. He fixed the problem with a flourish, saying any further difficulties with it or if she just needed someone to talk to sometimes, he'd be there for her; seriously, he cared for her. At the front door and time for him to go (suddenly he'd looked at his watch and jumped) she said she'd remember. *Could he replace her present lover?* She wondered. *He was now like a permanent piece of grit in her shoe.*

Then, in the time it would later take to eye Douglas's crotch and back, she blew a little kiss. In one movement he landed a full and heavy kiss on her lips. Just as quickly he shot out of the front door, leaving Stella wondering if it had happened at all; but it had. He'd kissed her and it wasn't just a peck.

* * *

Dr. Carroll's door opened and he stuck his head round.
'Stella!'
She went into the consulting room, shutting the door behind her.
He was waiting, offering his usual smile.
'Hello, well? What can I do today?'
She sat down and waited, unsure how to begin. Dr. Carroll, used to this, prompted her gently.
'Would this visit have anything to do with your hectic love-life? Come on Stella, what's happened now?'

Stella smiled, relaxing. 'You remember me telling you about Clive? He wants to have an affair I think. He fancies me but I'm not sure how to deal with it. Steve's convinced I'm seeing someone else, bangs on about it all the time – "you're not the same as you used to be, you're not interested if I'm here or not!" It's getting on my nerves, but I've been with him for so long…'

Dr. Carroll had a problem. He'd known Stella for a long time, he was one month and a day older than her and he liked her. He more than liked her.

'Steve's "tried and trusted" though, isn't he? He's safe sex, you need stability. This new man, you don't know much about yet, do you? It could turn out to be a disaster – drop Steve and you're left with nothing, which won't suit you. I'd try both for the time being, if you can cope with that, see how it goes.'

She smiled, fiddled with the corner of his desk.

'You never do straightforward do you? You never have.'

She stood up and he took her hand.

'You're worth so much more, Stella! Can't you see it? You don't value yourself highly enough that's your trouble! Just be very, very careful. Go on, off you go, see you soon!'

She left and he tapped his computer keyboard before admitting his next patient.

* * *

So Clive and Stella had continued, their emails becoming more and more explicit. However, for Stella at least, each snatched liaison never quite bore out the content. Something, a certain *'je ne sais quoi'* was missing from the clinches, although compared now to Steve's irksome efforts, Clive was rapidly superseding him.

For some months Stella vacillated. With heady excitement of *new* sex plus intelligent conversation on the horizon now, Stella could begin to plan for what was commonly termed 're-structuring of personnel'.

* * *

'Who should I choose? Steve's getting impossible and Clive really does want me, what shall I do?'

Dr. Carroll, debating for a moment, took a breath.

'This is too close to home, Stella, I can't get into this I'm sorry.' He paused. 'Stella, you must realise, you must know…'He spaced his words carefully. 'How-many-men-do-you-need-to-tell-you-you-are-beautiful-and-desirable? Make your choice – I could be yours and then it's an end to my being your doctor! It will finish completely, you know that: you know how I feel about you, don't you?'

She did.

'I need you as my doctor.'

'Choose then, Stella, and be careful. I can't help you here, sorry.'

* * *

Stella plumped for Clive.

He was head-over-heels, besotted now. Nothing of this kind had occurred *ever* in his life before.

Her emails promised such fulfilment (beyond his wildest dreams) he thought he was going mad. Could this really be happening? She was slim, unlined, an *ingénue*, of what age he couldn't guess. Surely (he convinced himself) he must appear a cantankerous fool?

Stella didn't think so. It felt as if, standing on the seashore and taking the waves, one that appeared from a distance to be as benign and as easily warded as the others, engulfed and soaked you from head to foot, all but knocking you over.

She was used to being found attractive by slightly older men; but this was different. Clive was professing undying, passionate love and was positive it was how he felt. So she went 'with the flow'.

Once again though, he wasn't free. The context of his relationship with Martha he'd kept to himself at first and then confessed: he'd been engaged to another woman, broken it off to live with Martha, then told her he'd regretted it ever since and the feeling was perfectly mutual. Money (or rather lack of it) bound them together now – nothing else.

To Stella she was the 'elephant in the front room' – not quite so easy to dismiss as Clive deemed she was. But his time at her shop (and Martha's tolerance of it) helping with the financial side, let Stella reconsider: she'd been a mistress before, several times over, so why change the habit of a lifetime – *someone* rich and 'single' (her operative word) would come along eventually and she'd be ready. Her Prince (albeit rather late in the day) would have arrived. It was what she was waiting for. Had she but known what was in store with the advent of Douglas, she might have stuck to the tried and tested, but then love is blind and when mixed with the potent concoction that is sexual chemistry, deaf and dumb as well.

* * *

In 1973, fourteen years after Valerie's death, Douglas had met Helen at a party. Recently widowed herself, Helen found Douglas pleasant enough. She'd enjoyed a very happy marriage, but feeling lonely, was missing attention and tenderness now. Douglas was polite and attentive, automatically carrying out those small acts of courtesy that separate the more urbane lover from the inept.

She hadn't thought of him in terms of becoming a lover, she'd warned him from the start her feelings weren't 'love', whatever love meant, but she wanted him, needed him. A few encounters in bed had persuaded her he wasn't unpractised, but was perfectly adequate, more than adequate. She agreed to live with him, share his bed, but not marry him.

She had a son by her late husband: James. Douglas had no offspring. They found a cottage called 'Watermead' in a quiet village, Little Denton, on the outskirts of Dreighton with the river

Dreight meandering nearby. Organising removals from Surrey, they moved in.

Helen enjoyed the sun, possessing a small apartment in Tenerife, escaping there whenever the English climate threatened to cancel warm weather, which was surprisingly often. This wasn't a problem for Douglas who, by coincidence, owned a villa nearby. For the present, the arrangement of living some of the time in the Canaries and the remainder in England worked well. They were a couple and enjoyed the easy laidback lifestyle that came with living comfortably abroad. The facts had yet to emerge: that Douglas, deep down, had more affinity with England than he cared to admit, and Helen for Los Christianos.

Before Douglas, there was one man with whom Helen had shared a much more deep-rooted alliance. Reggie Crifton. He'd still call her mobile occasionally, often when she and Douglas were together. By her body language alone, Douglas wasn't fooled, but his intense feelings for her, the fear of losing her, prevented his objecting too much.

Friction, though, was gradually increasing. The hidden facts emerging: Douglas as helpless as Canute was unable to prevent them.

One Friday morning in August things came to a head. Removing her nightdress, they'd begun making love, Helen suggesting afterwards that next time they went away they should spend longer in Tenerife. That did it. Douglas was furious: why buy a lovely cottage, with everything they needed, only to go and live abroad? What was the point? Flinging the covers from the bed and leaping naked out of it, she grabbed a robe from the back of the door and angrily covered herself.

'I've just about had enough of this! *Enough!*' she shouted. 'I thought we could compromise but it just isn't going to work; so *no more!* I'm going into the spare bedroom. Don't even *think* of following me unless it's for a reason other than just being downright awkward!'

Douglas was stunned. Rejected in the home he shared with the woman he loved: *'he loved'* now being the operative words. She'd stormed across the landing and slammed the door, farcically returning a few moments later, in order to go to the bathroom: this room not having the benefit of an en-suite. Emerging, she shut it a little less forcefully this time, but nevertheless with an air of finality that brooked no argument; this was it from now on.

The stormy weather reflected the brooding atmosphere. Thunder rumbling and then exploding; torrents of rain lashing down, hissing down the chimney in the sitting-room and dripping off the thatch. Fading and returning. On and on it went interminably; the noises of nature the only sounds emanating. Eventually, fed up with what seemed to him to be a silly (but for Helen a serious) turn of events, Douglas snatched up a raincoat and went out to the car.

On the outskirts of Great Denton was a thriving garden centre, boasting along with the usual plants and garden items, many more facilities including the Coffee Shop and Restaurant, which served particularly good food. Douglas enjoyed it. It was his 'Club'. He could bring his broadsheet and spread it out. He sipped his Americano, pondering.

Hysterical women, tears and tantrums, were not his thing *at all*. After another coffee he felt better and ambled over to the outside plant area where the sun was once again shining, drying all the puddles and warming his back. He returned home to find the place empty; dashing upstairs into their room, mentally correcting himself: *his* room, he opened the wardrobe – Helen's clothes were gone.

Feeling suddenly hot and sick, the coffee repeating and curdling bitterly in his throat, he flew across the landing to her room. There, in a heap on the bed, were her clothes; some fallen on to the floor, others sliding from the bed to join them. It was a recent pile, waiting for someone to pick them up and straighten them out. Feelings of initial relief that they were still there at all, rapidly turned to irritation and annoyance. The telephone rang; he leaped back into the other bedroom and grabbed the receiver.

'Hello; yes...who is this?' He waited.

A friendly voice asked him if he would like to win a holiday for two in the Caribbean.

'No, thank you very much, I would NOT.'

He slammed the phone down then listened; a key turned in the lock and the back door opened. Helen was home again.

Supper passed in comparative calm; inane conversations would begin simultaneously before he touched her hand and she didn't withdraw it. They agreed to call a truce. Getting ready for bed was an exercise in walking on eggshells, but eventually, when she was through the bathroom and in her own bed, Douglas tapped lightly on the door and stepped in. He walked over to where she lay in bed, kissing her lightly on the top of her head; she had lovely silky blonde hair.

'Night Douglas,' she said, 'Sleep well!'

'And you, darling.'

He closed the door and went back to his own room.

3

Douglas was anticipating the forthcoming lunch to which Stella had accepted the invitation and in *his* book this was tantamount to accepting seduction – it came with the territory.

Now in his sixties, and 'downsized', he still possessed charisma. His sexual radar honed by years of experience, had picked up on Stella from the moment he'd spotted her by chance, then some discreet enquiries disclosed she'd be at a luncheon for all the local worthies. He'd managed to procure an invitation. She'd exploded on him, was off the scale, but he knew how to prepare the ground for this little feast. He had offered her a lift home afterwards; nonchalantly inviting her to his cottage on the way, congratulating himself on this bit of good fortune. Then 'flu had followed soon after and brought her 'Thinking of You' card. Fate had done the rest. This was right up his street now: quite how far he could only imagine at the moment – but that was all part of the fun which, after the extraordinary and charmed life he'd led up until now, was in rather short supply.

* * *

'Friday 28th May. 12.30: Lunch with Douglas.' Stella closed her diary, paused a moment, then flung off the covers and nipped out of bed to open the curtains. The sky was a hazy blue, promising a fine day. Her body was tingling, gearing up for *something*, quite *what* it wasn't sure. She'd mulled over Douglas's sly innuendo: *'I'm sure we'll find something to do – discuss the meaning of life, perhaps…'* knowing it couldn't be further from the truth. At the back of her mind, she was already enjoying full sex with him: on his bed, on the floor, over the beautiful Shaker kitchen units, in his study…

Douglas had boxed clever on that first occasion following that convenient official luncheon when he'd offered her a detour to his home. He'd looked at her and asked casually,

'Would you like to go upstairs?'

It was innocently put; they'd just strolled round his well-stocked secluded garden and completed a tour of the downstairs. Stella had hesitated, unsure what to say or do. Douglas – as experienced, expert and practised as a brain surgeon – changed tack and folded his arms nonchalantly.

'Most women I know love looking all round houses, upstairs as well. I just thought you might like to take a look but we don't have to, if you'd prefer not?'

It was a suggestion, not a request. In order to make Stella feel idiotic had she refused? He was the master, she was the puppet; pull the right strings and…

'Yes please then, thanks; I would, very much.' He had smiled warmly.

'Follow me then, oh and watch your head on the beam on the way up!'

Upstairs was airy, light and quite luxurious. Soft carpets and exotic rugs; well-polished, unusual antiques, attractive ornaments, mirrors and pictures and two very large, comfortable looking bedrooms, each containing an accommodating, inviting looking bed. The second bedroom possessed the most magnificent en suite bathroom. A sunken ivory coloured bath with plain gold fittings – even the lavatory resembled some extravagant extra! It proclaimed luxurious debauchery. The lighting was effective: tiny spots of piercing white light. Douglas read the signs: Stella was 'sold', her expression rapt and shameless, he'd surmised correctly, she was wanton but not a push-over, not too 'easy', no fun in that. No, this would be deliciously exciting. Suddenly it was as if Stella had read his mind. She turned, walked out of the bathroom heading towards the stairs. He darted across the landing.

'In here's the third bedroom, a box room really, just a few odds and ends. Do go in…'

She had returned and peered round the door he was holding open. Lying propped up in the corner was a large framed photograph of him, taken a good many number of years ago at his practice in Harley Street. He'd been devastatingly, almost ridiculously, handsome.

'Is that you?' Stella looked at the picture.

'It was!' Douglas joked.

'Still is!' She'd meant it

'Let's go downstairs again shall we? And I'll take you home. I thought you might like a look, it's very cosy don't you think?'

'Very, I love the bathroom; it's wonderful!'

He was back in the driving seat. Stella had followed him to the car....

No sooner had he returned than the telephone rang.

'Hello!'

A woman, with the slightly artificial tones of a receptionist that wasn't quite out of the top-drawer but nursed aspirations, replied.

'Well? Was she there at the lunch? Did she come back with you? Did you take her upstairs, show her the bathroom?'

Douglas, irritated, was totally controlled.

*'Now listen, I've only just returned her to her home. This call's a little indiscreet, Rhoda! Discretion I said, didn't I? This won't work unless you let me arrange things **my way**. I'll call her in a few days, after we've had lunch at the end of the month, then take her over to the market the following Thursday, where you will have your stall that day and something suitable that'll take her fancy. She's small; a size ten or twelve at a guess and no doubt likes silk: have you anything that might be suitable?'*

The woman was snatched at his tone and admonishment.

'I've got a sea-green chiffon top with silk satin ribbon. I think it'll do. I'll arrange to be there, don't worry.' Then as an afterthought: 'And keep your hands to yourself if you can. Don't want to frighten her off and I know you of old, don't I?'

Douglas winced: his relationship with Rhoda Chambers was one of ambivalence. Right now he loathed her, but she was loyal and as sly as a fox. Without her help he'd have been in serious trouble and she didn't let him forget it.

'Thank you! I'm well able to control myself. The top sounds splendid. Next Thursday it will be. I'll see you then.'

* * *

Now Stella was returning to where she'd been invited officially. She let her mind drift back to that seductive bathroom, visualising herself in the bath with a tall glass of champagne. Lots of foam, hair piled up, Douglas walking towards her naked – *stop!!* She stared unseeingly out at the garden. It was **not** going to happen. Buried beneath these seductive fantasies lurked warnings that she was heading for trouble and as hard as she tried to suppress them, they refused to go away: '*come into my parlour, said the spider to the fly*' '*I don't think I'd trust Spencer though! I don't know what it is, but I haven't got a good feeling about him.*' A cloud obscured the sun and Stella caught her reflection in the window. She didn't look excited, about to go on a sexy date – she looked scared. It vanished in an instant. *Don't be silly!* She thought, rubbing at the smear on the glass and turning round.

Another friend, Jo, was arriving soon for coffee, then on to Douglas for twelve thirty so she'd got to get ready now. She tossed up the sort of look to aim for. Douglas would be assessing her possibly; her maturity, sexuality? She *had* to get it right.

Underwear first then: priorities? Removing a mint green and black lace set by Agent Provocateur, Stella examined it critically. It was tiny, revealing but not overtly so; it was her favourite set. The bra moulded each breast beautifully, presenting them perfectly, living up to the name: it 'provoked'. The thong hardly did justice to covering anything; a mint green lacy triangle topped with black, a black lace band passing between her legs, exposing her buttocks. Hardly an obstacle, it was just a token covering. Would she let him get that far? If he *did* get that far, she reasoned, he wouldn't be expecting 'big knickers' after the flimsy bra. Stella drew it on, her mind made up: her sexuality score was going to be ten out of ten.

The underwear chosen, she ironed a sleeveless cotton blouse in an attractive pattern of differing shades of blue with lime green leaves. It was startling and good quality, co-ordinating well with a close fitting designer skirt in cream. She finished it off with a silk pashmina, lime green pumps and jewellery –dramatic and original. An inspection in the mirror confirmed a good hair day. The doorbell interrupted her reverie. Jo was a true friend: dependable, practical and staunch. Always there in a crisis with exactly the right words to say. She was priceless.

'Stella, you look *won*derful!' It was meant, every word.

It was confirmed: she looked great. She was off on a date!

'Come in Jo, thanks. I'm quite excited, looking forward to it!'

They carried their coffees outside to the summerhouse, where Stella related all the details of the lunch – the excitement at the invitation she'd received, the conflict it was creating between her and Clive. She recalled *something* she'd heard about a friend of Douglas's called Helen, but hoped to find out more during general conversation with him. Changing the subject, they chatted then like the good friends they were until it was time to go.

Visiting the bathroom one last time, she reached into the cabinet for a small bottle of eau de parfum: *Magie Noir* by Lancôme. It wasn't chosen absently; it was tried and tested dynamite. Dabbing it quickly behind her ears and in her cleavage, on impulse she pulled up her skirt and rubbed a little under her thong and around the tops of her thighs. Placing the bottle back on its shelf, she caught sight of another perfume: *Halston* by Halston. That was for Clive. She paused for several long seconds, catching her reflection in the cabinet mirror. If there was a flicker of doubt at what she was doing, it didn't impact sufficiently to alter anything and she closed the little door, re-arranging her skirt.

* * *

'You put it there "on impulse"? Like hell you little tart! You're a bloody WHORE!'

Clive was incensed. Grabbing the bottle of Halston from his pocket, he smashed it against the tiles on the floor, filling the room with the reek of it. Stella trembled and rocked on her knees.

'It was! It was!'

'Go on, go on!'

'What's the point? You won't believe anything I say!'

'Try me.' Clive was very quiet. *'Just try me, darling, or was it "sweetie"? I'm waiting!'*

* * *

Stella climbed gingerly into the car, not wishing to crush the skirt further, putting her handbag on the passenger seat and checking her make-up one more time; it was perfect. She turned right on to the main road to Watermead; only a few minutes, the small clock on the dashboard reading 12.25.

He had taken her there before, now she was driving herself. She found the entrance and crawled down the drive. He was waiting, exhibiting some surprise that she'd come at all, she thought, but only *he* knew the true agenda. She wrapped the pashmina around her shoulders, collected her bag and wafted out. Lifting both arms in a greeting, he enveloped her; her hands on his shoulders, she aimed a kiss near his left cheek.

It was a warm day. The comfortable and stylish garden furniture around a table with an umbrella was attractive and inviting. A low stone wall bordered the terrace, supporting two ancient stone urns, each containing a tumbling mass of colourful plants. Everything was blooming and fragrant. Small birds were busy pecking at fat-balls hanging from a spreading blue cedar tree. Stella's initial feelings of nervousness and agitation evaporated as he led her to the table, upon which were two small dishes, one containing olives and the other macadamia nuts. It was all very civilized. She sat and he offered her one. Smiling, he replaced the dish and enquired softly.

'Would you care for some champagne? I have some chilled Krug, would you like a glass?'

Here Stella demurred, 'chilled Krug or not.

'I don't drink, actually, I'm afraid, it doesn't really agree with me.'

Douglas was taken aback and frowned slightly then tried an alternative.

'I have some organic ginger beer then, if you'd prefer? It was given to me as I like ginger, would you have some of that instead? We can have it in champagne glasses?'

Stella loved ginger too.

'Yes please, that would be lovely, thank you!'

He hesitated, the refusal was bugging him, '…but didn't you have wine with the lunch a couple of weeks ago? It's strange, I thought you *did*.'

'No I didn't, I had water. I just find it doesn't agree with me, I get tipsy very quickly.' *Have I fallen at the first hurdle?* She thought. 'I'm sorry if it's awkward, if there's a problem…' her uneasiness returning from its hiding place.

Remembering his manners, he smiled charmingly.

'Not at all, ginger beer it is!'

Striding indoors to the kitchen, he removed it from the fridge. Stella helped herself to some olives and a few more nuts and tried to relax and look around. He poured the beer into two tall glasses, observing her before returning. She really was ravishing and desirable.

Earlier that morning he'd carried out a more intensive toilette than usual. Guessing she might be 'adventurous,' he'd carefully shaved hair away from around his balls. It felt odd but not unpleasant, quite stimulating. He studied her again; a slight breeze was lifting her hair, which was an extraordinary shade of brown and incredibly sexy. He carried the glasses outside.

'I hope you like asparagus? I love it. I thought I'd go for something simple, take advantage of this lovely weather and eat outside.' He was chatting reassuringly, pleasantly.

However, continuing dipping into the olives and nuts **she** wasn't quite able to quell the feeling of uneasiness that was brewing away in the pit of her stomach. Was it pleasant anticipation or anxiety? She wasn't sure yet. Douglas affected her in a way she'd not experienced before. There was no similar experience at all – she hadn't 'been here and done this.' It was new, possibly a bit risky. On holiday, there were often slightly dodgy-looking smooth-talking people handing out invitations to Timeshare hospitality buffets where wine flowed and food was plentiful. Once you were well-oiled, the hard-sell would begin and the atmosphere changed. Now it was your turn. You were obligated – or made to feel that way. She felt glued to the spot. Although she was outside, there was that feeling that some doors had clanged shut, or what was it Lydia had said? *'Come into my parlour, said the spider to the fly...'* followed by the business of a lamb to the slaughter. She suddenly felt sick, so took a sip of the ginger-beer and squeezed the glass.

'What *are* you thinking about? You're miles away!' Interrupting her train of thought, he brought her back with a start. She looked up, flustered.

'No, no, not thinking anything really! I love olives!'

She picked the final three up and popped them in her mouth in quick succession. They were large; he stared, making her feel uncomfortable. Suddenly, almost with relief, she remembered Helen. She needed to know if there was a 'Significant Other,' however absent they were at the moment, needed to know how complicated this was going to be in the future should he ask her again. Covertly, despite the feeling of risk involved, she rather hoped he would. She could handle it, this wasn't the Costa Brava; she'd square it with Clive somehow. *Don't think about him now.*

'Do you have – 'she tried again, 'I've heard from round about that you have a friend; Helen?'

Douglas stared into the middle distance for a while.

'Ah *Helen* yes!' He scratched the side of his nose. 'Well, *Helen* prefers to spend *most* of her time in Tenerife, whereas *I* prefer it *here*.' He regarded her, his head tipped slightly towards her; making a point. 'She'll visit infrequently, stay for a week and then go back again. We used to be together, but not now,' he finished wistfully.

Stella accepted this. Living in two different countries couldn't make for much intimacy and there was no sign from Douglas she was sorely missed. He sounded fed up if anything; vague. She decided to drop it. Anything significant would materialize later, in its own time.

* * *

'My son will collect all my furniture. I shan't sleep here tonight or any other night come to that, I've had enough. You had your chance and blew it. It's over, Douglas; I'm leaving as soon as I can. I'm sick to death of rows and bickering all the time. I just cannot be 'bought' as you seem to think I can – trips to Barbados, pampering, expensive clothes and jewellery, you think they'll buy me but they won't. I won't marry you, I told you from the start how I felt and it hasn't changed. Oh don't look like that! You've no one to blame but yourself. Now if you'll excuse me? A van will be here in the morning. Goodbye.'

And she'd gone. The next day was farcical, her son trying hard to hide the embarrassment he felt about the whole thing. He'd not wanted the details; too much information there. This was his mother and her boyfriend. There wasn't a code of behaviour he knew that covered moving the furniture out of your mother's lover's house. He kept his head down, got on with it as fast as he could and drove them both away.

* * *

Snapping out of his daydream, Douglas remembered he had company and rose.

'If you'll excuse me I'll go and attend to the asparagus, won't be long, more ginger beer?'

He lifted the bottle towards her glass. Stella nodded with her mouth still full of olive.

Back in the kitchen he was humming, in control. The champagne didn't matter really, although a little alcohol usually assisted in oiling the wheels of seduction, but never mind, it presented more of a challenge and that was fine. He tended the asparagus spears, bobbing them gently in the simmering water, thinking his own thoughts. When they were ready, he carefully drained them and placed them on plates warmed from being over the Aga and carried them outside.

Watching, he wondered if Stella would eat the spears he'd served to her with her fingers. Not a stranger to etiquette, she picked the ends up and ran the spears over the melted butter, levelling her stare at Douglas in response to his waiting. He attended to his own pile then, before once again scrutinising her.

'Are you going to eat the *whole thing?*' he asked curiously. Stella bridled. 'No, not if the end is tough.' He winced as she took a bite. 'But this is tender, so *I shall!*' She was mimicking his pronunciation. He didn't appear to notice.

'Feisty little thing!' he thought. 'One thing I *like* about you,' he said, 'is you say *exactly* what you think. That's very good. I *like* that!'

Stella suddenly appeared vulnerable, almost childlike, in accepting this compliment. He wrestled momentarily over whether to seduce her or not. She looked almost innocent, quite incredible! She was a remarkable woman, but was this *conscience* troubling him, he wondered? That would never do! Vulnerable was good, win her emotions and he was home and dry.

Their plates emptied, he collected them and removed them back to the kitchen, calling over his shoulder.

'I hope you like the next course, won't be a minute!'

Stella waited. He returned shortly carrying an assortment of plates and dishes, setting them neatly on the table.

'Help yourself to tomatoes and potatoes. Would you like a fish knife? I know one should really, but I find them awkward. I'll fetch one if you wish?'

'No thanks, this is fine. I don't like fish knives much either, I think they're a bit pretentious.' forking some caviar around her plate.

Caviar; and not the inexpensive kind either. Something clicked in Stella's brain: 'How to seduce your Woman.' *First there should be available, some finest chilled champagne; second, some asparagus. For a main course try caviar (the more expensive the better) and mussels (all aphrodisiac so far!) Add perhaps a salmon steak or filet. For pudding (after she has sucked her way through the asparagus and swallowed the mussels) try large, ripe strawberries with lashings of cream, whisked and sweetened, served in a bowl. After that little lot, the rest is up to you!!*

After clearing his plate he rose, taking Stella's plate with his own, and headed towards the kitchen. Stella couldn't resist it, enquiring innocently,

'What do you have for pudding?'

He turned at the door.

'...there are some strawberries with fresh whipped cream and some sugar to sprinkle; naturally. I hope you like strawberries?'

'I bet you do!' thought Stella. 'I *adore* strawberries, thank you!' she said.

Once back in the kitchen, he tossed a strawberry in the air and caught it in the glass dish. *So far, so good!*

Stella wondered. Was this happening? Was it *real?* What was going to happen next? After the strawberries, after the washing up – no, too prosaic; the washing up would wait, but after that, then what? Surreptitiously, discreetly, so Douglas wouldn't see should he be looking and something told her he might, she needed to *know,* what she was convinced he would *also* want to know, *sooner or later* – was she aroused by all this?

Gently her finger hooked under the flimsy thong and pulled away sharply: she was. Did he know that? How could he, but something inside told her that he did: the telephone call and invitation. A rather voluptuous feast with champagne (had she accepted it) and now what? It was her call. Or her turn – shoving that thought to the back of her mind. Adjusting the front of her blouse where it had slipped open, she sat up. Douglas re-appeared with two glass dishes, the strawberries they contained, ridiculously huge. A moment later and he was back again with the cream in a separate bowl and a silver sugar shaker. He certainly had all the trimmings!

Stella, taking the lead, picked one up, dipped it into the cream and bit the end of it. The juice came dribbling down her chin. Douglas watched entranced, wanting to lick it off; he stopped himself, controlled himself.

'These are delicious, are you going to eat yours?'

'In a minute, you carry on,'

She rubbed her chin and her hand continued the path down, stroking her throat, then further down still, allowing her fingers to lightly brush her breast before settling once more on the glass dish. She seemed completely oblivious of its caress. Here was a woman completely at home with her own body: *very encouraging*, he thought. Taking a strawberry himself then, he dipped it in the cream as Stella had done.

He rested a hand on the back of hers and crossed his legs, unconcerned.

'I don't know what you fancy doing this afternoon (*I can't wait to find out*) but I've a large collection of videos. There might be one you'd like to see.'

This was unexpected. There was a good chance he'd suggest *something* in the afternoon, not in the *least* connected with discussing 'the meaning of life'! Considering this, Stella had thought about asking for a ride in his car, which wasn't ridiculous – he owned an Aston Martin after all. Not an every-day sort of car.

He'd deem it logical. Now there was something equally bland on offer and appealing, she enjoyed films as well.

I've a very wide selection. At one end, I have "Basic Instinct" with Sharon Stone?' He said this with a sidelong look.

Stella wasn't fazed. 'I've seen that at the cinema and on video.' She met his eye. 'I've just got "Oh What a Lovely War". I've always wanted that.'

He replied knowledgeably, 'That, I think, was originally written by Joan Littlewood as a play in 1963, it was quite controversial. I think it belittles and makes fun of the First World War, which was not, by any means, fun. I wouldn't wish to see it on principle.'

Stella countered him.

'No; I'm talking about the *film*, by Attenborough. It doesn't poke fun at all. It illustrates very well the tragedy of the whole thing and the old songs he uses poignantly. I find it quite disturbing to watch, very emotional.' *So there!*

He regarded her with increased interest. She wasn't afraid to state her own opinion even if it disagreed with his. That was good.

She continued in this more confident vein. 'I also have "Lady Chatterley."'

Momentarily thrown, Douglas coughed.

'Have you indeed?' The smile didn't reach his eyes. They were sharp, piercing her.

'Connie and Mellors, is it, with lots of fun in the potting shed? All that sort of thing?' His tone was snide and patronising.

Ignoring this she continued. 'It has lots of stunning nature shots, similar to David Lean's films. It's not a sleazy film. The only thing is, it's in French with sub-titles which are a bit of a nuisance, but it's very well done, I think. I could bring it sometime,' she suggested, 'plus the War one if you like?'

'But sex isn't *'sleazy'* though, is it? It's quite natural.' He regarded her. 'A natural thing between a man and a woman, at least it *should* be. Don't you think?' *Touché sweetie!*

He rose and collected together the remaining dishes and things on the table, slipping indoors to collect a tray.

'Shall we go in and take a look at the list then?' He paused by the door.

'Okay, I'd like to see it!'

She followed him. Depositing the tray in the kitchen, he opened a drawer in a large old bureau, removing a foolscap sheet. On it was a handwritten list of film titles. One jumped out at her, fairly middle-of-the-road, a safe, uncontroversial bet: "The Belstone Fox", with Eric Porter, among others.

He waited by the bureau. 'Have you found one?'

'"The Belstone Fox",' she announced,

'Good choice, have you seen it?'

She didn't think she had. 'It's presumably about a fox, hunting and that sort of thing?'

He moved next to her on the antique sofa.

'It *is* about hunting yes, a bit gory in parts, especially the beginning. But it's a lovely story.'

He opened the cabinet containing the television and video recorder and inserted it.

Returning, he slid an arm around her with assured confidence.

'We can pretend,' his tone risqué, 'we're in the back row at the cinema now, *can't we?*'

It was a challenge...

Stella was high on adrenaline, what was it they taught at school: fight or flight? Or was she getting confused? She didn't push his arm away, but was rapidly calculating how far she would allow this hand to travel on its journey. *Play it by ear; don't make a final decision yet.*

The film had begun: a nest of fox cubs was discovered then filled in, the young brutally battered with spades. Normally, under any other circumstances, it would have made her distinctly queasy, unable even to watch. Now rigid within his arm, she stared fixedly ahead at the screen. From the corner of her eye she saw him studying her; it was disconcerting. Having seen it all before, knowing what was going to happen, he was free to watch his own performance develop before his very eyes. That was *much* more exciting.

Moving his position slightly now, he held an elbow in each hand, her breasts within easy range. Either hand perfectly capable of opening the front of her blouse; *just take it very, very slowly. This was the crunch; one false move and his private production would shut down, possibly forever. He felt an erection begin and glanced down; it wasn't visible in his perfectly tailored denims. 'I know you of old,' Rhoda had said, 'so keep your hands to yourself.' He'd ignore this advice; having handled more erotic interludes than she'd had hot dinners. He could play this one like a violin. She had sex coming out of her ears.* The film moved on: 'first base' was reached, she decided. He'd grasped and was holding both her elbows in a resolved manner.

He hadn't moved for possibly ten minutes. She couldn't see her watch or a clock. Very carefully, with infinite precision like the practiced, experienced man he was, his fingers toyed with the edge of her blouse. Painfully slowly, they gently drew back the material, exposing breasts supported by mint and black lace. Controlling an intake of breath (*she was exquisite*) he whispered in her ear.

'You're a very, *very* desirable woman Stella, absolutely gorgeous...' He hoped this imbued just the right amount of sincerity without sounding too suggestive. She was breathing quickly '...quite perfect. Your breasts, hair; everything about you is perfect, darling!'

He'd reached 'second base,' she decided. He was slowly drawing back the lace now. It was the final obstacle to total exposure, her breasts and nipples too. Was she comfortable with this? Yes; a little further yet. The film was genuinely absorbing, but her peripheral vision was recording every move he made. She felt hot. Where would she draw the line?

It was a good three quarters of the way through; a particularly harrowing scene was coming, he warned her. She half covered her eyes as she'd done as a child during 'Dr.Who'. It wasn't necessary to go *that* far, he told her. She could see what was going to happen: the pack of hounds was racing up the railway track and a train was approaching at speed. It was all special effects, she said; they weren't *really* going to be slaughtered. Quite unashamedly and calmly fondling both her exposed breasts, he said he liked to get right *into* a film, feel all the emotions being portrayed in front of him, forgetting about the Special Effects team and the entire attendant filming crew to lose himself completely in the plot. *This may be true for you,* she thought, *but I'm only too aware of your increasingly wandering hands to allow* **me** *to be drawn into the drama.*

One of the actors said: 'You don't know what you could be letting yourself in for!'

'You can say *that* again!' she exclaimed.

Douglas paid her no heed, continuing to stroke, tracing the tips of his fingers round her nipples which, under their own volition, were standing proud and erect. It was absurd to allow this to continue without any comment at all. Without the help of discreet investigation she knew she was aroused, more so than she'd been during lunch. Yet she didn't fancy him really. Termination would be when (or if) his hands reached the waistband of her skirt, she decided. That would be *it* then, **no further.**

In as nonchalant a tone as she could muster: 'Not bad for my age, I think!'

Douglas agreed entirely.

'Oh, absolutely *not* darling, they're quite wonderful!' *What was her age?* He wouldn't try *that* one yet. 'They're the most perfect breasts I've ever *seen*, not droopy, too large or too small. They're completely smooth and unblemished, *exquisite!*'

The film reached its conclusion, the ending pleasing Stella, who was always on the side of the animals, caring quite passionately about them. With the ending came decision time. Jeeves was at home, no doubt wondering when he was going to get some food and a walk, preferably in that order. Feeling suddenly more in control, the reality of the situation dawned on her with all its implications: common sense kicked in.

Leaning forwards, she lifted both his hands from her.

'Douglas this is all very *well*, but surely you see it *isn't* and *cannot*, *go* anywhere!'

His smile was benignly condescending, as if he was listening to a seriously minded child explaining what they believed to be a profound truth with all the attendant innocence of childhood.

Irritated by this, she continued – he wasn't getting it. *So try a bit nearer the mark.*

'Douglas, I do **not** want to go to bed with you!'

Surely *that* was plain enough? It was. He sat up, folded his arms and had the grace to look more than slightly affronted, even hurt. *What she didn't realise, his plucky little sweetie, was the fact that his reaction was all stage-managed and she'd fall for it – he **knew**. Now, what was she saying?*

'I'm not a tart'

He controlled a smirk. Translated this often meant they were exactly that: and how!

'Of *course* you're not, darling, what a thing to *say;* a 'tart' indeed!' *Now what?*

'I don't just jump into bed straight away, not on the first time I come round.'

No! Of course not, but I don't think you'll wait long, will you? I can tell!

'I never expected that you would, Stella, not at all...' *Repeat it for impact.* '...Not at **all**!'

Should she now soften the bluntness of her statement she wondered, or is that leaving your options open? She wasn't sure which.

'I've *enjoyed* your company – I feel proud of my body too in a way.'

***Now** we're getting there, that's more like it!*

'You **should** do darling, it's the most *wonderful* body and I love looking at it. Even just your breasts alone....' Now he was considerate. 'I've enjoyed your company too, but *you* must call the tune, only do what you're *com*fortable with. I'll respect that, respect *you* for that.'

Respect, a key word in the lexicon of seduction – works every time, given time...

Leaning back in the corner of the sofa away from her, it was time, he decided, for the 'last act' of his private production that afternoon. He smiled.

'Now, *kiss me.*'

Hesitating, she leaned towards him, kissing him on the mouth. It was soft and yielding, very good to kiss in fact. He opened his lips and their tongues met. This kiss was **it**. He was an expert. She shut her eyes, wallowing.

Her body moved against his. Sitting completely still, he allowed her to rub her hips against him. He sensed the pent-up passion waiting to emerge. This wasn't the perfunctory kiss of a cold and sexless woman at all, this was the kiss of an inveterate giver and could she *give!* Quietly confident, everything would come to him if he waited and the wait wouldn't be long either, whatever she'd said. This kiss had sealed everything.

Moving away eventually, she stood up. She'd said what she'd had to say, although the kiss had rather undermined that now. Enjoyable – *no, a lot more than that* – intoxicating as it might have been, Jeeves would be bursting to get out, munching his way through his treats. He rose and followed her, delaying her by placing both arms around her hips, crossing his hands over her groin. She lifted them, determined and he didn't resist: *don't frighten her!*

She faced him. 'I'd like to keep you as a friend, Douglas. This sort of thing has an awful habit of turning sour! It'd be much better if we kept things on a sensible, friendly footing.'

In the same pose he'd adopted when she'd asked him to stay for a brandy, he spoke to her, his tone adult, conspiratorial and seductive.

'I'd like you to come here again. I don't *want* you to go now. It's very secluded and discreet here, you can put your car in my garage so no one will be able to see it or know you're here. We can enjoy each other's company. Give pleasure to each *other*....'

Stella pondered now. He was tall and *definitely* attractive, no two ways about it. However, either she'd missed something out or he just hadn't listened to a word she'd said. She needed time to consider.

'Thank you for a wonderful lunch, it was lovely, but I must get home and see to Jeeves, he'll be wondering what's happened. We'll no doubt speak again. Perhaps next time we could go out for lunch, I know some lovely places? I'd like to do that.'

Now in 'gentleman mode,' he replied, agreeing with her.

'Then that is exactly what we'll *do*. I want to make you happy, my purpose in life. I'll look forward to it *very much*.'

Opening her door she climbed in. He stood back and waved her goodbye. No date had been set for another meeting, but there was no doubt in her mind he'd phone soon to arrange something. More pressing was reporting this to Clive. He'd bet her a pound coin Douglas would 'try it on'. To him it was blindingly obvious – Douglas was a single man, Stella a nubile, attractive woman; it stood to reason. But she'd accepted the bet, nevertheless.

4

Clive called Stella in the morning as usual, curious to discover how the lunch had gone the day before. Having got to know Stella very well over the past fourteen months or so had persuaded him she was a strange but potent mix of innocence and sexuality: two completely different women in one body.

The trouble was there was no accounting for taste where women were concerned including Martha, *they* thought he was charm personified, God knew why, possessing a sort of carnal, earthy maleness simmering away under that elegant facade. His creepy 'Lord of the Manor' style didn't fool him for one moment but he could see it was cat-nip to a cat for women – drawn like moths to the flame. God, he really *detested* the man.

Stella read 'Clive' on the screen and answered the call.

'Good morning Clive! How are you?'

'I'm fine! How're *you*? How did the *lunch* go?'

He couldn't help the emphasis, it rankled to ask about it, but he *had* to know.

'Oh, fine...'

'Just "fine"?' He was suspicious. 'Is that it then? Just "fine"?'

'Well, actually I owe you a pound. You *were* right, he *did* try it on a bit, a little.'

No surprise there then. How much was "a little"?

'Can you meet me later this evening at six thirty, before Chess? You can tell me the details then. As long as you're all right, didn't come to any harm. I thought about you, hoping you were (*what?*) all right!'

'I'm fine,' she replied, sanguine. 'I'll wander along the footpath from about six fifteen, don't rush, I'll wait 'til you get there!'

'Thanks, I'll see you later then. Bye.'

He gripped the phone and cursed. How feeble was that! He so wanted her to want *him* but the odds weren't stacked in his favour. Douglas was obviously rolling in it, and flashing it around could afford to give Stella anything she asked for, while *he* was left having to account for every penny. He tried to view it objectively – what would he have told another man standing in his shoes? Not to be so bloody stupid probably, but then they might not be as emotionally involved as he was. That was the trouble, she had him round her little finger. The one positive that he could see here, was that Spencer had women like Stella for breakfast. In that way he did have an advantage; he'd be there to pick up the pieces that Douglas left on his plate when he'd finished with her.

Clive would receive an edited version, she decided. It was right to have drawn the line where she did, but that *kiss*! She admitted that age-wise he was older than Clive, *part* of the reason she'd prevaricated over further intimacy, but the *real* reason was would he be any good in bed? Possibly not, but *that kiss!* It was a pity such small things like the ability to kiss well were so important, but they were; undisputedly important. Clive's kiss (how could she tell him, she wasn't so unkind) just couldn't compare, *would never compare* to his.

Why was it, she wondered, that a man never came with the whole package? Did men feel the same, in reverse? Continually, some essential element one of them had was lacking in the other, always necessitating a dual relationship. Whichever way you looked at it, Dr. Carroll was right, she never 'did' straightforward, her life was always complicated emotionally, but was her recipe for the 'ideal man' *so* out of the ordinary?

* * *

At six fifteen she dawdled along the small foot-path he'd take on his way to Chess. Some years ago, she discovered certain times were sacrosanct: Chess. She'd wondered then if he had a mistress whom he visited on these occasions. To be completely incommunicado for those times every week of the year (including Bank Holidays) seemed, to her, an absolute rock solid alibi for a little extra-marital activity. Presumably his partners at the club would cover for him if a little checkmating of the sexual kind was offered.

Since getting to know him though, she'd discovered he genuinely liked the game. Not only that, it gave him time-out from being with Martha, 'saving his sanity' he'd said.

She spotted him before he saw her. Head down, it was impossible to gauge his expression. He'd worked in Intelligence and knew all the tricks: body-language, the lot. She'd have to tread carefully he was no fool; unless being in love cancelled that useful commodity out as it had, often so spectacularly, with men all through history, since the world had begun in fact.

He came straight to the point.

'How did Douglas try and seduce you then, what did he do?'

She was ready. 'Not a great deal really, (*the absolute truth in her vast experience*) he stroked me a bit, kissed me (*and how!*) and wanted more I think, (*know*) but I stopped him before he touched me. (Evocative word: touched).

'I said I didn't want to go to bed with him, told him straight (absolutely true) I wanted to keep him as a friend; that involvement, sexual involvement, always had this habit of turning messy. It was by far a much better arrangement to keep things platonic and friendly. I think he saw my point.' (Not).

Clive listened; she *seemed* to be telling the truth, wasn't *too* emphatic, protesting too much! He'd give her the benefit of the doubt, *this time*. It was early days.

'Did you make an arrangement to meet up again?' he asked casually.

This was an easy one.

'No we didn't; I think it was just to say thank you for my

inviting him to the supper we had. If he'd wanted to seduce me, it failed. No, I think that's probably it now. (*We shall wait and see*) You'd better get going, Clive, we'll speak in the morning as usual.'

Giving her a quick kiss he walked back down the path towards the main road. She looked, watching his receding back, but he didn't turn round.

* * *

The telephone call she was half expecting came three days later on Sunday evening. Fairly certain who it would be, she reached for the handset.

'Hello!'

'Hello Stella; it's Douglas!'

She moved to the sofa. 'Hello Douglas, how are you?'

'I'm well thank you, and you?'

'Well, thanks! I've just got back from taking Jeeves for his walk. I'll be getting something to eat in a minute.' Kicking her shoes off and tucking her legs under her, she made herself comfortable.

'I tried phoning earlier, but there was no reply,' he said, 'I assumed you were out with the dog, anyway, the point *is*, we didn't make any arrangement to meet again and without wishing to harass you,' He hoped he'd read her correctly and she was expecting a follow-up call. 'I wondered when it would be possible for us to meet again and when you'd next be free.' Before she could reply he continued:

'I don't know if Thursday would suit you, the third of June?' *Be positive; suggest a date.* 'I go to a sort of flea-market-cum-collectors-fair over at Great Denton and then on to Maple's Farm for lunch if you'd care to join me? You did say you'd like to go out for lunch somewhere, how're you fixed?'

This sounded a good idea.

'I was just about to say Thursday's good. I know the fair you mean, I've been there before and to Maple's Farm. I think it starts at ten. I've got a doctor's appointment at nine thirty in Great Denton, but I could meet you inside the hall and leave my car in the car-park.' Then she had a bright idea. 'Perhaps you could drop me back to it on the way home from lunch?'

Certainly; it was better than he'd hoped for.

'Well that sounds excellent. I think we *should* be discreet. When I come to visit you, I thought I'd leave my car a few streets away and walk. When you come here, you can put yours in my garage and no one will know.'

Hang on, she thought, he was assuming rather a lot, wasn't he? That she'd have him round to her home; leave her car in his garage...

'Hello? Are you still there?' Maybe a *bit* hasty, but he carried on.

'Shall we say you meet me after your doctor's appointment then, in the Public Hall?'

Stella agreed. 'I won't be able to be *too* late back because of the dog, but I'll look forward to meeting you after the surgery.'

He was relieved. 'I'll look forward to it too, very much, I'll see you *then*.' Stop while the going's good, he decided.

She stared at the handset for a moment; he hadn't said goodbye, was a little abrupt perhaps? *But make up your mind,* she thought, *one minute he was assuming too much!* No, the arrangements had been finalised. He obviously just wasn't one to chat. That was women, she smiled, recalling the lengthy conversations she'd held with her female friends.

Men phoned for a purpose and once the purpose had been accomplished, they hung up. She'd locate her diary and enter the engagement officially, not that she'd need to refer to it; she ran through her other appointments, looking to see when she was next going to see Clive: 'Friday 4th: 6.30 evening'. Martha was going to the theatre in Dreighton with friends, so he'd suggested that they had a curry together at her place.

5

Thursday morning was misty and damp, not very warm. The weather so far had been miserable for summer; it was supposed to be flaming June but the only thing flaming had been her gas fire. Rifling through her wardrobe again, she picked a fine crochet tunic in off-white, embroidered with dusky pink roses at the waist. With a few minutes to spare following her appointment, she went into the car-park and looked for his car.

It was there, the shiny black Aston Martin. She couldn't wait. Inside it was crowded. She spied Douglas over by an antiquarian bookstall, browsing, and squeezed through the crowd to join him. He stroked her back absently but didn't give her a kiss. Easing their way round the various stalls, they arrived at one selling vintage clothes. A brassy blonde behind it eyed Douglas from behind the rail, a tape measure round her neck and substantial bosom on display; a subtle, swift glance passed between them.

'Anything here you want to look at, dear?'

Her smile was warm enough, but her eyes were hard as diamonds and as cold as ice. Flicking along the rail, Stella felt rattled. Something about her wasn't right. It was hard to take in what was hanging up. Douglas, going through the motions, dismissed various garments until as if by chance, he held out a beautiful silk chiffon top. It was sleeveless, in different shades of sea-green, fluted at the hem and very unusual. Stella liked it, she was supposed to like it, that's was why it was there, *why they were there*.

Taking it, she looked for the price label. The woman studied her, her lips pursed. Quite the little stunner! Douglas knew his women all right! He'd told her she was a natural and my God he wasn't wrong.

Removing it Douglas casually enquired the price.

'That's thirty five pounds, sir, ta!'

Something significant was going on here, it definitely didn't feel right. Perhaps she was imagining it.

Now she was embarrassed, as she didn't have the cash and didn't want to be beholden to Douglas. She knew she was blushing. He looked at her.

'Is it your size? Would you like it? If it fits and you want it, I'll buy it for you.'

Rhoda smiled. *Dear silly little soul. It's exactly your size and you want it.*

She took a slight breath, resolved now.

'Thank you very much, Douglas, I'd love it, thank you!'

Reaching in his pocket he drew out a wad of notes and peeled four off. She dropped the top in a bag, gave the change to Douglas and passed it to Stella.

'Enjoy wearing it, my love, have a nice day!'

Too engrossed, she missed the glance that betrayed two collaborators: two *satisfied* collaborators.

He could be a bit officious, thought Rhoda, as he'd been when she'd phoned him the other week, but they went back a very long way. There wasn't a single inch of him she wasn't intimately familiar with. Once, long ago, it'd upset her that he didn't love her, he knew every intimate inch of her as well, but she was well over that, she thought. They had the *'arrangement'* which paid the bills and added welcome titillation to an otherwise mundane life. Waiting until they'd wandered on, she searched for her phone.

'Jed? I've just served them. They're on their way to Maple's Farm. I think you ought to take a look. Can you meet me there? As you're in the area, you'd be daft not to…hello?' She shook the phone; the signal had gone. Sticking it back in her bag she began packing up.

Douglas looked at his watch.

'Have you seen enough here, do you think? I'd like to make tracks. It can get a bit crowded at lunch-time.'

He led her through the milling crowd out to the car. He unlocked the doors, which clicked open with that unmistakeable sound of subdued luxury. Sauntering round and letting her in, where she sank into the leather, inhaling the subtle scent and resting her arm between her seat and the driver's, taking in an impressive array of dials as she did so.

The short journey passed in companionable silence. Stella slipped open the bag, wanting another look. She teased it out, feeling the soft silk chiffon. It was beautiful. She sniffed; it smelt slightly of perfume, but not unpleasantly so – a seductive scent to go with a seductive creation. She couldn't wait to try it on. Douglas fumbled around for his sunglasses whilst driving, the sun having decided to come out. Slipping them on, he glanced across.

'I think it'll suit you beautifully, it's as dramatic as you are, darling, and I look forward to seeing it on you.' He watched her smile. 'I'm glad you let me buy it for you. I want to buy you things. I'm unusual I think, in that I love shopping, and I'll *love* shopping with *you*! I'd like to buy you some lingerie perhaps. Do you like lingerie? (*Of course she did*) I'd thought maybe a corset to pull very tight. I'd like to control you and pull the cords very tight. Would you like to look for one?' This was slightly overwhelming, but she could get to like it, she thought!

'I love beautiful underwear, something small and lacy.'

'Do you ever go without any? *Would* you go out without any?'

He stared straight ahead, his tone neutral.

'I *have* done, on occasions.' she replied, 'I don't think I always need to wear a bra.'

She could hardly believe she was saying this! He was so easy to talk to. It didn't feel in the least embarrassing.

'*I* don't think you do either as I remember!' He smiled, making her feel at ease, 'Many women's breasts are droopy, but yours are still pert, they tilt up not down.'

Stella was going to lay a few ground rules down over lunch, but now she wasn't sure *what* she wanted. She gazed out of the window as they pulled into the car-park at Maple's Farm, right in front of the restaurant entrance. The car drawing a few covert envious glances, she felt almost tipsy. About to reach for the handle to open the door, it was opened for her.

This must be how a celebrity felt all the time. Pinching herself (*was this real?*) she heard Douglas's name. He'd appeared not to hear and was heading for the door to the restaurant. Whoever it was, seemed determined that they recognised Douglas and called again. This time he stopped and turned round. The stranger was bronzed and bulky, wearing a black Armani suit with a tee shirt, a huge gold watch on his thick wrist.

'Douglas? I thought it was and you look so well too! Are you goin' in for lunch?'

Douglas seemed strangely agitated as if wanting to escape, but there was nowhere to go except in. She stood by the door, unsure what to do, adopting a semi-smile ready to use if she was introduced, but she wasn't. Douglas held the door for her. Not in a proprietary way, but as if she'd just happened to be there. She was about to say something when he strolled past with the inquisitive stranger in tow, chatting now quite conversationally. Realising she wasn't required she strolled over to look at the menu.

As soon as seemed polite, Douglas extracted himself and meandered back to join her, leaving the man to wander up the stairs leading to a display of Agas and expensive bathroom suites. Stella decided to laugh it off; *he'd* invited her in the first place. Maybe it was a friend of Helen's, although he wasn't, she thought, the sort of man Helen might go for, but she wasn't about to make an issue of it, knowing instinctively he'd feel the same. Once shown to a table, she smiled sweetly at him and joked.

'You can't take me anywhere darling, can you?'

He smiled and studied the laminated menu card. She was right. The subject was closed.

Upstairs, among the glittering kitchen and bathroom displays, prices just a string of noughts, Rhoda Chambers was consulting with 'Mr. Armani.' She was tense and fidgeted with her mobile.

'Did you see her then? She's sitting down there now. He knows his stuff! Little Miss "butter wouldn't melt" with a slit as wide as the ocean, I bet, and as wet! Little madam, I don't know who she thinks she is. What's the betting he's dipped her already?'

'You're jealous, Rhoda, he can control his self. For your sake, make sure you do the same. Bringin' me here was dangerous, bloody stupid in fact *and* unnecessary, seein' as they're coming up to London soon. Jus' for God's sake keep out of the way and stop phonin' 'im – he hates it. If he wants you, he'll call you. Just make sure you're well gone before they get out of here, 'cause if 'e sees you – or *she does!* God help you, now clear off! I want a new bathroom, where's the sales guy?'

He wandered off. Rhoda was history, why was there never anyone around to serve?

About to descend to the restaurant she remembered who was there, so returned through the Agas and bathrooms to another exit. Mr. Armani had found an excited salesman, ignoring completely her passing wave. *Bastard,* she thought, *he's right, I am jealous. That bitch down there is just his cup of tea, fresh as a daisy.* Across the road she saw a garage with rows of polished cars on the forecourt. A large, flapping sign read: 'Quality Used Cars.' Rhoda laughed. *'Quality Used Women,' that's what he leaves behind, well, let him take her up to town, she'll find out soon enough, silly little cow!*

Lunch over, Douglas signalled to a passing waitress then turned to Stella.

'Do you want to go straight back to Great Denton now, or what would you like to do?'

During lunch they'd discussed a mutual fondness for antiques. Stella knew an excellent warehouse not half a mile away from where they were; five floors of antiques and bric-a-brac. Jeeves could wait a little longer. She hadn't yet been able to explain that all she wanted was to 'go out' rather than get intimate, but maybe he just hadn't *allowed her to*. He was very much in control still, she noticed. Had bought her that lovely top, hinted that there may be more where that had come from as well – lingerie, her 'candy', she loved it to death.

'Could we go into Copshall and have a look at the Antique Centre there? I'd like to get back by about four, so we have a little time yet, would you like to go?'

'That's a very good idea,' he agreed, 'yes, let's do that.'

He pronounced it 'Copsle' – believing that was the way it was pronounced by those who 'knew'. Douglas had provided all those sort of men with women more than ready for a bit of extra-marital sex, or rather (if he was honest) *Mrs. Chambers* had. Stella had all the poise and the elegance of the upper-classes; slightly *too* innocent sometimes, but he was satisfied she had four-star in her tank. She'd know what to do with a prick all right, he was convinced of that. She'd make a mint.

'I hope my parking fairy will be working today. Copshall hasn't got many car-parks. I'll try by the centre first and see.'

'Parking Fairy'– she liked that; it made him jollier, like Clive was. A pang of guilt struck. She hadn't thought about Clive. Explaining her plan of just going 'out for lunch' would salve any conscience for the moment.

Douglas's parking fairy was obviously flitting around; there was a space directly at the foot of the steps leading to the centre, and they drew into it. She waited this time, allowing him to open her door. Picking up her handbag, she walked up the steps to the ground floor showroom.

Putting his arm round her shoulder, he bent towards her ear.

'Just slipping across to the Lav, I won't be a sec. I'll come and find you, have a good look round!'

He headed down the steps and across the car-park to the Gents.

At the entrance he fished his mobile from his trouser pocket and pressed the keys.

'Jed! Douglas; I saw Rhoda's car in the car-park at Maple's Farm. Just keep her under control, will you? She doesn't appear to be doing discreet at the moment. It *worries me.* I've brought Stella to the antique centre at Copshall, her idea, then back to Great Denton. Nice speaking to you, sorry to ignore you earlier, I didn't want her to see you speaking to me. Hopefully she won't associate you when we're in town. Too busy dancing around in fancy knickers and silky things I suspect.' He gave a quick laugh. 'I must go! I'll see you later, bye!'

She was engrossed on the third floor, looking at a collection of pretty Victorian nightdresses and assorted underwear, mostly in white cotton broderie anglaise, 'naughty-but-nice' and innocently sexy. He slipped his arm around her protectively.

'Anything there you like, darling?'

She'd found a pretty white camisole, edged in cotton lace, with little strands of baby-blue ribbon running through it. Also an exquisite floor length nightdress in the finest gauzed cotton, again decorated with lace. She loved them and they were her measurements. This time she'd seen the prices, written on tiny white labels, innocently dangling from small gold safety pins. She put them back; this was pushing her luck *too* far. Picking up both items, he held them against her separately.

'Well these look very pretty! Do you *like* them?'

She did; but over a hundred pounds for both? That was too much. She chewed her lip. Douglas smiled, enjoying this, the total was nothing. There was more in his private account than she could ever dream of. He let her stew, then...

'Come on sweetie! Let's go to the desk, I can see you want them and they'll look *stunning!* Come on, over here!'

Before she could protest (she wasn't your average gold-digger, he decided), he opened his wallet and whisked out a card. The lady at the desk explained one paid on the ground floor, but she'd need to write the details down from the price labels into her ledger. This was carried out extremely slowly, the zealous assistant peering at Stella over the top of her reading glasses. The details entered, she passed the garments as if they were disreputable items from a sleazy sex-shop.

'The man will have a bag at the desk where you pay.'
Probably brown paper under the counter! Stella thought.

Back in Great Denton and sitting in Douglas's car, they consulted their respective diaries. She still hadn't broached the subject of a 'lunch only' system and now seemed as good a time as any.

'Douglas, I wanted to say I'd prefer it if we went out for lunch…' he looked at her strangely, hadn't they just done that? '..I'd enjoy outings in general, rather than rendezvous at your home? I enjoy going out; I enjoy your company.' Now what was coming he wondered. 'We don't need to go to expensive places, or even go out every week.' She'd try to make him see her point – she didn't want to be obligated. 'We could take turns to pay as well.'

He was looking at her tenderly, an expression a man might assume whilst looking at an animal that trusted him completely, before committing some violent act of cruelty upon it; knowing the animal would still offer him unconditional affection afterwards. It had been proved that animals were incredibly resilient and loyal — a large proportion of humans were no different if they loved you.

She was obviously used to paying her way. It wouldn't take much to make her feel incredibly spoilt. Good, he'd sweep her off her pretty feet. However, as a starved man should never be presented with an enormous meal at first, neither would he foist *too* much pampering on her at one go. One more date without sex he reckoned, then by the next one she'd have changed her mind and want to go to bed with him, almost certainly.

The next month should see them, all being well, in London and a meeting (a *business* meeting, he corrected himself) with Jed

Zeitermann and colleagues, possibly at the Café Regent. That would impress her, nice and handy for Soho — bright lights, entertainment, she'd lap it up…

'Douglas?' He seemed lost in a dream.

'What?'

Stella tried again. 'I *said* I'd be happy to pay my way and go Dutch, I don't want you to feel I am taking your paying for granted.'

He felt touched; she could be quite engaging.

'Well I believe the man should *always* pay. I wouldn't *dream* of you paying *anything*, it's my *pleasure* to escort you, *spoil* you. From what you've told me, it seems you need a bit of spoiling, so: *let me spoil you!*'

Stella couldn't recall ever implying anything of the sort. Perhaps she'd let slip some remark during that supper with Clive and Martha, or it *might* be a sort of 'fishing' to see how she'd respond to his suggestion. Whatever it was, it was a whole new ball-game and one she could get used to! Her feelings for him were changing; he was very kind and wanted her company. She hadn't got money to splash around on lunches and trips every week, so *let* him!

She gave what she hoped was an enlightened smile.

'*Thank* you Douglas; I'd thoroughly *enjoy* being spoilt actually.'

'*Splendid!* Then that's what I'll do. Now, when would you like to meet next? I see I'm free next Wednesday afternoon. We could go for tea somewhere?' he suggested, 'then the following Tuesday I thought we might try The King's Arms Hotel at Fords Bridge, near Melton Malsor, do you know it?'

She did; it was the beautiful old four-star hotel, featured in all the 'Good Hotel' guide books, a 'celebrity Chef' charging celebrity prices. She'd never been, but wanted to try it.

'That sounds great, tea on Wednesday's fine.' She jotted this down. Turning round, she suggested, 'Shall I come over after lunch some time, about two thirty?'

'That would suit me, yes.'

'Thanks, that's great. I'll look forward to it very much.'

He opened the door to let her out.

'I'll look forward to seeing those things on you too. Just the job, I think!'

Stella clutched her parcels wondering whether to offer a kiss or not – but diplomatic or boxing-clever, he closed the door, going straight round to the driver's side without waiting. Locating his sunglasses, he slipped them on and with a quick wave, eased the wheel of the car towards the road.

Stella, moving out of the way, watching him go and wishing she was still in the car, had the distinct impression that *he* knew that as well. The now familiar ache was there, up between her legs, yet she'd only just told him it was to be 'Lunches Only'. How could she change her mind? She'd have to stick it out for the time being or risk looking stupid and she certainly wasn't going to do that. Perhaps re-consider after a trip to the King's Arms, who knows, just see how things go. Monday afternoon she was seeing Clive. *Good job I live alone,* she thought, *this could get a bit complicated.*

* * *

Douglas phoned Jed from his swivel chair in the study.

'I've just dropped Stella off as I told you, I think she wanted to kiss me but I was too quick. I want her positively dripping by the time we get back from Fords Bridge *and she will be.*'

Jed laughed; his team and crew had got a cracking new gadget in the pipeline, putting all the new technology gimmicks in the shade. The tide was turning. It was possible to buy online machines that could actually simulate sex, with real sensations sent directly to every part of the body at the click of a mouse. People wanted the real thing again now, not a substitute, wanted to *see* the real thing again too. Well they'd certainly get a surprise at *his* club.

'She was a classy bit of work there, Doug, I've got to give it to you, plenty of style with nice tits and a small arse, a neat body altogether. Too many girls look like professional working girls, porn actresses. The whole point *here* is they've got to look like the stuck up bit of totty you see wandering down Sloane Street, or nipping into Fortnum's: all airs and graces on the outside, randy as rabbits on the inside. Well, like I say Spencer, you certainly know how to pick 'em, she's a little peach! Be careful she don't bruise too easily though. "Be *gentle* with me, Douglas!" Jeez! You're a lucky sod you are. Take care of her now!'

Douglas's jaw tightened. Jed was good occasional company and far richer than *he* was; a bit crude at times but that was the job. However, when it came to a certain *'je ne sais quoi'*, Douglas was your man.

'Yes, well, when we get back from Fords Bridge, I'm hoping, presuming really, she'll want to get to bed…after that, over supper, I'll put it to her we come up to town on the fifteenth July, a Thursday, first class naturally, on as early a train as we can from **Dreighton** .'

Jed noted this.

'Then check-in at the Élan, freshen up a bit before getting over to the Café Regent for say, one o'clock?'

'Yeah, sounds good so far.' He continued making notes.

'Meet you there, have lunch, then flip over to Brewer Street and impress her with some snazzy offices. Butter her up a bit and encourage her to express her sexuality – it won't be a problem, I can tell; *believe me.*'

'Oh I do!' Jed was excited. 'I believe you all right, no messin'. Our Rhoda's the one we've got to watch. If she gets a bit jealous and I think she is, she could muck things up completely.'

Douglas was adamant. 'Then don't let her. Or I shall *raise Cain*. She knows I want Stella for the Sirens weekend spectacular in July, does she?'

Jed swallowed. 'Yes she does, but don't worry, I'll keep her mouth shut. I'll be in touch before London, just to finalise things with you.'

'That's fine, nice speaking to you. Be in touch soon, bye.'

6

Friday the fourth of June and Stella was busy preparing for Clive's visit with the curries. She'd discovered tucked away in a drawer, a beautiful Chinese silk jacket teaming it with a tight skirt and satin camisole, pushing her feet into a pair of gold wedge sandals.

There wasn't a great deal to do really – the curries would go in the microwave and that would be it. She lit a couple of candles and fetched the plates out ready. It felt too domestic. There wasn't the sexual tension experienced when about to see Douglas. He had her sussed, seeing through the 'Goody Two-Shoes' image, he presented her with unadulterated lust. They were a mirror image of each other, each repeated reflection stretching into a sexual infinity.

Clive did what it said on the tin: honest, kind and dependable, with the end in sight. Now he was on her doorstep, curries in a carrier bag in one hand, bunch of flowers in the other: definitely 'Mr. Nice Guy.' Did she want that?

'Hello Clive, come in!'

Following her through to the kitchen, he stared.

'What have we here, let's have a look at you! Lovely!' He plonked a kiss on her lips, beaming all over. 'I love you!'

'Love you too!'

But did she? It was so – trite almost. An American TV ad of an archetypal ideal husband and wife: 'Hi Honey, I'm home! Here's the supper.' Ideal husband then kisses ideal wife and places ideal curry in ideal microwave, before an ideal evening together. Clive wouldn't see anything wrong in that, kind, wholesome man that he was – so what was it *she* wanted: *un*wholesome? No, but she'd spent a long time carefully applying her makeup; it wasn't 'tarty', it was subtle and sophisticated, as she hoped her outfit was.

If she was pushed to say *what* she wanted, it would be a sophisticated 'man-of-the-world' confident greeting; a serious face and a passionate kiss, a 'grown-up' kiss. *Douglas's* kiss, but she could hardly say *that!*

'Do you like my outfit?' she tried.

'Yes I do! Very nice, let me feel you!'

He lifted up her skirt but Stella hesitated; this was too early – the TV ad had lost the plot.

He chirruped, 'Oh yes, lovely, lovely; *very* pretty! Is that nice? Do you like that? You like that?'

Cringing inwardly, she smiled. The tone was more 'kindly uncle', not 'experienced lover'. Douglas would *never* use that tone to her, she couldn't conceive he ever would. That was the difference in a nutshell.

When the curries were ready they took them to the sitting room on trays, eating and chatting in the candlelight. He knew what time the theatre performance ended, but was a cat on hot bricks. It didn't make for a romantic atmosphere – one eye on the watch, even a surreptitious one.

No sooner had supper been dispensed with, he was keen to get down to sexual brass tacks. Never having found reaching a climax easy and quick (even more so when under a certain amount of pressure) what was her best bet, she wondered. Clive was creative in his attempts to induce an orgasm, believing her distracted manner was a mental effort to concentrate on achieving it.

Aware of the time, she decided to fake it. Could she imagine it was Douglas? Why not? The trouble was, the serpent had entered the garden and was tempting her with forbidden fruit. Already she was keeping secret the fact he'd phoned her and they'd made two arrangements to meet. It was secret because deep down she knew they'd go to bed together, if not on this next trip out to tea, then probably after lunch at Fords Bridge; no not probably, *definitely!*

The certainty of it and the fact she *wanted* it to happen, did the trick; no need to fake anything now. They both achieved satisfaction and pleasure for different reasons.

'I don't want to go, sweetheart, not now, but I must. They'll be coming out soon and I need to get there on time. I'll ring you as usual in the morning?' He was pleased with himself.

Stella nodded with one hand on the door.

'Yes, fine; thanks for the curry – and the flowers!'

He held her one last time.

'I've had a wonderful evening, I'll think of you all night, text me if you wake early. I'll keep the phone under my pillow.'

'Goodnight, and sleep well!'

She watched him go. Silhouetted against the light in the porch he couldn't fully see her, so gave a quick wave and shot off home, his mind full of his wonderful evening. He'd satisfied her, she'd go to bed contented, dreaming of him; no thoughts of Douglas encroaching on his territory tonight!

As the car tail lights disappeared around the corner, Stella looked at the kitchen clock: 9.15, not very late. She called Douglas's number; which was engaged, there was a request for ring-back if she wanted it; she tried again a few moments later and it rang.

'Hello?'

'Hello Douglas, it's me!'

Douglas smiled, he knew who it was.

'Oh! *Hello!* Isn't it past your bedtime?'

A naughty smile sneaked across her face, she felt skittish.

'It is *really*, but I called for a quick chat. I've been thinking…'

'*Have* you darling, what about? Do you want to tell me?'

She did. 'I've been reconsidering our little arrangement.'

'And what part, exactly, of our arrangement have you been reconsidering?'

She didn't want to stop and think, just get it out as quickly as possible. 'About our outings just being, well, trips out, really.' That sounded silly, spit it out. 'I was wondering if I might reconsider going to bed with you.'

Douglas was enjoying this.

'Hold on just one moment while I turn the television down a bit.' He rested the receiver on his desk, nipped into the sitting room, killed the sound with the remote control and retrieved his glass of claret.

'Do you mean you've changed your mind and *want* to go to bed with me? Is that what you're trying to say?' This was better than the drivel on the television.

Stella swallowed; a nervous reflex, what was she *doing*? Only yesterday she'd decided to 'just go out for lunch'.

'I *would* like it, I think, if we could do that, perhaps at some stage at least – well – *think* about it I mean.' She didn't know *what* she meant, sounding ridiculous even to her. *He'll think I'm an idiot.* 'If *you* would like to too, that is?'

Douglas could feel her squirming. He was getting hard and shifted his position. 'Well to be perfectly honest, darling, it's not something I've ever discussed – it's quite refreshing, actually.'

He loosened his belt. 'There's no rush though, sweetie!' *Go for it, Spencer!* 'Make your mind up after a few more outings, when you're absolutely ready and *sure* it's what you want to do. I'm not going to push you!' *That should do the trick.*

Stella felt lulled again; he was a gentleman.

'When we come back from Fords Bridge, when we'll have all afternoon perhaps?'

Bingo!

'Well, yes indeed if you fancy; let's just play it by ear, shall we?'

His erection was straining and uncomfortable, so he let down the zip. That was better.

'Now, don't you think you ought to be getting into your nightie, or whatever you wear in bed? Do you wear anything, besides Chanel No.5 perhaps?' He teased his shirt out of the way.

Stella knew she was blushing; he was streets ahead of Clive where patter was concerned. It never entered her head that it was due to years and years of practice. It made her feel grown-up.

Something, some imprint in her formative years, had left her feeling she'd never quite acceded to maturity, couldn't be considered a woman by an obviously mature man. At last she was being treated, spoken to as such a woman; it was intoxicating, she wanted it more than anything.

'I do wear a nightdress, sometimes just a T-shirt. I don't feel comfortable with nothing on at all, I can't get to sleep.'

This was wonderful. He felt around on his desk for the box of tissues.

'If someone was in bed with you, you might not want to sleep at all; want them to remove whatever you were wearing if it was getting in the way, wouldn't you think?'

Now it was getting painful. He passed the receiver into his left hand; the need for relief was mounting.

'I can't *sleep* if someone's in my bed. I need to sleep alone…' No! *What am I saying?* 'After making love I mean!' She suddenly felt tired and wanted the conversation to end. 'I do want to go to sleep now, Douglas.'

'Do you, darling?' He pulled out two tissues, ready.

'Well I think we've had a useful chat, thank you for being so frank, you'd better get some sleep and we'll meet next Wednesday, I'll look forward to it; bye now.'

He hardly moved as the tissues filled. Well, that hadn't taken her long; splendid, all systems go now.

'Goodnight Douglas, see you then.'

Replacing the handset, she rushed into the bedroom. Jeeves was asleep in his basket. When he had an irritation, or had done something he maybe shouldn't have done, he would rush away from the scene of the crime and she was doing the same thing, couldn't bring herself to look at the telephone by her bed and yet…she'd do as he suggested and play it by ear.

* * *

On Monday afternoon, Clive waited for Stella in the car park of Dalswood Village Hall, having skipped Chess once again. There was a phone-in programme on the radio about adultery. His hand went to the 'off' switch but then paused. A woman was speaking, had obviously phoned in. The programme interviewer was a man. He caught what she was saying and listened.

'I still love him, but no matter how much I try to pretend that I'm perfectly satisfied, I know I'm not and it causes tension which only makes the situation worse because my husband feels bad about it to begin with.'

Now the interviewer: 'Would you consider having an affair if it was just sex? Many men may argue it's all *they* want out of an affair and are quite happy with that, do you think that would be a solution?'

The woman replied: 'The thing about having an affair is that even if the man didn't get emotionally involved, I probably would. I wouldn't be able to help it; it's such an intimate thing, sex. Then I'd have to question if I still really loved my husband at all and it would only add more stress to the whole situation. Although I'm sure if the offer was good I'd find myself sorely tempted, I know.'

The interviewer came in again: 'Thank you for that; the time is now coming up to one thirty. We'll continue this after the News.' Clive looked up. Stella had pulled into the car park. He turned the radio off and waved, smiling. Inside he wasn't so confident. She was a very attractive woman, easily turned by some blah-blah-blah from someone like Spencer. He flinched suddenly with pain. His car keys crushed in his hand. He *hated* the man. Climbing out of her car, she looked sexy and desirable, about to step into *his* car, so what was he worrying about?

'Hi darling, love you!' He attempted to keep his tone from sounding insecure.

She leaned across and gave him a kiss.

'Mmmm! Love you too; where are we going, over to Caswell?'

'If that's where you want to go that's fine by me, whatever you want to do.'

Smiling at him, she sat back in the seat, contented. Clive was humming; equally buoyant.

'God, I was in trouble again this morning! Hadn't done this, hadn't done that. Then I'd trodden something into the carpet from the garden without noticing, but who cares now!' He beamed at Stella and winked.

The voice of Douglas returned, like the devil sitting on her shoulder, whispering in her ear: '*If the mood took one to go to bed; one just did: I can't recall it ever being discussed, this is quite refreshing actually; there's no rush though, sweetie…*'

She caught his smile, and then glanced sideways at him feeling guilty already.

After a comfortable amble round the small town, they were ready for a tea shop but for some reason they were all closed. Disappointed and about to give up, Stella suddenly spotted a pub: 'The Kingfisher' and suggested they went in for a drink. They could sit in the beer garden, which looked quite attractive and share a packet of crisps each.

Clive looked in his wallet. 'What do you want to drink?'

Stella thought. 'Half a lager and lime please and some salt and vinegar crisps for me. Which do you like?'

Ignoring this, he went up to the bar.

Stella went into the garden and waited. Clive emerged with the drinks and passed her the packet.

'Didn't you want any?'

'No thanks, you tuck in!'

She emptied half the glass straight away. The sun was hot and she was thirsty. Within seconds it had gone to her head. Clive was speaking whilst perusing his diary and she tried to concentrate but her head was woozy. He was asking something, his mouth opening and shutting like a fish gasping for air. She struggled to grasp what he was saying, so he repeated it.

'I said; what are you doing on Wednesday afternoon, this Wednesday coming?'

Before giving it a second thought, glad she could understand the question at last, it was out.

'I'm going out for tea.'

'Oh?' he said, 'Where are you going?'

The lager was taking over now.

'I don't know yet!'

Clive looked puzzled. 'You're going out for tea but you don't know where? Who are you going *with* then?'

Out it came, no equivocating.

'I'm going with Douglas, he asked me.'

Riled now, he raised his voice. 'When did he ask you?'

The lager continued like a truth drug, she couldn't fight it.

'Last week sometime, we're going out for lunches. He's taking me out and I want to go out with him. He's not attached and he can afford to take me!'

Momentarily on the ropes, he was back in the ring very quickly.

'Well OK, you go out with him then, but it's the end of us. I won't put up with it, I mean it! I'm not sharing you with *anybody*, least of all *him!*' He couldn't bring himself to utter the name. 'Is that clear? It's over!' He was furious with both of them, her and Douglas.

Stella's fuddled brain began to clear. 'Now hang on Clive.' She counted on her fingers. 'You have a partner and you're hard-up. Douglas is free and rich and I'm a free woman. If I choose to go out for lunch with a single man whose company I quite like, then I shall.'

The drink was making her waspish. 'You can't dictate to me who I see or where I go. If that's it then that's it. I'm being honest with you now – we're going out for lunch; that's what I told him I'd like to do (*before I changed my mind that is*) so really you can like it or lump it.' Swallowing the rest of the lager, she plonked her glass down.

Gawping and ear-wigging from fellow drinkers tempered Clive's response. He stood up to go.

'Have you quite finished? If so we'd better get back to the car and think about heading back.'

Later that evening he trailed over what Stella had said and concluded she was quite right. He had no authority at all. It was jealousy rearing its ugly head, that, and his concerns that Douglas's motives were nothing if not a little 'iffy'. There was no such thing as a free lunch in his opinion, there'd be a catch somewhere. He would try something. He fetched out his mobile and called her.

7

Wednesday the ninth of June dawned sunny; the sunshine was expected to last all week according to the forecast. Stella decided her morning would be given over to preparations for afternoon tea…and whatever. He'd be expecting her to make an effort, wouldn't he?

Taking Jeeves for his morning's walk, she decided she'd leave the French doors open later so he could get out if he wanted to, not knowing what time she'd be back. While he was snuffling around, she mentally reviewed the call she'd received from Clive a few days ago, consenting to dates with Douglas *provided* they didn't go to bed together. Well, this afternoon wouldn't be 'the whole way' that she'd suggested *possibly* on their return from Fords Bridge the following week. This could be a 'suck-it-and-see' if you like. Blushing suddenly at her own figure of speech, she doubted her own willpower. She'd managed an edited version before – she could manage it again if necessary. She looked at her watch, calling Jeeves back from his rambles.

Douglas watched as Stella climbed carefully from her car within the confines of his garage and walked towards him. She looked ravishing. She'd obviously taken him at his word. He was growing fond of her in the way one knew a cold was coming: caught early enough, it was sometimes possible to stave it off; neglected (when all the signs were there) you could be landed with a right stinker. He didn't want all that nonsense – stick to the plan.

He turned to open the door to the conservatory, playing for time. She looked different. There was more self-confidence. Putting his arms out to greet her, she smiled and kissed him.

'Hello Douglas, lovely to see you! What a lovely afternoon it is now!'

'It *is*, isn't it, and you look stunning; I love the blazer!' Releasing her, he ushered her through the door. 'I thought we might go to Caswell for tea? I've never been but I understand there's a good tea shop there, it's featured in one of the tourist books I have. Does that sound all right?'

What a coincidence! It was a tad close to home, having gone with Clive only the previous week. She wondered which one it was. She was willing to give it a try. Over tea she'd raise the subject of a rather strange mail that had arrived, the postmark too faint to decipher, but it wasn't local. Something about it smacked of Douglas, but how exactly she wasn't sure. She'd try to find out.

He was more edgy than usual, darting glances at her whilst driving. She opened the clip on her bag and poked inside, there was no sign of it immediately, so she undid the internal zip and felt; nothing there either. What *had* she done with it? She was *sure* she'd brought it. She closed the flap then turned the bag over. There was a pocket the length of the bag along the back. Pulling it open she found it and breathed a sigh of relief, relaxing in her seat.

'What were you looking for? Have you lost something?' He was still jumpy.

She stared at the road ahead as he usually did; utterly composed.

'I thought I had but I've got it. I'll show you later.'

* * *

'Hello?'

'Douglas? It's Rhoda; I've sent your little Ms. Maitland a flyer for the S.I.R.E.N.S website. I thought it might tickle her fancy!'

Douglas squeezed the receiver and drew a pencil from his desk-tidy – it snapped, he was so furious.

'You just can't help yourself, can you? You take the first thing that jumps

into your head and do it. I'm seeing her tomorrow and can almost guarantee she'll have it in her bag. If I deny any knowledge it'll look ridiculous when we discuss it in London; if I admit knowledge, she'll want to know exactly what's going on. Even decide to forgo the whole thing and leave! I'll call Jed and tell him that thanks to you, the trip's postponed and could he keep you informed as to any new developments. In the meantime, try thinking before you act? Goodbye!' He slammed the receiver down, fuming.

Now he'd have to plan tomorrow carefully. He picked up his mobile, scrolling down the callers list, found Jed and pressed the key.

'Jed! Douglas here; I've just had Rhoda on the phone, wonderful! She's posted a flyer for the Sirens Club to Stella, web address, the lot, in case it "tickled her fancy"! Now I'll have to concoct something that won't jeopardise the whole show. I know you can't watch her twenty-four seven, but you'd said you'd take care of things now she's in the know. Stella might be daft, but she's not stupid. I'm postponing the trip until I can see the extent of the damage. If I can corner her emotions and I think I'm well on the way there, then there's no harm done, but let's hope so!'

Jed was apologetic: 'It won't happen again, Doug; I'll sort it out. I think half her trouble's jealousy and I can't stop that, but I'll try to contain things, I…' Douglas cut him short: 'Just make sure you do!'

* * *

Pulling into a shady parking space, Douglas turned off the ignition, fiddling with the key a moment. Then with a hand on her knee he faced her.

'You know, darling, it's is a pleasure for me to take you out, we seem to have quite a lot in common. We *like* each other, don't we? I can say anything at all to you on any subject, absolutely anything. It's fantastic; you make me *feel* fantastic.'

Placing her hand over his, she stroked it with her thumb.

'It's a pleasure for me too. Yes we *like* each other! You make me feel very sexy and adult.'

He located his tender expression.

'*Do* I, darling? How wonderful. Well you *are* an adult you know and very, *very* sexy – quite naughty, I'd think. Adventurous even! Shall we have a wander round and try and find this place for tea? 'I'd like some Earl Grey, would you?'

Leaning across she kissed him on the lips, her perfume strong and oriental. He freed his hand and lightly brushed her breast as they kissed a little longer. From the corner of her eye she glimpsed an envelope on the back seat. Emerging from his side, Douglas was round to Stella like lightning, taking her arm at the elbow and closing the door.

'I just need to fetch a ticket, won't be long.'

Cupping her hand against the glass, she peered in. Resting on the rear seat, as she'd seen, was a white window envelope. It was opened but the contents had been replaced so the address was no longer visible. In the top right hand corner, she saw the logo print of a woman like a mermaid, in red, curled round a small black heart. It matched the logo on the post she'd received that morning. Glancing quickly over her shoulder, she saw Douglas about thirty yards away, queuing to get a ticket. A group just in just front of him appeared to be having a whip-round for sufficient change; he had his back to her, patiently waiting.

Keeping one eye on his back, she carefully opened the rear door and felt for the envelope. Snatching it up, she lifted the contents slightly, making out a handwritten signature. In a large, swirly but decipherable script, underlined, was the name 'Jed Zeitermann.' It meant nothing.

Douglas had fed the machine and was bending slightly, waiting for the ticket. She pushed the letter back in the envelope and dropped it on to the seat, carefully clicking the door shut. He was approaching. Her hand was still on the handle of the door. She pulled it away quickly and fiddled in her handbag, looking agitated.

'What is it now?' His pleasantness was deceptive.

Stella whipped out her mobile with apparent relief.

'I thought I'd left the phone in the car, but I've got it here, silly me!'

Displaying the ticket, he closed the door and locked it. With a dazzling smile he slid his arm around her. 'Shall we hit the tea-shops then?'

Happy, she looped her arm round too. He was in his soft denims again and a checked cotton shirt; the material felt luxurious, it wasn't cheap. Underneath his body felt lithe and muscular. The pavement narrowed, necessitating single file.

After passing a few shops they saw a thatched cottage, with a board painted black with white lettering, *'Cream Teas 2.00 – 5.00. 'Welcome'*. Underneath, another line read NO DOGS. A stainless steel bowl containing a dribble of dirty looking water sat below the sign. An archway, complete with rambling rose, had 'Entrance'; under this, a path led to a large lawn dotted with wooden tables and chairs. Some people were already having tea; a few children were excitedly watching ornamental fish in a pond surrounded by a low brick wall.

'I think this is the one we're looking for.' They strolled to an unoccupied table under a bower shady with clematis.

They sat for a moment, admiring the neatly kept borders before a raucous voice from a nearby table interrupted their peace.

'If you want tea, love, you 'as to go inside and order, they won't come to you. You got to go indoors like.'

Douglas turned. It was a large lady with lanky brown hair, wearing a low necked white top decorated with the 'Playboy' motif picked out in tiny sparkly stones.

He smiled, rising. 'Thank you very much, I'll go and see what they've got.'

Turning to Stella, brushing her cheek with his hand, he asked, 'Would you like the cream tea with Earl Grey?'

She smiled, contented; spoilt already.

'Oh yes thanks; that would be lovely.' She watched him cross the lawn in perfect measured strides.

'Mrs. Playboy' watched him too, her huge cleavage on display, and addressed Stella.

'Oooh, classy man you've got there, 'aven't you!'

Stella smiled, nodding; revelling in it. Mrs. Playboy was just about to make another comment, when one of the children shouted at her from the pond. He was up to his knees in water, splashing it over the others who were laughing and shrieking on the surrounding grass.

Without bothering to go over and remonstrate, she shouted.

'Jason! Just get out of that water, you little shit! Come 'ere and get your tea now! Them's new trainers you've got on, get over 'ere now the lot of you!'

Douglas, emerging from the cottage, was carrying a heavy tray. Just in time he lowered it on to their table as the young boy, soaking wet, collided with him, splashing dirty green pond water over the immaculate brick-coloured trousers. Mrs. Playboy immediately waddled over and bent down, exposing even more bosom, running a paper napkin ineffectively over the dark marks, smearing green water weed as she did so. A vein in Douglas's jaw quivered.

'Could you just leave it? The sun will dry it, thank you.'

Mrs. Playboy rubbed his calf with her bare hand. A male companion sitting at her table, with his head buried in *The Star*, looked up.

'You heard the man, Dawn, leave it!' He looked at Douglas. 'Sorry mate, who wants kids, eh?'

'Quite! Who does indeed?'

Struggling to her high heeled feet, she trundled back to the table where she continued to drool, watching him through half closed eyes, all four children now sitting round the table, slurping orange juice through straws.

Ignoring the family, he turned to Stella.

'What have you got there then, is this what arrived in the post? Let me see?'

Stella passed the glossy flyer: it was printed in black, white and red. At the top was a stylised picture of the figure of a woman like a mermaid, in red curved round a black heart. Underneath were the letters S.I.R.E.N.S. and beneath that there were silhouettes of men and women, the women printed red, the men black, in a variety of intimate poses: standing, sitting or lying down. The footer gave some contact information:

We are an exciting new club for adventurous adults: for more information visit our website: www.exploresirens@reflect.com or email us at: info@sirens.co.uk

Douglas studied it closely. Stella reached into her bag.

'It arrived in this.' She remembered the envelope on the back seat of the car and hesitated, leaving the envelope where it was. 'Oh, I don't seem to have it. I must have thrown it away; can you shed any light on it? Have you ever heard of them? Do you know what it is or who they are?'

He folded the leaflet in half and placed it on the table, buying time. Another tray, bearing a massive cream tea, was carried over by a tall, heavy, masculine looking woman with a red, shiny nose, short grey hair and wearing a very unflattering black skirt with a slightly grubby white shirt.

There was an odour about her which was neither sweat nor perfume. Stella sniffed, noticing it, wondering if Douglas could also. She glanced at him but he was helping to unload the items from the tray and didn't seem bothered. She was explaining.

'If you need any more cream just ask, okay?'

About to leave, Stella noticed the enamel pin on her lapel: the figure of a woman like a mermaid, in red, curved round a small, black heart.

Her eyes were mean and cold. Stella wracked her brain. She'd seen similar, but where? The woman at the market-stall, who'd sold her the green chiffon top, had the same hard stare.

Now she didn't feel quite so hungry, picking at her scone distractedly. When she'd had sufficient and without reference to the flyer in particular, she began again. 'Do you know or have you any idea, what SIRENS stands for?'

Thoroughly enjoying the spread Douglas paused, 'I *have* heard of it. I be*lieve* it stands for: sexually intimate rather exciting new sensations.'

Stella was dumbstruck. How on earth did he know that? Now she *was* curious, but a little unsure how to proceed. He carried on, totally matter-of-fact.

'I was wasting a bit of time on the internet and did a search for Sirens for no reason other than I was considering a cruise near the Med at the time. Up came this link and I opened it. It's based in London, with other links in the South East and South West. You had to log on to obtain access to, shall we say, more *specific* information. I didn't want to give my email address, so opted to "take the tour". It's for the more *broadminded* and adventurous adult, not for youngsters or those of a more prosaic sexual bent.' He grinned. 'But it's interesting; a bit different from the usual run-of-the-mill sleazy sites. Have you tried looking it up?' Not a trace, not a flicker of duplicity.

'No I haven't. I'm at a loss to know why it was sent to me at all. It was addressed with full postcode, everything, but nothing else came with it. I did think about looking at it but decided to wait and ask you today to see if you'd heard of it.'

Douglas, his tone still soothing, decided to go fishing.

'Have you ever subscribed to any *adult* publications? Perhaps bought something of an *intimate* nature that you can recall?'

Stella coloured slightly. He'd landed on target.

'I joined a site featuring exotic and erotic lingerie once and made a few, like you said, intimate purchases online, yes.'

Douglas was focused.

'Did you submit your address? I'm assuming you wanted whatever it was you bought delivered to *you* and in case it went astray, gave your full postal address, or how else would your purchase reach you?' His tone was reasonable.

Stella thought. It was possible – sites of a similar nature could share their mailing lists and anybody could find out a postcode nowadays. Her suspicion that something sinister was behind it was dwindling. She was looking naïve. She'd try and appear a little worldlier.

'I like to consider myself uninhibited and adventurous. I'm always willing to try something a bit different!'

She flashed a 'come hither' look, pleased at the desire in his eyes. It made her feel powerful and confident.

With a wicked grin he leaned back in his chair.

'Come on then, roll out your fantasies, have you got any? I'm sure you have!'

His easy manner was infectious.

'I often fantasise I'm a high class call-girl.' He was smiling encouragingly. 'I talk to myself while I'm getting ready to go out somewhere, pretending I share a flat with another girl and we're discussing clients. I like to pretend I'm offering excellent sex for which I'm very well paid.'

This was almost too easy. Perhaps Rhoda's slip-up was a blessing in disguise.

'Being paid large amounts of money in return for sexual favours turns you on then, does it?'

She was away now, the runaway train. Had Rhoda walked into the garden at that moment, he would have kissed her.

'Oh yes it does!' Then she added prudently, 'As a fantasy, that is!'

'But of *course,* darling,' He was glib. 'I wouldn't dream for one moment that you are anything other than *(What?)* exactly what you are; a very attractive and desirable woman.' *Let her make what she will of that.*

'I've never *paid* for sex,' he continued dryly, 'but as you say, I don't see anything wrong in it. I think it would turn *me* on to pretend I was, especially if it was very *good* sex. Personally I don't think there's anything that beats it, what say you?'

'Do you mean very good sex or paying for it? There's a difference!' she replied. 'Personally I'd endorse either, but which do *you* mean?' She raised an eyebrow. She'd got his measure all right, she was sure of that.

'Well, both I suppose, Stella.' He was happy to encourage her savoir faire. 'I find though, generally, it's virtually impossible to find someone with a sex drive compatible to one's own, would you agree? What starts out as something a bit different rarely bears out one's own fantasy: it invariably falls short of the mark. However,' with a twinkle in his eye, 'I live in hope!'

Stella, her appetite returning, took a bite of scone and cream. It was enjoyable talking about sex, especially with Douglas, he was so relaxed and open. Perhaps her earlier fears about him were unfounded. He wasn't being disrespectful, they were chatting about this as equals, what could be better? It never dawned on her there might be an ulterior motive at work. She continued. 'Oh yes I'd agree with that. I think *chemistry*'s very important. Without that, nothing you do is going to be fully satisfying, but *with* chemistry I think you can do *anything*. No holds barred.' She took another bite and licked her lips.

What was tripping off her tongue, completely unsolicited by him, surmounted his wildest dreams. He was on cloud nine. He'd obviously lit the blue touch-paper. All that was necessary was to hypothetically stand well back.

She tipped her head to one side.

'So just supposing someone got in touch with *you* from this 'Sirens' thing? Would you want to get involved?' She wanted to tackle him now. 'Do you imagine it would be up your street?'

She wiped her fingers, waiting. He paused. He'd seen her close the rear passenger door. Was she ferreting for an incriminating answer? He was prepared to bet she wasn't as clever as that. He was prepared to bet also that Clive wasn't proving man enough for the job. She'd set her sights on him quite obviously and wasn't going to risk throwing it all away, even if it meant entering denial over the coincidence. Nevertheless, the letter from Jed tossed casually on to the back seat was very careless. *Now* who was being indiscreet?

He prevaricated. 'In my former life I met a varied clientele, an eclectic bunch. One of them I still keep in contact with is a Jed Zeitermann.' He waited, but saw not a glimmer of interest – so he continued.

'He's an entrepreneur in the corporate entertainment industry and a very interesting man. Every so often he writes to me with news of his various business interests. We're rather isolated here and he knows I like to keep up with any gossip. In his business it's usually pretty hot, too!' This hit the mark, she was obviously impressed – good. My surmising is probably correct.

I'm listening to, she thought, *going out with, a man who has the most incredible contacts and might even take me to meet them if I'm patient and willing.* This would also tie up with and explain the letter in the back of the car: Jed Zeitermann's name was on it. She felt nosy. She should have left things alone. He didn't appear to have noticed anything, *so just leave it; harping on about it's only going to make him suspicious. Let it come up naturally next time, if it does.*

The demolished remains of their meal lay on the table, with no sign of the waitress who'd brought the second tray. Douglas stood up and felt in his back pocket.

'I'll go and settle up, won't be a tic.'

Inside the cottage, in the extended lounge-cum-dining-room, was a bar and till. Through a door behind it, came the rather mannish waitress. She'd applied some fresh lipstick. It looked incongruous on an otherwise makeup free face. She eyed Douglas and then looked at the receipts she had on a spike next to the till.

'Two cream teas with Earl Grey tea?'

'Yes. I recognised the pin and wondered if you belonged locally or in London?'

'Locally,' she replied, 'although I do go to London when I can, my name's Hazel. Do you know Jed?'

'Jed's a very old friend of mine,' he answered. 'I'll be seeing him quite soon actually, accompanied hopefully by the young woman with me this afternoon.' He raised an eyebrow and tipped his head towards the door.

Needing the cloakroom, Stella headed for the cottage, to look for a sign to the Ladies. About to ask, she caught the drifting conversation and paused to listen. So; he intended to take her to see Jed a very old friend of his. When? Why tell staff information like that? Did she know him or what? She hid behind the remains of the dividing wall, trying to catch more.

'Is she a member with you?' asked Hazel.

'I'm *preparing* her, shall we say,' he replied. 'It's not "grooming" as such although in some respects she's very child-like.'

Stella stiffened. 'Grooming' 'childlike'? What was he on about? She was an adult, he'd told her so. Was this to do with the Sirens thing, she wondered? 'She desperately wants to please and receive reward, but in other ways she's mature and, I would say, adventurous even. My instincts aren't usually wrong.' He paused. 'Did she appeal to *you?*'

What the hell?? She was getting desperate, but didn't want to miss anything. She clenched her muscles tighter and listened.

'Yes she did,' she replied with enthusiasm, 'she's got that innocence about her; innocent on the *surface* but deeply sexual underneath. In my opinion she'd take to the Club like a duck to water! Assuming you're not going to drop her in the deep end. That wouldn't normally faze a duck though, would it?'

Laughing at this little joke, Douglas replied,

'Quite! No, I intend to take this very slowly. My only concern at the moment is a letter from Jed on the back seat of my car. I was unusually careless and threw it there for later. I'm sure she saw it, which was rather unfortunate, although my guess is she didn't have chance to read it. Anyway, the point *is* she likes sex. That much is obvious. Now, how much was the tea? I can't be too long here or she'll wonder what's going on. It's been very nice meeting you though, Hazel.'

Stella was chary: so it *was* to do with the club then! The fact she'd seen the letter, he knew. Whether or not she'd read it, he didn't *and she hadn't*. Now she wished she had! All she'd seen was the signature – a man they both seemed to know. He'd addressed the waitress by name, so how much of this conversation had she missed, any of it? She didn't like the look of her. The whole situation was a bit weird, a bit surreal. Her head swam suddenly with nerves – should she trust him now? "I'm preparing her…" *for what?* "…did she appeal to you?" *in what sense?* Maybe Cathy was right about not trusting him. But she wanted him. She fancied him like mad. Another spasm necessitated immediate action. She crept back to the doorway making up her mind to pretend she'd just arrived, knocking the knocker on the opened door.

'I thought I'd come and find you,' she called, 'you seemed a while and I need the Ladies. Do you know where the cloakrooms are?'

'They're through there.' Hazel indicated a door to the left of the bar. 'Then second door on the right, the first is the Gents.' She looked at Douglas.

She followed the directions then found another door taking her on to the street again. She waited in the doorway and after a few minutes Douglas emerged looking for her. She felt excitement rise, it was true. She desired him every time she saw him. She resolved to go with the flow. Fate and destiny.

'There you are darling, shall we head back to the car now?' His tone was seductive. 'And go home?'

Smiling, she walked in front of him on the narrow pavement, back to the car park. The afternoon lay ahead; it was going to happen and they both knew it.

8

The drive home, heavy with sexual undercurrents, made conversation tense. On descending the hill before the turn to the cottage, the nerves tingled in her arms. Her throat was completely dry, nervousness causing her to swallow involuntarily, making her cough.

'Is everything all right?' he asked concerned, his clenched hands on the wheel the only visible sign of tension.

She struggled to get some moisture in her mouth and saw a bottle of water. 'Would you mind if I had a sip of this?'

Douglas smiled. 'Of course not, help yourself.' He swung the car expertly down the driveway towards the house, pulling up beside the conservatory. Stella remained where she was, not even undoing her seatbelt. Her hands trembled, dropping the plastic bottle.

Casually opening his door and ambling round he smiled in amusement.

'Are we getting out?'

Her legs felt they didn't belong to her. None of her limbs did. Sliding towards the door, she felt the belt restrain her. He leaned across, gently releasing the fastening. She smelt his aftershave, potent and arousing, pulling like a hook in her groin.

'We have to take this off, darling, or you can't get out,' He let it slide into its socket then held the door. 'Out you come!'

Making an effort, not wishing to appear completely foolish, she grabbed Douglas's hand and climbed out carefully. Douglas, a pillar of diplomacy, pushed the door shut behind her.

Inside, he walked through to the study and checked for any phone messages. There weren't any, so he wandered casually back to the kitchen, pottering around deliberately. Stella, tension fading like steam from a mirror, followed him. He picked up the kettle and gave it a shake.

'Would you like more tea or have you had enough?'

Stella didn't want tea, she wanted something else and hoped Douglas did too. Had she made a fool of herself already, though? Would he think she didn't want him? She did. Sidling over, she placed her arms around his waist before lifting her face towards him. Sliding a hand behind his neck, she tilted his face down towards her, kissing his lips.

He eased her away gently to replace the kettle, before whispering, 'What do you want to do now then, Stella? Where would you like to go, *mmmm*?' Running his fingers under her chin, he let them wander round to the back of her neck, gently pulling the fine hair at the nape of it, winding it around his finger. Stella tried again to kiss him, but he placed a finger on her chin, preventing her.

'Tell me what it is you want, Stella?'

She knew what she wanted now; she *knew*.

No hesitating, 'I'd like to go upstairs with you, to the bedroom.'

Taking her hand he led her towards the stairs.

'Let's go then, shall we? Up here.'

Stella followed a step at a time. At the top he led her into the airy and bright spare bedroom and her confidence drained away again. She stood closely in front of him and shut her eyes, her arms at her sides. Without saying a word, breathing steadily, he held the top of her dress, feeling for the zip. With one hand on the material to anchor it, his other drew the fastener down slowly, negotiating a belt at her waist, until it reached the bottom.

Poking his fingers in the opening under the belt, he gently stroked the bottom of her spine, just above her buttocks. Slipping a finger down between them, he traced the course of her thong, but avoided touching anywhere more intimate, pulling the elastic up slowly and tightly between her legs.

With her eyes closed and her ears ringing, she rubbed his back before gripping a handful of shirt from his waist. She pulled it up with gradual but increasing urgency, not caring now whether he'd ultimately be able to satisfy her or not. He was so erotic it wouldn't matter – it was completely irrelevant.

He was unbuckling the belt, gently easing the dress off and allowing it to drop to the floor. Her arms at her sides, he unhooked the back of her bra using both hands, unfastening it easily; discarding it to join the dress. All that remained was a half-buried thong. Sliding his hands down her hips, under the band of elastic, he drove it firmly down until she was completely naked. She lifted her legs to step out of it, holding his arms as she did so.

With a wrist in each hand, he moved her arms apart and studied her, drinking up the sight.

'Absolutely beautiful, aren't you? A proper Venus de Milo – the perfect woman's body – in and out in all the right places and a perfectly shaved mound just *wai*ting for me, how *won*derful!'

Releasing her wrists, he moved behind her, unfastening his shirt and slipping it off. Keeping her back towards him, she heard the rest go but didn't want to turn round. Not yet.

Then he called, 'Come over here and lie down darling, come on, turn round and don't be shy!'

She bit her bottom lip, ready for anything, ready to be *polite* about anything *(he'd be no good)* and turned round.

He heard the gasp.

'Oh my God...*Douglas!*' She couldn't believe her eyes. Was it *real*? It had to be! 'Did you? How have you...?' She wasn't making any sense at all.

He reclined, grinning; a wide, lascivious grin. Not needing to move an inch. 'I carry all before me as you see. Well, do you *want* it then, darling? I think it wants to take *you!* I want to impale you on the end of it, come over here and *hold it!*'

His tone was throaty, emphatic and coarse. He was still. There was just the one part of him quivering. Some women had legs reaching 'all the way up to the top' – this *thing*, his erection, went 'all the way *down*' to his balls, a long way down, a vertiginous way down. Stella didn't have a problem with vertigo. She moved to the bed and lay next to him.

Now it was his turn to be surprised, he'd never had it as good as this, ever. It could begin and end in a few seconds if he wasn't careful. He hadn't bargained for this, he'd met his match.

Placing his hands gently on her head, he twisted his fingers in her beautiful, shiny hair, holding her carefully. She was a pro. He noticed her teeth hadn't touched him all the way down. No gagging reflex, not a glimmer – her throat open and completely relaxed. Her tongue darted suddenly. She drew in half a breath. It was accurate. Air glanced that spot. Cold – then warm. He thought he'd died and gone to heaven. She fixed her eyes on his face. She was in control now, he realised, this sometime innocent looking woman was capable of propelling events forward or halting them in their tracks and he was utterly helpless to do anything.

'Oh *oh, oh darling, please! No! Oh yes; oh Stella, please no!*' He was babbling, completely incapable. Valerie, Rhoda, Helen, *Helen!* Nothing previous compared to this. How in God's name had *this* happened? How? He couldn't believe it.

He wanted to have her, bloody hell he wanted to have her. He was an inexperienced kid compared to this *professionalism*! Jed would go into orbit – suddenly, remembering that name, the plan, he began to shrink. He didn't want to share this little peach with *anybody,* let alone Jed Zeitermann. He forced the man to the back of his mind. She'd eased him from her mouth and was lying next to him, rubbing her hands up and down his back and squeezing his buttocks, pulling them apart, eyes dark and full of power.

'Was that good Douglas, did you enjoy it?'

He stared at her, the little minx. She *knew* he had, *knew* how good it was. And how good, more to the point, *she was*. He was almost the pupil now, instead of the master.

'I want to feel it inside you, I want—'

'*I want, I want!*' she teased, 'What about what *I* want, darling? Before it goes anywhere else, how about you pay a little attention to *me?*'

Her face was suffused with longing. As were those deep, lascivious eyes. He could refuse her nothing. He wanted to give her everything, use every one of his senses: taste her, smell her, look at her, feel her and listen to her. He wasn't used to being instructed, thought that he alone would be in control, but she was his equal in every way.

Propping himself up on one elbow, he looked down at her for a moment before lifting her legs, one on either side of him, sliding further down the bed. He could smell her arousal, smell her sex. He let one hand secure the top of one warm thigh, as with the other, he ran his thumb across, parting her, watching the glistening, welcoming anemone.

She'd felt his thumb exploring and closed her eyes as with a slight brush of hair he went down. Then it was nothing yet everything. She was lost. He was working her and she could hardly bear it.

Opening and teasing her with his lips, he used his tongue and teeth to torment her, his fingers squeezing and pinching her nipples above him. She felt the velvety sensations mounting then receding and the wonderful laxity that comes before a climax. In less than five minutes probably, he stopped precisely on the brink and looked up at her, knowing he'd timed it to perfection. Her whole face slackened, her lips numb, as after a visit to the dentist, her tongue lolling.

'Turn over, Stella.' It was a command, the balance of power passing back to him.

Struggling, she rolled over.

'Lift up a bit sweetie, *that's* it*!*'

He eased a cushion under her hips, stroked her buttocks and moved them apart: a tight little arse – the muscle clung involuntarily. She wriggled. He was getting hard again. He couldn't remember such an erection before and wasn't going to wait any longer. Moving, she tried to reach herself with her fingers.

'Are you ready to come, darling?' he asked, receiving a muffled affirmative.

She froze then yelped, as the length increased uncomfortably. Pulsating on to the bed, her face buried in the pillow, she gave little grunts of pleasure as he continued to push.

'Now it's my turn darling, *wait…now!*'

She lifted her hips. A few seconds later, his arms relaxed, she was covered from head to foot by his body. Shifting her head round to lie on her cheek, he kissed her gently near her eye. It was over.

The telephone was ringing, she could hear it, but he wasn't moving.

'The phone's ringing, Douglas, the telephone, are you going to answer it?'

'Is it?' He listened. It was still ringing. With a spurt of energy dredged from somewhere, he lifted himself up and swung off the bed, moving quickly to the other bedroom to grab it before it stopped.

'Hello?'

'Hello Douglas it's Helen. How are you?'

It was a drench of cold water. Immediately he was alert.

'Helen! Hello, how *are* you?' He felt for the door with his foot and pushed it shut behind him. 'I'm fine, thanks. I thought I might come down to see you next month if that's all right, there's something I want to discuss. I could catch the two forty seven train from Guildford, get into **Dreighton**, connections permitting, about five fifteen on Monday the nineteenth, could you meet me?'

Douglas thought fast. He had the trip up to London to organise. 'Any idea how long you want to be? Would it be a fleeting visit or something longer? Just so I can make sure I'm free, that's all, any idea?'

'I'd be returning on Saturday morning, the twenty-fourth. I've some other people to see while I'm down, so won't need you waiting on me every day. I need to know now though, if possible, so I can book the tickets.'

'Of course you do. Yes, that'll be fine! I'll meet you at the station on the Monday. I'll be there by five o'clock. Ring my mobile if you're delayed or there're any other problems.'

'Thank you, Douglas, I'll see you then. Are you keeping well?'

'I'm *fine* thank you, yes. See you, 'bye!'

Replacing the receiver, he heard Stella moving about, heard the lavatory flush. He was in a quandary, this was completely unexpected. What a day it was turning out to be! Opening the bedroom door he found her curled up on the bed, turned away from him. Without moving her position she spoke quietly.

'Who was that on the phone? Is everything all right?'

Padding over, he sat on the edge of the bed, resting a hand on her hip.

'That was Helen.' He stopped, she hadn't shifted beneath his hand so he continued, 'and it seems she's coming down to stay for a few days next month.' There was still no reaction. He changed his tone, 'How would you like to take a trip up to town with me before then?'

He stroked her hair. She stretched slightly, keeping her face hidden. He kept his tone light.

'It would mean an overnight stay, possibly longer, would you like to meet a few friends I still keep in touch with, have lunch at the Café Regent and perhaps find time for a bit of shopping? I don't know what she wants, but it won't interfere with our plans although maybe,' he suggested quietly but more firmly, 'it might be better she doesn't know about them while she's here. She's only coming for four days, not long.'

She absorbed this. Helen was coming to stay, but he was, in almost the same breath, offering to take her up to London. Introduce her to some old colleagues, go shopping – *stay overnight*.

She rolled over. He looked unflustered, quite normal, and had pulled a dressing gown on which suited him: stripes of Mediterranean blues and greens. It was very flattering. Stretching out fully on the bed, she arched herself like a contented cat. The sex had been fantastic, far better than she could ever have hoped for. There was nothing to think about.

'I'd love to go up to London with you, Douglas, and meet your friends. I think we'd have a lot of fun together. And especially with an overnight stay...' she added softly. Then leaned back on her elbows, chin down, eyeing him provocatively, 'You could hire me for the weekend! I'd happily be your escort, darling!'

Leaning across, he gently brushed her nipples. Resting his chin between her breasts he looked up at her as she slumped lower on the covers.

'*Would* you darling, will you be my very sexy escort and keep me company?'

'Oh I *will.*' she said slowly, decided. 'Do you think we can have a bath now perhaps, maybe some champagne even?'

With an impish grin he rose from the bed.

'Very good Madam, I'll go and run it and order up chilled champagne and two glasses,' He put a finger on the tip of her nose. 'Wait there, I'll call you!'

Lolling on the comfortable bed, she watched him as he left the room. In the kitchen below he was humming. She heard the clink of a couple of glasses and the fridge open and shut then climbing the stairs once more he walked through to the bathroom. In a few minutes the scent of pines wafted through into the bedroom with the sound of running water, then some music. It was a trombone playing soulfully on a CD from the next room. Stella vaguely recognized it, it was dreamy and relaxed. Getting up, she wandered into the bathroom, not waiting to be called.

He was bending over the bath, swirling the water with his hand.

'A warm bath, chilled champagne, romantic music, this is how it *should* be, darling. You look beautiful, climb in and I'll fetch you a glass of fizz.'

She sank down in the warm water, while he took the chilled, streaming bottle and eased out the cork. It gave a gentle pop and he reached for the glasses, expertly filling them, topping them up once the foam had subsided.

Joining her, he sat opposite, gave her a glass and tipped his towards hers in a toast.

'Well here's to us, Stella, and lots of happy times ahead!'

'I agree! To us! What's the title of this music? I know it, but don't know what it's called, do you know?'

His eyes crinkled at the corners. 'Oh I *know*, it's called, "I'm getting sentimental over you" it's Tommy Dorsey, from the nineteen thirties. Do you *like* it?'

'Yes I do, I love this sort of music; it's romantic.'

'Yes it *is*. We seem to like a lot of the same things and have a lot in common.' His eyes sharpened. '*Don't* we?'

She agreed, nodding and sipping her glass of champagne. You could get used to his way of speaking. Grow to like it in fact. She stroked his balls gently with her toes and slid down beneath the bubbles, gently swinging her glass in time with the music, relaxed.

'Isn't this civilized? How it *should* be....' A mischievous glint shone in his eye.

He traced his own foot between her legs.

'....is it like this with Clive?'

Startled, she looked up. He enjoyed seeing her slightly uncomfortable.

'Not quite, no; it isn't.'

He chuckled.

'Well you'd better enjoy it with *me* then, *hadn*'t you?'

9

Reggie Crifton aimed a friendly slap on Helen's naked bottom as she bent over to straighten the bedclothes. Reaching for his shirt, he began mimicking.

'Have you *"phoned Douglas"* pet, and has he *"said yes"*?'

Straightening, Helen scolded him, laughing.

'Now stop it, Reggie, don't be naughty! I called him to say I'd be going down on Monday the nineteenth of July and coming home on the Friday. All I said was there's something I wanted to discuss, that's all. He won't be very happy I don't think.' She pushed the fringe away from her eyes. 'He still loves me, that's half the trouble.' She wandered towards the bathroom and Reggie watched her, admiring her figure. He could understand her point.

He loosened his tie, turned up his shirt cuffs and continued with a wicked twinkle in his eye.

'Well, the point *is*, he'll have to get used to it then, *"won't he?"!*'

'I said stop it!' She peeped round the door. 'You are awful, you know!'

He leaned close towards her. 'Yes, but you *like* it, don't you? Can I come in?'

'No!' She closed the door. 'Go and sort out some breakfast, we've got a lot to do today.'

'Your wish is my command, pet! Don't be long, and tea or coffee?'

'Tea please, thanks.'

She had another peek at the solitaire ring, cushioned in its box on the windowsill and smiled. There was pop music now from the radio downstairs and Reggie's mellow voice, singing along.

Reggie had good cause to celebrate, having known her a long

time. He'd smiled as he recalled phoning her on her mobile, asking after 'His Excellency'. Knowing full well who was there, that the calls needled him, that his feelings were far too strong to risk rocking the boat by forbidding them. She'd told him how she'd tried to let Douglas down lightly before storming out completely.

It was at her recent birthday celebration, to which Douglas had been invited, that his fate had been sealed. What a farce that had turned out to be; it should have been on the stage. So blinded was Douglas with besotted love, he hadn't a clue which way the wind was blowing. All over Helen like a rash after the ignominious break-up and believing an olive branch was being waved in his direction. He'd arrived all dressed up like a posh dog's dinner, oozing champagne and gifts for her while Reggie had her pants in his pocket (his idea) and his pyjamas under her pillow. In the guest annexe, unpacking as meek as a lamb, Douglas had accepted Helen's towels or anything offered to him, as grateful crumbs from her table.

She'd insisted that in exchange for him pocketing her pants, Reggie had to behave himself, and not wind Douglas up as was his wont – and he'd agreed, well able to be magnanimous now. Yes, it was all falling into place. Soon he and Helen would be married, with homes in Portugal, London and the North East. He was a true Geordie, but had sung his way out of poverty – not quite Sinatra, but doing very nicely thank you now a new generation of youngsters from eighteen to thirty had discovered Swing and the old songs of the Crooners. Suddenly he was top of the pops, up there and the same age as Jagger, milking this new craze for all he was worth.

Looking from the kitchen into the garden, a spaniel was racing round the lawn; a present to Helen and another thorn in Douglas's side, having forbidden her a dog at their cottage, knowing her fondness for them but standing firm. While still an untrained puppy, it had got into the annexe where Douglas was staying, leaving a little packet on the bathroom carpet which, too late,

Douglas found with his bare foot. Reggie had nearly burst himself laughing, Helen cleaning it up, apologising. Douglas had been in a fix; revolted by the mess but ambivalent regarding Helen and little Buster: a gift from his rival. Loving dogs himself, he hadn't wanted to be tied to one at home…and he still loved Helen.

Reggie's reaction of mirth had infuriated him. They'd laughed 'til they cried in bed that night! Little Buster was curled up in his basket, having made his presence well and truly felt where, as far as Reggie was concerned, it really counted.

Tea, cereal and toast ready, he called Helen, scooping up the newspapers from the doormat and placing the *Daily Mail* by her breakfast setting. Opening his copy of the *Independent*, a glossy supplement fell out – a trailer version of a new magazine to be published called 'The Spice of Life'. It was boasting interviews and articles of a bohemian and controversial nature. This pilot issue previewed a new club that was garnering publicity, but had previously been discreet and shrouded in mystery.

Some information was available on their website, but anything *really* worth seeing was secret unless you forked out for membership. Members were as protective about the goings-on as the Brotherhood, but someone had obviously had enough and decided to blow the whistle (probably encouraged by a lucrative fee) telling all and causing a stir. The club was called S.I.R.E.N.S. which stood for (pointed out in bold copy) Sexually Intimate Rather Exciting New Sensations. Letting his tea get cold, cereal untouched, he began to read:

'The Club originally opened in 1959 in converted premises off Brewer Street. The aim was to gather together like-minded, sexually adventurous adults, in a congenial atmosphere, where any sexual experience, providing it was genuinely consensual, could be carried out and enjoyed to the full with no holds barred. Using all the current technology available, areas could be converted into virtual situations limited only by Members' imaginations. For example, if a Victorian Brothel was required, complete with every Victorian decoration and effect – even

down to 'pea-souper' mists swirling around, and the noise of horses and carriages outside – it could be provided. Every single fantasy that could possibly be conceived was available at the click of a mouse or flick of a switch, the only provisos being that no fantasy or scenario could involve animals or children in any way whatsoever. Anyone caught contravening these rules would have their membership instantly cancelled, and never be allowed to return.'

Helen picked up her mug of tea and wondering what was absorbing him so much, tweaked the pages.

'Got something interesting?'

'Aye pet listen to this!' He was excited. 'Someone's been kicked out of a club in London and been tellin' tales out of school. The name of the club's Sirens and sounds a little bit on the fishy side to me like!' He looked up and grinned. 'You might want to take a look, there're some names here as well.' He read them out, 'Piers Falby, no, don't know him. David Thorpe rings a bell, Jed Zeitermann I've never heard of either,' looking up, 'does he mean anything to you?'

Helen stopped in her tracks and replaced her mug carefully. 'Jed *Zeitermann* you say?'

'Yes, you know him?' Reggie was curious.

'The *name* sounds familiar.' She sat and clutched the edge of the chair. 'I think Douglas used him sometimes.' She became serious. The memory had made her squirm. 'It was all a bit sordid. Some of his patients from Harley Street days had a little side-line going with "discerning gentlemen of a randy disposition."'

He put down the paper, tongue in cheek and looked at Helen, not quite believing this.

'Believe me, it's *true!* I *suppose* if you had to be pedantic, it was a kind of pimping,' she said, 'but he'd disagree. He was pairing off women: rich, bored and wanting servicing, with discreet men who were happy to pay.'

Reggie was agog.

'There was him and a Rhoda Chambers, I think, met her once

and didn't like her. She'd got her eye on Douglas at one stage, but he wasn't *that* keen. Although they *were* quite close before Valerie died and a while after, then we met at a party and she wasn't mentioned again.' She was curious, 'Is her name there as well?'

He scanned the article, looking, and then found it on the second page:

'Regular staff at the club included Rhoda Chambers; she was in charge of interviewing and choosing suitable women wishing to work there as 'hostesses.' A Madam by any other name, this being hotly denied though, her argument being that they worked for a Members Club with strict membership rules and were not there as sex workers. Precise details appertaining to their duties were not forthcoming on interview, except that they enabled the smooth and successful running of the Club and were bound by contract to be unavailable outside the Club premises for any purpose whatsoever.'

He looked up, grinning now from ear to ear.

'Ho *ho;* I wonder if Douggie's seen this! I bet you he's mixed up in it somewhere, the maggot! It sounds right up his alley, sorry, *right up his alley*!'

He ducked as Helen aimed a swing at him, laughing.

* * *

Jed was just finishing a sandwich, feet up on his desk, when the phone rang. It was Katie, his Assistant; for some unfathomable reason they weren't secretaries any more.

'Jed, sorry to interrupt your lunch, but I have Reggie Crifton on the line, at least he *says* he's Reggie Crifton. Would you like a word or shall I tell him to call back later?'

Swinging his feet off the desk, he pushed the sandwich packet away. 'Reggie *Crifton* you say? Do you mean *the* Reggie Crifton?'

'So he says. Do you want a word?'

'Yes, put him through.' There was a brief pause, then Katie's voice.

'...Reggie Crifton for you.'

'Hi, is that Jed Zeitermann?'

'Sure is, is this Reggie *Crifton*? To what do I owe the pleasure of this call? How did you get this number?'

Reggie chuckled. 'Bit of a long tale. I'm calling in case you know a Douglas Spencer.'

'In what connection would that be?' Jed was cagey.

He took a gamble.

'It's the Sirens Club and Rhoda Chambers? I know Dougie of old, met up with him only a short while ago and he'd got that twinkle in his eye. Rhoda had a bit of a thing for him *before* he met Helen. He got a bit jumpy when I mentioned her name. I'm pretty close to Helen now, like. She's going to see him next month, she said that you and he were buddies a way back and I thought like, you know, I'd call and see what's cookin''

Jed was on thin ice here: Douglas *would* be jumpy about Rhoda because of the business with Valerie's death. That was dodgy. He didn't want to get into any *more* trouble discussing it where he shouldn't. He knew also, Douglas still carried a torch for Helen despite his interest in Stella and putting two and two together, she might be about to give him news he wouldn't want to hear. Jed had a deadline. He needed Stella, with the co-operation of Douglas as well. He'd have to be very careful until he knew what motive, the *real* motive, had prompted Reggie's call.

'Hello? Hello? Are you still there?' Reggie hoped he hadn't gone too far.

'Hi! Yes, just looking at an email, sorry.' How could he continue this conversation without landing him in more of a mess? Then he had a flash of inspiration.

'Reg, you told me just now you were calling *in case* I knew Douglas Spencer, what did you mean *in case?*' He neatly hit the ball back into Reggie's court.

There was a pause; Jed allowed himself a smile and a sigh of relief.

'I might be interested in this Sirens club. From what Helen told me of Douglas, I wouldn't have thought it was his scene! (*Not much!*) I thought you might be able to pull a few discreet strings like and let me see if it's what I'm looking for. In the entertainment business I come across some…*interesting* women. I'm sure you're a man of the world yourself; there may be a bit of business in it for you.'

Jed was taking notice now. He'd amassed a small fortune, but was as susceptible to flattery as the next man and if he'd heard correctly, not only might he be able to introduce a celebrity to the Club, but also land a few choice women as well.

It was times like this, though, where unlike Douglas, Jed's common sense flew out of the window as the dollar signs began going round.

'Reg, let's get this straight, can we? You're closely connected to Helen, who was going out – well, who was shacked up with until not that long ago, Douglas Spencer, who I go back with a long way too. You're interested in our little club, but wouldn't necessarily want Helen to know. Am I right so far?'

'Aye man, yes; you've got the picture.' Reggie recognised an easy touch when he heard one; Jed was no exception.

'And it *might* be you're not only interested in finding out about us here, but also supplying a bit of the old totty?'

Why he'd worried, he didn't know. Jed was priceless.

'Aye man, I do that, but we don't want to upset Helen with details, can I rely on your discretion here?' *Of course he could.*

'Say no more, Reggie, you sure can! Now, how do you want to play this? You say Helen's going to see Douglas next month? How about we meet up and I take you round on the tour. We can discuss anything over a steak and a drop of the old bubbly, what do you say?'

'Aye sounds great to me, man! Are you seein' Douglas any time soon, like?' It was a risky question but he'd got him sussed.

'Yeah, I am as a matter of fact! He's got a cracking new bit that can't seem to keep her knickers on for long, gagging for him by all accounts! They're up on the fifteenth of July. She was enough to rattle Rhoda. You said you knew about Rhoda as well?'

Talk about a canary, the bird had nothing on Jed. 'Aye, she had the hots for him years back and proved her loyalty, *at a price*.' This was a real shot in the dark, but worth the risk.

'Yeah right, *at a price*; I try to keep on the right side of her myself. She's got a bit of a trap on her, doesn't always know when to keep it shut either!'

Pot and kettle too! Reggie couldn't believe his luck. Wind this up and get out while the going's good.

'Can we fix a time, date and place to meet? I've got to go out in a few minutes.'

'Sure thing, Reggie!' Jed reached for his diary and opened it, finding July. 'Well, how about Wednesday the twenty first? Say twelve o'clock at Rosie's Bar, Raglan Place off Brewer Street, do you know it?'

'Not off-hand but I know Brewer Street, I'll find it. Twelve o'clock sounds fine. You'll recognise *me* and I'll wait to be introduced.' He paused. 'Wait a minute. Did you say Douglas was arriving on the fifteenth?'

'I did, yes, but did you really want to see him when you were up?' He hadn't wanted this.

'I'm keen to know what he gets up to on his visits. I'd keep out of his way, how big's this place?'

'Big enough and dark enough to hide if you want to – we've got observation rooms for members who like to watch. I'd keep you hidden, he'd never know.'

That sounded excellent.

'Aye just the job there then, Jed, I'll be up on Friday the sixteenth, leaving the following Wednesday or Thursday. Meet you just the same?'

Jed scribbled in the diary. 'I've got you down for Friday now and I'll meet you at Rosie's, thanks for calling, I'll see you then.'

Replacing the receiver, he sat transfixed for a moment then raised his fist. *'YES!'* Reaching for the phone again, he obtained an internal line, keyed in three numbers and waited.

'Hi, it's Jed. Tell me – is Miranda around this afternoon by the remotest chance? Yes I know; that's why I'm asking. Yeah, I'll hold.'

He shifted his position in the chair, reaching in his fly to adjust his underpants. That was better.

'Hello? She is? How about three o'clock...*where*, oh...' He thought a moment. 'Tell her I want a nurse...well the hospital-mode of course! What? A *baby*, I'm not a soddin' *baby*, darlin'... Yeah, maybe some guys do like that, but I want to suck a lot more than her tits and as sure as hell don't need a nappy, have you got that? Good. I'll be round at three.'

* * *

Douglas had the post open in front of him, he couldn't believe his eyes. Had he not known, he'd have assumed the circular was professional, such was the presentation. It was streets ahead in sophistication from the S.I.R.E.N.S. flyer. Stella was remarkable! Where had *this* come from? Talk about timing, it was clockwork. Grabbing a pen, he read through what was in front of him; in a very classy format it was an unbelievable offer:

'Je ne Sais Quoi'

Exclusive Women for Discerning Gentlemen

'Je ne Sais Quoi' was established in 1952, as a facility for those with the resources to receive their requirements. It holds a well maintained reputation for those essential qualities: discretion and fulfilment. Gentlemen requiring that indefinable talent in a female Escort are guaranteed to find gratification within our exclusive domain. There are three levels of Membership: Candide, Justine, Rose. The subscriptions, paid annually, reflect the level of service which can be expected from each. However, **all** levels are filled with carefully selected ladies, trained and qualified to entertain the most discerning of gentlemen, holding the highest expectations. Along with offering the highest standard in Escorts, is the expectation of a high standard of Clientele. Personal grooming should be exemplary and should extend to appreciable sartorial elegance. In return for these provisions, we supply a unique opportunity to fulfil any manner of personal requirements. Below are the current rates for 1994, all credit cards/cheques accepted.

Candide: £10,000 Justine: £15,500 Rose: £25, 000

Rose

£25,000 inclusive of VAT

For Gentlemen with the means,
this is the ultimate level of Membership.

All previous services mentioned are available with additions. It should be noted that although this is the 'no holds barred' level, any serious harming of our Escorts will not be tolerated and if serious enough would be considered grounds for reporting as assault to the appropriate authorities. It is understood that what is acceptable on any matter of intimacy is agreed between Client and Escort, before proceeding. The list below is by no means exhaustive – imagination setting the only limits.

If required the Escort can live-in for 12 months of the year.
All forms of intercourse are offered: oral sex including anal
Role play, bondage, S & M, usage of all forms of sex toys/aids

Golden showers
Sensory deprivation: Blindfolding

Rose's chosen punishments for not providing services in accordance with her client's wishes are included on a separate sheet and should be studied carefully. They have all been approved by Je Ne Sais Quoi.

Douglas looked out the application form for the 'Rose' Membership and began filling it in. On completion he found an envelope, signed and dated the form, put it in the envelope and sealed it. As the form requested he addressed it to Madam Collette Michelle Dubois, c/o 17 Patrick Way, Little Denton, Dreightonshire, NA4 2HT and stuck a first class stamp on it. He picked up his mobile and pressed 'call'.

Stella had just accepted a mug of coffee from her friend Cindy when it rang. Seeing Douglas' number she answered it.

'Hello?'

'May I speak to Madam Dubois, if she's there please?'

Stella bit her lip. 'Speaking, who's calling please?'

'This is Douglas Spencer. I've received a communication from you this morning and I'm *very interested.*'

Sitting next to Stella, Cindy whispered, 'Clive?'

She shook her head quickly and stifled a giggle. 'Ah yes, I know. Who would you wish to speak to? For which Membership would you be enquiring about, please?'

This poor imitation French accent had her intrigued. She leaned forward, trying to listen.

Douglas replied adamantly, 'Oh I think, Madam Dubois, it has to be the *Rose* Membership. Is there anyone available to speak to me right *now* perhaps?'

'I can let you speak to Rose; *oui! Un moment s'il vous plait!* ' She pushed Cindy away with a finger to her lips.

'Hello, this is Rose speaking; can I help you, sir?' She clutched at her breasts.

'Possibly, I was looking to employ your services as soon as you were available actually. I've just submitted my form for approval. The money isn't a problem. I was wondering if you might be free next Tuesday, I need an escort to accompany me to London. I'd like to meet you beforehand to find out if you offer all you *say* you do!' *This is very erotic and right up my street.* 'Would you be available for inspection?' Douglas paced his study.

'It's rather short notice, but as it is the top level, I think I can say yes and you require an outcall. Can you tell me your address now, sir?'

'Certainly.' He gave his address. 'Shall we say ten thirty, for coffee?'

'I'll check with Madam Dubois, but unless you hear to the contrary, I'll see you next Tuesday, sir. Thank you for using 'Je ne Sais Quoi', goodbye.' She replaced the receiver exhilarated, her eyes very bright.

'Right, so tell me now, what was all *that* about, Stella?' Cindy found her voice. 'What on *earth* are you up to? Who was that on the phone?'

'Hang on Cindy, don't worry.' She lifted an appeasing hand. 'It's a bit of a long story. Something I've always *wanted* to do and, well, now it looks like I'm *going* to do. It's a bit of an adventure in a way, a new journey.'

'Oh yeah?' She remarked dryly. Concern nibbled her. She cared about Stella. 'Mind if I tag along then? Can you *tell* me about it, where you're going? You might find you need someone to talk to.'

She picked up her mug and peered at her friend. 'How long have you got?'

'Long enough, Stella...' She sat closer. 'Come on, spill!'

Stella frowned, trying to get her head round what she'd just done. Cindy waited. Then she decided.

'Wait there a minute, there's something I want to show you, I won't be a tic.' She got up and went through to the kitchen.

Cindy studied the flyer for 'Je Ne Sais Quoi', her mouth open. Feeling awkward, slightly embarrassed, Stella sat in an opposite armchair and waited.

'First of all, who were you speaking to on the phone just now? Do I know him? *Presumably* it's a him?' She fanned the flyer slowly, and looked at Stella. 'Secondly' squinting down again and reading it over, 'I'm assuming Clive knows nothing of this. If he *did* he'd be a bit upset to say the least and lastly, though I know it isn't really my business, but how many people have you sent this to? Well?'

Stella ran her tongue over her teeth, debating, and then explained slowly, just enough to put her friend in the picture. Cindy didn't interrupt. Just as Stella was beginning to wonder if telling her had been a good idea, that possibly she'd even taken offence, she burst out laughing, falling back on the sofa, arms stretched out, hooting.

'Stella, my God, *Stella*! You're so wicked, you know that! You've sent this to this man Douglas, and he's opened it and replied? Bloody hell Stella, this is amazing! What are you going to *do?*'

Somewhat relieved, she told her.

'Exactly what it *says* I'll do! I'm absolutely crazy about him, he's the most fantastic lover I've ever had and that's saying something! He's so...oh I don't know, *adult,* I suppose. Yes, adult and sophisticated and sexy, good looking.'

'And married?' She knew Stella.

'No! That's the whole point you see, he's *not* married! There's a friend called Helen he sees occasionally, who he used to live with, I believe, but they're not together now, in the relationship sense I mean.'

The laughter stopped, her friend sat up.

'Are you sure? You don't think he's just *using* you do you? Taking advantage of you? I'd hate to see you *hurt,* Stella, I really would. What's the state of things at the moment apart from this?' She waved the sheet of paper. 'When are you meeting again? Is there anything else about him, or this, that you haven't told me? Come on! I want to know everything. I'm your friend, you can trust me. There's more to this isn't there? Tell me.'

Stella nodded. 'A flyer came in the post the other day for a sex club I think, of sorts, not sure. Douglas was a bit vague about it to me, but I overheard him talking to a waitress at this tea shop we went to the other afternoon. He called her Hazel and she seemed familiar with it. *Then* he said about taking me up to London in July and meeting some of his friends. That's when I produced this Agency 'Je Ne Sais Quoi'. He sounds really excited about it. I'll be accompanying him as his escort. Do you want to see the Sirens thing too?'

Feeling disorientated suddenly, Cindy looked at Stella. She thought she knew her friend pretty well, but obviously not *that* well.

'Yes, if you want. Whatever sex has to do with sirens I can't imagine, except they were supposed to be female and lure in the men, but come on, I'm open to suggestion!'

Going into the kitchen, she removed the flyer from a drawer and passed it over. Cindy read it carefully.

'Are you completely mad, Stella? Or crazy perhaps, totally off your trolley?'

Feeling a mix of guilt and indignation, she retorted.

'It may *look* a bit, well, *different*, but I'm an adult and so's he, very definitely. I'm flattered he thinks I'm enlightened enough to appreciate something like that.' A note of desperation crept in. 'He really does *love* me, you know.'

It was her insistence. Cindy glanced up, worried.

'This sort of thing doesn't show that you *love* someone Stella! It's just sex *I'd* say he's after, he's a *bloke*. I *might* be wrong but well, has he actually *said* he loves you?'

'Of *course* he has *and does*. He's said it lots of times.' Her tone still sounded petulant, like a child. Cindy's expression was doubtful.

'He *has!*' She wasn't going to admit it. Her friend had hit the nail on the head. Those longed for words had never left his lips.

'Anyway, we're going up to London on Thursday the fifteenth of July and home again on Sunday. I'm really looking forward to it. It's what I've always wished for. We'll have a brilliant time.'

'I'm sure you will, Stella!' She was conciliatory now. 'A lovely time…what about Jeeves?'

She'd forgotten Jeeves.

'Cathy can have him to stay. It's only for three nights after all.'

'And four days!' Cindy reminded her. 'Well, if Cathy can't have him don't worry, I'll look after the poor thing, but fancy forgetting him! Take your mobile with you, won't you? I'll want to keep in touch, make sure you're okay,'

She saw Stella's expression. 'I'm sure you *will* be, but you never know. Text me anyway, I'll want to know all about it when you get back. I'm probably just worrying too much, have a great time and enjoy yourself. One *last* thing: you forgot Jeeves, have you forgotten Clive as well? What're you going to tell *him*?'

Stella hadn't forgotten Clive.

'I'll tell him the truth; I'm going up to London and staying a few nights. Martha wouldn't let him come anyway, so there's not a lot he can say or do to stop me really.'

Cindy shrugged, feeling sorry for Clive; she liked him. He was considerate, a gentleman. She hadn't met Douglas, wasn't overly impressed with what she knew about him so far, but would reserve judgement until she had. Stella needed sexual excitement in her life and even liking Clive as she did, she realised he wasn't exactly the sexiest man she knew. Stella needed the 'edge' and Douglas might provide it.

'Well, apart from poor Jeeves, you seem to have got it all worked out. I just hope you know what you're doing, Stella!'

She smiled, relaxed and happy.

'I do. I've got him, Douglas I mean, exactly where I want him – putty in my hands.' An explicit image flashed through her brain. 'Except for the fact he isn't putty at all! He's stiff as a board, huge in fact!'

'Oh gross, Stella! Too much information, *please!* God! You are awful, quite bad!' she laughed.

Stella giggled. 'I know, and Douglas *loves it!*'

10

Rhoda Chambers had finished hanging her washing out and was sipping a cup of coffee in her lounge when the phone rang. She answered it.

'Hello?' A pause, then a voice she recognised. Smiling, she sat down on the settee.

'Hello Rhoda, are you well?' It was Douglas

Rhoda felt very well indeed. His cheque had arrived yesterday in the post and was waiting to be paid into the Building Society. She was certainly in the mood for a chat.

'I am darling, thank you. What can I do you for today?'

'Could you manage a trip up to London on Thursday the fifteenth of July, in time for lunch at the Café Regent?'

Rhoda was amazed – he was full of surprises.

'With you, you mean? Is it to do with your little friend? I thought that might get a bit mixed up…'

'What do you mean mixed up?' He was quick.

She wanted to bite her tongue off, stupid woman. Jed had filled her in, all excited with the news about Reggie. Not wanting Douglas to know in case he took over in his usual fashion when after all, Reggie had rung *him* first. Now she'd nearly blown it and roused his curiosity. She thought quickly.

'….with Helen coming to see you and all that sort of thing.' She always managed to get in a mess; it was the effect he had on her, even after all this time. She still hankered after him, albeit she knew, it was very much one-sided.

'How did you know about Helen? Have you been talking to Jed?'

Rhoda hoped for the best. 'Only a quick chat, he mentioned that she was hoping to see you. That was all, nothing else. Should he not have told me?' *Push the blame across.* 'He was on about the club mainly, just this and that, you know, nothing in particular. I thought you'd be juggling rather, with your young bit *and* Helen coming.'

'I'm perfectly capable of juggling, sweetie! What I need *you* for is something I hadn't envisaged but is rather opportune. Stella's even *more* adventurous than I'd thought she was, quite extraordinary really. She wants to have a go at being an Escort, has even produced a very professional advertisement and the owner – the Madam's, a Michelle Collette Dubois.'

Rhoda was unsure. 'Madam Dubois? Do I know her or something? Who is she, the name's not familiar.'

Douglas sipped his Earl Grey tea.

'You don't know her and neither would you've heard of her, because she doesn't exist. I'm hoping you might be able to lend a bit of substance to the name. The point *is*; would you be able to *be* a Madam *for* her? So she can meet a *real* 'Madam Dubois', could you do it? She has the most amazing potential and would be a terrific asset at the club for our more *prestigious* clients, I think, not just anybody.'

Rhoda was interested, this sounded brilliant. He could rely on her for this little job. She gripped the receiver, riveted. He continued.

'I'm sure you could produce the right amount of motherly care at the same time as whetting her appetite for some serious sex.' *She won't resist that.*

'She's vulnerable, as you saw, which men will find attractive, but an absolute pro when it comes to technique. (*That will make her jealous.*)

'I'd want to introduce you to her over lunch, before we take a look round the premises. It might be an idea to wear a wig as well. She may be vulnerable but she's not stupid and she might remember you as the woman who gave her the top at the market.

I know you can manage a different appearance quite well. You fooled the Inspector at the time, which due to considerable advances you couldn't manage *now*, but we'll just be more careful darling, *won't we?'*

Rhoda was in a dream, her coffee cold and untouched. Be business-like and alert, what an opportunity! She hated the little bitch, envied her figure, her manner, everything. She hated her even more now she'd obviously given Douglas a run for his money. She knew the moment she saw her he'd have her, couldn't resist it, but she'd certainly let her know what it was *really* all about. It would be a *pleasure*.

'We *will* be careful Douglas. I'd *love* to take her on. Show her what's what. I'll make sure I'm there for one o'clock and join you for coffee or something if I'm a bit late and don't worry, she won't know who I am, but I'd better have a name other than Rhoda, what about Zena? Zena Fortune? It sounds very James Bond.'

Douglas smiled. Good old Rhoda, she had her uses.

'That sounds *splendid*. I'm glad you can help. I'll look forward to seeing you *then*, bye now!'

He replaced the receiver, sat back in his chair and finished his tea. A rather good weekend coming up and Helen as well next week, whatever *she* wanted; things were looking pretty peachy, pretty good.

* * *

In the offices across the road from him, four stories up, a couple were kissing, the woman leaning back against the window, the man nearly eating her. Boxes were piled up on either side of them. He'd slipped the top from her shoulder and was eating his way down her neck. One arm was trying to hitch her skirt up and she was obviously wriggling but there didn't appear to be a sill to rest on.

Reggie watched them idly and pondered over the Sirens club

and what it all entailed. This Jed sounded a little gauche to be in charge of an enterprise boasting what it did, but maybe he was a bit old fashioned. He could picture him without having seen him: gelled hair, collarless shirt, Armani suit and dripping with gold, a huge oyster Rolex on his wrist, expensive aftershave and Italian leather shoes.

Would he be married? No, divorced in all likelihood, his first wife having been the sweet little thing from next door and perfectly adequate, until Jeddy-boy hit the big time and decided it was time to upgrade in the wife department. Now he'd either have a glamorous blonde bimbo as a wife, or a series of girlfriends he could wine and dine and have fun with. Nevertheless, he'd got where he was – a sizeable fortune – with a good head for business. He shouldn't be too flippant.

What he wanted was to infiltrate this world that had Helen's former lover in its thrall. Ever since she'd met Douglas at that party at the Hampton's place, she'd not been the same. It was this charisma, animal magnetism. Once you'd fallen for it you were sucked in for good. She'd certainly been all over him when he'd taken her to Barbados, but somehow, despite his best efforts, she always managed mentally to keep 'one foot on the floor' so to speak, had never told him she loved him. Just by doing that single thing, she had Douglas exactly where she wanted him; a friend but nothing more.

Something about the man got up his nose. He had to admit he wasn't looking forward to waving Helen off from the station next week, knowing she'd be staying in his cottage where presumably they'd got up to all sorts once upon a time. Now he wanted to know what. He and Helen had a very good sex life he believed, quite enterprising and exciting enough for *him*, so what was it that turned this man on? He thought it'd be quite fun to find out. One thing he was sure about; it certainly wouldn't be dull.

The couple across the road had now sunk to the floor out of sight. He turned back to face his desk, checked his computer for a moment then got up and wandered into the office lobby to search for Paula. At five feet eight inches tall in bare feet, she was very clearly visible, the heels she wore taking her up to the six foot mark. She was over by the cold water dispenser in the corner; bronze leather shoes with high heels, navy skirt, a wide bronze leather belt and a crisp white shirt. Highlighted auburn hair reached her shoulders where it flicked up at the ends, shining like a shampoo advert. Holding the beaker, she turned and smiled at Reggie. With perfect white teeth and just a trace of a sun tan, she looked striking as usual, leaning against a chair in the lobby, eyebrow raised.

'Well Mr. Crifton, what can I do for you this afternoon? I'm surprised to see you actually, wasn't Helen going to drag you round the stores in preparation for the big day?'

Reggie smiled, but was professional. 'Can you spare me a few moments in my office? Something I want to discuss. Can you transfer my calls for a moment, Lucy?'

Lucy smiled obligingly; she was new. 'Certainly, Mr. Crifton!'

Bringing her water, Paula followed him and he closed the door.

'I'll come straight to the point, have you ever heard of the Sirens Club?'

From the mystified expression on Paula's face he could see she hadn't.

'Reggie, are you having me on? The Sirens Club, you must be kidding surely? Did I hear you right, *sirens club?*'

'Yes you did, I know it sounds odd. It's a new club in London, well when I say *new* it originally opened in the sixties, but was fairly unheard of. Jed Zeitermann was running it, still is. It received a mention in a new magazine that's coming out. It's raised its profile a little now. I wondered if you'd come across it, like.'

Paula was curious.

'And what *sort* of club are we talking about here, loud hooters blaring? Those old air-raid warning things you mean? Gas masks? Tell me!'

He laughed. 'It could be anything, including using gas masks I suppose, but I think they mean those legend half-women who used to lure the sailors like! I have some information about it here.' He passed her the glossy ad from the newspaper and, she stared in disbelief.

'Bloody hell, Reggie, what are you into now?'

'I thought you'd be surprised pet, actually it's not *me* entirely. Someone I know from back a bit's involved in this somehow and I want to know what he's up to, just for fun, like, you *know*. There's something not quite right, goes back a long way, a hushed up death, caused a bit of a scandal at the time!'

He raised an eyebrow, continuing. Paula was taking it all in.

'It was all over the papers and the man involved in it, the man I'm interested in, was the apple of Helen's eye. Personally I think he's a creep.' He rubbed his face. 'But he's a very rich creep and still wields quite a bit of power. Helen's mine, but she just can't leave him alone, keeps fussing about him and returning. He's like a magnet to women. I can't see it, but then I'm a man. I don't know what this'll turn up, where it'll go, but I am on his case. I don't trust him an inch.'

Paula narrowed her eyes and considered Reggie. If she was honest, she quite fancied him herself. Although in his middle sixties, he was a bit older than the men she usually went for; she liked them young and fresh. Reggie was the exception to the rule.

'Well, now you've told me, where do *I* fit in this plan? What do you want me to do, Reggie? Is this the sort of thing your publicity machine should get hold of, do you think? Can't imagine you want this stuff on your website, you'll have to be a bit careful; Helen'd hit the roof, wouldn't she?'

Reggie studied the faint outline of Paula's lacy bra showing through the crisp white shirt, visualising what lay underneath.

She shifted suddenly, making him start in surprise.

'What? Oh Helen, yes she would. Go nuts. Keep her at bay if she asks anything. She knows I was interested in the article this new magazine published, but apart from that she's too busy thinking about telling him we're getting hitched and what he's going to say. As if it matters!' He rolled his eyes. 'Honestly! She's finding material for curtains we just don't need and furniture that's perfectly serviceable, she wants to replace!'

Perched on the corner of his desk, he tried to avoid staring too blatantly.

'Where *you* fit in, should you be willing, is perhaps organize three or four girls with heart-stopping looks and bodies, broad minded enough to indulge in a little sexual fantasy, entertaining Mr. Spencer. He's got a young*ish* I think, protégée at the moment that he's bringing up with him, who dotes on him and whom, I'm in absolutely *no* doubt, will be treated like the proverbial once she's served his purpose!'

He rubbed his nose and shook his head. 'He's a hard hearted old maggot, needs bringing down a peg or two. Why I want to make it my quest, I don't know really.' He shrugged. 'But like I said at the beginning, he's always rubbed me up the wrong way and needs sortin'.'

He folded his arms and asked her, 'Would you be up for it? There're some fit girls around here at the moment. I was thinkin' around their early twenties maybe?'

Standing up from the desk, he looped his thumbs into his trouser belt. 'I'll make sure they get a good screw, like.' Paula raised an eyebrow. 'Money, I mean! I'll make it worth their while; you're magic at organisation, pet. Three or four girls, real crackers, on the seven fifty train to London, on Friday the sixteenth July.'

Reggie was about to open the door but Paula stopped him, catching his arm. 'Just one last thing, Reggie, don't make yourself a fool for Helen to find out. I'm sure this man deserves hassle if he's as you say, possibly more, but don't jeopardise what you have with her.'

She squeezed his arm, pleading. 'She obviously feels *some*thing or wouldn't go back and see him. If it gets back what you're up to it could back-fire big time. Men like this Spencer always come out smelling of roses, yeah? You'll end up smelling like what they put *on* them, but having said that, I know *exactly* who I can ask.' She released him and winked. 'I'll sort it!'

Reggie patted her shoulder and smiled.

'Aye, pet! I'll be really careful, thanks, you're a star!'

11

Stella carried her tea and muesli back to bed, where Jeeves jumped up to join her. Balancing her mug carefully on the bedside table next to a lamp, she saw the flyer for 'Je Ne Sais Quoi'. Next to it, her clock glowed seven forty-five, plenty of time yet.

Just emerging from the shower her mobile rang – it was Clive, eight-fifteen. She pressed to accept the call.

'Hello Clive, good morning. Are you okay?'

'Morning, sweetheart, I'm fine thanks, and what are you up to today?'

Stella took a breath; resolved. 'I'm having lunch with Douglas at the old hotel near Fords Bridge, The King's Arms, at Melton Malsor? I expect we'll take our time getting back afterwards and stop somewhere for tea. I'll leave a message for you on the mobile later.'

Dead silence. She looked to see if the signal had gone or something.

'Hello? Clive, are you there? It's Tuesday; my lunch date?'

'I'm here, though whether that means anything's beyond me.' He was fed up. 'I might just as well be in Timbuktu for all you care.' As a bus lumbered up the hill, he considered stepping out in front of it. Stella was ready.

'Clive, I thought we'd got this all sorted out? You can't stop me from seeing whoever I want, remember?'

He remembered. Someone had just shoved past him on the pavement. He was in everyone's way lately. What was she saying now? '…I've never been to the King's Arms there, and I do like a treat out. You rang me to say it was fine as long as I didn't sleep with him and I told you that I wouldn't.'

Yes, and how stupid was that, he thought. 'You did, yes, but–'

Stella interrupted. 'No buts. I haven't and *will* not sleep with him.' She looked at Jeeves curled up on the bed; animals never lied, 'But I *will* go out for lunch with him. If we can't agree on that now, then we might as well stop this altogether. You'll just have to trust me, Clive.'

Looking at her flyer again, she winced. She didn't *like* doing this, but Douglas was different. She wouldn't deny herself having some time with him. For the sake of being 'Rose', something Clive would *never* be able to comprehend, although come to think of it, she was expecting rather a lot, wasn't she? A bit drippy – letting her have sex with someone because they were possibly more satisfying than you were. No, she could see his point. Equally, it meant she was selfish – that was the other side of this coin. Oh hell! She wanted both of them for different reasons. Was she jealous of Helen? How would she even feel if *Clive* got fed up and left her.....or found out she was two-timing him? Then what? He was very strong...

Clive was quietly patient. 'Fine then, yes, you can go out with him and I'll trust you until I find you out. But God help you if I do, both of you for that matter. You'll be very sorry. I'll warn you now.'

Stella looked at the clock again: eight thirty-six.

'I'll catch up with you tonight, okay?'

'Okay. I'll look for your message this evening, but I won't want a résumé of the day's events.' He felt a fool; a fool for love.

'I understand. See you later then!'

'See you later.' And he was gone.

At precisely ten thirty, Stella pulled into the opened garage at Watermead and got out. She was dressed for business in a black and cream suit, with a camisole under the jacket and black patent heels. Douglas was waiting. Wearing the suit he'd worn for her supper only a few months ago. Now it felt a lifetime ago, so much had happened. She felt very sophisticated, soignée, *adult*.

Douglas greeted her, folded his arms and looked on appraisingly.

'Well! Rose, is it?' He rubbed his chin and raised an eyebrow. 'You *are* Rose I assume, from the Agency?'

Stella's sophistication was skin-deep. Playing a role she'd devised didn't quite square with how she felt emotionally. She looked at his eyes, the window to the soul: they were passionate, affectionate, looking at her and liking what they saw. He was just teasing. *He loves me, he really loves me; he doesn't need to say it, it's obvious from how he's looking at me, the 'look of love' is there all right and I love him too. He's all I've ever wanted and I'll do anything for him, anything he asks, I'll do.*

Douglas waited then motioned her towards the door.

'Come in, Rose, would you like some coffee? I've made some fresh and a few biscuits,' He pulled back a chair for her. 'I propose we leave for the King's Arms about eleven thirty? I have a booking for one o'clock. Now, can I take your jacket or would you rather keep it on?'

'I'll keep it on, I think, for the moment. I'd love some coffee, thank you.'

Douglas poured from a cafétiere. 'You can help yourself to the milk and biscuits.'

At nearly eleven thirty, she excused herself and slipped to the downstairs loo to check over her makeup. When she emerged again, lipstick refreshed and hair pinned up, Douglas was at the sink washing everything up.

'Do you have an apartment somewhere near here?'

'I do, if you wanted an in-call sometime.' She sounded tense.

He looked at her from the sink before wiping his hands on a towel, and then went to set the alarm.

'Wait outside please, Rose, I won't be a sec!'

She did as she was told, but something wasn't right. A small dark cloud sat on the horizon of an otherwise brilliantly blue sky. She'd devised this 'Je Ne Sais Quoi' as a joke and to shock him a bit and it had certainly done that. Now he was taking it just a little too literally. She didn't want him losing sight of the fact she was Stella, *playing* at being Rose, 'playing' being the operative word.

He opened the car door and she climbed in, remembering how on the last occasion she could hardly climb out for excitement. This time, apart from kissing her cheek, he hadn't given her any embrace at all. It was hard to conceive that not *that* many days ago they'd been as intimate as it was possible for two people to get. He could certainly turn his emotions on and off it seemed, like a tap.

She'd fastened her seatbelt when Douglas turned, curious.

'A penny for them?'

She jumped. 'What? Oh nothing. Just daydreaming that's all.'

With hardly a purr from the engine, they turned from the drive and set off. Douglas broke the silence as they approached the old cobbled streets and houses on the outskirts of the small, up-market town of Melton Malsor.

'I think I'll go in this short-stay car-park. The Hotel's only a few yards away, can you manage all right in those shoes, do you think?'

Stella turned her ankle and looked at them. They were quite high.

'The street's a bit uneven with the cobbles. I note with approval, though, that *Madam Dubois* requires her girls to wear heels. They're much sexier, I think. She's quite right to stipulate them; well done.'

She smiled, he was 'playing the game'. It was what she wanted – to be an Escort. No, she'd join in and play the part. He slipped the ticket in the windscreen and opened her door. Once out it was obvious he'd been right. Watching her stumble for a while, he held her elbow in a vice-like grip until they entered the lobby, when he placed his hand in the small of her back, directing her, whilst looking around for a sign to the restaurant. Within seconds, a man in a morning suit appeared, to lead them to the covered loggia area where lunch would be served.

It was airy and surprisingly spacious. They had a table near the window, with a good view of the walled courtyard garden. Elegance abounded: heavy white damask napkins and reed thin stemmed glasses. A waiter delivered the napkins over their knees and presented two menus. The prices, in discreet small print, were way above average, steak being exorbitant as usual.

'Anything there you fancy, darling?' Douglas watched her. 'Choose whatever you want.'

Stella liked duck and steak, but as both were so expensive she settled for the poached salmon with hollandaise sauce.

'You won't have a starter then?'

'I'd prefer the main course and a pudding I think, if that's all right?'

'Of course it is. I shall do the same, I think.'

He pored over the list as a wine waiter hovered.

'I see they do champagne by the glass, would you like some with the meal?'

Stella had planned to have a drink and some champagne sounded good.

'Thank you, yes I would please.'

'Good, that's splendid.' He turned and passed the list back to the waiter. 'Two glasses of champagne then please, with a jug of water.'

Twitching the crease in his trousers, he then regarded her over his elbows on the table. With just a shadow of a smirk, he began the interview.

'So, tell me then, Rose, do you usually lunch with your clients first? Is this your way of getting to know them? How long have you been...doing this sort of thing?' He sat back again, confidently, and waited for the answer.

She swallowed then cleared her throat.

'Well, yes, I like to have a meal first, to break the ice before anything more...intimate. I haven't been doing it very long, I-'

Douglas was quick, replacing the slight smirk with a look of aggrieved confusion. 'You haven't been doing it for very long? But I thought I was getting the Rose Membership? Which I was led to believe was the top level in fact. Are you telling me I've been palmed off with a girl of no experience?'

She clenched her fists under the table. She couldn't do it. 'I'm sorry, Douglas, I can't keep this up, I'm afraid. I know what it said on the form, but I really en*joy* what we do together. It isn't *work* for me, it's a pleasure.'

Douglas stared, cynical now.

'A *pleasure* you say, Rose?'

'Yes.' She smiled uncertainly.

'Then tell me sweetie,' with another smirk, 'what would I be *paying* you for?'

'*Paying me for?*' She frowned, not quite registering. 'What do you mean?'

Douglas continued. 'I'm *paying* you! The top, a dress, then those gifts from Copsle and a trip to London next month...I'm *paying you* darling. You *say* it's a pleasure, but you might find *some* of the things I'll expect you to do unpleasant, even painful perhaps. I read the list of punishments for Rose carefully as requested and they're uncomfortable to say the least, let alone rather demeaning. I can understand a payment of some sort is entirely reasonable. Are you now telling me you're not only without much experience, but no longer wish to be my escort either, Stella?'

His use of her real name made her sit up.

'No, not at all, Douglas, I love the idea and think it's very sexy. I think that *you*'re very sexy. It's very *grown up,* isn't it?'

'Yes it *is,* darling. You seem to have a thing about being "grown up". Do you not *feel* grown up ordinarily?'

The conversation was interrupted for the champagne. The waiter poured some water then lifted the wine glasses, hovering. Douglas waved them away.

Stella warmed to his apparent interest. He really did *care* about her.

'No I don't. I suppose it could be because I've not had any children. I don't seem to ever feel I'm a grown up woman. I know it sounds odd.'

He chuckled and crossed his legs.

'Well I can assure you one hundred and ten per cent you are *totally* a woman, absolutely no question about it. You're a woman through and through. I've never ever *known* a more total woman. You're incredible, I think.'

Stella sipped the champagne, the tiny bubbles bursting on her tongue like the little bubbles of pleasure bursting in her head. Here she was, in a classy restaurant drinking champagne, opposite an attractive and sophisticated man who was telling her what she'd so hoped to hear. It wasn't possible, was it, she reasoned, to have done what they'd done and not be feeling passionate love as well! She was in heaven.

The waiter may have caught the tail end of Douglas's conversation, but his face remained passive. He'd heard it all before, a hundred times probably.

'Are you ready to order, Sir?'

'I think so, are we?' Stella smiled. 'Yes we are. Well, the chicken for me, please, and you wanted the salmon, was it?'

She nodded. 'Yes please, and the vegetables rather than salad.'

'And another two glasses of champagne if you could, please?'

'Certainly, Sir, that's no problem.' He removed the menus and extraneous silver and left.

Stella's heart lurched, love and desire hurt. She lifted the flute by the stem, sipping some more, it slipped down easily and was enjoyable to drink. He was so relaxed and poised. She wanted to be the same, a character from an Audrey Hepburn film. This was so remote from every-day reality.

Suddenly, his shoe was running lightly up over her ankle and down again, the effect making her wriggle. She blew a little kiss just as the food arrived on steaming plates. He was *her* man and she loved him, adored him. She peeked provocatively from beneath her lashes: a champagne lunch preliminary to making love, what could be more 'grown up' than that? This would last forever. She just *knew* it.

Over coffee in the lounge, Douglas returned to the subject of Helen. He spoke in a confidential manner Stella found rather heady, confiding in her as an equal, adult to adult, albeit about a woman due to visit the very next week. The way Stella read it he was talking about her because he didn't feel the same any longer. Helen was his past and she was his future.

In the car going home, his hand climbed up under her skirt reaching the top of her stocking, stroking her bare thigh. After two glasses of champagne, the discreet atmosphere and sophistication of it all had gone to her head and she willed his fingers to travel further, which they did. A sudden slowing down of traffic required both hands on the steering wheel. A glistening trail slicked over it and he looked at her, amused.

'You're a little wet! Not long now and we'll see what Rose is really made of, won't we?'

Going through to the kitchen and removing her shoes, she heard a faint click. He turned and smiled. 'We don't want any interruptions now, do we? Well Rose, shall we go upstairs, do business? *Come on, off we go!*'

She took his offered hand, heart racing. The first time they'd made love in this bedroom, everything had looked pretty. Now it was different. The curtains were drawn, large ornate mirrors ranged around the bed and the bed itself was swathed in sheets of thick black satin, like the sex videos she'd watched with Steve which now seemed centuries ago.

Doubts were stepping in as he released his grip. She looked warily at a pink quilted Ottoman at the foot of the bed. On it were some black cords and a box of cling-film. Set slightly apart was a shiny gold coloured vibrator, probably eight inches long, and thick. Undoing his shirt, he watched her.

'Don't look so nervous, sweetie! I'm sure you've come across all this before in your line of work? Madam Dubois informed me you were a most willing young lady. Only too happy to accommodate a discerning Gentleman's *requirements,* isn't that right?'

She tried to hide her jitters. It wasn't *quite* what she'd expected.

'Douglas, this *is* just a bit of fun, isn't it? I mean, you do *know* I'm Stella *really,* don't you?'

Quick to reassure, he went over and put his arms around her.

'Of *course* I do darling, I'm just entering into the spirit of the thing. You're a very adventurous and sexy woman, Stella. Would you *rather* I called you Stella and not Rose? Is this all a bit much for you? A bit too, how shall we say – *grown up,* perhaps?' *That should do it.*

She felt stung. 'No! Not at all Douglas, it's exciting. No, I don't have any reservations. And call me Rose; I *am* Rose after all, your escort. I'll take my clothes off and pop to the bathroom. I won't be a tic.'

His voice flowed like warm syrup. 'You can take your clothes off, but I'm coming to the bathroom with you.'

She was in her underwear, just removing a stocking.

'Well you go first and I'll follow you afterwards.' She removed the other, not looking at him.

Suddenly he was beside her, one hand feeling between her legs, his thumb massaging her gently.

'You don't get it, do you sweetie? I want to watch you, touch you. Do you like my thumb up there, Rose? Do you like that, does it feel *naughty?*'

She was blushing and getting wetter, his thumb penetrating to where it joined the palm of his hand. Straightening up from unfastening her stocking, she turned and met his lips. He kissed her hungrily, probing his tongue around her mouth, over her lips and face.

Everything was red as she slid to the floor, pulling him with her. They were kissing roughly, wildly, when suddenly she tasted metal and drew her face away. Rubbing her hand over her lips, she saw the blood.

'Douglas, I'm bleeding, I think you bit my lip.'

He rubbed it roughly and took her arm.

'Better come to the bathroom then, hadn't you? I don't think it's very much.'

Propelled through to the bathroom, she waited while he dampened a flannel then held it to her lip. She looked at the toilet and clenched her legs.

'Bursting to go are you Rose?' he breathed. 'Wait there while I fetch something.'

He returned with the gold vibrator, the end of which was a large shiny knob.

'Straddle the lavatory facing me; *no*,' She'd sat down. 'Stand up, lift the seat up and stand over it.'

The urge to go was unbearable. She held on, not knowing what was coming.

'Have you ever had an orgasm while you're *peeing*, Rose?' he asked, 'It's impossible for a man, but I want to *experiment* on you. Get your hands out of the way and when I tell you, I want to watch you. No, when I *tell you*.'

He moved the shiny head of the vibrator nearer.

'When I turn this on you'll start to go.'

She heard the buzz before she felt it. The pulsating made it difficult to keep her balance, so she rested her hand on his shoulder. She could feel splashes on her legs and looked at him expectantly.

'Lie down *now!*' It was a command. 'No, face down and lift your hips up.'

Before she knew it he was tearing her. Then it was his thumb again, rubbing over her anus before the tip of the vibrator replaced it, the vibration of it passing through and she heard him moan. Her face was pressed hard against the carpet, the top of her head hitting the lavatory bowl with each thrust.

'This is hurting me, Douglas. Can we go back to the bedroom?'

He grunted. 'This is work, Rose; it's what you do and what I'm *paying* you for. When I've finished, *then* we'll go back to the bedroom. We've only just *started!* I've got a contract with *Madam Dubois* and I'm getting my monies worth. I said it might be painful didn't I? A little more thought before giving me that list perhaps? I'm afraid it's a bit late now!'

She shuddered; her back ached and the carpet was rough on her knees. His hands pressed down on her shoulders and she could hardly breathe. Suddenly he pulled out and stood up.

'Get up and come back to the bedroom, come on! *Rose!'*

Relieved, she scrambled up, catching sight of herself in the mirror. She looked 'brazen', that was the word. Her cheeks had flushed, her shiny hair mussed up. Her breasts were red from lying on the floor and she stung between her legs. She felt wanton, but something was missing: affection. He wasn't calling her Rose with any affection or feeling, but then it was all part of the game – she was an escort and he was paying her, had taken her out for a slap-up lunch and now she was doing her job. Wasn't that what she wanted?

He was calling. 'In here, Rose, are you coming or do I have to *drag* you?'

'No, I'm coming, Douglas.'

'Oh, I don't think "Douglas" is on. Sir will do nicely! Now, lie down on the bed. No, this side, that's fine.'

Obeying, she heard him fiddling about and half sat up to see what he was doing. He had the large roll of cling film. It was shiny and yellowy and looked stronger than normal, on an industrial sized tube.

'Lie down Rose, with your legs together.' He paused, considering. 'And your arms above your head, I think. Lift them up and hold your hands together. That's fine.'

Wrapping the sheeting around her ankles several times, he bound them together, slowly moving up towards her thighs, lifting her up off the bed with one hand as he went along. Just below her hips he stopped. Dragging her to the edge of the bed he tipped her feet to the floor.

'Put your arms round my shoulders and stand up. Come on now! That's it!'

He paused. 'Put your arms up again now.' Reaching shoulder level, he stopped. Tipping her back on to the bed he reached for the shiny black cord; plaited with a tassel at each end. One end he fastened around her neck, tying it in a knot and the other he slid round an arm supporting the bed head, pulling it down until it was taut, tying it securely. She watched; his eyes were intent on what he was doing. They were piercing, frightening.

'It's just a bit *tight*, Douglas, I...'

Dropping the tube, he yanked her down the bed. His voice was low and menacing and his expression cold and angry.

'What did I say to call me, Rose? Not Douglas, was it? What did I say, Rose?'

The cord was constricting, making her lightheaded. Her throat was dry, she wanted to cough.

'What did I say, Rose?' he repeated slowly.

What did he mean? She was getting confused. What had he said? She couldn't remember.

'What did I tell you to call me, can't you think?'

It came to her, her tongue felt all thick. 'Sir, *Sir!* This is a bit tight round my neck and it's making my head ache, can't you loosen it just slightly, *please?*'

He paused. Beads of sweat glistened on his forehead.

'Sorry, I'm afraid I can't do that. You'll just have to put up with it, *won't you?*' He took hold of the tube again, paused, and wiped his brow ruminating. 'I *could* put this over your face...but I don't think I will. The cord's *not* too tight,' he said, yanking and testing it, 'so don't make a fuss.'

He continued wrapping above her head, humming a tuneless noise. When he reached her wrists he unrolled a length before tearing it, neatly wrapping the remainder around her. It was looking a bit on the tight side. Her hands were turning red and her arms very white, but he left it.

Her heart sank, she could feel it again. She'd ask, but he was never going to undo all this. She'd try to humour him.

'Sir, *please*, I've got to go to the loo again, I need a wee and I'm a bit stuck!' She felt a giggle erupting, he was getting too carried away…

His eyes sparkled at this. '*Do you* darling? I'll watch you again then. I'm certainly not removing this just for that. That *would* be a silly waste, wouldn't it?'

Moving nearer, he was aroused again. He was close to her face.

Stella froze. 'I don't want what I *think* you're going to do either. I think I'd rather stop now, *Sir!*'

He wasn't interested. 'I'm not going to stop *now* darling, this is *much* too exciting. I'll be forced to complain to Madam Dubois and then have to punish you,' he said. 'Can you remember what your punishments were? I don't think any of them were very pleasant, were they? It was you who wanted to *play* the escort, remember?

'*You* wanted to do it. It *"turned you on"* you said, didn't you? *"I want to be a high class call-girl, play the escort."* Well darling, *now you are,* and this,' holding himself, 'is what they do.'

Right by the side of the bed now, he slid her round until she faced him and straddled her. Stella tried to shift, move her face, but the cord cut tighter. Her head was spinning as she opened her mouth for air. It was just what he was waiting for.

'Good *girl*, Rose! Open wide, *open wide NOW!!*'

Stella struggled, she could smell and taste it and retched, then her head seemed to explode and she was floating away.

'Wake up, Rose!'

He slapped her cheek, her eyelids fluttered then opened, her head was throbbing. He reached for the cord and untied the knot, watching the blood rush back down her neck, flushing her chest, but her face was pale. Coming round, she was aware of an uncomfortable wetness between her thighs. There was no feeling of urgency, she'd been.

'Look at you.' He held up a mirror. 'A beautiful little spirit level and you're lying quite flat, just *perfect!*' Putting the mirror down, he glanced at his watch. 'I shan't be a tic. Relax for a moment. You were very good, *very* good. I won't be long.'

Slipping a shirt on, he went downstairs. He fancied a drink after that. Finding his bottle of claret, he poured a glass then checked his fridge and larder. He pulled a couple of plates down from the rack, putting them on the worktop, then put some music on – 'In Romantic Mood' it said on the CD. It would do, he *did* feel quite good. Remembering Stella was wet, he grabbed a roll of kitchen towel and with his glass in the other hand, tripped back up the stairs.

Stella had had enough, she was messy and uncomfortable. She could just about see herself in the mirror he'd propped up. The whole scene debauched, like something from a pornographic video. She heard him come back and twisted her head.

'Please can you sort me out, Sir? Will you untie me now, my arms are killing me!'

Ignoring this remark he rolled out several sheets of kitchen towel, debating. At the moment, the film contained the liquid, but it was copious and would go everywhere. He left the room again, she heard him opening a drawer somewhere then he was back with what appeared to be an enormous plastic bin-bag but opened into a plastic sheet. Moving across, he opened it out and gripped her ankles. Raising her off the bed, it flowed towards her waist.

Awkwardly, with his other hand, he spread the sheet underneath her then lowered her on to it. Unrolling sheets and sheets of kitchen paper, he padded them along her sides and under her legs. Now he could start the business of unwrapping. He looked at her face. She was close to tears.

'What's the matter, Rose, I've put some music on and I'm sorting you out. You can have a shower and then some supper.

I've no cause to complain this time. Your Madam will be pleased with you, you're doing very well.'

He took hold of the film from around her arms and began unwrapping. Next he wiped her face with some kitchen roll. She relaxed with relief as her arms, cold and numb, were beginning to tingle back to life.

'Give me your hand, darling, and get up slowly. Don't worry about dripping, stand on here a moment.' He indicated some paper spread on the floor. 'There's one more thing to do before you shower and we can have supper.'

Stella couldn't think and she watched him anxiously. What was there left to do? He knelt down next to her, taking her hands in his.

'Don't look so worried, sweetie.' He licked his lips, leaning closer.

'No *please*; just let me shower now, can I? *Please* don't, Douglas, Sir. I thought you said it was all over.'

'I don't think I did, darling, what I *said* was "you're doing very well". I didn't say you'd finished. That's lovely, Rose, you taste good, *very* good. '

'You're getting wet again, aren't you, Rose? You know you are. This is turning you on now, isn't it?'

She realised nothing so far had given her an orgasm, but now she felt that rushing feeling. She grabbed his shoulder for support.

'Oh darling that's wonderful, keep going. *Lovely.*'

Suddenly 'Rose' kicked in. All apprehension forgotten, she wanted him to touch her. Her knees buckled and she slid to the ground, Douglas supporting her.

'Please kiss me, *Sir*, please *kiss me!*'

Hungrily he found her mouth and her tongue met his, tasting her own juices. When she felt his erection she pulled him on top of her. She couldn't get enough of it.

'Do it, just do it Douglas, please, hard, I want it hard *now!* As hard as you can, Douglas, *please!*'

Coming quickly this time, he rolled off and lay by her side. The evening sun warmed his back. Music wafted upstairs. He reached for his glass of wine and propping himself up on one elbow he sipped it while looking at her. She lay with her eyes closed, a flush suffusing her face and chest. Dipping his finger in the wine, he traced it round one of her nipples then another dip and round the other one, they stood up erect. Placing his glass on the floor, he leant over and sucked them. She opened her eyes.

'Do you want some supper now, sardines as usual? Grab a shower and I'll go down and get it ready. See you later.'

She went across to the second bathroom, which had a shower, and wondered about the mess left in the bedroom, now reeking of sex, but decided to leave it. Turning the switch, she let the hot water cascade over her, soaking her hair and body. The soap stung like mad.

She hoped she wouldn't go down with cystitis and if she did, would Clive guess the reason? She paused a moment; she hadn't given him a second's thought. Maybe she ought to text him. She turned the shower off and looked round for a towel. On the back of the door were a couple of toweling bathrobes: why two, she wondered, choosing one and unhooking it.

The collar looked a bit on the grubby side and she gave it a sniff; perfume: strong and expensive. She sniffed again and thought she vaguely recognized it; someone had worn it, obviously not Douglas. She smelt it under the arms. It wasn't unpleasant, but it smelt of another body and she didn't want it. She removed the other one, recognizing his aftershave. She was nearly dry now but put it on to go down for supper. She found a smaller towel and twisted a turban. Douglas had prepared supper.

'I thought we'd sit in the conservatory. I've got claret, would you like some squash or something? I've got lemon barley or orange, which would you prefer?'

'Lemon please, Sir.'

Douglas smiled, his eyes twinkling now. 'You can drop the Sir, darling, you're Stella again, but we can discuss business if that's all right?'

He preceded her to the conservatory with the two plates, placing them on the table and returning for the drinks.

Stella suddenly felt quite hungry. 'Did you want to discuss London? It will soon come round; did you still want to take me?'

'If you're willing, of course I do; but there are things to discuss first. How has all this made you feel? Did you enjoy it? Would you enjoy that part of escort work, do you think?'

She pondered. Did she *really* want to give this sort of thing a go? It would be an experience and under relatively safe conditions. She trusted Douglas to keep her safe.

'If you're talking about the Sirens Club I'm interested to go. But I'd like to know a bit more about it first. Did you say I'd meet a *real* "Madam Dubois"?'

He studied his plate, a mental image of Rhoda Chambers suddenly projecting itself.

'You'll meet Mrs. Zena Fortune and if you're keen, you could earn quite a lot of money. You can choose the name Rose or any other name you fancy. It's a very professional, *adult* set up.' He threw her a glance. 'You'd be able to live out any fantasy you wish. You can tell me about a fantasy if you like. I'd be happy to help make them come true for you.' She was looking wary. 'As true as you are happy to *make* them of course! What's the sexual fantasy which persists in your mind but has never been realised; is there one?'

Not even a pause for breath:

'Yes there is!'

'Come on then, tell me, what's it all about? Let's go through to the sitting room and I'll bring the coffee.'

Settled on the sofa with Douglas next to her, she began.

'Where I worked in Harlow once, there used to be a boardroom with a huge board table and once a year they'd hold an Annual Meeting. It sat twenty, the table, and the room was oak panelled with a chandelier. After the meeting I'd serve coffee and liqueurs and some would smoke. It was all men; no women. The male ambience fascinated me. Soon I was having fantasies about it.'

Hardly daring to move, he prompted her gently.

'What *were* the fantasies then, Stella? Are you going to tell me?' *Of course she is, silly woman!*

'Well, after business, as they smoked and drank, I'd imagine entering the room wearing a white silk dressing gown and nothing else.' She eyed him wickedly.

'I'd step on a small stool, climb up to the table and then remove it. The men would sit back, contemplating me.' She rubbed her arms, in thought.

'I'd go to the chairman first, at the head. He'd want me to kneel on all fours, facing away, with my legs as far apart as I could, my chin practically on the table, forcing me up in the air, completely exposed, yes?'

He nodded, engrossed.

'He'd feel me between my legs, lubricating me. Then he'd pull me apart with one hand while easing the thumb of his other hand up my, my bottom.'

He noticed she didn't say 'anus', couldn't she say it? He'd remember this.

'Then he'd take his Mont Blanc fountain pen, rubbing the nib gently to where his thumb was before removing it, turning it the other way round and replacing it where his thumb had been.'

'And where was that?' he asked keenly.

She stared. 'Up my bottom, do you mean?'

'*Mmmm*, could be?'

She tried again. 'Well, up my arse then?'

He was right; she couldn't (or wouldn't) say it, *that word. Don't let on you have noticed.*

'And then what?'

'After that, after he'd removed the pen, I'd go round to each of the nineteen other men in turn, presenting myself to each one.'

She wriggled. Was this too much information she wondered?

'On the opposite side, men would reach across, not very far, to fondle or grab my breasts. At times I had all of me filled with one man's fingers and then' – demonstrating across his knee – 'with my head held up like this, another man could stretch and pinch my nipples.'

He gently fondled her breasts, allowing her to carry on. 'I was used for their entertainment. Moving and positioning myself however they wanted me. Occasionally I might have to kneel up and stick my own finger up my bottom, really stretch myself.'

There she goes again; I'll try something.

'Stick a finger up where? Bottom's a bit twee darling, where did you stick it?'

'I told you, up my arse!'

'Yes, but what's another term for "arse"?'

She squirmed beautifully, he'd landed on target.

'All right then, up my backside?'

'*Yes* and another term? Come on, don't you want to say it?' *No, she definitely did not.*

'You know where I mean! I *can't*, I don't *like* to say the word *you* mean; I can write it, but can't say it. Anyway, I'd move round to each man in turn and they'd do whatever they wanted to do to me; except full sex.'

He'd store this invaluable piece of information. For now let her sing away!

'How did the men receive satisfaction other than your allowing them to finger you then, if they weren't allowed to screw you?'

'After I'd been round the table top, the men would be aroused. I'd climb off the table and crawl underneath it. They'd all be waiting for me.'

'What, you mean all twenty of them?' He tried not to sound too amazed. He didn't want to startle her, *but my God!!*

'This is a *fantasy*! I haven't actually *done* it. Don't think I'd want to either, but I don't mind *talking* to you about it. Do you want to know the rest?'

'Please! Yes, just carry on!'

'As there *were* twenty like you said, I took it very slowly, performing the best I could on each one. I'd decided to, to…' She blushed and stopped.

'You decided to do what, darling?'

He smiled as she snuggled closer and whispered in his ear then drew away.

'Do you know how I mean? Do you follow?'

He did. His brain was racing as to how he could arrange this little orgy in London. He was so excited he wasn't following what she was saying. *Bloody hell! How had this happened? No two ways were the same! Who would they ask? Not a problem, Jed would fix this up easily; no man with red blood would turn this down.* He resumed an expression of quiet interest; she was rattling on, digging her own pit, except she didn't know it and he would hold her to it…

'Darling all this is wonderful, you're getting me very aroused again, but I think we've had enough for one day. I don't want your friends wondering where you've got to. Won't Jeeves want his walk?'

She hit earth with a bump. Jeeves had been forgotten. Everything had been forgotten in the heat of the moment, perhaps she could try a version of this.

'Douglas, I'd love to come with you to your club and just have fun; I need to make some arrangements, towards the end of July I think you said?'

'I did, darling, nearer the middle actually, the fifteenth we'd travel up. I'd like to buy you a white silk dressing gown. I know a little boutique in **Dreighton** that might have just the thing, would you like that?'

Stella leaned across and kissed him.

'I'd love it darling, thank you and now I must get going, put my clothes on again. It's been a wonderful day today. I've got a lot to think about!'

He stood up, anxious to see her leave, think about how best to arrange things. He had her in the palm of his hand. He wasn't going to slip up and lose her now.

'Off you go then!' he said, patting her briskly. 'Leave any mess up there, I'll sort it out. Get yourself ready and off home again.'

He was already through to the kitchen, completely preoccupied. It was so disconcerting, no continuous affection; suddenly turned off. She really wanted him, wanted to please him and wanted to be with him, wanted him to want to be with *her*.

She went up to change, scouring for anything she'd left behind. Suddenly her mobile beeped a text. Clive. 'Read now?' She pressed OK: 'Are you at home? I have half an hour free from 7.30?' She looked at her watch – it was ten minutes past; 'I'll be home at 7.30! See you later.' She was whacked, but Clive wasn't much trouble. Back downstairs again he was waiting, the garage door was open; she paused with her bags.

'Will you ring me about going shopping, then?'

'I shall. Come round for coffee as usual and we'll go to Dreighton and look round. Pick up some lunch and see how we feel, shall we?'

'That sounds good; well, thanks for today, it's been great. I enjoyed it.'

'So did I Stella, very much. I think you'll do very well in London. Keep up the good work!' He waved her off.

12

'Meet me by the bandstand at half seven then.'

David wasn't going to give up. At any moment, Clive could have picked the phone up and Martha was tense.

'Seven thirty then, Davina, just for half an hour or so, I'll see you later.'

'That was Davina, Clive,' she called upstairs; 'I'm popping out to meet her. There must be something she wants to tell me, I won't be long. Did you hear me?'

'I heard, see you later.' He was looking around for his mobile, he hadn't met Davina. He assumed she was one of her Pilates friends.

'I might pop up to Bill's then in that case; he's just got a new Audi, an A5, huge thing with leather seats and tinted windows.'

'Bill Johnson, Colonel Johnson do you mean? *Clive?*'

'Yes! He said I could go round for a drink sometime. If you're going out, I could go round there.' *And might have long enough to see Stella,* he thought.

Martha racked her brain; where did he live? If it was near the park...this was getting too complicated, but she couldn't give it up yet. If only there was something she could pin on Clive, but he was too clever. Sooner or later she would have him and that would be IT, he could clear off and she could have David. If he was prepared to wait that long for her.

Jeeves's delight at seeing Stella was short-lived as he found himself stuck out in the garden. She brushed through her hair and washed her hands. Despite the shower she felt soiled. How would it feel when she was doing it for real in London, at a sex club? The nerves tingled down her arms and she felt a bit panicky. Clive must never know about this. She'd better see Cindy and have a good chat with her. Only Cindy would know where she was going. She'd tell Cathy she was going to London for a break. A car drew up outside and she peeped through the window. It was Clive.

'Hello my sweetheart, how are you?'

'Fine; can we take Jeeves for a walk, do you mind?'

'I told Martha I was going round to see Bill Johnson, he's got a new car. I can trust him. Would you like to go round there? We can be like a normal couple, what do you think?'

'Okay, is it far?'

'No, up on the Cogen Estate, ten, fifteen minutes' walk perhaps? Jeeves will get his exercise and we can be together.' He smiled agreeably. 'Did the lunch go all right today? You went to the King's Arms then?' *Be civilized about it; don't rile her.*

Stella went to fetch Jeeves's lead not looking at him, feeling guilty. 'We did yes, it was quite nice. I had a glass of champagne.'

'Did you!' he said 'Hi Jeeves, come on then, where's your lead? Go to Stella.'

They trudged up the hill towards the estate on the edge of the village.

'Do you know Bill well then?' Stella was curious. 'I haven't heard you mention him before.'

'He's an old friend. We keep in touch.' He kicked a pebble into the gutter, making Jeeves pull against his lead, straining after it. 'He's a lot younger than me and divorced.' He turned anxiously. 'I'd better watch you, hadn't I? I don't want to lose you, Stella. I do love you, you know.'

'I *know* you do Clive and I love you too.'

'*Do* you?' His eyes were hopeful.

'Really, Clive, I do, yes.' And at that moment she believed she did – it just didn't last.

The house was detached, four bedrooms and maybe five. It was modern with white plastic doors and windows, with a conservatory at the rear and a neat and tidy front garden. The black car was in the driveway, very shiny.

Bill was at the front door, with a broad smile and holding a glass of Guinness.

'Hi Clive and who will this be then? No Martha?'

'No, she's gone to meet a friend from her Pilates I think.' He slipped an arm around her shoulders, giving her a hug. 'This is Stella and her dog Jeeves.' Jeeves was sniffing a curb stone. 'Can he come in?'

Bill held his glass out in a welcoming gesture. 'Sure he can. Come in, I'll find you a drink,' he invited. 'Go through to the conservatory, the dog can go round the garden, he can't get out. What would you like to drink, Stella?'

She liked him. He was Irish with piercing blue eyes and dark wavy hair, strong and muscular, with his shirtsleeves rolled up to the elbows.

'Oh, a glass of tonic please or a squash I don't drink usually, alcohol I mean.'

'Is bitter lemon okay?' He opened the fridge and studied the bottles.

'Yes, great, that would be fine, thanks.'

A letter from the Sirens Club was on the hall table, open. She daren't look too closely at it. It was an invitation for some time in July.

'What have you seen there then?' The drink was ready in his hand, he was watching her. 'I'm terrible for leaving things lying around so I am. Here's your drink,' passing her the bitter lemon, 'shall we go through then?' He scooped up the letter and shoved it in a letter rack.

* * *

Martha skimmed through the leather address book by the phone for Colonel Johnson and found he lived on the Cogen Estate – the opposite direction to which she was going. That was a relief. It was tense and exciting heading for the park and the bandstand. There were two paths that led there. She saw him leaning against the wall, watching the other path to which she was on. Inside, she realised, you never felt any different from when you were young. It was just the body that got older, not your emotions. She wanted him and there was no one else around. He heard her approach, her heels tapping on the path and turned to meet her. They kissed quickly, looked around and found a shadowy corner behind the shrubbery borders.

'Dearest Martha,' he began, 'I'm so glad you could come. I was missing you, I *need* you!'

He reminded her of Peter O'Toole, with his quaint way of making conversation. No one called her 'dearest' these days except David. She could smell his aftershave, and cigarettes on his breath.

'Can we sit down? I can only spare a short while.' She took his hand.

'Over here, it's dry on these grass cuttings. Come here.'

She was doubtful. 'I'll get covered in grass there…'

'Then I'll brush it all off you! Come and sit down woman!'

Once down, the grass was forgotten. He slipped her sarong open, sliding his hand in. It felt good. His kiss tasted of mint and tobacco. They both spoke together then and laughed. David smiled at her.

'No, go on, after you.'

'David, I might have to keep you waiting for ages,' she said. 'I'm convinced Clive's involved with Stella, but so far he hasn't put a foot wrong that I can prove. If I just sit back and let it play out, he's going to slip up sooner or later then I'll have him where I want him.'

'Not in your bed I hope!'

'Oh God no, perish the thought!'

'However long it takes, Mattie, I'll be here waiting for you.' He thought, 'Can you skip a class one day, or has he any plans of going anywhere?'

Martha scoffed. 'Is he *going* anywhere? Well I don't know what with, he says he's never got a penny to his name. If he does, you'll be the first to know.'

She considered this idea. 'I *might* be able to dodge a class. Meet you when he goes to Chess.' She poked in her bag and pulled out her diary. 'What about next Thursday, the twenty fourth?'

'Is it the twenty fourth? Nearly out of June already! That would be wonderful,' he said, delighted. 'I could pick you up in the car from the hotel if you like.'

'I think that will be all right. Look, I'm going to have to go in a minute,' brushing down her skirt, 'I must get all this grass off....'

'Ten more minutes. Come closer.'

* * *

'What did you make of our William then?' They were walking back to Stella's.

She chose her words carefully. 'He is quite attractive, I liked him.'

'I thought you would...' He paused. She guessed what was coming. '...more than me?'

She just *knew* he'd say that; it made her so *angry*.

'*Clive!* I've only just *met* him, for half an hour, you're paranoid!'

'I'm in love with you, aren't I' he appealed,

Stella fought down the irritation. It drove her mad.

'I've *said* I love you this evening. I'm with you now. Don't keep pushing.' The trip to London slid into her mind like a TV commercial. She wanted more than one night with Douglas. She wanted to stay in London a bit longer if she could. 'I might go away next month, just for a few days, I'll have to see.'

Immediately Clive was on edge.

'On your own you mean? Where would you go?'

Stella was vague. 'London possibly, I'm not sure, somewhere anyway.'

He couldn't help it, the lack of confidence in his tone. These exchanges were always the same.

'To get away from me you mean, don't you?'

Now she looked at him, a pang of guilt suddenly – he was so *nice*.

'Of course I don't, darling, what a thing to *say*.'

She listened to herself. She was even *sounding* like Douglas now. They had reached her front door, she unlocked it and Jeeves rushed in.

'Come in for a minute, Clive.'

He peeked at his watch. He was with Bill. He could spare another five minutes. She dropped the lead and slipped her arms around him, pulling him towards her, reaching up to kiss him.

'Look, Clive, I do love you, I really do. You're comforting, safe. I don't want to get away from you! I just want a few days away to do something a bit different, that's all.'

'I know you do, I'm just an old worry-guts! I don't want anything to hurt you.' He gently stroked her hair. 'You're very, very precious to me. You do understand that, don't you?'

'Yes I do.' She held her arms against his chest. 'You could stay longer, but you'd better get back to Martha, hadn't you? I'll speak to you in the morning as usual.'

He took hold of her hands and squeezed them. The last person he wanted to get back to was Martha. She always used that to rub in the fact he was tied, as if he didn't know.

'I'll call you at the usual time, yes. It was lovely to see you tonight.' He was heading out of the door. 'Speak tomorrow then, bye my darling.'

'Goodnight and lots of love!'

In bed she thought about the letter from the Sirens Club that she had seen. It was so distinctive; she couldn't have mistaken it for anything else. He must be a member too and had been invited in

July – was London or another branch, she wondered. He was very nice. Sexy and charming! What *was* the matter with her, she was sex mad. She turned over and went to sleep.

13

On Monday morning on her way to the shop, Stella made a plan. She wanted to get sorted in her own mind what this trip was all about and Cindy's advice would be useful. She needed someone to confide in and apart from her, the only other person was Dr. Carroll. She might give him a sketchy version. Monday's were usually quiet. She arrived to find her sorting out stuff to go into the summer Sale.

'Morning Cindy, do you think we could have lunch today? I want to discuss my trip, maybe have two hours?'

She was collecting a huge bundle of clothes and taking them through to the stockroom at the rear. 'That sounds like a good idea; I hoped you'd tell me what it's all about. Whereabouts would you suggest?'

Stella climbed into the window display.

'How about the Spritz Bar, bag a corner table and have some jacket potatoes, do you fancy that?'

'Yes that sounds OK,' she called from the stockroom. 'We'll go at twelve and stay 'til two. Can you stay out the front there a while? Then I can sort these things in here. Give me a shout if you need any help.'

Having just attached a scarf to a stand, she stared out at the street. Suddenly her heart jumped a beat. Douglas was striding up outside and deep in conversation with his mobile. Her stomach flipped.

She scrambled up and shot through the doorway.

'Hello Douglas, fancy seeing you here! Were you going to sort out when we went shopping together?'

'He looked startled. 'I said I was going to ring you and I *shall*.

Busy working today I see?' He glanced briefly at the shop, 'You'd better go and get back to it then. I'll *call* you, bye!'

He continued walking. She was glued to the spot; paralysed almost.

'He loves you then Stella, does he?' Cindy leaned in the doorway, straight-faced, watching.

'Yes, yes he does. We're going shopping soon. He's buying me a white silk dressing gown. He's fine when we're together, but other times we have to be discreet.'

'Why?'

Stella hadn't worked that one out either.

'I don't really know, but he wants to keep me a secret. I wouldn't want *Clive* to think there was more going on than we agreed about!'

'What had you and Clive agreed then?' Cindy was curious.

Going back inside, she fiddled with a shelf of sweaters.

'He agreed I could go out with Douglas, as long as I didn't sleep with him.'

'*I* see;' she couldn't quite believe this, it was so obvious. 'And he thinks that's going to work then, does he? Knowing you like he does?'

'He trusts me, Cindy, but we've said about this before. He's just not enough on his own. I need a sexual edge, a bit of a challenge. Douglas provides that and I'm very excited about London. Anyway, he's got Martha to think about – Douglas is unattached and...'

'Except for *Helen* though, don't forget!'

'Helen was in his past, she barely sees him now. I'm not worried about *her*.' Anxious to change the subject for the moment, 'Shall I carry on sorting things here and then we go to lunch at twelve?'

'Yeah, I'll be in the back' she replied, 'just give a shout if you need me.'

At twelve they shut the shop and headed down towards the Bar.

Inside, compared to the bright sunshine, it was gloomy and smoky. They walked through to the courtyard and found a spare table with an umbrella.

'I'll get these, Cindy, my treat. What would you like?'

She looked at the menu on the table. 'A tuna and sweet corn jacket with no butter or mayo I think, thanks.'

'I'll have the same. I'll just go and order.'

Walking back into the bar, she heard a voice. Bill. She looked around. He was sitting at two tables pushed together in a corner, with a group of at least eight other men, quaffing a pint of Guinness, while the others were drinking lager. Empty pint glasses littered the table and three men were smoking, the two ashtrays filled with stubs. They were engrossed in something and hadn't looked up as she went in, then she saw what it was – three flyers for the Sirens Club. The barman had served a customer and Stella was next. She turned back to the bar and placed her order.

'What's your name?'

'Stella.'

'I'll give you a shout when it's ready, knives and forks are out there on the table by the wall.'

The bar was crowded with others waiting to be served and the group of men still hadn't looked up. She didn't want to catch the Colonel's eye and carefully edged through the crowd back to their table.

Cindy sipped her white wine, the ice clinking in the glass, cold and refreshing.

'Well this is nice, thank you.' She scraped her chair a bit closer to the table, 'So come on now, tell me all about this trip, when it is and what it's all about.'

Stella took a gulp of lime and slipped her sunglasses on. She relayed the plan first, and then told her about meeting a Madam Dubois. 'I think Douglas is intending I go with her to this club they know, the Sirens Club. I've shown you the flyer I had for it, haven't I?' Cindy nodded, listening keenly. 'Officially I'm his escort, but he thought I might enjoy trying my hand at a bit of *real* escort work.'

Cindy replaced her glass precisely, on a beer mat, and then held it a moment before raising her eyes slowly. Stella cocked her head.

'Why look at me like that?'

'Well, I'm just curious to know how you can let a woman you've never met, introduce you to strange men to work as an escort. You do know what escorting *is* I presume?'

She shot up straight, her cheeks colouring slightly, 'I'm not being a prostitute if that's what you mean. It's a high class club with respectable clients, escorting isn't just lying down and opening your legs you know, you have to have conversation as well.' She paused, 'I think I'll be quite good at it.'

Cindy sniffed pointedly and considered what to say.

'However it's dressed up, Stella, you'll be expected to give strange men, men you've never met before who may indeed *be* strange themselves, sex. And any way they like and I *mean* any way they want it. Do you catch my drift?'

Stella shuffled in her seat, pushing her hair behind her ears. The sign she was nervous: good, she ought to be.

'But I'll be with Douglas,' she said defensively, 'and I'm sure this Jed's businesslike and as for this Madam, well, they can't *force* me to do anything, can they? *Can* they?' she asked, suddenly alarmed.

'You tell *me*, Stella, you're the one that's going. If I'm honest, I don't like the idea at all and I'll worry about you the whole time you're there. But you've obviously thought about it. I won't try to stop you, but one thing I ***will*** ask,' she said, with a wry look, 'what are you doing for protection?'

Stella was uncertain. 'Protection? Do you mean will there be bouncers there, that sort of thing?'

'*Stella*!' Cindy spluttered her drink; *what was she like?* 'I mean protected sex; condoms. The risk of infection these days is tremendous. I'm talking about hepatitis, Chlamydia, H.I.V., haven't you even *thought* of that?' Now she was worried. Surely she couldn't be *that* naïve?

'Oh I'll take some with me, I got some at Morrison's,' she replied airily. 'They're bound to have more there anyway, seeing as it's a sex club and anyway,' she concluded, 'as I said before, I'll have Douglas with me. He'll look after me, I'm sure he will.'

'Well as long as you're sure.' Her tone was unconvinced. 'But I wouldn't hold your breath if I were you. For God's sake keep in touch, Stella. Promise me you'll just run for it if you need to get away, *promise* me! Why on earth you feel the need to do this though, I've no idea.'

'Stella!' The barman had their order ready.

Cindy watched sadly as she walked back to the bar. She was so green about some things. She hoped nothing would go wrong. There was a warm heart underneath this façade. She just needed to meet the right man and she hadn't yet, but this wasn't the right way to go about proving anything. She was sure of it. She was heading for deep water.

Collecting the meals, Stella heard her name again and recognizing the voice, she peered towards the gloomy corner.

'Well if it isn't the same lovely Stella that caught my eye before! What're you doing here?'

Her cheeks reddened as the other men ogled her. She felt naked.

'I'm sitting outside with my friend Cindy, having a spot of lunch, fancy seeing *you*!'

She heard a comment about 'fancy' and a crude snigger. One of the men whistled at her.

'*Two* fine ladies sitting out there then. *I'm* wondering will you be coming here again. Do you like to come here, Stella, lovely lass like you?' More raucous laughter followed.

'Sometimes I do…'

'Go on then! Let's see you come!'

She heard the whisper, it was vulgar and suggestive.

'Don't upset the lady! Sure she's a fine woman. Look after yourself now won't you Stella?'

She stalked back to the table and plonked the plates down with an air of finality.

'Now I *know* why I'm going!'

'Oh yes and why's that then?' she asked.

'I need to grow up, really. I'm too soft. I need to know how to handle men like there were inside, whistling and trying to embarrass me. Hopefully this trip to London will make me tougher. It's what I need, changing.'

Cindy stretched out a hand. 'Well I, and I'm sure all your *real* friends, love you just the way you are. You're fine as you are, but it's up to you. If you think you can keep safe.'

'Yeah I'll be safe! It'll be great fun and I'll tell you all about it when I get back.'

'You're going on the fifteenth you said, how long were you planning to stay?'

'I might come back on the Sunday with Douglas. I'll see how it goes but I'll keep in touch. Now,' changing the subject, 'the shop, will you get some help in, because the Sale will be on then?'

'Don't worry about the shop, Stella, just worry about yourself. Let's enjoy this now and I'll get you another drink.'

'Bye then Stella,' A call to their table. 'You do what I say and look after yourself now, won't you?'

Stella had her back to the door but she knew who it was.

'I will. Thank you, Colonel.'

'Bill to you my sweetheart, go safely now.' He went back indoors.

'And who was *that* then, Stella?' Cindy asked, intrigued.

'His name's Bill Johnson, he's a colonel and Clive knows him. I met him the other evening. He's just got a new Audi. He's Irish. I liked him.'

'Oh Stella, please be careful!' she implored.

Spluttering over a large piece of hot potato, she replied.

'I will, don't worry.'

14

Rhoda looked in the back of her diary to find Hazel's number, she could never remember it. She answered straight away.

'Hello?'

'Good morning Hazel, it's Rhoda. I've got a bit of news. A friend of mine, Douglas Spencer's just called, to say he and a,' – she paused, wondering how to describe Stella – 'a friend of his, Stella Maitland, will be coming up to the club in July. I don't know if you've heard of him at all?'

'I *think* I might know who you mean. By coincidence I think they're the couple I served with a cream tea some weeks ago. Would he be tall and quite striking? His friend was dark haired and very attractive, I thought.'

'That's the one!' Rhoda was delighted. 'I wonder if you might teach her a thing or two when they come up. If you could get there that is? Saturday the seventeenth I think she'll be starting. How do you feel about it, you thought she was quite attractive, you said?'

'Oh I did, *very!*' Hazel was in no doubt about that. 'It sounds quite fun. From what Douglas was saying, I don't think she's done this sort of thing before, but shows promise.'

Rhoda remarked with relish, 'I think she's up for it as far as straight sex is concerned, but hasn't got the first idea about what women can get up to together.'

'Well don't worry,' replied Hazel, 'she won't be in the dark for long. It'll be a pleasure to initiate her into some of the finer points of lesbian fun!'

Rhoda, determined to make the most of this, insisted, 'Well don't spare the horses, will you? Give her the whole lot!'

'Not a problem, Rhoda,' Hazel assured her. 'Is she a friend of *yours* particularly?' she asked, with a hint of sarcasm.

Rhoda scoffed, 'Ha! Well not exactly, no! One thing I must ask you, can you make sure you call me Zena in London? I'm *Madam* Zena Fortune. I want to teach the girl a lesson, silly stuck-up tart!'

'I'll remember that! I'll look forward to it, goodbye now!'

Hazel underscored the entry in her diary and tapped her pencil, thinking.

Many men enjoyed watching two women together.

* * *

Reggie was out in the garden when the phone rang. Helen picked it up. 'Hello?'

'Hi! Is Reggie there please, could I have a quick word if he is, it's Paula, from the office.'

She looked out of the window.

'Just one minute, he's outside, hang on and I'll fetch him.' She placed the receiver on the table and went into the garden.

'Paula, how're you doing? Have you found anyone for the trip yet?' Reggie asked.

'I have yes, Mandy, Tracy and Tamsin. I said we were going with you to the Sirens Club in London. Tamsin had heard of it and was keen to go, but the other two hadn't, so we looked it up on the website and now we're ready.'

Glancing out of the window, he saw Helen picking dead heads off the roses with Buster at her heels. He continued.

'I've a feeling it's blondes that do it for Douglas. Remind me, are these girls blonde or what?'

'Yes, Mandy and Tracy are platinum and natural. Tamsin's light brown with blonde streaks. They've all done glamour modeling. No inhibitions, any of them. They're the best I could come up with, Reggie, I'm sure you'll approve.'

'I'm sure I will, pet, they sound great, thanks. As far as I know, our Dougie's gettin' up there on the fifteenth in time for a lunch at the Café Regent. I suggested we came up the next day, on the Friday. Jed was going to keep me quiet and you girls can blend in and let him introduce you to Spencer. We'll have to play it a *bit* by ear.'

Paula had a question. 'Reggie, what is it you're exactly hoping to find out? Has Spencer done anything actually illegal that you know of?'

'Well the rumours have it Valerie his first wife didn't die accidentally.'

Pushing his hand in his trouser pocket, he leaned against the sill.

'I don't like the sound of his bringing a young lady up who might not know what she's in for. Somethin' tells me I should be around to watch the show and if I can find out what happened back in nineteen fifty nine, so much the better.' He looked out. Helen was still intent on gardening,

'And I su*ppose* like, I want to try and find out what it is that makes him tick; what it is that has Helen still after him. I'm not sayin' she'd go back to him like, but he has something the women seem to find irresistible and I'm curious to know what it is. I'm going to try and get talking to his friend Rhoda – if anyone knows what *really* happened, *she* does.'

Helen returned with her trug and wandered into the kitchen.

'Paula thanks for phonin', I've got to go now, but we can discuss it more next week. I'll be in the office on Tuesday, so see you then.'

* * *

Douglas wanted to make two calls. He tried Jed first.

'Jed, Douglas here; I just wondered how many replies you'd received, if any, in response to the Fantasy Day on Saturday when I'm up with Stella.'

'Bees round a honey pot, Doug. Funny you should call now. I've only just hung up on Colonel Johnson. He's got eight guys interested and the money's already received. Another four have sent cheques, making twelve so far and a few weeks to go yet. I'm taking it that your Stella doesn't know she's Queen of the Show?'

'I'm calling her next and arranging a trip to get her a white silk robe. I've also heard about Hazel Makepeace.'

'Yeah, get her fixed up with a dyke as well. They can watch her after. Great idea that I think; brilliant! I've organised a room as near as she describes in what you sent me. Bloody great table for twenty – nine each side and one at each end. I can see it already. Do you reckon she could do two goes at it?'

'Heavens, you mean forty men?'

'If me maths is right, yeah!'

'I would suggest it was over two days then. I've spoken to Hazel and I think the best idea would be to have one sitting on Saturday and another on Sunday in the same format, but with the addition of Hazel. That would seem straightforward to me, could you arrange that?'

'I can give it a whirl. She could be with Rhoda in the morning for some of the V.I.P's then do you think, yeah? Make a cool little packet. Do you want to talk money now or wait until it's all set up?'

Douglas kept his head. *Be cool and calculating. It was time Jed learned breeding stood for something. He'd waited long enough for this – he might not be of the 'old school' like Clive, but neither was he a jumped up nouveau-riche like Jed. No, this weekend would see changes in the management structure and a 'nice little earner' as Jed would say, for him.*

'I'll wait until I'm there, but I would assume one third to me, one to Rhoda, who's going to be Zena Fortune on this occasion, and one to the club, as a bonus to those mainly responsible which would include you, of course. When we see the figures, the directors can decide. I think it should be a shareholder's decision.'

He grinned. He didn't hold the majority shares – yet. Jed

couldn't argue with that one. By the time they tried to call a meeting…well.

But Jed didn't like the sound of that. Big deal! He was after a bit more than just over thirty three percent. He wouldn't argue today.

'We'll sort it when you get here then. I'll remember about the "Zena Fortune" bit too. I suppose she'll be in a wig and a different get-up as well?'

'I told her she mustn't be recognisable as the woman who sold Stella the green chiffon top, yes. If anything though, she's more likely to remember *you*, when you appeared at Maples Farm that time. Be careful what you say, won't you?'

'Yeah I'll be careful, but there's no way you're goin' to get *me* sportin' a rug. I'll p'raps grow a bit of stubble or somethin', but I don't think she's goin' to recognise me. It'll all be so new to her that she'll just follow what she's told to do, don't you think?' He waited, then ploughed on 'I'll just keep her mind buzzin' with what's goin' on, I reckon. It's goin' to be good and I get a hard-on every time I think about it. There's just somethin' I want to run past you though, Doug?'

'And what would that be?'

'Our boys in the technical department have come up with this thing that we use normally in the hospital-mode. It isn't to everyone's taste but I thought I'd run it past you, whether you want me to use it when she's here and in action.'

Douglas waited to hear, not sure what was coming. Jed obviously needed a prompt. He wondered what on earth it could be.

'Well come on then, tell me or ask me if you're going to. What is it?'

Jed had seen it; it had even made *him* feel ill at first so amazing it was in its originality and design: the latest thing in Intimate Entertainment and an asset to the Club. Because of the small amount of radiation involved, the girls had to be sure they weren't pregnant, but apart from that, if it was your cup of tea it blew your mind. Douglas flicked his cuff and glanced at his watch. He wanted to catch Stella as well this evening to round everything off and he was growing impatient now.

'Are you going to tell me, Jed? I've other calls to make this evening. Spit it out if you're going to?'

Jed took a breath. 'Yeah right, well, it's a kind of X-ray thing. I don't know how it works exactly, but when a girl's lying on a table, whether she's naked or not, on a screen in a viewing gallery that the punters can watch, you can see anything in graphic detail that's pushed up inside her.'

'Jed, what exactly is new about that?' Douglas was bored. 'Even the most basic porn movies show a guy's prick pumping in graphic detail and Technicolour I might add. For Heaven's sake, I thought you meant something original.'

Jed was quick to explain. 'Yeah, but only from the *outside*, you can see close-ups of penetration. What *I* mean is you can see it pumping right up inside her body. You can see through her body and really watch her getting fucked, buggered or both.

'She might be lying there under a sheet or something on the show floor and you can't see nothin,' but the camera shows it all on a screen what's bein' done. As I say, it's not everyone's cup of tea perhaps, but it goes down well in our 'Operating Theatre' and it's makin' a bloody fortune. Whad'ya says to that? D'ya think it's a go or not?'

Douglas wasn't bored now, he'd never heard of such a thing. He asked a question.

'Does the girl know anything?' Then he realised his error. 'When I say '*know* anything' I mean know it's being transmitted to a screen? Obviously she knows about penetration.'

Jed sensed his interest, saw the money coming in.

'No, the woman doesn't a know anything like what you mean. It suits the voyeurs too, of course. They can watch something the girl is completely unaware of, and when she comes herself – bloody hell, you can see it all for real.'

Douglas was sold.

'I think we could come to an arrangement about this. I would suggest we enquire discreetly among the clientele as to who wishes to view it. They would pay an additional fee, of course.'

'You're singin' from my hymn sheet there, Dougie boy!' Jed felt hot with exhilaration. This was going to be a winner.

Douglas winced at "Dougie boy", but he admitted a grudging admiration for this innovative creation. Jed obviously knew the right techies in the business. It was sordid but it paid. If it wasn't felt by the girl on the table, then he agreed – it was all the more exciting to watch. He sensed also that Jed might try to crank up his share of the profits for this little extravaganza. Well, if it was sponsored well enough and drew the crowds, then they might be able to negotiate.

'I'll be in touch with you again before we arrive, but shall leave the organisation of the event to you. I must call Stella, I'll catch you later. Keep me up to date with anything else you think I should know about. Bye for now.'

'Bye Doug thanks for calling. Just leave everything to me!'

Douglas was still in business mode and serious. Stella was a commodity, a highly lucrative commodity which needed handling with care and respect. Respect? Inasmuch as her earning potential demanded respect, but emotional respect; no, he'd no emotional entanglements there. He called her number, his diary open and his finger on the following Saturday.

'Hello?'

'Stella, Douglas. I hope I'm not disturbing you?'

Stella dropped her book and sat up.

'Hello Douglas, no, not at all, is this to do with our shopping trip for the dressing gown?'

'That's right darling, yes. Are you free this Saturday?'

'The twenty sixth, yes, I am.'

'*Gooood*, I'll collect you at ten thirty and we'll go over to Dreighton. I'm sure we can pick up the most gorgeous white silk gown. It'll look very flattering. We don't want anything cheap and tarty looking for London. We'll go straight over to this shop I know, have some lunch then I'll I drop you back.'

This was deliberate. He heard the intake of breath. He could play her like a violin. Stella swallowed, she wanted to go to bed with him after buying the gown and here he was implying that he'd be leaving her high and dry.

'I'm free all day that Saturday actually, should you want a home demonstration. A little fashion show when we get back-'

'Jeeves'll want a walk though, won't he? I'll see it on you soon enough darling, you could always try it out on Clive perhaps? I'm sure he'd *love* to see it on you. He's got the hots for you, hasn't he?'

He stretched his long legs out, crossing them at the ankles, thoroughly enjoying this little exchange. It was making him feel randy. He wanted sex now, and he didn't want Stella. He twisted round, reaching for a small black book from a drawer in his desk.

'I'll see you on Saturday, Stella, goodbye now!' Ending the call without waiting for a reply, he opened it, flicking over the pages and finding a number. He entered it and waited.

'Oh hello, it's Richard, I wonder if I could speak to Rachel? Oh is she? Who's there available at the moment…yes, just outside **Dreighton**…Mandy! Is she blonde? Platinum and natural! *Splendid!* No, that isn't a problem, yes, overnight please, splendid, I'll look forward to meeting her, thank you. Yes, on my account please. Many thanks, 'bye now!'

15

'Paula? It's Mandy. I've had a call to go to a Richard Spencer just outside Dreighton. You don't think it's any relation to Douglas, do you? The one Reggie's investigating? He wants me overnight and is excited I'm blonde. I'll let you know what I think.'

Paula was apprehensive. 'Be careful, darling. Reggie didn't paint a very good picture of him. Just do what you have to do and if it *is* the same bloke, don't for God's sake give anything away. If we meet him again in London, it'll be his look-out. He's used a false name and won't want to shout about it, that he's seen you somewhere before, I shouldn't think. Let me know what you discover. Oh, and one more thing...'

'What?'

'Enjoy!'

'I will, don't worry! See you later, Paula.'

The following morning Paula checked to see whether it was Douglas Spencer or just coincidence. She'd see Reggie again in the office the next day, Tuesday, to report her findings. The answer-phone was on until midday and she left a message. Just beginning to feel a bit concerned she hadn't received a reply, her phone rang, it was Mandy.

'Hi Paula, I'm sorry not to call you earlier, but I've only just got back and found your message. Before you ask, yes, it *was* the same man. Richard Spencer and Douglas Spencer are the same. I think without doubt as well, that there can only *be* one Douglas Spencer, whatever his name is. I'm shattered and I must be at least thirty years younger than he is.'

'You're joking! I'm seeing Reggie tomorrow and I want to be able to fill him in on this-'

Mandy interrupted. 'Well I can tell *you*, he certainly filled *me* in, just about everywhere and then some. He's one perverted cookie and kept coming back for more. I suppose being a former gynae *could* have had something to do with it.'

'Well go on then, don't keep me in suspenders! What did he do?'

'Are you havin' your lunch?'

'Just finished, why? Was it as bad as that then?'

'Well, just that he liked to improvise a lot, not to say he wasn't well supplied. It must have been at least eight inches if a foot!' She giggled. 'No, he wanted to use bananas, cucumber, salami…'

'A baguette?' She suggested.

'No. Why do you ask that?' she asked, interested.

'Could have filled it and had a snack?' She sniggered. 'I'm only joking!'

'Good, because of where he wanted to put the salami!'

Paula shrieked, '*No!!*'

'He is *seriously* kinky, but business is business!'

'Apart from that, did he say anything else I should know? How did he give himself away that he's also Douglas?'

'I was very careful what I said, but I did happen to mention the Sirens Club apropos the salami, saying it was certainly an " sexually intimate and rather exciting for me" as far as *I* was concerned. He said he was planning a trip up very soon. Then he boasted about Jed and a number of other senior colleagues and that once he'd also been a Harley Street gynaecologist. I figured it had to be one and the same man. I'm as sure as I never want to see a garlic sausage again, that Richard Spencer is Douglas Spencer. The proof will be when we're all up there.'

'Certainly will! Well thanks Mandy, at this moment he'd deny it of course.'

'Well, to coin a phrase: he would, wouldn't he? See 'ya later, babe!'

Paula laughed and hung up. Tomorrow couldn't come quickly enough.

As soon as Reggie had settled himself at his desk the next morning, he heard a knock at the door and Paula poked her head round. She walked in carrying two mugs of coffee then perched on the chair in front of his desk. Today she had a very tight black skirt on, a sleeveless silky top with an unusual pattern of black and white circles on an off-white background, and knee length sixties style, cream patent leather boots, she looked amazing. Reggie transferred his calls and stretched back in his chair.

'You're looking tasty this morning, Ms. Greenway, and bursting to tell me something by the look of you, so come on, pet; spit it out!'

Paula crossed her long legs and noticed Reggie's eyes flash their way quickly up and down. She had a sip of coffee and then put the mug down on his desk.

'Douglas Spencer has a false name, Reggie, he's *Richard*! He's also got an account at Magic Moments Escort Agency.' She grinned from ear to ear.

'Bloody hell, pet!' Reggie was astonished. 'How did you find this out, tell me!'

'He called them on Sunday night and wanted to have Rachel but she wasn't there, so he was offered another girl, platinum and natural.'

Reggie was all ears. 'Yeah, so who was she then?'

'*Mandy!* Mandy who's coming up with Tamsin, Tracy and me to the Sirens Club next month, I believe?'

'Oh good God, Paula, this is crackin', have you spoken to Mandy since, did she give you a report like?'

'She did yes!' Paula was enjoying this. 'He'd got a whole selection of goodies out apparently,' she paused a minute, 'healthy eating!'

'Healthy *what*?' intrigued, he waited.

Paula reeled them off.

'Oh all sorts – bananas, cucumber and carrots...salami!'

Reggie was unsure that he'd heard correctly.

'Did you say salami?'

Paula nodded.

'Ouch! Bet that hurt!'

Paula nodded again.

'I'd think so! Mandy said she never wanted to see one again!'

'I can quite believe it! Oh my god, a salami *sausage*. I have to give it to Mandy though, I bet she coped.'

'Mandy's nothing if not professional, Reggie. Shall we tell Tracy and Tamsin, or leave it just between ourselves? That he uses an agency?'

'I think leave it, Paula. He's not Mr. Nice Guy and I think we should all be aware of that. That's just a bit of private information we'll keep secret I think.'

'Okey-doke Reggie, now, if we can leave that aside for a moment, can we get on with the other things to arrange next month?'

'Aye we can. Just remind me again when we're off up to London can you?'

'Hang on I'm just looking.' she relayed the plan 'All right so far?' He nodded, so she continued.

'The girls and I can make our own way back, so no need to worry there. It just depends what you want to do about Helen coming home again. Only you can decide that one!'

'Yeah, thanks Paula, now back to less entertaining concerns. Can you get the BBC on the line for their Comedy Classics show and put them through to me?'

'Will do Reggie, see you later.'

16

Martha was in a tizzy. She remembered what she'd told David: Thursday the twenty fourth. Clive was due to go to Chess at one and pick her up from Pilates at five fifteen. It had always worked well. This time she wondered whether to cancel him taking her there or collecting her. Should she say she didn't feel like going at all? Then she remembered David was collecting her from the hotel. She'd stick to the usual routine, making sure she was back in time for Clive. If she was a bit out of breath, so much the better, she'd put it down to a more strenuous session than usual.

Clive was completely distracted these days, in a world of his own. Not that it bothered her much. Sooner or later he'd slip up and she'd have him bang to rights as far as Stella Maitland was concerned.

She looked at the time in the kitchen – half past ten.

'Are you up there, Clive? Do you want a coffee?'

Clive was emailing his sister. Stella had been even more offhand when he'd spoken to her that morning. She *said* she wanted him, but there was no enthusiasm. Douglas was at the bottom of it somewhere. He'd try and see her on Saturday. Martha was talking of going into Dreighton for the day, which meant they could go out. He'd suggest it tomorrow.

'*Clive!!* Do you want a coffee?'

He started with a jolt.

'Yes please, I'll be down in a minute, just been emailing Gina. The weather's awful in Florida, Hurricane George is wreaking havoc and the noise is terrible. The dog-house blew away and nearly took Monty with it apparently. Poor dog must have been terrified. They have him inside now.' He logged off, 'I'm just coming.'

He picked up his mug and then stared at Martha.

'You look nice today, Mattie! Were you wearing that first thing? I didn't notice.'

Martha shrugged this off. 'I was, yes. I bring it out when the weather's good.' She turned round and fiddled with things on the immaculate work tops.

'I've decided I'll go into town on Saturday on the bus. I want to see if any sales are on yet. Bentley's might have one and House of Fraser. Jacobs might as well. I'd like some new undies and nightwear and they have some good brands.'

She picked up her coffee mug again, turning it round and round. 'What did you fancy for lunch today? If we leave at one, we could have something light. I don't want indigestion this afternoon. Shall I fix a quick salad? I've got a mushroom quiche which I could stick in the oven, or you could have it cold. Which would you prefer?'

'That would be lovely, yes.'

'Which would you prefer then?'

'What do you mean "which"? I said yes!'

'Hot or cold, do you want it hot or cold?'

Clive felt he couldn't care less and neither really could Martha.

'Oh, hot then please. Crisp the pastry up a bit, so not in the microwave. I'm going back upstairs and have a sort through my files. There's a chess competition coming up soon.' She didn't move, 'Why don't you go and sit in the garden or something, closeted up all afternoon in that room on a lovely day like this.'

He went back upstairs. Shortly after, he heard Martha open the conservatory door (which stuck) and go out into the garden. He took his mobile and looked for Stella. He couldn't wait for tomorrow, he'd ask her to go out with him on Saturday *now*.

Stella was sitting on the banks of the river Dreight with Jeeves, throwing small pebbles into the water.

'Hello Clive, I'm with Jeeves by the river. What do you want?' She tried not to sound too irritated.

She was frustrated Douglas had ended the call so abruptly, still not knowing whether she'd be able to see him after buying her dressing-gown.

Just occasionally it crossed her mind that he was using her. Clive could be a safer bet after all. She was using him really. Then she remembered their times in bed together, so exciting and different, Douglas kissed her and touched her all over. Sucking, pushing his tongue where she'd never had it before and 'that place' she found so difficult to say, but he was *making* her say it. She squirmed with the remembrance....

'I was calling to tell you that Martha's going into Dreighton on Saturday. I thought we could go out somewhere if you weren't doing anything? We could go almost anywhere you wanted, providing it isn't there. She's going on the bus, so I'll have the car; this Saturday, the twenty-sixth?'

Stella knew the date. She was going into Dreighton herself. Suddenly it was crystal clear.

'Sorry Clive, I'd've loved to, but Cindy and I'll be going too, we thought we'd mooch around the shops. Another time would be fine, but we've already arranged it. You *could* come with us, but then we'd risk bumping into Martha, so maybe leave it. Never mind, I'm sure we'll find another day, yeah?'

Clive felt cursed. She was a minx and knew exactly how to twist the knife, using Martha to goad him at every opportunity. Well he'd show her. One day he just *knew*, she'd be begging him on her knees to have her back, once that *man* had finished with her, and would he have her? He thought for a moment. When she was without all her make-up and fancy clothes she was beautiful and loveable. Of course he'd have her back. She was a part of his body as much as an arm or a leg was. Oh well, he'd find something else to do. Go and take some photos with his new camera or something, another opportunity would present itself.

'Yeah, okay Stella. Don't go spending too much money though. Don't let Cindy lead you astray.' He heard Martha returning. 'I'll call you first thing in the morning as usual, darling, love you!'

'Love you too; have a nice day, are you going to Chess this afternoon?'

'Yes, I have to go, we have a competition coming up soon and I need to sort the teams out, but I'll see you as soon as I can then.'

'....If you say so, Clive!' This was Martha, arms folded, in the doorway.

'Who will you see so soon, exactly?'

Clive closed the call. 'That was Stella. She's got a problem with her computer again and wanted me to fix it, but as you probably heard, I can't go today as I've got to go to Chess, so I said I'd see her as soon as I could. It's hard being without your computer.'

'Why can't she take it to Northbytes, why do *you* have to do it?'

'Because she's my friend and I like her. I like to help my friends. You have friends at your Pilates, don't you?' he retorted, 'Who's the man I see you hanging around with, chatting to when I come to collect you? I saw you the other week while I was waiting. You looked animated enough then. Stella's a good friend. I may go over on Saturday while you're gallivanting around the sales. It's probably something quite simple.'

Martha decided to leave it there. It was a warning not to natter too much to David, they must be on guard. She went back downstairs.

As they approached the hotel, Martha was more apprehensive. She couldn't see David's car. She worried Clive would pick up on her anxiety. He'd stopped and was waiting for her to get out but she seemed fixed to her seat. In the end he spoke.

'Do you want me to collect you at five fifteen? What on earth do you do with yourself before the class starts? You're there for over three hours.'

It had never occurred to him before that she had all this amount of time – the class itself couldn't be more than an hour, so what did she do with the rest of it? The stress of worrying when David was going to show up made Martha more snappy than usual in her reply.

'It's a hotel, Clive, The Royal Oak Hotel. They have a pool, a Jacuzzi, a sauna, a bar and a very comfortable lounge. I relax and enjoy myself away from your company for a change.' She glared, 'I can even chat to my friends without having inane comments made about them and totally chill out before returning home again. *You* sit in front of a board covered in black and white squares, in silence, moving silly bits of white and black wood around. It's whatever turns you on, Clive.'

She grabbed her sports bag and swung open the car door, climbing out.

'I'll see you here at five fifteen as usual!'

She shut it with more force than she intended, so she smiled briefly at him through the window before going up the side path. Clive watched her for a moment, and then grated the car into first gear before moving off, the engine roaring before scraunching itself into second gear.

When she was sure Clive had gone, Martha returned to the car park. None of her other friends had arrived, for which she was grateful. She felt a cat on hot bricks. She was checking her watch again just as his car drew up level with her and he put the window down.

'Hello Mattie, looking good. Are you ready?'

Martha opened the back passenger door, threw in her bag then climbed in the front. He'd got some different spicy aftershave on which she didn't recognise, it smelt very good. Why was perfume and aftershave so evocative? This scent, whatever it was, turned her on, and want to eat him. She'd bought something for Clive once, very expensive at the time and when he wore it now (on the rare occasions he'd bother) it left her completely cold. There had to be physical chemistry between the two people concerned for it to wax its full potential. The chemistry shared with Clive was all but dead, she decided.

'I'm ready for anything, darling!' She leaned over and gave him a kiss on the cheek, breathing in some more.

Checking his driving mirror, he pulled out on to the road.

'Where do you fancy going, Mat? I wondered about that National Trust place on the way to Leighton Bridge. It's not too far. I packed a few rolls and a bottle of champagne in the cool box. We could find a shady spot and then if you like, go for a wander round the rose gardens there, what do you think to that?'

Martha considered, weighing up the pros and cons. It sounded good, but there'd be other people with exactly the same idea. She felt so frustrated. She knew the blooms would go unnoticed while she simmered with repressed lust. David glanced across and noticed her frowning. Misinterpreting, he wondered what he'd done wrong. He put a tentative hand on her knee, and she grabbed it with such force he nearly swerved off the road.

'Hey steady on, you'll have us in a ditch if you're not careful. What's the matter, have I said something wrong? We don't *have* to go to the gardens, it was only a suggestion. If there's somewhere else you'd rather go, just tell me, dearest.'

They were driving through the countryside now and just coming up to land owned by the Forestry Commission.

'Slow down; slow down David, please.'

He looked in his mirror and saw a car close on his tail. Indicating towards the side of the road, the car shot past. Just ahead was a track. He crawled a little further forward, up to a five bar wooden gate. Next to it was a smaller opening for public access and a sign warning about the dangers of starting fires.

'What about here? Are you all right, Martha?'

He turned to face her, anxious now as she looked so tense and had gone pale. Cars were swishing past on the road every few seconds. She undid her seatbelt, grabbed his shoulder, pulling at his shirt. As she kissed him, he felt her whole body tense. She pushed against his mouth as hard as she could, clawing and pulling his tie. Suddenly she stopped, her face flushed and her eyes bright.

'I just wanted you so much, David. I couldn't bear to stand in a queue to look round a garden. I'm sorry if that sounds silly, it's a very romantic idea, but I want to be alone with you. I'd love the rolls and champagne, but only if there're no other people around to disturb us. Shall we take them in here, take a rug as well?'

'Of course we can, I suggested the gardens because I didn't want you to think that on an afternoon off, all I wanted to do was make love to you. I wanted to take you somewhere I thought you might like to be. If you'd rather find somewhere here, where we can be private, then that's absolutely fine with me.'

He took the key from the ignition and opened the door. Outside it was warm, with the fragrance of pine trees – a slight breeze was blowing, but the temperature was just right. Martha walked round to where David was removing a red cool-box with a white lid.

'Can I carry anything, the rug or the box?'

'You can take the rug if you like, everything else is in here.'

She took the rug from the boot and he brought the lid down.

'Let's go then, shall we?'

They set off up the path towards the trees, the pine needles and soft undergrowth muffling all sounds. It was very still and inviting. After walking for about fifteen minutes, the pine trees gave way to deciduous forest and dappled light, where ferns and lush grass looked promising. The pine trees were planted in serried ranks, with little or no undergrowth to speak of, but here there was fresh, bright grass and the sound of the birds again.

David pointed to a spot beneath an overhanging oak tree.

'How about over there where the sun's coming right through, what do you think?'

Martha looked and agreed. She followed him over and shook open the rug, treading it down over the bumpy surface, and they both lay down. They kissed again for a while, slowly, languorously, and then David pulled away and looked at her.

'Do you want me now, do you feel relaxed enough here? You know I want you now. You must feel it!' He grinned, it was very obvious.

Martha teased, screwing her face up with indecision.

'Er…possibly, I'm not sure!'

He grabbed her skirt, laughing, and hitched it up. Underneath she was naked. It didn't take long. Martha stared up at the sky and could feel him relax in her, grow heavier and breathe normally again. She felt warm and comfortable and relaxed herself, all the tension gone. Suddenly, as each sensation returned, she felt as if she was returning to earth again.

She felt the itchy rug underneath her bottom, over the uneven ground and the slight prickles and bumps. She could hear him breathing and feel his heart beating rhythmically, smell the grass, the leaves, the earth and his aftershave still and the tangy scent of the perspiration forming on his forehead in small beads.

With an unpleasant start, she realised about the time. She peered at her watch – it was only three o'clock. She breathed a huge sigh of relief. David felt it, lifted up slightly and looked down at her.

'What was that for, Mat, that huge sigh?'

'I was looking at the time, it's only three o'clock. I thought it'd been hours.'

'Well let me see now, the time doesn't seem to be flying, but are you enjoying yourself?'

'Oh I *am! Very* much, are you?'

He looked down at her and shrugged.

'Er…possibly! Not sure!'

Then she laughed as she smacked at him, grinning too. He rolled off and felt in his pocket for some tissues and cigarettes, passing her the tissues.

'Need these, darling?'

She took one and smiled, loving the intimacy of it all.

'Thanks! I feel hungry now as well. Shall we have those rolls and open the bubbly?'

'Now that's a good idea, let's!' They lifted out the various cool packets, carefully wrapped. David took a bite of roll, then lit a cigarette and leaned against the tree. He exhaled slowly.

'In my Sunday paper about a month ago, was an article in a magazine it was promoting, about a club in London called the Sirens Club.' He flicked the ash and paused.

Martha stared at him and then choked on a crumb.

'The *Sirens* Club?' she exclaimed, 'You mean sirens? As in those fish-women?'

'Yes, it stands for Sexually Intimate Rather Exciting New Sensations.' He smiled at her.

She sat up, astonished.

'You're *joking*, such as?'

He grinned again, inhaling, chuckling.

'*I* don't know, it's only what I read. It's a club in Soho that promises a very hi-tech sexual experience, or experiences. It's a member's only club, mind you. At least I believe if one wants to take full advantage of everything there is on offer, one has to be a member, at any rate.'

'Are you planning on joining then?' she asked, amused.

'Who, me? No, much too expensive I expect. It looked very different from the usual strip joints and peep-show things that used to be around that area. If such a thing *can* be up-market, this was. I remember when they first made sex shops legal. Now it's all computerised and hi-tech, as I told you.'

'Good grief! I've never heard of it! Don't think I like the sound of it either, but I expect it makes money as you said. Did it say where it was?'

David thought a moment.

'Brewer Street I think, or near there. It has a website that gives a bit more information too, I believe, but it looked and sounded from the article a rather sordid affair.'

Martha finished another glass and brushed the crumbs of the roll away, not looking up.

'You read it all through though, obviously.'

David hooked a finger under her chin, lifting her face.

'Well, yes I did, why not? I know I said it *appeared* a bit sordid, but I was curious to know what it was all about, from what I could read about it. I'm curious about sex, we men are you know, brute beasts, some of us…'

He put down his glass and wiped his mouth.

'Come here, Mattie!'

17

Saturday morning was warm and humid, but pouring with rain. Heavy grey clouds covered the sky and looked set in for the day. Clive emerged from the bathroom smelling fresh coffee, and heard the radio. Martha was humming along, preparing breakfast. He rubbed his hair vigorously with a towel and went into the bedroom to sort a shirt out. He felt low and depressed. Martha was going into Dreighton, which on the face of it was good. He wouldn't have her company for the morning at least, possibly the best part of the day, but so was Stella, with Cindy, so would probably be there for the day as well, just his luck.

He looked out of the window and stared at the clouds as if by glaring at them, they would thin and allow a patch of blue sky to show. Photography would be hopeless today. Martha had been on at him for long enough to fix the door to the conservatory, an ideal job to do today, but he felt rebellious. Why should *he* be the only one working, while Martha and Stella were out? He'd ring Bill before Martha had the chance to say about the door.

'Bill, hi, it's Clive how're you doing? Yeah, isn't it, and looks set in for the day. I was just calling to see if you were busy, only Martha's going into Dreighton and probably expecting me to fix that door in the conservatory.' He scratched his head. 'I don't feel like doing it really, least I *might* do later as it *is* a bit of a nuisance, but in my own time. Not let her think I've got nothing else to do all day…what? Oh, *Stella*! Yeah, well, just my luck *again*! She's in Dreighton as well, with her mate Cindy, so *that's* out…great! That sounds good…yes I know, just along from "Nothing to Wear". I'm surprised the girls have closed it on a Saturday, I'll meet you there about twelve then, that's great, yeah, cheers!'

Stella was rushing, having taken Jeeves for a longer walk than usual, just in case Douglas changed his mind and they had the afternoon together as well. But as it was raining, the flimsy, filmy summer dress she was going to wear and had all ready to slip on, would look silly now. Her hair was frizzy with the humidity and dampness and now at nearly ten o'clock, there was no time left to sort it as she had to choose something else. She opted for black; a black sleeveless dress and a shiny PVC Mac in a raspberry retro print she'd found in their own shop.

She screwed her hair up into a twist and fastened it with a large clip and looked in the mirror. It looked pretty good, all things considered. She found some black shoes, and then a bit of lip gloss and a smudge of eye shadow. Applying a quick spray of perfume, the first one that she grabbed, and she was ready. She heard the purring engine from his Aston Martin, found her keys and put them in her bag then opened the door. Instead of getting out of the car to open the passenger door for her, as once he had, he remained in his seat.

'Are you ready to go?'

He adjusted the mirror and reversed from her driveway, the wipers intermittently brushing the windscreen as the rain began to ease a little, although there was no encouraging brightness in the sky. It was just on 'pause' before the next lot moved in.

'Yes, thank you.' She settled in her seat and fastened her belt quickly. 'I'm looking forward to this trip,' she said brightly, turning to him and smiling, but his eyes were on the road ahead. Trying to elicit some conversation, she added, 'Do you think white silk or satin, I mean as in shiny like satin or…not shiny I suppose?'

He could see her perfectly well from the corner of his eye and sensed her rather forced bonhomie, but he wasn't going to respond immediately, instead he switched the radio on, fiddling until he found Classic FM.

The Emperor Concerto filled the car and he returned his hand to the wheel.

'We'll just see what they have, shall we? You can slip a few on and get what you feel most comfortable in,' He looked slyly across. 'I don't think you can make a decision until we see what there *is*.'

Stella sat back in the seat and tried to relax, there was an imperceptible shift in the alliance today. She shivered and rubbed her arms, tingling and nervy again.

'Chilly?' It was a statement.

'Err no, I'm all right thanks.'

'I like your coat, darling, it suits you – looks very good.'

It was a small compliment which had Stella in ecstasy. A small crumb had been dropped to her from the master's table. She snatched it quickly.

'*Do you?* I'm so glad. I didn't know *what* to wear really. I got ready in a bit of a rush. I took Jeeves out for a longish walk and we got rather wet. '

'Why did you walk him so long in the rain?' His tone was admonishing. 'I don't suppose he enjoyed it. We won't be *all* that long. I said we'd have a bite to eat and then I'll bring you home again. It could be clear this afternoon.' With a deliberate, sidelong glance, 'So that was rather silly, wasn't it?'

She wriggled in her seat slightly and fiddled with her hair clip.

'I suppose it was really. I thought we might have done something else this afternoon, as well as getting the dressing gown.'

'Did you, such as?' His fingers moved on the wheel, in time with the slow movement, a beautiful piece of music.

It made her stir inside and sent prickles down her spine. 'Make love, perhaps? I do love you, Douglas.'

It was out. The words tipped into the silence like great lumps of rock and like rocks just sat there, incongruous. They couldn't be tucked away somewhere now, they were there, until something else was said. The music continued; the piano playing quietly into the silence. Douglas looked straight ahead. It was getting busier outside and more commercial as they entered the town and headed for St. Peter's Way. He'd heard, but chosen to ignore it.

'I thought we could park here and have, oh,' looking at his watch 'three hours should be enough? Two fifteen? If we need more we can think again, but the shop I had in *mind*, is Jacobs of Dreighton.' He unfastened his seatbelt. 'Wait here while I go and fetch a ticket, won't be long.'

Stella didn't know whether to feel grateful he'd ignored her comment or not. There was no sign he'd felt uncomfortable about it and he must have heard. He was striding back now. If only she could keep her emotions in check! She just got more and more confused: did he love her or not? Why was it so important to *know?* Because she *knew* deep down, very deep down, there was hidden that tiny grain of knowledge. Fact: he didn't love her; never had done and never would and like him, but for a different reason, she would ignore it.

He opened the car door this time and took her elbow as she climbed out.

Martha was quite enjoying herself despite the drizzle, looking round Dollings department store. She'd stopped to look at the saucepans and kitchenware. They always attracted her, the stainless steel so bright and shiny and the pristine tea towels and oven gloves. She decided to have a coffee in the in-store coffee shop and then go along to Jacobs until she saw the queue. Changing her mind, she had a cursory look along the racks of underwear on offer on the next floor, just to satisfy herself that she *had* looked, before taking the lift to the ground floor, out through all the perfumes and cosmetics and left down St Giles' Street towards Howard's Lane and Jacobs.

The shop was small and consequently a little intimidating. No prices were visible on the items on display. The sort of place to window-shop and move on unless there happened to be something specific you wanted. A 'Reduced Items' rail stood like an embarrassed poor relation at a posh wedding in one corner and served a dual purpose: somewhere for the wary to look first before committing themselves further and a place for the confident to pointedly breeze past it as unworthy of their attention.

Martha placed herself in the latter category. With one foot on the bottom stair to ascend to the first floor and the lingerie collection, she paused. Above her were voices she recognised. The female one she had heard recently, the male's not since the supper back in May. Marie, the assistant, was obviously up there providing assistance, so for the first time, purely so she could hear what was going on, she poked along the Sale rail and listened.

'We do have this in white as well as the ivory, sir, if you would like to see? I can also offer to lift the hem a little. Cut as it is on the bias, it's important to do it carefully so as not to lose the flow as it falls from the hips.'

The man, Douglas she realised, sounded full of admiration.

'Very nice, darling, it suits you *perfectly*. I love the way it flows when you move. Quite *char*ming! Do you *like* it?'

'Oh I do, yes. It's beautiful. The weight's perfect, looks very glamorous, nineteen-thirties almost. Don't you think?'

Martha wished she could see, but that was impossible.

'I do darling, yes, but the point *is*, are you *comfortable* in it, *happy* with it?'

'Oh yes, Douglas, very, it's lovely!'

'*Good*, well that's settled then. Except for the alteration, how soon could you fix the hem?'

'I could have it ready for you by next Saturday, the third of July?'

'That would be *splendid! Thank you.* Will you take this card?'

'If I could do that downstairs sir, please; if you'd like to follow me? I won't make a charge for the alteration. Above three hundred pounds we don't make a charge.'

Martha searched hurriedly for somewhere to hide. Over in the opposite corner was a changing cubicle with a heavy curtain in front, secured by a tie-back. She dodged inside and pulled the curtain across. Through the slight gap, she watched Douglas Spencer and Stella. The transaction completed, he put the receipt carefully into his wallet and moved to open the door.

'Well thank you *very* much you've been *most* helpful. I'll collect it next week and you have my telephone number if there's any problem. Good day to you. Stella?' He waited.

'Thank you Douglas, it's perfect.'

They walked out to the narrow lane and the door closed with a discreet click.

Marie was about to return upstairs when the sound of the curtain drawn back startled her and she turned round in surprise.

'Good heavens, my dear Martha! I had no idea you were there! Can I help you at all?'

'I'm sorry to startle you, Marie, I know the people who just left and didn't want to bump into them particularly. I hope you didn't mind.'

Marie was solicitous. 'Don't worry my dear, it's a pleasure to see you, was there anything particular you were looking for today?'

'Well actually I wanted to see your lingerie collection and was on my way up when I recognized the voices. Small world isn't it?'

'It can be I'm afraid, yes. Well let's go up and I'll see what I can find for you, shall I?'

* * *

As Clive passed 'Nothing to Wear' on his way to the Spritz bar, he glanced in the window. Placing a pair of sandals in front of a displayed summer dress was Cindy. She looked up, gave him a friendly wave then carried on with what she was doing. For a moment he stood and stared. Then she called to someone.

An assistant he hadn't seen before appeared, bringing a small stand with slots in it and a handful of small white tickets with numbers on. Engrossed in finding the correct prices, the girls didn't look up again so he walked on.

So! Stella wasn't with her after all and yet at eight fifteen that morning she'd told him she was rushing to give Jeeves a decent walk before Cindy called for her at ten thirty. *Liar!* He walked quicker, furious. He bet he knew exactly who she was with, *bloody man*...where had they gone *this* time? He swallowed, livid.

He was losing touch with everything, everyone was laughing at him behind his back. Why hadn't she told him? He thought about what she'd said when he'd told her Martha was going into Dreighton, so they could therefore go anywhere but! Of *course!* He'd said exactly the right thing. Douglas had taken her to Dreighton too! Martha providing unwitting cover for both of them! GOD he was mad! He swung open the door of the bar in a temper, looking round for his friend.

The Colonel was at the bar holding a pint. He turned round as Clive came crashing in and over to where he stood.

'Now where can the fire be, Clive? Slow down and let me buy you a nice drink. What will you be having?'

Clive was certain what he wanted. 'I'll have a whiskey please.'

'And would that be a double there, Clive?' He sensed this had been said with conviction.

'Please. Yes, a double whiskey and no ice, thanks very much.'

Bill ordered the drink and handed a note over, passing the glass to Clive. 'And now tell me what all the trouble is. You're looking pretty angry to me. What seems to be the problem? Would it be your women grieving you?' His Irish lilt was calming.

Clive cast about for a table and pushed through to one in a corner with three empty chairs. They both sat down. Clive kicked off, after a large gulp of liquor.

'Do you know Douglas Spencer?' He raised a quizzical eyebrow and glared. 'Bloody man, I can't stand him, yet women think he's God's gift. Ha! Typical isn't it? He's a slimy bastard.'

'Martha will be thinkin' he's God's gift you mean, and this man Spencer's not married!'

Clive took another mouthful and swallowed. 'Yes and no. He's not married, bastard!'

Bill sipped a few more times at his Guinness, deliberating. The name did sound familiar now he came to think about it. It was possibly on the small print at the bottom of the letter he'd received from the Sirens Club, where all the names of the Associates and Directors were.

When he got home he'd look. This was all fitting into place. The letter had been in the hall when Clive and Stella had called. Stella had spotted it and tried to gloss over the fact. If what he was suspecting was true, Stella, Clive's little friend, was involved with a man procuring business for the Club. A club he'd already made arrangements to visit in a few weeks' time for what was promising to be a spectacular event. Stella must *know* about it, surely? Yet she'd looked as if butter wouldn't melt! Holy mother of God, what would he say now? He felt sorry for him. Love did terrible things to you, all ways round.

18

Jed Zeitermann rolled over in bed and looked at the naked woman lying next to him fast asleep. Her fair hair was fanned across the pillow, shiny and luxurious. She was very slim but not thin, just petite. Her breasts were large compared to the rest of her body, her skin tanned and unblemished. A small trace of pubic hair ran across her mound, stopping just short of the cleft. She was beautiful and not the property of the Sirens Club. Jed had met her on holiday and she came over to stay with him when invited and when her job in the Swedish Tourist industry allowed.

She was the best woman he'd ever been to bed with and that was saying something. Her wit amused him, her body and what she could do with it – do to him, left him breathless. It was the closest to love he thought he would ever get. If anything happened to her, he'd never find another like her and he knew it. It would devastate him, he realised, really finish him. He was very careful to keep her away from the business of the Club. She knew all about it, in the main, but remained aloof and left the workings of it entirely to him, happy enough to hear occasionally of anything that Jed considered important.

This coming weekend would certainly fall into that bracket. It was Thursday the fifteenth of July. Douglas and Stella would be boarding the train for Euston (first class) as he lay there looking at her. As if she sensed his stare, she opened her eyes slightly and smiled, then wrinkled her nose and reached over towards him, the tip of her tongue tracing her lips as her fingers reached for him, crossing his thigh and touching the end of his penis very lightly.

It sprang to attention immediately so she left it and gently began to work his balls into the palm of her hand. He groaned, resting his hand on his hip, watching her, but aware of the time passing. Today, these next few *days* would see history made at the Club and more money than it had seen since it opened. Everything had to go like clockwork, his job depended on it. As much as he wanted to let her continue, he reached for his mobile with one hand and gently extricated himself from her grasp with the other.

'Sorry Erika, I've got to make some calls to the guys. Why don't you go grab a shower and fix some breakfast? It's going to be one hell of a few days here, babe!'

Erika climbed out of bed. Padding naked across to the en-suite bathroom, she pressed the knob to turn on and heat up the shower to a correct temperature. Jed had all the latest designs in bathrooms and kitchens and she loved the luxury of it. How his money was earned didn't much concern her, the Club was just a fact of life. She was sure he indulged himself at times, but that was Jed; he was like that. It didn't mean anything, they'd been together now for nearly four years and she sensed he didn't want to lose her and that was good enough.

No man liked a clingy woman and her job kept her out of the country for longish periods at a time, which meant they could keep the relationship fresh and new. In an industry that was often tawdry and de-humanizing, women became commercial goods and the explicitness of it meant that personal relationships could suffer as a result. For as long as she could show that she depended on him for nothing and was there when he really needed her, she would have him, she decided. What she did in her *own* time was another matter entirely.

He pressed Piers on speed-dial and waited.

'Hiya, Jed here. Just checking that we're all meeting up at the Café Regent for eleven forty five yeah? Douglas an' Stella should be on their way now and Rhoda's meeting us there, except she's *Zena* and not Rhoda remember…yeah. I'd like to have a quick run through sometime today, just to get everything up to speed. I'm meeting Reggie tomorrow with the girls at Rosie's Bar. I'll have to juggle a bit, as he's not to bump into Douglas. I want to keep it as low profile as I can that he's there at all really...sorry? No, *he* knows that *Douglas* is coming. Douglas isn't to know that *he's* there, got that? Good, that's fine.'

Erika was holding up a tea bag in one hand and a jar of coffee in the other with a 'choose' expression. Jed pointed to the coffee. The next items were a frying pan and a packet of cereal. Jed wavered a moment, fluctuating, then went for the pan. Moments later the aroma of coffee, bacon and eggs filled the room and his stomach rumbled.

'This room,' he continued, 'the room for the table scene. I want the table in the middle with a bloody great chandelier over it and boardroom chairs round it. The mirrors above the panelling I want disguised as leaded Tiffany glass, to look as much like an oak panelled boardroom as possible. Nothing modern at all, a stool so's she can get up on the table and twenty fountain pens, one at each seat...yeah, yeah, blotters too would look good. I'm going now, me breakfast's ready. I'll see *you*, Andy and Dave at eleven forty five and any problems between now and then, give us a bell, yeah? Okay, cheers mate! Bye.'

* * *

Rhoda checked around one last time before catching the bus to the station. She'd churned over in her mind about the wig. It wasn't a terribly good fit and needed tugging into place. She felt so self-conscious in it too. In the end, so as to get the correct makeup to go with it, she decided on first thing in the morning. As a consequence, every time she'd looked in a mirror since, she'd had a surprise. She'd wondered also what a real Madam wore.

She'd trawled round the local Charity shops in search of inspiration and had come across a mint green suit – jacket and skirt – and a low cut sleeveless white top in very shiny polyester satin. She already had quite a respectable tan and these colours complimented it, as did a pair of high heeled pale green shoes in just her size. She added a few gold chains, a gold bracelet and some gold hooped earrings. Now she opened the front door, pulled up the handle on her case and wheeled it to the bus stop.

Once aboard the train she relaxed. It was tempting to walk through the first class section to the buffet car and see if she could spot them, but decided Douglas would be furious if she did. It wouldn't be worth it. He was putting her up at the Élan after all, so she wouldn't rock the boat. They'd agreed to stand at opposite ends of the platform and not make contact until the lunch. He'd said not to go to the hotel first either, but make her way to Piccadilly in time for one o'clock and join the others.

She folded her arms, crossed her legs and stared out of the window, catching her reflection. She was frowning and pursed up with spite. Who did Stella think she was anyway? She'd show her. She inspected her nails, brushed her skirt down and hoped Douglas would appreciate the effort. The moving message above the carriage doors indicated the train was on time and she marked off the number of stations left before Euston.

* * *

Moving through the doors to the first class section of the train, Stella looked around at the other passengers already seated, all of whom were either reading the papers or staring out of the window with the studied nonchalance peculiar to first class passengers anywhere. Their seats were opposite each other. Stella sat by the window and studied Douglas, engrossed in the business section of his broadsheet, expensive looking reading glasses perched on the end of his nose, paying her no attention.

She'd spoken to Clive first thing, who, although he sounded a bit grouchy, had nonetheless said he hoped she would have a good time and enjoy herself. He'd see her when she got back. She'd told him she would call him again from London, but he hadn't replied. She'd thought the signal had gone and had tried again, but the phone was switched off. Cathy had collected Jeeves for a walk and put his bed and toys in the back of her car, ready to take him home until her return. Now she was left with her own thoughts.

Last night she'd given herself a thorough make-over. A bikini wax leaving her skin a bit red had toned down reasonably. Her hair was in a French pleat and looked elegant. What she was wearing had been taken out and pressed probably a hundred times – a perfectly tailored navy linen dress with a very fine peacock blue thread running through it. The bolero that went with it was also navy linen with a peacock blue trim all around the edge.

On her feet were gold leather sandals with a small wedge heel and a sparkling blue stone between the gold leather straps. They were ridiculously expensive, but unusual. Douglas had made no comment about anything and she'd felt loath to ask. She'd be undressing and going to bed with him that evening, so had chosen her underwear with care too. The jolt of realisation must have caused her to make a noise, as he rattled the sheets of the paper and looked at her, for the first time that morning it seemed.

'Did you want a coffee, darling? They'll be coming through in a minute. Are you all right?'

'Fine, thank you. Yes, a coffee would be lovely. You look very nice today.'

'Oh just the usual…' brushing this off. 'So do you, especially the shoes. You have excellent taste in shoes, Stella, I'm sure Madam Dubois would agree. You look very good indeed.'

Stella waited as the coffee arrived and the steward moved on down the carriage.

'This Madam you talked about, does she work for the Sirens Club? Does that make the club a glorified brothel? I thought that was against the law.'

Douglas smiled. 'Zena's job is to look after the female club employees. She's a form of supervisor, I suppose. Most of the management are men and Zena looks after the interests of the women, representing them to the board. She deals with other matters of personnel as well, disputes, admin, that sort of thing. But her special responsibility will be *you* this weekend.'

Gazing out of the window, he continued. 'The club is licensed for the purposes of adult entertainment with a restaurant and drinks license as well. It's been going since nineteen fifty-nine, well established now.'

He pulled at the crease in his trousers. 'Jed Zeitermann, whom you'll be meeting, is the overall manager there. I think he'll be bringing a few other representatives with him today.'

He put down his coffee and smiled. 'I hope I've managed to organise the sort of experience you'd like to try darling; only *this* time it'll be for real.' He leaned forward. 'You know that, don't you?' He was serious; dead serious. 'You understand you're not Stella the *pretend* whore now? If you have any doubts about what's going on, what you'll be required to do, you *must* say so. It's an adult club, Stella.' He studied her face intently. '…for grown-ups *who know what they want.'*

She leaned back, her arms on the rests. 'That won't be a problem, Douglas, I assure you. I'm looking forward to meeting your colleagues.' She crossed her legs, making circles with her foot, the stone sparkling as she moved, eyeing him evenly.

'Well just so long as you know.'

He sat back again, looking out of the window at the passing scenery before resuming his paper. Suddenly he reached in his coat pocket, his mobile was vibrating. He looked at it and pressed the answer key.

'Jed, good morning, is everything going to plan?' He glanced up and angled himself slightly from Stella.

'Fine Doug, yes, Piers, Andy and Dave are coming with me. Rhoda's called to say she's on her way and should be there for about one. I just wanted to check one thing over with you. It said on the tickets for tomorrow that the dress code was business suits, for sitting at the table. Was that right?'

'That's absolutely right, yes, as formal as possible. If any of them smoke, cigars are preferable; if you could say that to them?'

'Sure can and fountain pens for all of them as well, yeah?'

'Correct. That'll be splendid.' His tone was even. 'Stella's with me now and looking forward to meeting you so if we could save any further discussion for another time perhaps?'

He looked from the corner of his eye. She didn't appear to be listening to the conversation. Jed took the cue to shut up.

'Sure thing Doug! Understood. See you later then!'

Alighting carefully from the train at Euston, Douglas slammed the door behind her. It sounded final. Now she didn't feel so sure. Everything was large, bustling and impersonal. The London mainline station had a smell all its own: hot, dusty and dirty. On impulse, she considered calling the whole thing off and boarding the next train home, but she was committed.

She looked around at the other people wandering across the huge, impersonal concourse, particularly the men. She swallowed nervously. There were all sorts – all types and ages, some attractive, some not. What had she said she would do? She couldn't remember. Had she said she'd carry out her fantasy, the one she'd told Douglas about? What about the conversation over that cream tea with the waitress? The one she suspected of being a lesbian. Oh God. She felt sick. Douglas, cool and together, had his and Stella's luggage and was casting around the station also, to see if he could spot Rhoda. He saw her suddenly. She was walking briskly towards the underground. *Good girl.* He picked up the bags and headed for the taxi rank.

'We'll take a taxi to Albemarle Street, check in at the Élan and freshen up a bit. Then make our way to Piccadilly. The table's booked for one o'clock. Are you with us?' He waited, amused at her expression of bemusement. 'Over this way, darling, you look all in a daze. Is everything all right?'

'Yes thanks, just a bit tired from the journey, I think. I'll be fine once we've had something to eat. I could do with freshening up.'

'You should be excited, darling!' There was a slight reproof in his tone. 'I think you'll enjoy yourself very much. You've got the chance now to show off that beautiful body to men who'll appreciate it, I can vouch for that.

'I can hold my hand up, Stella, and repeat, you are one hundred per cent woman, with a body and sexuality crying out for attention. With the Sirens Club you'll find some real appreciation of your talents.'

They joined the queue, moving up slowly. Douglas gave the address to the driver. Sensing her sudden disquiet, he stretched an arm around her shoulder as they pulled out and headed towards the hotel.

'I keep telling you,' he said, mollifying her, 'there'll be nothing to worry about. Zena will look after any concerns you might have and I'll be very proud to sit and watch you perform, and be pro*fession*al.'

He stroked gently up and down her arm, sliding his hand to the back of her neck, gently pinching her there between his finger and thumb. The effect was immediate, she could feel it. He could see it.

'You're a *wanton* darling; you know you are really, don't you?' He lowered his voice. 'I'm betting you'd like to fuck me right now, *hmmm*?' He whispered in her ear, putting the tip of his tongue to her lobe, slipping it towards the inside before retracting it and sitting up.

Stella looked at the rear of the driver's head, wondering if he could see in his mirror, or hear what was going on. It was all so intimate, but if he could, he gave no indication as he wound his way through the heavy late morning traffic.

The hotel had an imposing yet restrained facade. Their luggage was taken by a nimble porter as soon as the taxi stopped. Inside it was hushed and efficient, the check-in taking moments. They took the lift to the third floor, then along to their room where the door stood open, their bags on luggage stands. The bed was huge and dominated the room, which smelled fresh and clean. The lighting was unobtrusive, white voile curtains hung at the tall window looking over the street and a winged chair, an armchair and a low coffee table sat beneath it.

Opposite the bed was a writing desk and chair in a highly polished dark wood. On top there was information about the hotel, some writing paper and magazines and a vase of sweet scented fresh flowers. This completed the furniture, except for the built in wardrobes that filled the opposite wall to the window. Stella walked back towards the door and looked on the right where a door led into a beautiful bathroom of black marble, glass and shiny chrome, with a white tiled floor.

Huge fluffy white towels were on racks and two towelling bathrobes were on hooks on the wall. She looked at her watch: twenty minutes to twelve. They had left at eight thirty and now they were here. She dithered between having a quick wash, or a shower in the black marble cubicle with glass and chrome doors.

Douglas appeared, naked, in the mirror behind her. He opened the glass door to the shower and stepped in.

'Are you coming in, Rose, or do I have to *drag* you?'

Her mind now made up, sexual recklessness overwhelmed her and she tugged her clothes off quickly, tossing them on a stool, climbing in as the warm water surged out and sprayed them. With urgency Douglas sucked and pulled at her lips and tongue, so when she breathed the water went up her nose and stung. She kissed as hard as she could and placed his hands around her waist, writhing in desperation to feel him push inside her.

She could feel it hard against her stomach, squashed between them. She tried to lift herself against him but wasn't tall enough, and he wasn't going to lift her or make it easy for what she wanted.

'Please! Please can I have you? Please!'

Taking his penis in her hand, she lifted her leg against him but he grabbed her wrist and held it. Reaching for the dish on which it sat, he dug his nail in and quickly slipped off the plastic film from the soap which was ribbed, oval shaped and ivory coloured, with the hotel logo engraved in the middle. He manoeuvred them away from the shower's direct hit and reaching round, pulled her buttocks apart, sliding the bar in between. She gasped as she felt the pointed end of the oval.

'Now then sweetie.' He grappled with her surprisingly firmly, his tone authoritative. 'Where is this soap going, *hmmm?* Where's it heading Stella, tell me!' he ordered.

She knew what he wanted, but she *could not say it!*

'It's going up my arse, Douglas, and it hurts. It does really, it's *hurting!'* Wriggling, she tried to stop him but his grip was like iron.

'If you say it,' he bargained, 'say *that word,* Stella, you know the one I mean, then I'll stop. Now, say it, *loudly, darling,* so I can hear you!'

The soap was sliding in easily, stretching her. The ribbed edges were rubbing and it stung, burning. He twisted it around. She bit her lip, mumbling into his chest, warm against her face

'I can't hear you. You'll have to say it louder than that, darling. Now come on, *shout it!'*

She shut her eyes and said it. No way could she shout it.

'Anus.'

'Louder darling; much louder, then I'll stop. Go on!'

She tried again, '*Anus; ANUS!'* She shouted it, feeling tears of humiliation pricking now. Immediately he removed the soap to the dish again, replacing it with his fingers, rubbing and soothing there, turning the shower head on her once more, washing it all away. He kissed the top of her head, her hair wet and shiny.

'That's very good, darling. We just have to remember who the boss is I think, don't we, *hmmmm?'* He opened a small bottle and shampooed his hair vigorously, rinsing it off. 'And now we have an important lunch to get ready for, so get into 'Rose mode,' Stella and think what you're doing. You really must grow up if you're going to do this, not be a silly cry-baby.' He had one last rinse. 'That was only one word and if you can't manage that, we'll have to wonder if you're up to the task at all, won't we?'

He climbed out of the shower, turning it off and grabbed a towel from the rack, leaving her dripping in the hot, steamy room, vulnerable again, listening to the steady drone of the extractor fan. Why did she get these conflicting feelings? She wasn't immature, she desired like a real woman and he'd *told* her she was.

She looked down at her body, flushed rosy from the shower. It spoke for itself. She was a healthy woman with a very healthy sexual appetite, an appetite about to be assuaged at one of the top sex clubs in the country.

The mirror was fast losing the steam and she saw her reflection, sharp under a small, brilliant spotlight. Men, decent men with the same sexual urges she had and probably stronger, were going to thoroughly enjoy her, revel in her and desire her above all others. She was the best. She was Rose of the Rose Membership! However many there were waiting for her this weekend, she'd do it *and how!* She'd show Douglas Spencer.

She stretched up and toppled a fluffy white towel from the rack, wrapped it around her hair in a turban and strode naked back to the bedroom, where Douglas was brushing back his still-damp sleek hair. He'd changed into his lightweight grey suit jacket over a white shirt and a pink and navy patterned heavy silk tie. As he bent to remove his trousers from the bed, he felt Stella behind him. Deftly she pulled down his shorts and slipped her hand between his legs, cupping his large balls, heavy and warm from the shower.

Before he could say or do anything, she commanded, 'Leave the trousers where they are and step out of these.' She tugged at his shorts and he kicked them away. 'Bend and put your hands against the wall, flat, palms against the wall. Walk back three paces.' His coat and shirt rose up his back as he leaned forward and stepped back, his feet slightly apart.

'Stay there and don't move.'

She knelt down between his legs, stroking his balls and lightly scratching the base of his penis with her nails. It became erect as she continued to stroke gently. She stretched him apart as wide as she could and bringing her face up to him, made circular motions with her tongue, just the tip. His back was beginning to ache slightly, but the mounting sensation from his groin was stronger; much stronger. He'd denied her in the shower and now he wanted to have her.

'*Darl*ing, darling; can we move to the bed or floor or somewhere? Darling, I'm going to come in a minute!' His calling was increasingly urgent. '*Stella!* I want you here now, let me…'

'*Stand where you are and DON'T MOVE!*' she shouted.

'Darling, if you keep doing that I'm going to come; please.' He was secretly enjoying it. 'Oh! No, Stella!' It was sudden; the point of no return. 'I'm…oh God I can't stop it, I can't stop it!'

She withdrew her hands, watching him helpless against the wall. She passed him a handful of tissues grabbed from a box on the bedside table.

'Pull your shorts up and put your trousers on. I'm going to dry my hair and then it's time to go.'

They continued getting ready in silence. As he opened the door for them to leave, he turned to her and kissing her briefly bit her lip, hard. She yelped in pain. It said she was his. He owned the proprietary rights and wouldn't let her forget it.

19

Surfacing from the underground into Piccadilly Circus, Rhoda stopped for a moment to get her bearings, looking for Eros. It was such a landmark the statue, yet surrounded as it was by tall commercial buildings and lights, it looked dwarfed and insignificant, almost out of place entirely. Nelson's column and the lions of Trafalgar Square were much more imposing. It was a good statue in its own right, just placed in unsympathetic surroundings. An anachronism except for the fact it depicted Erotic Love – sex really. In this area, sex certainly made the world and money go round. She leaned against the railings, slipped one foot out and then the other from its shoe and wriggled her toes.

The shoes had rubbed the back of her heels, causing blisters. She had half suspected this when she set off and managed to purchase a small packet of sticking plasters from a kiosk in the underground. Now having carefully applied one to each sore spot, she waited at the traffic lights, crossed over to Regent Street and ambled up towards the Café Regent. It was hot and crowded, the heat shimmering off the pavements, the sky a bright, intense white. She opened her handbag and burrowed in it for her sunglasses. Her wig – a dark shiny brunette – was making her head hot. She longed to tear it off.

She hoped the air conditioning was working in the club or it would be unbearable. It was one o'clock precisely as she pushed open the heavy doors of the Café. Inside it was plush, dark and cool. She recognised Jed first, but not the three other men dressed in lightweight business suits with regulation white shirts and broad pastel ties. Standing slightly to the left of this little group was Douglas with Stella, whose hair formed loose waves around her perfectly made-up face and who looked very attractive. His arm was draped casually round her, his hand resting very lightly on her hip. Jealousy jolted her and she felt a mess, a hot, flustered mess.

Jed turned as she approached, his hands shoved in his pockets, pushing the edges of his coat back, not bothering to remove them as he addressed her.

'Hi Zena, it's great to see you!'

The name sounded strange, she would have to get used to it.

Stella turned, clutching Douglas's hand.

Gently but firmly extracting himself from her grip, she watched as he greeted this woman, kissing her on both cheeks.

'Hello, Zena, you look charming as always.' He began the introductions. 'Jed I think you *know* and this is Piers, Dave and Andy.'

The men turned and acknowledged her, smiling. She studied their expressions for any hint they found her attractive. Some men preferred the older woman (and at fifty five she didn't think she was completely over the hill) but there was nothing, they were just being polite.

'And I'd like to introduce Stella!' He grasped her again, easing her slightly forward.

She extended her hand and endeavoured to sound confident.

'Hello, Zena. Douglas told me about you. I'm very pleased to meet you. I believe you're going to introduce me to life at the club.'

There was no move to take her hand, so she retracted it, flustered, gripping her opposite elbow, her body language defensive.

Did she think she was royalty or something, thought Rhoda, *silly, nervous little bitch.*

'I'm looking forward to learning something and having fun this weekend. Thanks for offering to explain everything.' The woman's face remained impassive so she tried harder. 'I really *was* looking forward to meeting you,' she enthused now, 'Douglas has made it sound *so* exciting; I can't be*lieve* I'm really going to do this!'

She sensed everyone was looking at her then, she was babbling. She shut up.

Rhoda was reassuring.

'You'll be fine, honey, you look very sweet.' She appraised her with a hint of mockery. 'I love the dress. Relax dear, that's very important to do that, relax. The more you tense up, well,' she smirked, 'just relax.'

The men looked down, lifting their toes and studying their shoes avidly, hands shoved in their pockets, jiggling the contents and waiting. Douglas lifted an arm to shepherd the little group.

'Shall we go up and find our places now we're all here? Zena, Stella, after you.'

They climbed the curved staircase to the next landing and into the dining room. It was cool and pleasant, the room welcoming and airy after the heavy atmosphere in the foyer below. The wine waiter arrived to take their order. Douglas studied the list.

'Now what does anyone fancy, champagne?'

He looked over his reading glasses at the assembled party, confident.

Jed, elbows on the table, agreed. His colleagues also approved, but although slouched back, their expressions betrayed their discomfort.

'Zena, Stella? Champagne all right for you too?' Douglas, oblivious to any strain, was on form.

Rhoda replied chirpily. 'Thank you Douglas that would be lovely; lovely and chilled.'

He removed his glasses, closing the list. 'But of *course*. Two bottles on ice of the Bollinger RD '97 first I think, if you could?'

'Extra-brut there, Douglas!' This was Piers. 'I'm sure the ladies are sweet enough though, especially Stella.'

There was a general murmured chuckle. He opened the corner of his mouth to Andy. 'But how long she *stays* dry is another matter completely.'

He smirked, ogling her. Douglas added an imperceptible wink.

Despite anti-perspirant, the stage whispered aside caused burning prickles under Stella's arms. She put her elbows on the table, cradling her chin, striving again at sophistication.

Rhoda was enjoying being seated next to Douglas. She scraped her shoes off carefully and moving her foot ever so slightly, felt his shoe. Pressing a little bit further, she left it there. His foot didn't move. She raised it very slightly, feeling the leather under her little toe. Leaning forward, resting his chin on his hand, he placed the other one on her thigh, his thumb moving round in small circles, massaging over her skirt. His expression relaxed, was giving nothing away.

She smelled his aftershave and recognised it. It was all she could do to sit still. This was her reward for behaving herself on the train. He was pleased with her for sending the flyer to Stella, although he hadn't been to begin with. But since then, if it hadn't been for that, the silly girl might not have been sitting here with him now, waiting and keen to spread her legs and suck cock. Did she know that was really what it was? What she'd *really* have to do? Somehow she doubted it, well she'd soon find out, she thought with malicious glee. By the time Sunday came....He removed his hand as the menus came round and a large bucket of ice sat by the table containing the champagne.

Stella studied the menu, choosing what to have, deciding on the lobster followed by salmon, when prompted by Douglas.

David looked up. 'Are you workin' this afternoon, love?' Jed, Andy and Piers sniggered.

Stella looked blank. 'What do you mean? I don't think so, am I?'

She looked across at Douglas, who was smiling, before covering his mouth to hide a broader grin.

'I don't think so sweetie, not this afternoon. Not until tomorrow. If that's what you want, then have it, darling.'

He frowned at Jed, who aimed a kick under the table at David.

'Make your minds up guys, we're all waiting.'

While the five men were in conversation waiting for the starter, Stella asked Rhoda what David had meant. Was it apropos of her ordering all fish? Rhoda turned and whispered confidentially.

'It could turn your wee fishy dear, make it smell fishy, that's what he meant.'

Stella didn't understand.

'Why should that matter, if it smells fishy?' Suddenly she *did* understand; '*Are you working this afternoon love?*' She was flustered, embarrassed for being so naïve.

'Don't worry, dear, take no notice, you'll be fine. I'll explain everything later.'

Stella caught the steely look in the woman's eye before turning away. She was sure she recognised her from somewhere, although that woman had been blonde or streaky blonde, and Zena's hair was dark, so it couldn't be the same. She looked around the table now with fresh eyes. Did she recognise any of them? It was difficult to tell, but she felt uneasy, alone. Perhaps the drink would make her feel better. Douglas was leaning across and filling her glass with the pale bubbly wine. He lifted his glass.

'Here's to the Sirens club, the weekend and success!'

Everyone joined in.

'To the Club!'

* * *

Back at the hotel, Stella, Rhoda and Douglas sat in the lounge, the lunch having gone well as the atmosphere relaxed with the effects of the champagne. Douglas, sitting comfortably on a sumptuous sofa with his arm arranged across the back of it, examined Stella shrewdly.

'So then Stella, now you've met Jed and a few of his colleagues are you happy about tomorrow and Saturday? Is there anything you wish to ask me before I go back in a while to see Jed and finalise arrangements?'

Stella shook her head. There was nothing she wished to ask Douglas.

Looking across at Rhoda in a chair opposite, he gave her a sly wink.

'I think Zena here will fill you in on any more *personal* things you may wish to discuss. So if I can leave her with you, Zena, I'll head back and return in time for dinner.'

He rose, patting Rhoda on the shoulder whilst giving Stella a peck on the cheek.

'I'm sure there's plenty you can ask and learn, Stella. I'll leave you to it. Don't get up to mischief though ladies, this is a respectable establishment.'

He grinned at them before moving towards the door, acknowledging a waiter on his way out.

Stella scanned Rhoda's face for any hint of warmth, but saw none. She hunched up her shoulders, and then tried to relax as she'd been told, before braving her first enquiry.

'What advice can you give me for this weekend then, Zena? I haven't done this before and want to get a good idea of, well, *you know*. I need some inside information really.'

She smiled affably, shooting her arms out and hugging her knees, appealing to a possible better nature, but it was an uphill struggle.

Rhoda considered her prey. Not much of a challenge, but it could be entertaining. She must play her cards right and keep herself in Douglas's good books. She could still feel his hand on her leg, the recollection stirring up an almost painful throbbing. She'd better change her attitude and do 'kind' before she lost Stella's confidence. Tipping her head back, she surveyed the ceiling, placed an arm on each rest and crossed her legs, allowing a shoe to dangle off the end of her foot, swinging it on her toes.

'Inside information…well let me think.' The ceiling held no inspiration, she closed her eyes. 'The best advice, as I said before, is simply to relax, you'll save your energy and appear more…

professional.' She opened them and smiled more encouragingly now. 'I'm not saying look bored with the whole thing! Expression, facial expression, is very important. Let whoever you're *dealing* with feel he's the only one you're interested in if that makes sense dear?' She watched as Stella mirrored her body language.

'I see; yes, I'll try and do that. There's one other thing I wanted to ask, although you may not know the details.'

'What's that then?' She cocked her head. 'Ask me, I'll tell you if I know.'

'I think I *might* be asked…at least I *think* I could be asked…' She couldn't prevent the colour suffusing her face, twisting her fingers together in her lap, 'if I'd perform with another woman. Two women I mean, or more than two, without men involved at all. Do you know anything about that?'

She did. Hazel Makepeace was arriving tomorrow and they were going to play out a little scene in the Schoolroom. Stella would be in need of a little light admonishment if she couldn't do her lessons.

'Douglas mentioned it, yes. I think you *might* have met the other woman concerned earlier in the year, but you may not remember. Again, the best advice I can give you is relax.' offering another reassuring smile. 'Women are best placed, I think, to know another woman's body.' She spoke easily, woman to woman. 'With men it's just satisfying their need to climax, more than your own pleasure if you see what I mean. Men, as I'm sure you know well, aren't often expert at bringing pleasure to the woman and letting her orgasm.'

She paused to let this sink in. 'As important as relaxing, I'd say make sure you can *fake* convincingly too. Nine times out of ten the man is hopeless and faking is all part of the job, boosting their egos.'

She was almost caring now. 'Would you like a cup of tea at all, or a cold drink from the bar?' She could tell by the change of expression on Stella's face, she felt accepted and taken under her wing. Good; so far so good.

'That'd be nice, thank you. I'd love a cup of tea, Earl Grey if they have it?'

Rhoda glanced around until she caught the eye of a waiter who came over immediately.

'Could we possibly have a pot of Earl Grey tea for two?' She looked at Stella. 'Will you have anything to eat as well?'

'No thank you, still full of lunch!'

'Just a pot of tea then please on room...? What is your room, dear?'

'Three four three, I think.'

'Three four three, please; thank you.'

'Now where was I? A woman on the other hand, knows *exactly* how to stimulate and bring excitement. Are you relaxed with your own body? Do you like touching yourself, feeling yourself *intimately?*'

At last a connection; she loved the feel of her own body, holding and playing with her breasts and touching herself. She liked the scents. There wasn't anywhere she didn't know. She knew what tipped her over the edge into orgasm.

'I *do*, yes. I *love* the feel of myself, but I've never felt another woman.'

'Do you think you might *like* to? It might, if it's a new experience to you, turn you on. Help you to have a very *intense* orgasm. I'm sure you'd enjoy the feeling of power that comes with precipitating orgasm in another woman, don't you think?'

Stella was aroused. Rhoda was helping her to be more open. Everything was going to be all right. She understood her, was her friend.

'I think you may be right, I'd love a new experience like that. I feel turned on now. You've made me feel more confident, thank you.'

Job done! Rhoda smiled to herself. 'You'll be fine dear as long as you remember: relax, be convincing in what you do and most of all *enjoy it!* Not much use otherwise, love, is it? You might just as well!'

The waiter came over bearing a tray of tea and a receipt, placing the cups and saucers, pot and milk jug on the table in front of them. Rhoda signed the slip and took the pot.

'Do you have tea first or milk, dear?'

'Tea please, I only like a dash of milk, thanks.'

She handed the cup over and poured one for herself.

'Now then, anything else you want to ask at all? Feel free, nothing will shock me, "been there and done that", as they say…'

* * *

Businesslike, Douglas enquired, 'Can we just have a look at how things are going to go tomorrow and Saturday? I want to be sure in my own mind what the programme is, if you could just run that through for me?'

Jed tapped his computer and got the timetable up on screen.

'Right, well *tomorrow* I thought breaking Stella in *gradually* would be a good plan: I have the Hollywood Suite room free from ten thirty, and eight of our members are keen to have a crack at 'er!' He peered up at Douglas from the screen. 'I thought spread it out a bit and have four in the mornin' and four in the afternoon yeah? What d'ya think?'

'I think that sounds a good idea, yes. You're right she needs to be introduced slowly. Presumably you have the act with Hazel on Saturday morning and then the Table Fantasy in the afternoon, correct?'

Jed scrolled around on the screen, hoping Douglas couldn't see the scheduled meeting with Reggie and the girls tomorrow at twelve o'clock.

'Yeah that's right. Hazel's coming tomorrow and staying with friends of hers in the Tottenham Court Road, she said that she'd bring them along as well. Nina and Joanie, they *are* members and I'll see if any of the girls here are free, if any more are needed. They're in the Schoolroom from ten thirty again on the Saturday.

On view to members, usual lesbian action: strap-on, corporal punishment, girl-on-girl, okay?'

'Excellent, Jed; sounds fine. I think that'll be enough then for one day. I know you have forty men interested, but to be fair if they're all paying extra for this, she needs to be up for it and fresh for the second lot as much as for the first, so postpone the second group over to the Sunday, I think, if you could?'

Jed considered this, it was asking a lot. Stella was new to the game and twenty men might just be her limit, full stop. He wanted the money, wanted to keep sweet with Douglas, but after meeting Stella today he had his misgivings. He studied the list of the twenty men he'd chosen to be at the first sitting, the best of the bunch, men he knew well. The remainder were a bit of an unknown quantity. Douglas was restless. He needed to say something quickly.

'Yeah, just leave it with me Doug, then Sunday morning there's the possibility of the Victorian brothel, with Rhoda puttin' her through her paces. Then a rest before the next Fantasy in the afternoon which about wraps it up I think.' He leaned back in his chair away from the screen, hands clasped behind his head, smiling.

'Thank you that sounds splendid. Now,' looking at his watch, 'it's four o'clock. Have you anyone available at the moment? Blonde if possible, all this has had its effect on me and I could *do with something.*'

Jed changed programmes on the screen and looked. Anything that would get him out of the office, Stella had got under his skin and his opinion of Douglas was diminishing fast. He moved the mouse around.

'I have Melissa free at the moment: blonde, thirty-five, well experienced and happy to discuss your requirements. Sound about right? She's in the main club, second floor, stairs or the lift if you want. Room twenty two and available now, I could give her a quick buzz, tell her you're on your way?'

Douglas stood up from his chair, pushed his hair back, adjusted his trousers and straightened his tie.

'Do that. I'll see you later and thank you. Second floor you say?'

Jed picked up the phone and pressed a number; nestling the receiver under his chin, he reached for a pen. 'Yes, second floor, main club. Enjoy!'

He watched Douglas leave and close the door as his call was answered.

'Hi babe, Melissa here, you've got business for me?'

'Sure have! Spencer's on his way up, look after him darlin', you know what he likes…bubbly bath and good shag, piss…'

'No worries, I'm gettin' ready! Will it go on his account?'

'On the house, love, and let him know that, yeah?'

'Okay, see you later.'

'Thanks; see ya babe.'

He looked at the closed office door, then out of the window towards Chinatown. He'd had enough of today. He'd head back home now and find Erika. Douglas was turning his stomach, maybe he was getting too soft. Tomorrow he'd meet and talk with Reggie, who sounded a much better guy altogether. It was funny how your opinions can change. He slung his coat over his shoulder and headed home.

20

Reggie called Paula on the internal phone.

'Are you all set for tomorrow? I just thought I'd give you a quick ring.'

'Everything's ready, Reg, meeting up with Jed twelve o'clock at Rosie's right?'

'Aye, spot on Paula, I just tried to get Jed at the office but he'd transferred his calls and gone home. We'll soon find out what's going on, I wonder how Stella got on today. She's up there now with Spencer!'

'Poor kid, Mandy said he was voracious! I expect they'll share a room. She's going to be worn out before she's even started at this rate!' Paula laughed. 'He'll enjoy himself and then get the news from Helen, which won't make him a happy bunny, will it?'

'I shouldn't think so, no. She was a bit curious about what I was doin' up in London for four days like, I said I wanted to do my own pre-nuptial shopping and not to worry about me. Just enjoy herself with Dougie.'

'What did she say to that?'

'Just gave me a look. She's busy getting ready to go anyway. I don't think she'll suspect anything.'

Paula bit her lip, debating.

'Reg....'

'Aye?'

'Are you planning to join in any of this at the weekend? I don't want to be nosy, but if you want us to make ourselves scarce at all, just let me know, won't you?'

Reggie pondered this and chuckled.

'No pet, there's no one I fancy really apart from our Helen – maybe with one exception, though!'

Paula smiled into the phone; she was curious, wondering.

'Oh, and who might that be?'

Reggie grinned back at this.

'Ah now, that would be telling wouldn't it? That's for me to know.'

'And for me to find out?'

'Maybe, Paula, maybe. I'll see you tomorrow then?'

'See you tomorrow, Reggie, have a good night.'

* * *

At seven thirty, Stella decided to get ready for dinner. Douglas hadn't returned from the club and Rhoda had changed and gone out for a walk, leaving her with a magazine and a suggestion that she should rest while she had the opportunity. She perched on the bed and tried Clive on her mobile, receiving the voicemail. She waited for the beep.

'Hi Clive, Stella; I just wanted to say that all's okay here and I've got a nice room to myself. We had a good lunch and I spent the afternoon with Zena Fortune, a friend of Douglas's. We're not far from Bond Street or Regent Street, so plenty of good shops around. I'll try and give you a call in the morning. I'm getting ready for dinner now, say hello to Cathy for me if you see her. I hope you're all right. I'll call you again, lots of love, bye.'

She held the phone in her lap, staring into space. What was she doing here with these people? How had it come to this? All from one dinner, one suggestion that Clive had unwittingly, by dint of his text to her, caused her to offer and now here she was. She'd told Clive she might stay on longer, but now it didn't seem such a good idea. Surely Douglas wasn't going to put her up here in luxury on her own after he'd gone? He hadn't said anything about when they were going home. She'd go back on Sunday and try and get things sorted with Clive again. He'd be pleased to see her and want to kiss her and 'make love' again.

She sat waiting in her outfit for dinner, a lovely strapless white dress with a pattern of yellow roses which hugged her body. Who would she *prefer* to go to bed with, Clive or Douglas? Who understood her sexuality best? There was no question really and she'd been over and over this a hundred times in her mind, it had to be Douglas. Douglas was available, eligible, sexy, and rich. Was that her criteria? Yes it was. If it meant she was going to experience life (for only a weekend after all) as a 'call girl' of sorts, then so be it, she would live the life for a few days and enjoy it. Worry about tomorrow when it came. She was putting the final touches to her makeup and hair when Douglas returned. He grabbed her as she looked in the mirror.

'You look *delicious*, darling! I'll just have a quick wash and we can have dinner. I've spoken with Jed. You start work tomorrow at ten thirty in the Hollywood Suite. Don't worry about what to wear. I suggested you arrived at ten o'clock, and then Zena can look after you and give you a change of clothes from the wardrobe there. She's used to that.' He wandered into the bathroom.

'After dinner I think you should come up and have an early night. I want to speak to Zena, ring Helen and possibly slip out for an hour or so. I'll try not to disturb you when I get back. I won't be a minute; you can wait here or go down.'

She stood listening to him, busy in the bathroom. So that was it! She stared miserably at her satin nightdress in a champagne colour with black lace trim, tossing it on to the floor. What was the point of hanging around here?

She called out as she opened the door, not knowing whether he heard.

'I'll wait downstairs and join Zena then, see you later.'

He heard it close. Smiling, he finished rinsing the soap off and grabbed a towel.

* * *

Stella was in a strange dream, a roaring train was heading towards her from the underground as she stood naked on the platform, surrounded by strangers taking not the slightest interest. In her hand was the gold vibrator. There was nowhere to hide it as the train approached the station. In the driver's cab she was surprised to see Douglas. He was calling to her. She could hear him above the din of the engine. She tried to run away and find the exit but it always managed to lead her back to the platform. She knew he was chasing her and was gaining on her. Her legs wouldn't move properly. She felt a hand on her shoulder and screamed.

'Wake up sweetie, there's breakfast here and then it's time to get you ready for your first day.'

She stirred and awoke. The dream was still fresh in her mind for a moment before it began to melt away like dissolving celluloid.

'I heard a noise. I dreamt I was in the underground and a train was coming in and you were driving it, I…'

He wasn't listening, returning to drying his hair. That must have been the noise she heard. He wore a suit she hadn't seen. It was a very dark blue. His shirt was pale blue, with double cuffs and gold links, his tie dark blue silk with pin prick size white dots.

Over on the table under the window lay a tray with breakfast on and a pot of coffee. She climbed out of bed naked and helped herself to a bowl containing a small packet of muesli, a glass of orange juice and some toast and marmalade in a small sealed jar.

Douglas patted on his aftershave and turned to her.

'I'll come with you and Zena to the club, we can find where you have to go and then I'll leave you to it. I think the plan is that you have four members this morning….' He burst out laughing at his unintended pun, Stella uncomprehending.

'I said four *members,* sweetie! Cocks, dicks or pricks whatever you like to call them! You'll have four in the morning and four in the afternoon. We want to ease you in gently, darling, because, well the point *is*, we're not sure whether you'll quite be up to the mark for the fantasy; the main feature of this weekend.'

It was a pose of deliberately contrived nonchalance: one hand resting on the chair back, the other casually in his trouser pocket, his leg bent across the other, shoe resting on the toe and one eyebrow cocked.

'I said to Jed when we ran through the timetable, I didn't think you'd be much good at what was required. You've never done it before and you could even damage the reputation of the club.'

He held his arms across his chest, frowning.

'I told him that in my opinion it would be far better to let a more experienced woman perform this and lend *her* your dressing gown.'

He could see his words were hitting home, as she stood open mouthed.

'Playing Rose with me at home was one thing, Stella, but playing a role here for real, with real money at stake's a different matter.'

He stood in front of her, dwarfing her in her bare feet.

'I'm not convinced now that you have what it takes. But you can have a little go today.' He patronised her. 'I'm sure you can manage eight men over a day without *too* much difficulty, but if you find by lunchtime that you've just had enough...' He opened his eyes wide, his face sceptical.

That was enough. He'd done it. Stella was furious.

'I can *DO IT!* How *dare* you suggest otherwise. I can bloody *do it* and show you I can. Do you intend watching or taking part? Because I can tell you, if you take part you'll come like you've never come before, no matter how many men there are involved!'

'There'll be twenty actually, as I understand it!'

That shook her; she carried on.

'Okay then, *twenty*, whatever, *just bring it on! I'll DO IT!*'

Having won that little battle, manipulating things to suit him, he was soft and placatory.

'Finish your breakfast then, darling. If you're *really* up to it then no one will step in your way. You can just prove me wrong, can't you? Now hurry up and get ready, I'll go and read the paper and breakfast with Zena. We want to be there by ten.'

He opened the door and was gone.

The Hollywood Suite comprised a large oval shaped room in the centre of which was a huge bed. Just above picture rail height ran a succession of gleaming mirrors framed elaborately in gold. The ceiling was covered in draped white silk, which met in the centre where there hung another large mirror, right over the bed. To one side of the bed was a sunken bath incorporating a Jacuzzi, which was already surging and bubbling; on the other side, an enormous white fluffy rug and an ottoman with a pink velour quilted lid. Stella, Douglas, Rhoda and Jed were seated in a gallery made up of two rows of chairs as if in a theatre, looking down at the room through the two-way mirrors which surrounded it.

'Any member can sit here and watch what's going on through these two-way mirrors. You won't be able to see the people. They'll just look like mirrors from your side.' Jed was running through the morning's agenda. 'The Jacuzzi's kept at a reasonable temperature. Just mind if you're using it you don't slip. The chest has all the usual toys and stuff, some cords as well for restraint. Just help yourself. The vibrators and plugs are all shrink wrapped and enough in there for each member if they want to use them. Don't use the same one twice with another person, okay?'

'Is there a loo where I could go if I needed to, in between visits?' Stella asked.

'Yeah, just follow me round a bit here. You see that door down there, just behind the trunk?'

Stella looked. 'Yes.'

'Well follow me round to that side.' He set off ahead. Here some steps went down to the level of the bathroom, which was perfectly visible. The lavatory bowl was shaped like a huge heart with a pink heart shaped seat, the point of the heart at the front. The bowl itself was created from transparent pale pink glass with pink liquid in the bowl. The floor and tiling below the mirrors was also pale pink. A white sparkling washbasin stood behind the lavatory. Stella was stunned. She'd never seen anything like it.

'Is this what I use if I need to go to the loo,' she asked, 'or is there another private one?' Hoping.

'This is it, love, don't worry, you won't know if anyone's watching you. A lot of members love to watch and hear a woman having a pee. We thought this was great actually. It's solid glass and cost a bomb. The acoustics are good too and there's room enough if the guy wants to come in with you and watch or whatever.'

Stella felt Douglas's hand on her bottom, rubbing it. It was quite dark and they were all standing close together, Zena next to her. 'I think this tour's been very useful, Jed, Zena will take care of Stella's wardrobe and be on call, but do you have any other questions, Stella, before we leave you to it?' He was rubbing her more firmly.

Stella pushed towards his hand, moving her hips. Remembering the earlier conversation that morning she was certain.

'No I don't think I'll have a problem with it at all, Jed.' She ignored Douglas's question on purpose.

'Zena, is there anything else before we go?' Deftly, he slid his other hand inside the waistband of her skirt and she was unable to shift. *That's how he likes it*, she thought, *in perfect control, total control.*

'I'm looking forward to getting started. I think it's time I got Stella changed and ready to go. When's the first one arriving?'

'It was ten thirty,' Jed said, 'but he had to get here from Weybridge and the traffic's heavy. He reckoned about eleven. It pushes things out a bit but shouldn't really be a problem. The other three for this morning are all local; straight from the office, so should be on time. You get an hour for lunch to yourself and we bring it to you, okay, sandwiches or something and a drink, then you start again after. Anything else just ask Zena, who can find me if necessary. I'll have my mobile open but I'm going out to lunch from twelve to two.'

He turned to Douglas, now standing relaxed.

'Are you staying here, Doug, or what had you decided?'

'I think I'll stay and watch the show for a while with Zena if she doesn't mind.'

Rhoda was delighted. 'I don't mind at all.'

'Then Melissa said she was free and I'm taking her for lunch to Covent Garden, a wonderful little restaurant I know there. I'll pop back later in the afternoon and see how things are progressing. Shall we get started, ladies?'

* * *

Stella slipped out of her dress and accepted what Rhoda was offering her – a white satin Basque with black satin trim, fine black fishnets and a white satin thong. It all fitted to perfection and to finish it off she put on a pair of elbow length stretch satin gloves and a pair of black patent leather laced ankle boots.

'Come and sit here and I'll fiddle with your hair a minute.' Rhoda pulled a spindly chair back from the mirror in the cramped changing room. 'You need it tarted up a bit, love.' Removing some diamante slides from a small, worn cardboard box and a couple of fancy black hair combs, putting these on the shelf below the mirror, she pushed a few hair grips in her mouth, holding them there while she tugged and brushed at Stella's hair. 'You better drink this as well if I were you.' She placed a tumbler in front of Stella, which held a clear liquid, which bubbled slightly.

'What is it?' Stella peered at it uncertainly.

'It won't hurt you, it's vodka and tonic. If you haven't had a punter before, it's better to be under the influence, believe me. If you look here,' she indicated a flat screen next to the mirror on the wall like a television set with controls underneath it. 'You can see your first customer coming into the club. I just press here,' indicating a button below the screen 'when you're ready to receive him. He hasn't arrived yet, so drink up, he should be here any minute.

Stella took a sip. It didn't taste very strong. She swallowed the whole lot in a few gulps and put the glass down.

'Here 'e is now, do you want to look or not?'

Stella took a quick look at the screen, which was covered in a fine layer of dust. The image was discernible; he was tall with gelled dark hair and full lips. He looked quite young, hardly thirty at a glance, with glasses. His face was quite pale and he wore a short sleeved blue shirt, a pale yellow tie and dark trousers. Not good looking but not bad looking either. The camera caught the whole of the area; he was sitting on a chair, checking his watch.

'Are you ready then? I'll press this button as soon as you're out there. You look okay, so off you go.'

'Will I know if anyone else is...watching me?'

'No, love, you just see the mirrors like Jed said. Go on, get going, I'm going to press it now.'

Stella moved quickly and nervously sat on the huge bed. Moments later, through another door (hidden in the wall from this side) stepped the man she'd seen on screen.

'You must be Stella. Hi, I'm Greg!'

'Yes I'm Stella and, and I want to please you this morning, so you must tell me what you want to do.' It sounded a reasonable introduction, there was no script to follow; she hoped this didn't sound too wooden or clichéd.

He undid his tie and slipped his shirt off. 'You're very pretty and I want to do *you* right now.' He tugged at the belt on his trousers then let them fall to the floor. He had tight shorts on underneath and was already poking out of the fly. Stella lay back on the bed, resting on her elbows.

'Do you want me to take this off or anything?' She watched as he peeled his shorts off. There was no hair around his balls, which looked large.

'No, keep it all on. Just kneel up for me on the edge of the bed.'

The drink was working, making her relaxed and drowsy. Kneeling on the edge of the bed, she felt a damp hand on her hips and her thong carefully moved to one side. Sliding his hands up the Basque towards her breasts, he clutched at them, kneading. Stella didn't know what to say now, feeling awkward, moving slightly. He wasn't making a sound. In the end she tried to face him.

'Is it okay for you?'

He sounded breathless. 'Great. I'm going to come out in a minute…then I want you to rub me with your gloves on. Keep them on…don't take them off.'

Stella waited and about ten seconds later, he turned her over so she was lying on the bed. He climbed on and knelt beside her.

'Can you take that thing off, your corset or whatever it is?'

Stella undid the hooks and eyes that ran down the front of it and pulled it off.

'That's wonderful! Now just rub me…closer…I want it all over you. Then we'll go in the Jacuzzi, yeah?'

Stella looked at him; his face was now red with exertion and he'd closed his eyes. She wondered briefly if he was married and what his job was. Then suddenly she felt warm drips over her chest and stomach, slowly dribbling down her sides in a little stream. He lay down beside her for a moment, recovering. She looked at her gloves and peeled them off carefully. Tentatively, she rolled towards him and put her arm around him. He opened his eyes and began to kiss her. He tasted good and could kiss well. Then suddenly he'd stopped and was pulling away.

'Shall we go for a dip and clean up a bit? I've another ten minutes or so before I'm due back in the main club for something else.'

Stella wanted to ask what that was, but decided it might be etiquette not to.

'Sounds good, let's go,' She removed her thong, stockings and boots.

Once in the warm surging bubbles, which massaged with some force, and sitting close together, Stella decided to ask him something. There'd been no conversation to speak of and it felt strange to her to have been so intimate with someone and hardly say a word.

'How old are you, Greg?'

'Twenty seven, how about you?'

Stella demurred now. 'Older than you I have to say, by quite a bit! Are you married?'

'I'm engaged. I joined here when I was twenty and I've been coming here about a couple of times a month since then. Sometimes to meet someone, like you this morning. Or sometimes just to watch. It's a funny sort of atmosphere,' he mused, 'it's not cheap, quite upmarket, so mainly businessmen. And they all seem to look like naughty schoolboys doing something they shouldn't, hoping they won't get caught out. In the bar and lounge some of them say they're only here for a drink and not anything else, as if they're embarrassed you'll think they're waiting to go and do something.'

'I suppose some *might* just be there for a drink and something to eat and just like to be able to say outside they're members here, even if they don't *do* anything,' she suggested, stretching out in the bubbles.

It was lovely and warm, quite luxurious. He was chatty now. He had a funny manner, almost like an old woman. She wouldn't enquire about his fiancée; perhaps he wanted to get a bit of experience before settling down. 'Do you know the staff here quite well? Do you know Jed or Zena, or Douglas?'

He thought a moment. 'I know Jed; he's a good guy really, quite a laugh. I've never heard of Zena, but Douglas Spencer I know works here and I've come across him once or twice. He thinks he's better than anyone else, yet he's still here for the same reasons *we* are most of the time, nothing to get snobby about. He does have friends here, though, I think you either like him or you don't and I don't.'

He moved over to the small rail by the steps and pulled himself out, picking up a towel from a pile on the floor.

'Got to get moving now, been nice meeting you and you're very pretty, whatever your age is. You take care now and look after yourself.' He pulled on his clothes and slung his tie around his neck. 'Are you busy today?'

'I think I've got a few more to come, yes, another three this morning and four this afternoon!'

He was over by the door now. 'Should keep you busy then!' He winked. 'Well, thanks very much and maybe we'll meet again, 'bye!'

'Thanks, yeah, we may do, 'bye!' And he was gone.

Stella picked up her gloves, stockings, thong, boots and Basque and went back to find Zena, who was waiting.

'Your next one's already here now so stick these on.'

Stella took a bright red bra and pair of matching briefs.

'And these.' She handed her a pair of thigh length red patent leather boots with a very high platform heel. 'And this.' Popping a red mask trimmed with red sequins and small feathers over her eyes. 'He'll tell you what he wants; it's in the trunk there by the bed. He's German and his name's Karl. Don't look so worried, you did really well for your first go, look there he is.'

She pointed to the screen and Stella looked once more. He was a huge muscular man with a very short haircut and who looked about sixty.

'Off you go, I'm pressing the button now!'

Up in the gallery Douglas joined Jed who was watching.

'How's she doing, duck to water?'

'Real good, Dougie boy, real good. Greg was an easy starter, now she's moving up a bit with Karl. He likes a woman to do as she's told. He'll want to tie her up then suck his dick. Good practice for tomorrow and I can see how she does.'

'I think she'll be fine, Jed, just splendid. I had a word with her at the hotel and she insisted she took full part for the whole weekend, shouted she'd do it in fact. I wouldn't want to deny her the *pleasure*!'

Jed rubbed his chin and pushed his hand in his pocket.

'You mean all forty men? You told her there was that possibility?'

Douglas didn't miss a beat. 'Oh yes, absolutely! She doesn't want to miss out on anything. I'm certain she'll have the stamina required. No question. She's a pro.'

Jed had his doubts, something wasn't kosher. For some reason he felt uncomfortable about asking him about the money. Douglas was a hard nut; he'd thought *he* was. This club was a business and he wanted it to be successful, the best there was. Right there at the cutting edge of the sex industry. But he realised now he had *some* feeling, compassion perhaps. That's how he ran a happy club staff-wise. He always tried to be sympathetic in a dispute (which was a rare event, most gripes were sorted out before they got that far) but where sympathy or compassion would normally be, Douglas had a great big hole, a compassion bypass. He looked at his watch. He'd be going off to meet Reggie in half an hour and had things to do.

'Did you say you were going out with Melissa or did I imagine it?'

'*No*, you didn't imagine it. I'm taking her to Rawls at Covent Garden, traditional British food. I enjoy going there, I've never been disappointed. The food's excellent. Well, she seems to be coping so far.'

He looked down to the floor below, where Stella was cuffed to the bed with red linked chains and a small padlock, her legs spread, briefs gone but her bra still on. Karl was bending over the opened trunk, sorting through the contents. He removed a red handled whip with numerous long fronds falling from it and closed the lid. Jed turned and squeezed past Douglas.

'Great, well, have a good lunch. I'm going back to the office for a while. Catch you later.'

'Very good.'

Douglas viewed Stella, enjoying it. He could manipulate her anyway he wanted to. How he loved being in control. He could snap his fingers and have Stella, Rhoda, Helen; all at his beck and call. Melissa was a slightly different matter, but she was still obliged to ask 'how high' when he said 'jump'. He'd make sure she wasn't wearing pants this lunchtime then he could touch her while waiting for his delicious game pie. He could feel an erection which would have to wait. A cry made him start and he stared down. Stella had about four livid weals across her back that he could see. Oh well! She'd just have to deal with it. He turned and walked away. Once outside the club he scrolled his mobile and pressed a key.

'Andy? Douglas here, I'm lunching at Rawls for an hour or so. There was a matter which we discussed earlier about the shares? Could you, Ray, Jim and Ian meet me at Holborn Kingsway station at three o'clock? Then it's only a short walk to where we can have a meeting and finalise arrangements. I've notified my accountant and everything's in order…good. I look forward to meeting you *then*. Goodbye!' He scrolled and pressed another number, waiting.

'Gloria? Hello, it's Douglas. Are you on reception for the weekend? You are, good, I wonder if you'll be kind enough to hold on to the payments and receipt copies for today, Saturday morning and afternoon events. The ones concerning Stella Maitland…somewhere in the region of fifty receipts I think, possibly more…Paula and who? *Reggie? Hello?*'

The line suddenly went quiet. Gloria looked at her screen and saw the flag next to the names and felt sick. She thought quickly as Douglas was still there.

'Hello…hello, Gloria? Paula and *Peggy*,' he asked, confused. 'Who in God's name are they? Oh, no, never mind then…yes please if you could, no hang on a minute, could you leave the Sunday ones with Rhoda? Thank you so much, I shall ind*eed*! Goodbye!'

He turned to see Melissa gliding towards him, looking very chic. She was about to take his arm when he whispered to her and she turned back into the club, returning moments later, handing him a small lacy bundle which he slipped discreetly in his inside coat pocket as they walked towards the underground.

* * *

Jed picked up the phone. 'Hi Piers, it's Jed, I'm calling about the Sunday afternoon session that Douglas wants for the other twenty men who weren't on the first list. He wants to milk this one for all it's worth and although he *says* he's spoken to Stella and she's happy about it, I have my doubts. I wonder if you can arrange a stand in, an understudy if you like, in case of any problems there.'

He quickly scanned his screen as pictures of women appeared.

'I'm thinkin' maybe Thalia, or…' scrolling down the list, 'Justine or possibly Gina even, would be okay? Same build and nice tits… yeah! If you could see what you can do, have a word and see who'd be up for it if necessary. Personally I think Stella will've had her fill of this by Sunday, what? Yeah, in more ways than one, yeah! I'm off to meet Reggie, Paula and the girls now…yeah…er, Tamsin, Tracy, and Mandy I think. They'll be workin' in the hospital-mode and needing the operating table in full working order for those who want to watch the screen. That's ticket only that one if you could remind them on the desk, yeah, an extra fifty quid there…Who? Hazel? Yeah, she's arrivin' today as well with a couple of friends of hers. Can you get Gloria to look after her until I'm free again, she's on for the weekend, they'll be working in the mornin' in the schoolroom. Look I've got to go now or I'll be late, call the mobile if there's any problems. I'll leave it with you, cheers!'

21

Reggie said goodbye to Helen, hoping she'd have an easy time of it telling Douglas the news. She was also seeing her son and a few other friends in the area, so it wouldn't be *all* Douglas, he knew that because she'd told him on the phone. Nevertheless, they'd decided, he wouldn't be expecting to learn they were getting married! It would still come as a shock. He pondered this on the train as it drew into the station where Paula and the girls were waiting to get on. He saw them on the platform and waved – they were all looking knockout. The other passengers turned as Paula sat next to him, Mandy and Tamsin opposite and Tracy just across the aisle. Four highly attractive women suddenly descending on one man who looked remarkably like a man off the television (but no one in first-class was brave enough to ask and find out) was slightly suspect.

'Mornin' girls, it's great to meet you! I'm delighted Paula managed to persuade you to come in on this little party. It'll be quite a show. I think we're due in at eleven forty and meetin' Jed at twelve at Rosie's Bar. Douglas and Stella are already there.'

Interest from the passengers, however covert, prevented further associated discussion, so conversation reverted to general topics.

Once packed in a cab and bound for Brewer Street, Reggie was able to continue. 'Jed's going to meet us and we'll have lunch. That was him on the mobile back then. Dougie's gone to Covent Garden with some woman but not Stella and should be gone for a couple of hours like. He'll get us into the club and hide me away from him while you and Tamsin meet the other girls. Mandy, you can't be seen by Douglas either at the moment because of the escort association.'

They laughed and continued to chat until they reached Soho. Jed was waiting for them and waved.

'Reggie Crifton, it's a pleasure! Hi girls, I'm Jed, as I expect Reg here's told you. I'm hoping a quick lunch will suit you? It's not haute cuisine, but I'm paranoid about bumping into Dougie or anyone who might tell him you're up here. It's close to the club and we'll have time for a good look round as I promised before he returns, does that sound okay?'

'Aye man, that sounds great.' He looked at the others. 'Suit you lot?'

Paula replied. 'Fine thanks, just the job!'

The others nodded, following Jed into the bar.

* * *

Hazel pressed the buzzer on the door-entry system of Alfred Mansions, Tottenham Court Road and waited. She was very hot, the tube had been crowded all the way from Oxford Circus and she'd had to stand.

After a few seconds, although a bit crackly, she recognised Nina's voice. 'Hello?'

'Afternoon, Nina, I'm rather hot out here, it's Hazel. Can you let me in?'

The buzzer sounded again and the door clicked open. Pushing it, she stumbled into the stuffy hallway.

'God, it's hot, lovely to get here at last! Is Joanie okay?'

'Here, let me take that for you…' Grabbing the bag, their hands touched; Hazel's hot and damp, Nina's cool and dry. For an awkward moment they paused; then Hazel reached for Nina's shoulder and looked at her.

'Good to see you, Nina, been quite a long time; kiss?'

She kissed Hazel's offered cheek.

'Good to see you too and looking forward to the weekend! I hear we're going to have a bit of fun at the club!'

Nina wheeled the case, bumping it up the two flights of stairs to the next floor and pushed open the door to number five. It was cooler; the windows were open somewhere and a breeze was blowing.

'Hi Joanie, we're here…this is your room.' She pushed open a pinewood door in the hallway and went into a bedroom with twin beds, decorated in pink, with a soft dark blue carpet. Pink, white and dark blue striped curtains were drawn against the sun, the breeze from the opened window sucking them out gently every few minutes.

'Hello Hazel,' Joanie poked her head around the door.

Hazel removed her jacket, dropping it on one of the beds.

'Good to see you again, come and tell us all your news and what's in store this weekend. Neither of us has been to the club for ages, have we? We were excited to get the letter. I hear we're part of the show! I'm just fixing some iced tea if you'd like a glass? Do go through to the living room, I'll be there in a minute, Nina'll keep you company.'

The living room was in the shade, decorated in cream. A pinewood base sofa with large, rich, oatmeal coloured cushions and a couple of brown and orange silk scatter-cushions, sat in a corner on a pine laminate floor on which lay some colourful rugs. On the walls were expensive looking pictures of an abstract design. Hazel dropped down on to the sofa, exhausted, and Nina sank into an armchair opposite.

'Did you say we were going to meet a Stella Maitland? Was that the name?' she asked. 'It sounds intriguing!'

Hazel nodded. 'Yes, that's the one. I think we're in the schoolroom, which I haven't seen since it was refurbished last year. Have you?'

'No I haven't, as we said, it's been ages since we've been along. Is it just the three of us or will there be anyone joining us, do you know? It would look more realistic if we had a few more *students*, so to speak, don't you think? Especially if any of them require discipline. I assume there'll be a certain amount of that involved, or they wouldn't have invited *you*!'

Hazel laughed. 'You're quite right there! I spoke to Douglas Spencer back along, May I think it was or maybe early June, he had Stella with him. A beauty with the most extraordinarily coloured dark hair, really glossy and so many different shades, lovely big blue eyes....'

Joanie carried in three glasses of iced tea on a tray and a full glass jug. 'Hang on a minute, wait for me before you begin all the good bits!' Placing the tray on a coffee table between them, she handed a glass to Hazel and one to Nina before taking her own over to a brown leather recliner in the corner.

'So...lovely big blue eyes and luscious hair, yes, carry on.'

'Well, he told me he was introducing the idea slowly, intending bringing her up to London in July, which he has done apparently. I'll be very pleased to meet her within the walls of the club, different from the tea shop!'

She took several long draughts of iced tea, the ice clinking against the glass.

'I don't think he wants us to "spare the horses" from what Rhoda said to me when she rang me. Plenty of action! '

'Irrigation perhaps?' enquired Joanie.

'Hmmmm, I know what you mean, but she's a beginner; probably not. *Some* anal play perhaps yes, in context with her lessons.' She put down her glass and sat up. 'I understand from Douglas, she has an aversion to saying the word anus. It's very difficult for her to say it...deliciously so, apparently, he recommends she be taught to say it more easily,' She licked her lips, 'or accept increasing discipline until she does.'

Joanie's interest was aroused. 'That sounds very good to me!'

'And me...how old is she, do you know?' Nina was curious.

'Well I thought she could have been anywhere between thirty five and fifty, it's difficult to tell nowadays, very attractive anyway.'

Nina sipped her tea. 'Well I'm really looking forward to it. I'm sure there's a lot we can show her and the visitors'll like to watch. I assume they still have the gallery, do you know?'

Hazel was positive. 'Oh they'll have that, all part of the fun! Do you remember the last time we went? I think we all stayed in a hotel together, a good few years ago now, but I remember how stimulating it was.'

They relaxed, finishing the refreshments.

'I'll just go back to my room and unpack a bit in a minute when I've finished this,' Hazel said. 'Could I possibly beg a shower? I feel a bit hot and sticky from travelling; you know what it's like.'

'Of course you can, make yourself at home,' beamed Joanie, 'it's great to see you again.'

Nina drained her second glass and replaced it on the table. 'When's it all happening? Do you know the timetable at all?'

Hazel looked in her handbag, a large black canvas square with wooden handles, removing the invitation.

'Saturday morning at ten thirty in the Schoolroom, it says, then it mentions a Zena Fortune who'll be there assisting and organizing...the name was a new one on me until Rhoda told me, Rhoda Chambers, do you remember? Very close to Douglas at one time, before he met Helen I think, though can't be sure, long time ago now. Anyway, I think I'll unpack and have that shower, see you later. I brought a towel with me in the bag.'

'There's a large pink one on the bed, if you prefer a large one!' Joanie winked.

'I shan't answer that, Joanie!'

* * *

As the fourth client of the morning took his seat in reception, Stella wanted the lavatory. She'd wanted to wait until lunchtime when she'd have an hour to herself but now at half past twelve, she couldn't.

'When do I get to have lunch, Zena, do you know? How long does this client have with me?'

Rhoda gloated. She'd been forced to wipe her acquired red marks down a little. Karl had been a bit on the rough side, but she'd survived. The one after was a doddle, practically impotent, he'd needed sympathy more than anything and now there was Joe. Anything in a skirt did it for him and he liked to watch you go to the loo…she'd been paying attention in between doing her crossword. Stella hadn't visited there yet. She'd had two vodkas and a large coffee, so by rights should be in pretty urgent need by now. She'd organised Joe as the last of the morning's visitors deliberately. Stella was shy and didn't want to be watched. Well *hard luck!*

'Do you need to pop to the loo, love? You have lunch after this one, Joe. Go quickly and I'll press the button,' Watching, as she opened the door to the bathroom, 'right now!'

Within seconds Joe was there, leaning against the jamb.

'Open your legs, kid, I want to watch…come on love; you can do it. Do it for me. Let me give you a little kiss.'

He had a ruddy complexion and wet lips with short wiry grey hair and piercing blue eyes. Stella cringed. She was bursting and yet couldn't manage to go; aching with the effort. He reached for her knees, gently but firmly easing them apart.

'Come on now, let it go, it'll only hurt if you don't. I'm waiting, Stella, and we haven't got all day. Sit up and stick your tits out, very pretty. Now let it come. Shut your eyes if it might help…'

She looked up at the mirrors, wondering if anyone was watching. He was growing angry and fed up with waiting – she could sense it. Then the first trickle came.

'That's a girl! Let it all go now, come on, it's only a pee! It won't hurt, you silly bitch, spread your legs wider and sit up. Go on, chin up, that's it, good!'

She shut her eyes tight and tried to relax. This was the last one and then it was lunchtime and an hour off. She jumped as she felt a finger, then another.

'When you're all done that'll be my cock...but not up there.'

She chewed her lip and finished. Instinctively she looked up again, but only saw her reflection. She reached for a tissue then washed her hands.

'Come on, come on, wasting time! Get in here.'

As she re-entered the room, she saw him rolling on a bright pink ribbed condom. She lay on the bed, waiting.

'Not like that, darlin'.' He finished what he was doing and looked up. 'Roll over and come to the edge of the bed...that's it. Now where is it? I've dropped it.'

She turned her head and saw him looking around on the floor.

'Ah here it is! Better have this.'

He squeezed some lubrication from a small blue sparkly tube onto his finger. It felt slimy but not cold. She knew then what was coming and he'd looked big. She gritted her teeth. With hardly a pause, she felt the teat end of the condom against her before a sharp, searing pain like a knife.

She screwed the bed cover up in her fists, clenching her jaws as he touched her inexpertly at the same time. Then suddenly his rhythm changed. He'd found the right spot and despite everything, she felt different for the first time that morning. She released the cover and moaned. She heard it escape and so did he.

'Enjoyin' this now, aren't you? Like it up your arse then, do ya? Must say you took it well...*oh!* Oh hell! I'm comin'....'

Stella felt the waves shudder over her. She'd done it! She was almost enjoying it and then it was over. She lay still on the bed, listening as he tidied himself up. He laid a hand across her bottom, gently.

'Thanks, love, that was great, really! I hope they keep you on, I'd like to see you again, what's your name; Stella was it?'

She rolled over. 'Yes it is, although I'm only up for the weekend, then I go home again.'

He was all dressed now and looking at her.

'Are you a member here then or what?'

'Not a member, no. I'm a friend of Douglas, Douglas Spencer.'

'*Really*? He's a lucky bugger, isn't he just! Oh well, 'bye now and thanks. See ya later!'

She watched him go through the door and flopped back on the bed, disturbed within seconds by Rhoda with a round of cheese and ham sandwiches and a large carton of orange juice.

'Here, take this, you've got an hour now, love. I'll give you forty five minutes and then fix your hair again and sort you out for the afternoon. How's your back now after Karl, feelin' better at all? Let's have a look.'

Stella hadn't thought any more about it. She looked up and could see her reflection in the mirror and a few red lines were visible. She stretched her arm round and rubbed there as Rhoda studied it cursorily. It felt a bit sore, but not too bad. She did feel hungry though, and picked up a sandwich.

Rhoda peered more closely before dismissing it.

'Hmmmm, you'll live! I'll be back for you at quarter to two. You start again at two thirty, all right?'

She didn't wait for a reply.

22

Douglas kissed Melissa goodbye outside the restaurant then found her pants in his pocket as he reached for his phone, swiftly passing them to her with a smile.

'Well it's been *lov*ely, darling, thank you. I look forward to seeing you again soon. I hope you have a good afternoon!'

He inclined his head as she left him, then looked in his contacts and found Rodney Horsely, his accountant. He called the number.

'Hello, Rodney? It's Douglas. I'm expecting Andrew Sears, Raymond Hinckley, Ian Pulver and Jim Knight…yes I shall…we agreed twenty five percent I think? Splendid, just wanted to make sure…I'll be in touch, thank you so much…yes, will do; 'bye.'

He walked briskly along to the underground station, taking the train to Holborn Kingsway then waited on the corner of Southampton Row. The four men, deep in conversation, nearly bumped into him as he stepped out to greet them.

'Hello, so glad you could get here! I've booked a room for the meeting, just a bit further along at Bury Place.'

Once in the lobby of the hotel, he enquired at the desk and the five took the lift to the sixth floor. The doors opened on to a corridor with dormer windows on one side and three sets of double doors on the other. In between the sets of doors was a selection of etchings of old London, framed in unfussy gold frames. Douglas opened the first set of doors, switching on some wall lights which lit dust motes floating in the hot air.

He ushered the four men inside. The walls were panelled and there was a large leaded skylight above, dimmed by grime and pigeon droppings. The group pulled back gold conference chairs with blue padded seats and sat down. Looking quickly up and down the corridor, Douglas closed the doors, turned on a fan which swirled the dust further and pulled out the chair at the head of the table, two men on either side of him.

'Right, well now we're together, gentlemen, I'm sure I don't have to remind you of the implications of what we're about to do. Does anyone wish to change his mind?'

He glanced around the table but no one indicated a change of heart.

'Well in that case I think I have something here to interest you.' He unzipped a maroon leather Mulberry document case and withdrew a wodge of paperwork. 'Shall we do business now?'

The other four removed a similar amount of paperwork from envelopes or cases and spread it across the table in front of them.

'Providing we're all in agreement, I think I said I'd pay you each twenty five percent above the current price today which is...' He checked a slip of paper, 'two hundred and seventy pounds and twenty pence.' He peered over his glasses at them, their faces avid; the distant murmur of traffic audible six floors below.

He shot his cuffs, placing his forearms on the table, and then consulted the papers in front of him, his cheque book sat nearby like a siren luring the four men, who were trying to concentrate on the conversation.

'Each of you has seven hundred and fifty shares, correct?'

They nodded, breathing faster as he reached for the book and pulled out a pen, removing the lid.

'I make that a cheque each then, for two hundred and fifty three thousand three hundred and twelve pounds and fifty pence.' He bent and wrote them out, tearing each one carefully and passing it across the table. 'Now if you would be so good as to pass me the certificates?'

Four lots of share certificates came back. He slipped them carefully into his case and smiled.

'Well then, I think that concludes the business, any questions?

'Do we send our letters of resignation straight away?'

They looked at Ian in agreement. It was a sensible question. They wanted to know.

'If you could wait until *after* this weekend it might be more prudent, although I can assure you the cheques will clear within five working days or whatever the bank says now.' He gave a confident grin. 'And perhaps let the dust settle a little before returning to the club and bumping into Jed. It might be more *tactful,* shall we say.' They chuckled.

'I'll let you know what's happening after I've called a General Meeting, but until then, enjoy your riches, gentlemen. Now, shall we have some champagne?'

He eased his chair back over the dusty red carpet and over to a table in the corner and an ice bucket containing a bottle of Cristal under a white damask napkin. Five glasses stood next to it.

'No one knows of this yet,' he continued, easing the wire cage from the cork, 'I'll notify the club in due course as to the new management structure. I don't foresee too many changes with the exception of Jed, who'll now be directly answerable to me and his position,' he floated his hand, 'is flexible. You should address the letters to him, as company secretary, by the way.'

He released the cork with a controlled pop, carefully filling the glasses and handing them round.

'"Under new management", as they say!'

Five glasses clinked in approval.

Douglas walked swiftly towards the High Holborn branch of his bank to deposit his shares and consider the state of play. He now owned sixty two and a half percent and could call the tune. The entire tune, a whole concerto! But he wouldn't call a board meeting *just* yet. He hoped he could rely on the discretion of the others. The only one perturbing him was Andy, a respected member of the technical side of things. He could just be running with the hare and hunting with the hounds and unless kept on board like Rhoda (he glanced at his watch) could just tip Jed off about a possible takeover bid. Well, he'd bide his time at the moment until after the weekend. Once that was over and he'd collected the ticket money and receipts saved by Gloria, Rhoda having collected the remainder, he could then afford to be a little more high profile about the whole thing and start hiring or firing as he saw fit. Nothing could stand in his way.

There was something else niggling him; infuriating, what the hell was it? He glanced at a newsstand on his way to the bank and one word in a headline jogged his memory. 'Paula.' That was it! He was sure Gloria had said, 'Paula and Reggie' to begin with and had then changed it to 'Peggy'. Why? What was that all about? He only knew one Reggie and that was Helen's, surely it couldn't be the same one?

Douglas Spencer was never known for taking silly risks – he'd risked enough today already, costing him over a million pounds. He wasn't going to take any more chances. He stepped into a doorway, cutting out some extraneous noise, and found the number of Reggie's office. How he still had the number he couldn't remember, it may have even come from Helen, but no matter. He changed the mode to 'number withheld' and pressed 'call'. He was reminded that a recording may be taken of his call to be used for training purposes: they all said that, but in his experience there was always at least one bimbo who was polishing her nails when it came to training on security issues. He hoped she would answer today.

'Hello? This is Reggie Crifton's office. And how may I help you?' The inflection in her tone confirmed all he needed to know. Some men, he decided, were just born lucky.

'Oh hello; I wonder if you could tell me if Paula's in today.'

'*Paula?* I'm afraid not, she's gone up to London. Can I help you perhaps?'

Oh I think so, sweetie. 'Oh dear, well is Reggie available then in that case?'

A hand slid over the mouthpiece and a call to see if Reggie was available. He held his breath.

'Reggie's with Paula apparently, up in London as well. Is this to do with his next production?'

It could be, darling, in a manner of speaking.

'Not entirely, no, don't worry, I'll leave it for the moment, thank you, you've been most helpful.'

'May I ask who's calling?'

How he hated these modern phrases, but blessed the woman repeating them today.

'You *may,* my dear, but I'd prefer it if you didn't. Goodbye.'

He ended the call. So; Gloria had been right the first time, *Paula and Reggie*! Two bimbos, *well!* Quite a day!

* * *

Jed was enjoying himself toting Reggie and the girls round on the 'Tour' and they'd just left the hospital-mode. He was glad the X-ray machine capable of depicting 'internal penetration' was a success, none of the girls showed any signs of reluctance towards it. He tried to keep his mind on the job in hand, but Paula had picked extraordinarily beautiful women and excitement was mounting. He was looking forward to seeing Erika this evening, sitting out on the decking, a dip in the hot tub. A take-away of something exotic and then…His mobile sounded and he excused himself from his guests. It was Gloria.

'Hi, Gloria, what's the problem? Got Reggie and co with me still, can it wait?'

Gloria wished it could. She ought to warn him just in case.

'I had Douglas on the phone a while back and I accidentally let slip about Paula and Reggie. I told him Paula and *Peggy*, that I'd made a mistake. He asked who they were, then said it didn't matter, but I thought I'd better warn you. I'm very sorry, Jed, hope no harm's done!'

He rolled his eyes. Paula and *Peggy*, just brilliant! 'Well it's too late now so don't worry, love. What's done's done, but thanks for telling me, yeah! See you later.'

He squeezed the phone up in his hand and rested an arm on Reggie's shoulder.

'This could be tricky! That was reception, she's told old Dougie boy that Paula and Reggie are here then changed it to Paula and Peggy. We might be safe, but he's a sharp tool. We'd better just be on our guard and in fact that just about rounds up the tour now. I'd offer you all tea or drinks if you wanted in the restaurant, but it might be safer to head back to your hotels and see you in the morning.'

He pulled out a piece of paper from his wallet and passed it to Reggie. On it was printed six numbers.

'If you come round to Raglan Mews entrance tomorrow and use these numbers you'll get in. He could be wanderin' around. Girls, if you could get here by half nine? Then we'll get you sorted with costumes or whatever.'

Paula kissed Jed.

'We'll be here and thanks for the tour, it looks great. We're staying in Bayswater, here's my number if you need it at all.' She handed over a business card. 'Otherwise see you in the morning.'

Jed ushered them towards the exit. 'See ya guys! Have a good evening.'

He walked into reception as Gloria was leaving and stopped her.

'If you see Douglas tomorrow, it's still Paula and Peggy, yeah! Don't make it bloody worse telling him it was Reggie all along. Let's hope he's forgotten. He's got Stella with 'im and dipped his wick more times than a candle-maker since he's been 'ere, so don't say nothin' unless he pushes it, okay?'

'I won't Jed, I'm really sorry, he always gets me in a tizzy and I didn't think straight. Sorry.'

Jed was about to go, then stopped.

'What did he want anyway, in the first place?'

Gloria dithered, unsure. She'd made one faux pas today, a biggie possibly. 'He wanted to know something about the money for the weekend events, the ones that involved Stella. I said I'd keep a record of them for him to see.' She hoped this was in order.

'Oh did 'e now? Thanks for tellin' me, don't worry, love. See you tomorrow and don't forget what I said, right?'

Gloria breathed a sigh of relief. 'I won't. Thanks, bye Jed.'

Jed was already heading back to his office and he gave her a distracted wave.

'Yeah! Bye Glo.' He kicked the office door shut with his heel and grabbed the phone on his desk.

'Is that Piers? Jed. How much had we set the ticket price for this weekend? Including all and anything to do with Stella plus the table fee…have you got a full list of who's coming and paying for what? Good, can you email me as soon as? Thanks, bye.'

He replaced the receiver and held it. As soon as he could, he'd ask Douglas just what cut he proposed to give him for organising all this. It was bloody hard work and he deserved his share. All Douglas was required to do was supervise Stella, not exactly hard graft. The rest of the time he was workin' his cock off or seemed to be. He'd tackle him about it tomorrow, right now he'd had enough for one day. Rhoda would take care of Stella. She must be on her last punter by now. He'd get back to Erika and that hot tub…

23

The dining room at the Élan was low-ceilinged luxury, tranquil but productive. Stella had been to some smart hotels in London, but this outshone all of them. The napkins were heavy linen and springy, the glass and silver sparkling. It seemed a world apart from the Sirens Club, although in the restaurant and lounge areas there it was all deep pile carpet, the carpet a rich royal blue and the walls covered in something that appeared to be red velvet and the woodwork a light oak.

Sitting with Douglas and Rhoda, she gazed at the large menu for the evening of the sixteenth of July. She was already living out her fantasy – this wasn't real life at all. She looked down at her dress, another gift from Douglas back in June – a sleeveless white shift, the bodice a semi-transparent organza silk with a silver thread running through it, costing the equivalent of one night's stay here on full board in a superior room. She felt in a complete daze. Douglas had summoned a waiter and was ordering.

'Stella…What do you want this evening?' He leant towards her.

She scanned quickly for something that took her fancy.

'I'd like the duck terrine, the grilled chicken and a mango sorbet, please. Thank you.' She handed the menu back to the waiter.

'And what would you like to drink, darling, a glass of champagne perhaps?'

'Yes please, one glass and some water, thank you.'

Douglas poured some water from the jug on the table and she glimpsed his wrist beneath a pristine double cuff, remembering how he'd held the jug on her table at home at the dinner party. There was no likelihood of lumpy orange sauce here. So much had happened in such a short space of time since she'd left home. The orders taken, the three sat back and waited.

'So, Stella,' Douglas sipped his champagne approvingly. How did things end in the Hollywood Suite? How was your introduction to the world of escort work?'

He smiled, leaning back in his chair, immaculate; his hair gleaming and his aftershave floating across alluringly.

'Was it what you expected? You have a big day tomorrow and Sunday, work's not over yet. Do you think you'll be able to stay the course after today?'

He studied his fingernails, flicking them absently with his thumbnail before lifting his eyes stealthily towards her.

Stella rested her elbows on the table; her face drawn and tired.

'I'm sure I won't let you down Douglas, I'll be able to carry on.' She returned his gaze. 'This is what we'd planned and I'm quite happy to continue, although I don't think I'd want to do it again.' She paused. 'But I'll see this weekend out.'

She took a few sips of champagne, letting the bubbles dissolve. It tasted wonderfully sharp and dry.

'What's the plan for tomorrow and Sunday actually?'

Rhoda fiddled with the stem of her glass as Douglas eased the toe of his shoe over her foot and up her ankle. He didn't look at her as he continued to address Stella.

'You're meeting Hazel and a couple or so of her friends, fellow members, tomorrow morning. Members of your own sex shouldn't be too taxing.' He raised an eyebrow. 'And then, as you know, you wear the silk dressing gown in the afternoon for the little display that Jed's organized.' He stared straight at her now, unblinking, forearms resting on the table, the palms of his hands together as if in prayer. 'I've informed Jed that you wouldn't need *rescuing* from that. You wish to fully partake of the whole thing, yes?'

Stella crossed her ankles and sat up, eyeballing him.

'Yes, definitely, I said so. I won't go back on my word.'

'Very well, that's Saturday, then I believe Zena has need of you again on Sunday morning in one of the club zones and I'll check with Jed again for the afternoon's activity. Then,' He brushed tiny crumbs from the table. 'I think we're due home again. I'm collecting Helen from the station late on Monday afternoon and will be incommunicado. You remember she called me at home when we were otherwise…*engaged?*'

Stella blushed, avoiding his eye.

'Yeah, I remember.'

A waiter appeared with the colourful and appealing starters, and then topped up the glasses. Stella put a hand over hers, declining any more before picking at her duck terrine and light salad.

Rhoda had a sudden urge to touch Douglas's arm, and she longed to put her hand over his, becoming aroused by his continuing foot play under the table. She *had* to get him in her room, somehow. As if sensing her frustration, he slid his glance to her and smiled.

'And what did *you* think of Stella's performance, Zena? Was she up to scratch, do you think? In your, how shall we say, *professional* opinion?'

'I think she did very well considering it was a first effort, very well indeed,' she replied approvingly, 'We didn't receive any complaints anyway. One of them, Joe, wanted to see her again, I believe. He was very *satisfied.*' Her eyes bore into him in an effort to convey a subliminal message.

Stella shuffled in her chair, slightly uneasy. Zena seemed extremely familiar with Douglas this evening, at odds with her position, she thought. Something was incorrect, how come she was sitting with them at all? Like a gooseberry. She wanted Douglas to herself and felt angry. Swallowing a mouthful, she put down her knife and fork and asked peremptorily:

'Wouldn't you normally eat at the *Club*, Zena? Is this a special weekend for you, to be staying *here* I mean and eating with *us*?'

Rhoda's glare was like ice and too late, she realised how rude this probably sounded. She looked hastily at Douglas – his face was granite. He used his napkin, replacing it carefully over his knees.

'Zena Fortune works at the Club as I told you and has agreed to be your supervisor on this occasion.' He fingered one of his cufflinks then brushed invisible fluff from his sleeve. 'She's my guest this weekend as you are, dining with us at my invitation until we leave on Sunday, with or without *your* approval.' He finished.

The waiter removed the plates, hiding Stella's mortification. She dug her nails into the palm of her hand and clenched her teeth. She hadn't been adult. She wanted the earth to open up; a classic little prima donna.

'I'm sorry, Zena, that was very rude of me, I'm sorry.'

Rhoda and Douglas exchanged a covert glance. She offered Stella a thin, disdainful smile.

'I've known Douglas a long time, dear, a lot longer than you have. We like to catch up every now and again, don't we darling?' Finally, she placed her hand over his, stroked it with her thumb then picked up her glass. 'Perhaps you're feeling a bit tired this evening and need an early night.' She glanced up as Douglas shot her a sly wink.

'We'll excuse you immediately after dinner if you want to go to bed; I'll see you later…ah, here comes the main course.'

The moment's discomfiture having passed, Stella ploughed on with the meal. It had been put down to overtiredness, now just forget it. She'd have Douglas's company all night, be satisfied with that. She risked a wary glance at Rhoda, who was busy eating and appeared unruffled now, so without catching Douglas' eye again, she began the chicken.

After pudding had been removed, she excused herself. Douglas was charming, rising as she bade them goodnight.

'I'll come up later and have coffee. I'll order some decaffeinated.

Go and have a good relaxing bath and I'll see you later darling, you do look rather tired.'

He blew her a kiss and she grinned. Everything was going to be all right again.

Rhoda had just finished drying from her own bath when she heard a discreet tap on the door. A peek through the spy-hole confirmed who it was. She stepped out of the way as he slipped in and closed the door. Douglas eased Rhoda backwards along the small passageway, past the bathroom, guiding her towards the bed.

'You're doing very well, Rhoda, very well. I think you want me…*don't* you?'

She grabbed at his suit, feeling his lean body through the soft, fine wool. His shirt felt cool and crisp to the touch. Preventing her grappling with his belt, he pushed her back on to the bed.

'I haven't long, I've had some coffee sent up to our room but I wanted to see you first.'

Undoing his fly, he left the belt fastened as Rhoda stretched out.

He raised himself from the bed, ignoring Rhoda's slight bewilderment, 'Well that was wonderful,' he grinned, 'but I have to go, I'll see you in the morning!'

'But I didn't think you. I don't think you; did you?'

Carefully adjusting his trousers, he turned, un-answering this remark. She was still recovering and was trembling.

'Stella *did* behave herself today, I hope? No other little outbursts like this evening's little fit?'

'She managed,' Rhoda replied, shrugging her shoulders, 'reasonably I suppose, but she thinks she's better than anyone else there, little madam. She needs to learn who the boss is, if you know what I mean, but otherwise okay, no complaints.' *That should fix her!* 'Yes, see you in the morning at breakfast and thank you too, it was wonderful for me.'

He headed for the door, still aroused and semi-erect. The corridor was empty and he took the lift up the remaining two floors and found his key card. The door clicked open and Stella was sitting up in bed wearing a very attractive grey and turquoise silk nightdress. He pulled the covers back and took her wrist.

'Come here, a present for you.'

It was very sensitive to the touch. Stella, opening her mouth, recoiled, repulsed and unsure.

He stood over her, ordering her.

'Take it Stella, rub it then, you spoilt little child.'

She lay down, lifting her nightdress and opening her legs. She'd been waiting for him, wanted him. He poured two cups of coffee from the silver pot on the tray nearly to the rim.

'I'm *not* a child Douglas, I lust after you. I want you. Need you; so fuck me then, *please!*'

He closed his eyes, concentrating.

'Are you sorry for this evening? Sorry for how you behaved to Zena? She told me you needed to know who was boss, do you think you do? Do you want me to teach you a lesson, Stella?'

She clutched at his buttocks, drawing them apart, forcing him into her.

'I'm sorry, very sorry. I want you and desire you, yes, teach me a lesson, you can do whatever you want with me…'

'You little whore; you love this don't you, love it, I…*Oh!*'

Abruptly he sprinted over to the tray. Stella watched, half in fascination half in horror as he stood adroitly over the coffee. He poured a little cream into the other cup and passed Stella the first one.

'Now drink it! Drink it my little whore, go on, this is your lesson, sweetie. Behave yourself in future. There's more of this tomorrow, I want to watch you, so come on now…just a sip. Do you want the sugar perhaps?'

Stella was revolted but curious, the two liquids marbling in the cup. Shutting her eyes she lifted it, taking a small sip. It tasted of hot coffee, nothing else. It was scalding hot and she took another sip, then swallowed some more. There was a tang at the back of her throat and she gagged.

'I can't take anymore. I've had half of it and learnt my lesson. I won't be rude to Zena again, I promise, but I don't want any more, could I have another...unadulterated this time? Please?' She handed the cup and saucer over to him.

'Of course, yes.' He took it and stood up from the bed. 'Well done Stella, Rose would be very proud of you, to say nothing of Madam Du*bois* who'd be delighted I should think!'

He rinsed them under the tap in the bathroom. Stella heard a text come in on her mobile and foraged in the bedside drawer to find it. She pressed the key, saw it was from Clive and opened it.

'Hi hope you're OK. Shall try and ring in the morning. Fed Jeeves and took him for a walk. Cathy is taking him again tonight. All else is OK. Sleep well. Much love xxx'

She deleted it, dropping the phone back in the drawer as Douglas returned and poured her a fresh coffee. He picked up the small cream jug and held it over the cup.

'Cream?' He twitched an amused grin.

Stella brushed her hair back and smiled.

'No thanks, black with two sugars please.'

Later, with Douglas on top of her, her mobile sounded again. He reached out an arm, opened the drawer and pulled it out as it rang, peering at the small screen.

'Do you know a Clive, darling?'

Warm underneath, she smiled. 'No!'

He pressed the busy key and put it down.

'Good girl, we're learning, aren't we? No more coffee. Do you like hot milk?'

Stella could feel him giggling.

'I love hot milk, actually.'

'Splendid. Hold on then, I think it's coming!'

24

Hazel woke as Joanie brought in a mug, placing it on the bedside cabinet.

'I thought I'd bring you in some tea, I've just had a call from the club.' The rings clinked together as she pulled back the curtains. 'Gloria wants us by nine thirty. It's only seven, so plenty of time, but I didn't want to rush. Nina's in the bathroom at the moment. I'm all ready, so when you've had your tea it's all yours.' She sat down on a chair by the window, a hand on each knee.

'I'll go and prepare a bit of breakfast. What would you like? We usually have some muesli and a slice of toast, but I could fix an egg or something if you'd prefer?'

Hazel sat up, blowing on her tea, her pajama jacket straining across her chest. 'Muesli and toast sounds fine to me, I'm quite excited.' She smiled at Joanie then replaced the mug, wiped her mouth and looked more serious. 'I was mulling it over last night; did you want to be the schoolmistress or a student today? I assumed Nina would be happy to be a student? Obviously Stella as a newcomer will be, but had you any preference at all? I honestly don't mind one way or the other.'

She glanced down but her expression betrayed her. Looking up she saw Joanie beaming.

'I wouldn't *dream* of denying you your role, Hazel, that would be cruel. No, you've met Stella and you're obviously interested.' She saw the gleam in Hazel's eyes. 'Make that *very* interested in educating her, so there's no question about it, you'll be in charge. But you won't hog her *all* to yourself! Gloria said the other regular girls there would be Sally, Caz, Misha, Pearl and Sorrel. That should make a nice little number.'

The door opened a bit more and Nina appeared, dressed in a skimpy tie-dye mini dress and flip-flops.

'Bathroom's free when you're ready, Hazel.' She looked at both of them curiously. 'What's been going on, have I missed something?'

Hazel patted the bed for her to sit down.

'We've just been discussing who wanted to be the schoolmistress. I think my expression rather gave the game away though, so if it's okay I'll be at the blackboard.'

Nina smoothed her dress then arched her back, stretching.

'That's *won*derful, Hazel. When do we have to be there? Nine thirty did you say, Joanie?'

Joanie rose, heading for the door. 'Nine thirty yes, I'll go and get some breakfast, see you in a minute.' She disappeared and pulled the door to. They heard her bustling around in the kitchen.

'Have you finished your tea?' Nina peered in the mug on the cabinet.

'I have and I ought to go straight to the bathroom.'

Nina pinched the edge of her dress with two fingers seductively and lifted it slowly. Underneath was a tiny pink thong and nothing else. She drew it up further to just below her nipples, her breasts two honey coloured cones, like miniature beehives. She leaned further forward over the bed, until the nipples peeked out, tantalizing, then waited, mouth slightly open, and her tongue resting on her top lip. Hazel tipped forwards and took the right nipple between her teeth and nipped it. A volt shot straight between Nina's legs and she pressed her lips together to prevent a cry. Hazel released it and nipped the other, a little harder. Nina watched, as at exactly the same time, she tweaked down the elastic of the thong. She sunk down on the bed, her eyes rolling, her body moving in spasms as she bit her lower lip, hard. Hazel drew away, sucking her finger.

'First lesson Nina, only one orgasm at a time please! Now I'm going through to that bathroom or we'll be late.'

* * *

Douglas, Rhoda and Stella climbed into the taxi hailed by the doorman. No one spoke at first, staring out of the window as they travelled the short distance to Brewer Street. Douglas broke the silence.

'I'll take Stella through to the schoolroom. It's going to get busy. Gloria might need some help with checking the tickets, there're a couple of names I'm interested in should they appear. I'll tell you which they are. If you could stay with Gloria all day today I'd be grateful, there wasn't anything needing your attention I think, just the brothel scene tomorrow.'

This wasn't Rhoda's plan at all. She wanted to watch the action, see his little protégée really come unstuck. She'd find out the names and then ask Gloria to text her if they turned up.

* * *

Reggie entered the six numbers in the entry system at nine fifteen and pushed open the door. It was a claustrophobic warren of passages and a hive of bustling activity. Men strode indifferently past half naked glamorous women; all in a day's work. The technical side of life in the sex industry bordered on the tedious it seemed to Reggie. They found their way to Jed's office and he knocked on the door. Jed opened it immediately.

'Hi come in, coffee?' He indicated a steaming pot on his desk and some mugs, taking a hasty swig from his own and wiping his mouth.

'If I can just run over a few things first with you...' He perched on the corner of his desk, sleeves rolled up, shirt open and gold glittering on each strong, hairy wrist.

'Firstly, Gloria as you know, made a bit of a boob-boob telling Dougie that Paula and "Peggy" were coming here today, yeah? Not brilliant of her, but she's a good worker, we all like Glo', so I told her to keep it that way, Paula and Peggy...'

Paula's mobile trilled and she fished it from her bag. It was Lucy from the office.

'Excuse me one moment, I'd better take this.' She went into the passage outside.

Jed continued. 'Yeah, so it's Paula and *Peggy* if he's interested. Secondly, I'm not very happy with Stella doing two stints on the table. When you called me, Reg, I got the impression you wanted to find out more about Douglas Spencer and what made 'im tick? Well in all fairness, it's probably what makes other guys tick too, it's making money and gettin' his rocks off, except where *I* try to have at least *some* leanin' towards, well, feelin's I suppose, this guy ain't got any. I mean a complete feelin's lobotomy yeah? The guy's just a sadist, I think.'

Paula opened the door, waving her phone.

'Lucy's told him, Douglas, she's told him, he knows.'

Jed rubbed his face with his hand.

'What do you mean? Who's told 'im what, sorry, what's happened?'

'Douglas rang the office yesterday; they have a recording of his voice. Terry got suspicious when Lucy asked first about me and then about Reggie. He listened to the recording and recognised it from how Reggie used to imitate him in the office. No one else in the world speaks like he does. He knows we're here!'

Jed finished his coffee and set down the mug, quietly.

'He now *suspects* you're here. He don't know for *certain* and as far as I'm concerned, he ain't bloody *goin'* to know either!' He looked at all of them and curled his lip. 'The more I hear about Dougie Spencer, the less I like him. We're still one step ahead of the bastard and that's how it's goin' to stay, agreed?'

They agreed.

'Good!' He rubbed his face and carried on. 'The next thing is the money.' He looked round at all of them. 'I don't trust Doug now as far as I could kick him. I used to have respect for him when we first started together, thought he was a bit of a lad, but now I dunno. It's taken a while for this club to get where it is now and in all fairness, Doug's played a very large part in contributing to that success. He knew the right people, knew how to butter them up, he was great at that, the old charm. He knew how to sell a name, a brand...'

A buzzer sounded from the phone on his desk and he flicked it, picked up the receiver, whispered an apology then answered. 'Hi! Jed. Yeah? They'll be there in a second, Miranda...er, two I think first in the morning, Tamsin and Tracy. Mandy'll be there in the afternoon when Douglas is watchin' the table scene...because he may remember her that's why, I'll tell you another time...well they'll just have to go over and watch something else for a while, darlin', I'll have them along in a second...yeah. No, give all ticket stubs or slips to Gloria can you......Thanks, catch you later.' He replaced the receiver.

'Sorry about that, it was Miranda wanting you over in the hospital-mode, so I'll be quick. As I was sayin', when he puts his mind to something, he does it, big time. I can't deny that, but this club's a business and I keep it going on a day-to-day basis. This is a big promo this weekend and a lot of money. I mean a *lot* of money and some big names who want zero publicity that they're here, yeah?'

He tapped on his computer quickly. 'That takes organisin' and isn't cheap. At the moment he's sayin' the money will go three ways: the club, which could mean anyone who works here – the directors'll decide and give out a bonus – Rhoda and him. How he works that out I'm not sure, he don't own the shares to have much clout but like I say, I just don't trust him one bit. As for Stella...' He moved his eyes to a large calendar on the wall for July, a little curled at the edges, depicting a well-endowed, bronzed woman staring defiantly at the camera, her long tongue poised impossibly near her chin.

He placed a strong hand on each knee. 'She's a novice and determined to manage this afternoon, but I've prepared a stand-in for tomorrow just in case she's had enough. It's gettin' it past Rhoda that's the trouble. I reckon he's stuffin' her as well.' He shook his head and heaved his shoulders.

'If I can do anything to help you like,' Reggie was keen, 'I will and if the worst comes to the worst, I'll take her home again when we go tomorrow. I'll have a word with you later about it, but we'd better get going now or we'll have Dougie here.'

Jed opened the door carefully, looking each way.

'Okay girls, down the end here you'll see the sign to the hospital, turn right and it's the second one down. There's a picture of a nurse on the door. Miranda's there and she'll see to you, then Paula and Reggie if you'd like to come with me.'

25

Sherrie heard the buzzer and opened the door to the schoolroom. 'Hiya, all right?'

Nina smiled. 'Hiya Sherrie, yeah we're fine, Hazel's going to be in charge.' She looked round the room. It had a worn, polished wooden block floor and cream walls. The skirting boards and other bits of paintwork were a dull shade of bottle green, also a bit chipped and worn looking.

Sherrie was moving desks around, which were made of a light pine in a traditional shape with an inkwell. Each desk had a matching school chair.

'I don't know where you want things, what you want to do first. Gloria said we'd got Sally, Caz, Pearl, Misha and Sorrel plus a Stella and you. I make that ten in all.'

Hazel was writing on the blackboard placed at one end, the walls curved horseshoe shaped around it.

'I think if we have Sally, Pearl and Caz as a three, then Misha, Sorrel and you perhaps with Nina. Then Joanie and I dealing with Stella.'

She underlined 'Stella' with the chalk. White dust fell with the pressure of the full stop. Looking at the small piece, she searched along the base of the board for any more.

'Could we have some new chalks as well, do you think, and a few of the slates to write on perhaps?'

Sherrie was making a note. 'Fine, that's no problem, anything else?'

'Is there a light-weight cane here?' Hazel surveyed the room.

Sherrie found it by the desk and picked it up.

'We've got this one? It's not the toughest one.'

'Fine,' Hazel tweaked it, 'that'll do, and finally some mats to lie on, gym mats, rubber or coconut matting if you have them?'

'Sure I can find those, how many do you want?'

She considered this. 'Three I think, then I think that's it.'

Sherrie counted up on her list then held her pen out, pondering.

'What do you think about a strap-on, vibrators, anything like that? I can fetch a few from the store.'

'What do you reckon,' Hazel asked, 'three vibrators and a strap-on perhaps?'

'I think five vibrators, plus a strap-on,' agreed Nina, 'Show Stella how to use it when we're lying on the mats.'

'Right, five it is then Sherrie.' She turned, 'Okay with you, Joanie?'

'Fine, let's get going!'

Sherrie looked at her watch. 'Stella should be here any minute. I don't know much about her except she's something to do with Douglas Spencer. Has anyone met her?'

'I met her back in May I think it was, at the teashop. She's very attractive, sexy in an odd innocent sort of way…'

Nina was jealous.

'She can't be *that* innocent coming here with *him* I would've thought? Anyway, we'll soon knock that out of her. Rhoda said we weren't to spare the horses.'

Sherrie jumped in smartly. 'She's *Zena* not Rhoda, Nina. She's Zena Fortune this weekend. Jed told me it's important she doesn't know it's really Rhoda. I think she's going to be with Glo' on the desk though. Today's the main day, we're booked solid I think. There was a waiting list for this afternoon apparently, so they're doing another stint tomorrow. Advanced bookings have made over fifteen thousand for the whole weekend, plus ticket money that's coming in today.'

'How much of that will *you* see though, do you think?' Hazel asked.

Sherrie hugged her clip board and stood relaxed.

'Oh enough I think, fair do's, the board are usually quite generous with their bonuses.'

They were interrupted by the door. Sherrie opened it to Douglas and Stella, who was dressed in a short navy gym slip over a white shirt, her hair up in bunches and fully made up. She tottered into the room, her feet in frilly white ankle socks and pushed into very high black platform heels.

Hazel could feel rivulets of perspiration trickling down her neck. She looked delicious.

Douglas continued addressing her.

'You'll be watched from above as before,' indicating the mirrors above the cream painted walls, 'through that door's another loo the same as you had before if you need it, a bit smaller with a pull cistern, but still see through. There are nine here this morning to look after you.' He winked at Hazel. 'So just behave yourself and you'll be fine. If you're *not* and I get to hear about it you'll be in trouble! There's a lot of money here this weekend and we don't want disappointed punters.'

Stella was very nervous. The smell was the same as she'd noticed in May from the waitress. It was that very same waitress who was now standing by the blackboard and wearing a black trouser suit over a large white T shirt, cropped grey hair, small, mean eyes and a large nose. There were three other women, one with a clip board, in a red sparkly stretch top over a very short black skirt, heading for the door where Douglas was still speaking to her.

'You'll finish here at half twelve, then an hour's lunch before the board room at two o'clock. I've got the dressing gown. Are there any questions?'

Sherrie returned with the required items. A tall, muscular man with an indifferent expression, in a black open necked shirt and black trousers had the mats over one shoulder. He dropped them on the floor without a glance, shutting the door behind him. Stella pulled at her short skirt.

'No I don't think so, thanks, except I could do with the loo. Right now actually?'

Douglas looked at Hazel questioningly. 'Is that okay?'

Hazel frowned, her hand pulling at her chin.

'Very well, just the first time. Then get back here fast, *actually!*' she added, mocking her.

As quickly as she could she went to the door Douglas had shown her. Opening it, she automatically peered up at the mirrors which surrounded her. Was there a movement or did she imagine it? She crouched, slipping down her white cotton briefs, bursting. She tried to relax, shutting her eyes.

Behind the mirrors in the gallery, Reggie watched. So this was Stella. He felt moved and sad. He looked across at Paula.

'What do you reckon?'

Paula stood with her arms folded and looked away.

'*I* reckon she's bitten off a whole lot more than she can chew quite honestly. If she gets through today it'll be a bloody miracle.'

'So you think my idea of helping her tomorrow's not goin' to be far off the mark then?'

Paula was positive. 'Certainly not, no, I think if we discuss it with Jed later we can work out a plan to get her out of here without arousing too much suspicion. I've a feeling Jed's on our side, if only from a mercenary point of view, his jobs on the line if the punters aren't satisfied and Douglas is on the board. He probably owns a *few* shares, but Jed's richer than he is.' Reggie looked surprised so Paula confirmed it. 'He told me and that must rankle…we'll have to play it by ear and see how it goes. Oh, we have company I think.' She looked behind her. 'Seats are filling up. Shall we go and watch what's going on?'

They climbed the few stairs to the gallery and found a couple of seats on the end of the second row. It was filling up rapidly, the air heavy with aftershave and a masculine miasma.

Hazel grasped Stella's elbow and steered her to the front of the class before two rows of four desks.

'Stella's new here this morning,' she explained. 'I want us to welcome her and later we'll all get to know her quite well, so,' pushing her forward a little, 'say "good morning"!'

Stella repeated this and the eight students replied, 'Good morning, Stella!'

Releasing her elbow, she explained how things would proceed.

'First of all we have a little spelling lesson. It should be easy, there's only one word. Stella has a problem with it...' There was a wicked glint in her eye.

Paula turned as a seat was lowered above her, and she looked up. It was Douglas, intent on the proceedings below. Speakers allowed every word to be heard and he had an excellent view. She whispered softly but urgently to Reggie.

'For God's sake don't turn round, Douglas is above you. He won't recognise you if you don't, the light's too dim.'

Reggie nodded, sinking further in his seat, pulling his mobile from his pocket.

Hazel turned and picking up a piece of white chalk, she wrote in large capitals the word ANUS. Stella's heart sank. How did they know this?

Reaching down and picking up the cane, she pointed to the letters.

'I'll ask the class first, what letters have we here?' She pointed to them individually on the board. Each letter was called out in turn. Tense, Stella watched.

'Well done,' she smiled encouragingly. 'Now then,' more sternly now, turning to Stella, 'I want you to read out each letter that you've just heard and then spell the word. Loudly, so we can all hear, dear, off you go!'

Her tongue felt three sizes too big. She began in what seemed to her a loud voice.

'A...'

'Much louder, Stella,' Hazel demanded, 'that was nowhere *near* loud enough. Now, start again and...'

'A...'

'Better, now carry on...'

'A-N-U-S'

'Good dear, that was better. Now,' her eyes sharpened, 'what does it spell altogether, out loud please.' She smiled meanly.

Paula could hear Douglas breathing, felt his shoe kick the back of her seat as he crossed his legs and shifted his position. She glanced at Reggie, who was texting into his mobile, not even looking.

Stella swallowed and scanned the mirrors. Was anyone there? They must be by now, was Douglas there?

Hazel was grim. 'No good looking up there, Stella, that's not helping is it? Now then,' she ordered, 'say it, nice and loud please.'

It came out in a small croak. 'Anus.'

'I beg your pardon?' She bent her ear. 'One more chance then you'll be punished until you *do* say it. Now – say it!'

In the gallery, his shoe clipped the back of Paula's seat again, he was obviously agitated. She peered across at her neighbour in the gloom, a large man with a beard sitting with his legs wide apart. She felt a bit sick, it was very claustrophobic. Stella was struggling already.

She tried again.

'*Anus!!*'

Her eyes opened and she waited.

Hazel seemed satisfied this time.

'Very good, Stella, you're learning, aren't you? Now then, I want you to demonstrate to the class where it is, show them. We want to know, don't we, girls?'

They were all leaning back in their chairs, eight women, probably about her age. What was she meant to do, though? Did she mean draw it on the board?

'I'm sorry. I don't quite know what you mean by "show it"?'

They were laughing, not unkindly, but as if they thought she was playing a game. Hazel wasn't laughing.

'I mean dear, lower your knickers and display yourself so we can all see. Do you understand now? You're going to show us something.' She glanced at the mirrors. 'What is it you are going to display to us this morning Stella? Say it again. Say "I'm going to show you my"…go on dear!'

She froze. Something inside her head was telling her *for goodness sake, chill out and enjoy it*. But she couldn't. Hazel was growing impatient and was flexing the cane threateningly.

'Come here.' She pointed in front of her. 'Come here and bend over. **Now!**'

Paula heard a sharp intake of breath all around her. She covered her eyes, heard a swish, a whistle of air and then another and another, the seats around her creaking with movement. Reggie was now scribbling something down in his diary, his phone still clutched behind it. She heard the woman's harsh voice again repeating the words she was waiting to hear from Stella.

'I won't ask again, Stella, now go and do it.'

Her poise ungainly, she trotted to the middle of the room, bent over, lifted her skirt and pulled down her knickers. There was a gasp from the two rows of desks directly behind her, the lighting was good. She grabbed a buttock in each hand and pulled them apart. Her face flushed from bending over, and her bunches hanging down, she announced in a clear, loud voice:

'I'm showing you my anus, here.' letting one buttock go and pointing with her finger – 'right here, I hope you can all see!'

Hazel was as excited as her bright eyed students.

'Would you like a closer look if I hold her for you? Come up here one at a time and then you can have a better look. She looks nice and juicy to me.'

Stella let out a cry as she felt Hazel's expert finger. She couldn't straighten up. She heard the chairs scrape back and footsteps approach, then a pause. She shut her eyes again, wondering what was coming next.

'Sorrel, if you'd like to come forward and see what we have in class this morning?'

Opening one eye and struggling in Hazel's vice-like grip, she saw a pair of legs in black fishnet stockings walk towards her. She bent further down, just catching sight of the bottom half of a similar gymslip to her own, barely covering the stockings. She felt exposed, it was all so new. With a whiff of not unpleasant perfume, a pair of hands, presumably Sorrel's, held her buttocks apart then seconds later she felt a tongue and the tip of a finger.

'Misha,' it was Hazel, 'will you come up to the front to join us please?'

Sorrel moved to one side and Stella saw a second woman step towards her. She was feeling dizzy and her back ached. She struggled to straighten up against Hazel's arm.

'Sherrie,' Hazel called, 'Stella's trying to stand up. As the third of your group, could you come here and give her something to lean against?'

She tipped her head to one side. 'Do you have something to show her yourself perhaps…' adding suggestively, 'I'm sure Stella here would like to *see*.' She looked up at the mirrors. 'Our audience is looking forward to the "Show and Tell" part of our lesson this morning.'

Stepping in front of the desks, Sherrie tore at the velcro that was holding her skirt in place and slipped it off, leaving the red sparkly top. Underneath she was naked and smooth, gleaming in the bright lights.

'Thank you, Sherrie.' Hazel smiled, pleased. 'If you could now step round here in front of Stella,' she prompted, 'I'll tell her what's next.'

Sherrie positioned herself in front of Stella and stood with her legs apart, her hands on her hips.

'Stella,' Hazel released her hold slightly and pulled Stella up, in line with Sherrie. 'I'm going to tell you what to do. You simply follow my instructions, is that clear? Do you understand? Say yes if you do.'

Sorrel was seated on a stool at the right height to reach her, her face buried. Misha was using a pincer movement between finger and thumb. Stella closed her eyes. Her knees felt weak now and the lights were hot, there was no air. Immediately in front of her she caught the scent of Sherrie, involuntarily licking her lips; she had a good idea what was coming.

'Yes; yes I understand you…'

And she waited.

Paula covered her face, this was difficult to watch. She glanced across at Reggie, who appeared to have fallen asleep, slouched well down in the chair. She reached into her handbag and pulled out a flyer for the club and began fanning herself. There was a faint hum of air conditioning but it wasn't very effective.

She looked round at the speakers relaying Hazel's voice and caught sight of Douglas again in the gloom, his eyes gimlet sharp, his mouth set in a hard line. He looked cruel, she thought. How had Stella become involved with him in the first place? He had a *certain* charm. There was something distinctive about him, but not her cup of tea. She watched as Stella was instructed to put out the tip of her tongue. Hazel, with a supporting hand, tipped her forwards.

26

Rhoda, impatiently waiting in reception with Gloria, was listening for the names she'd been asked for, but so far they hadn't materialised. Gloria had denied a Paula and Reggie being on the list and she should know. On Jed's instructions she'd deleted them and she knew if pushed, it was Paula and *Peggy*.

Rhoda wanted to know; Gloria might be able to tell her.

'The women Stella's with at the moment, do you know if they're *really* lesbian or are they just club employees who do this sort of thing for the money? Do you know?'

Gloria was cursing the fact Rhoda was there at all, she couldn't take to her. Just because she was 'in' with Douglas Spencer, she thought she was better than everyone else. She doubted that he felt anything for *her*. He looked the sort who'd use a woman for his own purposes and then ditch them. Rhoda went back a long way with him though, way before she'd got involved with the club. She'd heard rumours about his first wife, a bit of hushing up. Maybe he couldn't trust her so kept her 'on board,' maybe that was what it was.

They were pouring through the door now, members and day visitors, who were paying premium rate to sit in the gallery that afternoon.

Rhoda tried again – perhaps she hadn't heard. It was very busy. She couldn't catch all the names either as Gloria was hogging the screen.

'....I said, do you know if the women are really *lesbian* or just employees?'

Gloria was desperate for a cigarette and a break.

'All of them except Hazel, Nina and Joanie work for the club and just do it for the money as regulars.' She could smell cigarette smoke now and like a Bisto kid to gravy, was drawn to it. 'Hazel and her two friends are members, hadn't Douglas told you?'

'He'd told me about Hazel, yes. I just wondered about the others. I thought I might go and take a look when it slows down a bit.'

Gloria was sarcastic. 'Yeah, like you've *really* been rushed off your feet! Hardly stopped have you?' She poked in her bag for her cigarettes and lighter. 'Why don't you take over here a while and look for Paula and *Peggy,* was it? I'm going to have a ciggie. I'll be back in about twenty minutes. *Then* you can have a look.'

Jed hurried in and stood behind the desk as the queue was mounting. No one was allowed further on the club premises until either a membership card had been shown and any additional payment made, a receipt checked on the screen, or 'day membership' paid in full. Regulations limited the number of members in any gallery at one time – there was no 'standing room'. He spoke crisply to Gloria and Rhoda.

'The schoolroom's full to capacity. Send the next receipts to the hospital-mode where there's plenty of room.' Then he turned away from the crowd and added in a hushed tone, 'Anyone with a ticket for the weekend Spectacular we've advertised, can use the private facilities at the hospital with one of the new girls today *and* be guaranteed a front seat in the gallery at the table event this afternoon, but *only* if they answered the flyer. The forty sitting at the table have gold edged tickets.'

The queue was getting restless. Rhoda was slow and unused to the new till system. Gloria interrupted.

'I *know* that already, Jed, but look, Douglas told me *he* was using the private facilities *and* sitting at the table this afternoon at the first sitting with no club pass.' She stopped for a few tickets before continuing. 'I know he's "management",' Her voice was infused with sarcasm, 'but everyone else here has to pay employee rates, or show a pass and he has nothing…thank you, sir,' She smiled obligingly, 'if you could go to the hospital-mode through to the left now please,'

She announced to the others, 'All those with the weekend flyer tickets, if you could go to the other till please?' indicating Rhoda, 'and all the rest come to me, thank you!' Returning to Jed whilst working, 'Did you okay *that* with the board? I mean,' she calculated, 'that's nearly four hundred quid for members and what does he get, a forty percent discount?'

Working efficiently now the queue had been sorted, she continued,

'He's not all *that* popular here either. It might just cause resentment. Tony and Piers both wanted passes and paid *their* money, if *they* knew Douglas had had the lot for nothing at all – *well!*' She turned her nose up, irritated, snatching the money now and stabbing at the till.

Jed placed a placatory hand on her shoulder.

'I know Glo, but let it pass this time, yeah? I'll be speakin' to him about the money sometime this weekend and sortin' the bonuses out, so don't worry. He's been with the club a long time, right from the early days really, ain't he? He's not particularly a mate of *mine* either, but I think where the Club's concerned I can trust 'im....'

'*Ha!*' Gloria scoffed. 'Well, that's all right then, *ain't it?*' she added sarcastically, 'just as long as *you* can 'cause *I'd* want to hear a fairy fart before I trusted him an inch…. thank you sir, to the left please!' Her cigarette was forgotten for the moment, her posture brooking no argument.

Jed patted her shoulder again. 'I hear what you're sayin,' Glo, I hear what you're saying. I'll sort it so don't worry. You're doin' a terrific job today, brilliant, keep it up!' He headed back to the offices before she had a chance to comment.

Rhoda looked, once Jed had disappeared. 'That was a bit cheeky, wasn't it? Considering the reason I'm here is because you slipped up by telling Douglas "Paula and Reggie" and had to change it to Paula and *Peggy*. Not that I've seen either appear on here. I suspect they're already here and this is just a waste of my time. I'm supposed to be with Stella, his posh tart!'

She smirked at the thought. 'Not that a morning in the schoolroom's going to leave her much to be stuck-up about and come this evening, well! I don't know about *"come this evening"* now! She'll have enough *come* this afternoon to last a lifetime, *he-he oh dear!'*

She chuckled at her own little joke. The crowd having dispersed, she decided to ask Gloria once more, she would try to get back to Stella as soon as possible.

'Is it all right to leave you to it now? This afternoon's going to be a big affair, I ought to go and sort her out. They spent a few bob doing the place up for it didn't they, have you seen it yet?'

'No I haven't,' replied Gloria. 'Only pictures that Jed showed me. I think they were from something cooked up by Douglas,' Curious now, she asked Rhoda, 'Do you know where the idea came from originally? What's behind it all?'

'I think it was from some fantasy she told Douglas, when he was pumping her for ideas.' Rhoda looked at her nails, sniffing her wrist for perfume. She'd sprayed one on that Douglas liked, had used to comment on. 'She thinks he loves her, I'm convinced she thinks that, but the only woman he *really* loves is Helen, but *she* always fancied this celebrity television star. Oh what was his name…?' She tapped her head in concentration, '…somebody Crifton…' Then it came to her in a flash. '*Reggie*, Reggie Crifton!'

The two women looked at each other for a moment as the same thought dawned on each of them, animosity laid aside.

'Oh my God, Rhoda!' Forgetting herself and fumbling for her packet of cigarettes, Gloria took one out, tapped it on the box and lit up, sucking hard and exhaling through her nose. 'Do you reckon he's here with a *Paula?*'

'Could be, Douglas was very particular I kept an eye open for Paula and Reggie.'

'Well, to tell you the truth, Rhoda,' an air of feminine solidarity prevailing, 'Jed asked if I'd delete Paula and Reggie and if you asked, say it was Paula and Peggy.'

She took another long drag, exhaling slowly from the corner of her mouth, holding the cigarette up and away from Rhoda.

'I nearly shit myself when I realised what I'd said to Douglas when he called, I mean...' She pointed at the screen with her long red fingernail, 'it was flagged brightly enough, but when he speaks to you, you lose all common sense. Something about him, I dunno...' She looked up at the ceiling before taking another puff. 'Well put it this way, if he asked me for shag, which isn't very likely, but if he *did*, I wouldn't say no. Certainly wouldn't kick him out of bed.'

She squinted down through a puff of smoke, a sly glance.

'Would *you*?'

Feeling the momentary truce was drawing to a close, Rhoda was on her guard and cagey.

'Douglas uses a lot of women, but you won't catch him using me. I've known him a long time and I can tell *you*, the one woman he's using at the moment and who hasn't got a bloody clue is Stella.'

Gloria's expression changed again, her eyes twinkling with demonic mischief. She flicked the ash into a plastic cup.

'Why don't you show her?'

Rhoda was puzzled.

'Show her what?'

Gloria took one last draw on her cigarette before stubbing it out on a metal desk-tidy.

'He's booked a private cubicle in the hospital-mode with one of the new girls,' she glanced down at a list on the desk. 'Tamsin, got her from twelve thirty to one thirty. It's private to members, but staff has got access for the safety of employees.' She opened a drawer and removed a ring of keys, removing one and passing it to Rhoda. 'Get it back to me for God's sake, but this will get you in. Go through the door marked Private next to where it says Examination Suite, up the stairs and it's the first door on your right, with a number one on it.'

She looked at her watch, 'She should just about have finished with Hazel and the girls, so you can nip her up there and still have time to get her ready for two o'clock, you know Douglas'll be busy until one thirty anyway!'

Rhoda grinned. 'Thanks, Gloria, I'll do that, if I don't see you, shall I slip it back on the ring in there again? It won't be locked, the drawer?'

'It won't, but I should be here today and tomorrow morning. I'm leaving the Sunday receipt collecting to you in the afternoon I think, so Douglas said anyway. He wants all the ones for today as well, but Jed knows about it because I told him. Off you go now or you'll miss it all!' Then she remembered something else. 'Hey! Where are you going to watch the show this afternoon, do you know yet?'

Rhoda paused. 'No I don't. I want to, where would you suggest?'

Gloria fished out another key.

'This is for the security room behind the cloakroom here. It's not used in the afternoon. You can watch it on the monitor for CCTV. The camera will catch everything you want to see, make yourself at home, but get the room locked and the key back in here before Security come in this evening, don't forget!'

Grateful, Rhoda flashed a warm smile.

'Thanks Gloria, I won't, see you later!'

For the last fifteen minutes or so the women, divided into three groups of three (excluding Hazel), had been performing to a full house. Each group was positioned so wherever you were sitting in the gallery you had maximum view of one of them. Reggie, awake, with his chin resting in one hand and still slouched well down, half whispered from the corner of his mouth to Paula, who bent down to listen.

'By tomorrow mornin', she's goin' to be finished, pet, and I mean *finished!*'

They stared at the triangle that was Stella, Sorrel and Misha, now all three completely naked. Every so often either Sorrel or Misha would change ends, Stella remaining on her side, accepting either girl.

Every few minutes or so, Hazel would inspect for finesse, punishing with the cane if some action wasn't completed well enough. Stella had been beaten again at least six times in fifteen minutes. Suddenly, the chair behind Reggie tipped up. Paula turned and watched as Douglas flew up the stairs, two at a time and along the passageway at the top towards the exit. She peered at her watch; twelve twenty-five. All nine girls, with Hazel supervising and handing round remaining toys, joined together in the centre of the room.

'That was Douglas leaving,' Paula whispered, 'and I guess this must be the finale. I wonder where he's shooting off to, probably one of my girls over at the hospital.'

Reggie sat up, pulled at his tie and rolled his shoulders, stiff from slumping for the best part of an hour. The scene over, the mirrors became opaque, the house lights brightening. Everyone was leaving. He stood up and Paula followed him out. Standing outside in the corridor was Mandy, waiting for them.

'I've just seen Richard Spencer!' she giggled. 'I don't think he saw me, he was in a terrific hurry.' She kissed Paula's cheek. 'He's going over to the hospital-mode, Tamsin texted me to say she had him from twelve thirty to one thirty. What do you want to do now, we've got until two o'clock when it's the table do.'

As if on cue Reggie's phone, on silent, vibrated. He read the screen.

'It's from Jed – the three of us are to meet him at his office at one fifty, when he'll get us into the gallery for the main show.'

Paula grimaced. 'I don't know about you, but I feel pretty sick from that last performance! How about we find a pub and discuss the rest of the weekend?' She looked at the other two.

'Fine by me,' Mandy said 'I fancy a drink and a bar meal, that sounds like a good idea.'

'Reggie?' Paula asked.

'Great idea pet, aye, let's see what we can find.' He ushered the two women in front of him through to the reception. Gloria looked up from the desk, just as they breezed through. She was quick.

'Excuse me! Excuse me, are you…?'

But they had gone.

Rhoda was waiting as Stella stepped out of a shower in the changing room. She handed her a large, fluffy white towel. She looked strained and tired, Rhoda thought, her mouth was red and she was patting gingerly between her legs with the towel.

'Hurry up! I've something to show you before this afternoon's little performance if you're quick. Something I think you ought to see, dear.'

Stella felt a shiver of déjà vu, where had she heard that voice before? *She had, but where from?*

'Zena?' She stared, distrustful. '*Is* it Zena? I thought I remembered you from somewhere else.'

Rhoda gathered together Stella's wrap and sandals, anxious, but not flustered by this query.

'Well I don't know where, dear. I've been helping up here for years. Now slip these on and follow me.'

She hurried her along a maze of passages until they reached the hospital-mode. She opened the door by the Examination Suite as Gloria had said and sped up the stairs. Stella followed, unsure what this was all about. Slipping the key into the lock and turning it, Rhoda pushed open the door into the darkness. While their eyes adjusted to the gloom, Rhoda fumbled around for a light switch and a dim red light came on. In front of them was a narrow window. Still hesitant, Stella stepped across to the window and peered down.

Below was a stainless steel walled cubicle about twelve feet square. The floor was carpeted with deep purple carpet tiles. A trolley, carrying various stainless steel instruments shaped like probes of various sizes, stood within easy reach of a purple covered examination table. Stella barely noticed these things as on the table (which appeared to be firmly fixed to the floor) naked, was Douglas, with a very slim and agile blonde. Her head was buried between his thighs as she lay beneath him, both hands holding his buttocks, her long blonde hair trailing off the table. His head moving and working between her thighs, Douglas was evidently lost to the world. Rolling and lifting, he performed all the movements that Stella knew only too well. She put her hands on the window, too stunned to feel anything at first.

With one movement, he swung off the table and fiddled with the bits on the trolley, deciding which to choose. He picked up two, both looking like large shiny bullets. It was difficult to tell, but they appeared to be ridged. Covering them generously with lubricant, he inserted them as she lay with her knees up and apart. Once inserted, he twisted the ends. This seemed to have some sort of an effect, as the woman began to writhe and rub her breasts provocatively. Controlling both instruments with one hand, he put his fingers in her mouth and sucked at her nipples, nipping at them and lifting her breasts. He looked almost animal-like, his eyes wide, his expression ravenous. Yanking the instruments out, he dropped them to the floor and climbed on top of her, entering her swiftly, urgently. As they kissed, their faces locked together. Stella looked away, visibly shocked, dropping her arms to her sides. She stumbled backwards towards Rhoda.

'Why show this, Zena? Why did you want to bring me to see *this*?' she asked weakly.

Rhoda fixed her with a cold, unblinking stare, her lips a thin line, her face an unearthly red in the dim light.

'I don't think you've ever been hurt by a man, Stella, not really hurt, have you, but Douglas will do it for you. He's going to be your downfall. He wants you for sex, Stella, that's all. Sex and profit but you don't see it do you, because you think he loves you. He'll hurt you, Stella, really screw you up and then dump you when you're burnt out because he's cruel like that.'

She saw the blank expression of disbelief on Stella's pale face, in the light of so much evidence. She shook her head and laughed, a loud hollow sound, hands on her hips.

'I've been around you see, I've been with men like him,' jerking her head towards the window, 'I've offered men like him sex over and over and been hurt more than you'll ever know. I'm happy now on my own, but you're too soft and star-struck by all his charm and the size of his cock.'

That word did it. Stella winced and keeled backwards as if she'd been slapped.

Rhoda continued. 'Oh, I've been there, seen that dear, not bad, is it?' she added spitefully, 'It usually goes with the man and he's tall. Didn't he tell you that? Oh come on, don't look so shocked, it's like I said, you've probably been around, but never been hurt. Well,' she ushered Stella nearer, looping an arm round her waist, as she stood, waif-like. 'Let's just say I've taught you something, shall we? You live and learn, Stella. If you get involved in all these sorts of games, with men like him, you need to be savvy and I thought you needed a lesson. I'm doing you a favour. You don't have to believe me but the evidence is there to see, isn't it?'

She tipped Stella's face up, with a finger under her chin. Her eyes were watery, her expression drawn and vacant.

'Do you want another look? He's booked her for an hour. He enjoys sex, Stella, didn't you know? You can stay and watch if you want to. Or we can go and find a bite to eat and get ready for this afternoon, your dressing gown's all ready for you, it's back to work at two o'clock.'

Stella fought the overwhelming dizziness – she could feel herself going but she wasn't going to faint. Not in front of Zena, not in front of anyone. This was a nasty shock, but she could handle it. Douglas needed sex but he also needed *her*, didn't he?

It was why he'd brought her here for this weekend, more than Zena or anyone else, he needed *her*. *As long as I can keep that thought and hold on to it,* she thought, *I'll cope.*

'Okay then,' she said, more nonchalantly than she felt, 'no, I don't need to see any more, let's find something to eat and get ready.' She pulled the wrap more tightly around her and grinned. 'I can do it, twenty men, no problem!' *Hold on to that thought. I must hold on to that thought: he needs me, more than anyone – he needs **me**.*

27

Clive walked briskly down the street towards 'Nothing to Wear'. He'd heard nothing since Stella had cancelled his call late on Friday evening and he was worried. He pushed open the door to the shop. Cindy was behind the counter and he marched up to it.

'Have you heard anything from Stella?' He was trying to hide the anxiety in his voice, but his concern was obvious.

Cindy called through to the back room for assistance at the till and took him to one side.

'All I've had, Clive, was a text this morning that she was okay, was going to be busy this afternoon and coming home tomorrow some time and looking forward to it. That's all, nothing else, not even a quick call.'

Clive scrutinised her face.

'So what am I supposed to make of that?' he shrugged, 'Looking forward to being *busy*, whatever that means,' he sneered, 'or looking forward to coming *home*? I called her quite late last night and her phone was on but she just went to answer phone.'

'Did you leave a message?'

'No I didn't, I was annoyed but now I'm a bit worried as I can't get through at all. Cindy?'

She'd been dreading this coming. Stella was her friend but she'd warned her. She couldn't bring herself to look at Clive.

'Cindy, do you know something that Stella hasn't told me? Is she in any trouble?' He took her arm, very agitated, '*Danger* even? Please *tell* me if you know something,' he pleaded, conscious of the curious look from the young girl at the till. Releasing her arm, he coughed, controlling himself, 'Please tell me.'

A customer was at the counter now, occupying the assistant. Cindy looked at him.

'I'll level with you, Clive, I do know *something.*'

'I *knew it,* right.' He folded his arms angrily and placed his feet apart, rocking on them. Cindy touched his hand, soothing him and looked at the assistant who was once more idle, taking this all in.

'Can you carry on here for a while, Pat?' She ignored the downturned mouth and sulky expression. 'We're not exactly rushed off our feet are we? Give me a shout if you need me, I'll be through the back.'

She motioned Clive to follow her through to the back yard and into an office where she closed the door. She could feel Clive nearly bursting with aggravation. She turned to him.

'Please sit there and simmer down, Clive, I'm sure she's perfectly fine – '

Clive was having none of it.

'So why can't you look me in the eye and tell me what she's up to, because I want to know.' He kicked at a wicker-work basket full of trimmings and various accessories. 'I knew she was up to some sort of mischief or *worse.* If he so much as *touches* her I'll – '

'*Clive*! Please, just simmer down a minute and get a grip. She's an adult woman and in all fairness, you *are* in a longstanding relationship with Martha. Douglas,' She raised a hand to continue before Clive could interrupt, 'much as I don't like the *sound* of him –'

'Have you *met him?* He's a complete bastard – '

'CLIVE, *please*, this is getting us nowhere. Either you let me speak to you reasonably or not at all.' Hoping to God Stella was safe herself, she cursed her silently for placing her in this invidious position in the first place. She hated seeing the hurt in his eyes.

'All right, all right.' He lifted both hands in surrender. 'I'll be reasonable, okay? *Reasonable*, but it'd better be good. I want to know everything she told you about this little trip to London. She hasn't got a single room for starters, I found that out – '

'What did you say?' She was alarmed. 'Did you call the hotel then?'

She was apprehensive now; how far was he likely to go? Not only that, but it would have annoyed *her* in the same situation, being checked up on: an infringement of privacy really. Oh bloody hell, what a mess!

'I asked if a Miss Stella Maitland was staying with them and they declined to comment saying it was against hotel policy so that proves it, doesn't it?'

Cindy was mystified.

'Sorry, proves *what* exactly, that – '

'That she's *sleeping* with him, it's obvious!'

He flung his hand up then saw her expression and resumed an exaggerated relaxed stance, slouched with his knees apart and arms folded, mouth firmly shut, waiting.

'Clive, all I know, *is* that Stella and her...*friend*, Douglas, have gone up to London for the weekend in order for him to meet a few ex-colleagues and he thought she might like to accompany him.' *See how that goes down*.

'What *kind* of ex-colleagues might these be then? Do you know? Did she say? I don't even know what he did.'

Cindy decided this wasn't the right time to say he was a retired gynaecologist to the rich and famous; it smacked too much of scandal somehow.

'She didn't say who they were except one of them was a woman. Zena, I believe.'

'Oh whoop-de-do we have a woman! Yes, I think she *did* mention that to me! Well that makes everything hunky-dory then, doesn't it, and is there anymore?'

'Not really. I'm sure, knowing Stella, she'll be doing some shopping, occupying herself while he's in meetings possibly. Or sightseeing with Zena, you know, along the Thames or something, on a boat trip...' He narrowed his eyes, so she eyeballed him innocently, hating herself. 'And that's really all I know, Clive, quite honestly and anyway,' she said more brightly, 'she'll be home tomorrow, so I wouldn't worry. Honestly, you'll only wind yourself up and it's only a weekend for heaven's sake, not like she's decamped for a month's cruise to the Far East, is it?'

For the first time since he'd set foot in the shop, he now felt slightly ridiculous. Cindy was Stella's best friend and if she'd told anybody it would be her. They would probably laugh about this when they met up again, laugh at *him*. Well, he thought bitterly, *join the club*, everyone else does. He would leave and retire with what little dignity he could muster. This was obviously a stock room of sorts. He glanced up at the shelves and caught sight of a bottle of perfume he thought he recognised. He stood up and fetched it down it was *Halston*, by Halston, their favourite.

'Stella likes this one!' He looked at Cindy. 'How much is it?'

'Oh, stick it in your pocket, Clive, I'm sure she'll love it and be thrilled to see you too. Come on you silly chump! You'll have Pat spreading gossip all over the town! Hang on a minute.' She fetched a key. 'You can go out the back way.' She unlocked the back gate.

'In disgrace you mean?'

'Nah, I think she's lucky to have you caring for her, really, Clive.'

He smiled at her hopefully and it tore her heart.

'Do you think so?'

'Absolutely, off you go!'

She locked the gate behind him and felt sick. She would tell Stella what she thought tomorrow if she had a chance, certainly as soon as she could. It was time she grew up and got her priorities right. Sometimes boring is safest – Clive was in a relationship, which should satisfy that part of her that hankered after unobtainable men; he was possibly boring, perhaps not ideal, but he loved her very much and in this life, two out of three ain't bad.

28

Jed was nervous, very nervous. He headed for the cloakrooms, tucked his shirt in his trousers and rolled his shoulders. There were some very smart suits in there this afternoon as had been requested. Douglas, fresh from a shower and changed, had informed him that his was the Savoy Tailors Guild and he'd looked very impressive. He'd only just finished with Tamsin according to the computer, where *did* he get the energy from? He must be knocking on towards his late sixties, yet looked fitter than *he* did! No spare tyre, looking down at his own expanding waistline.

The other men were a pretty elite bunch too, almost an officer's Mess. He'd vetted all the names for any gentlemen of the press who'd have had an absolute field day today and trusted Gloria with the list of gold edged tickets. She could be a trial at times but knew which side her bread was buttered…he hoped. *Still,* indulging in this sort of thing and being in a position of high public profile, you're sticking your head above the parapet and sooner or later your number will be up – for all to see. Nothing is one hundred percent safe, especially not in this game, but the Club had a good reputation and a trusting, well-heeled clientele. He hoped Stella would be up to the task: today, definitely, but tomorrow…he would check to make sure the substitute was arranged.

His watch was coming up for ten to two. He nipped back to his office where Reggie, Paula and Mandy were waiting.

'Hi guys! Mandy love, I'm sorry, but now Douglas is here, can you get over to the hospital-mode and help there this afternoon? We're really booked up and they could do with you now. I could only get two seats for Reggie and Paula.'

He flicked a switch on his desk and a television screen flickered into life. 'I'm watching it on CCTV myself.' They all peered at the screen, the image a bit grainy, but identifiable as a board room par excellence with a huge board table surrounded by sombre suited men, some puffing on cigars.

'That's Douglas there, as you see.' He indicated the head of the table and then looked at the clock on the wall.

'It's time to go, guys.'

He went to the door, opening it.

'…After you, Paula, Reg.'

Despite endless applications of anti-perspirant, Stella was sweltering now, sitting naked in front of a lighted mirror, accepting the final attentions of a hairdresser and make-up assistant. Her confidence was growing. She looked fabulous, all blemishes masked and the colouring was perfection, her lips darkly tinted with long life gloss, her eyes smoky and seductive. She looked amazing. *If Clive could see me now…*she lurched forward suddenly, jogging the make-up girl's last minute efforts and apologised.

The hairdresser had finished some painful teasing and was wielding a massive can of lacquer.

'Shut your eyes, love!' She sprayed for about twelve seconds.

'Here you are, now pop this on. It's nearly two o'clock.'

Carefully, trying not to get make-up on it, she slipped her arms in the sleeves. It felt so smooth and luxurious.

'Don't worry if you're hot, love, there's air conditioning in there. Has to be, they're all dressed up in suits and it's baking outside. If anything you'll be chilly.' She smiled cheerily.

'And don't look so worried, darlin'! You look great, go and enjoy yourself!' She held open the dressing room door. 'That's the door there,'

From behind it there came the soft murmur of voices; low, masculine and an occasional burst of raucous laughter.

Stella held her breath, counting to ten and then firmly opened it. The murmuring stopped. Twenty males turned towards her, eager and anticipating, their faces blurred. She swayed a moment and gasped. At the head of the table and facing her directly, was Douglas: *how was he there?* Wasn't he still at the hospital-mode? Well apparently not. She hadn't ever seen the suit he was in. It was intimidating.

'And here we are gentlemen.' His cufflinks glinted in the light of the chandelier, his shirt a rich ivory colour. 'After our meeting I think it's only right we should receive some entertainment.'

He looked up at her, his expression misleadingly congenial,

'I believe you're here to entertain us? You look exquisite and tiny enough for this table, so why don't you step up on the stool and get up here where we can see you? Gentlemen, perhaps you could assist her at that end?'

Two men moved their seats and made way for her. She saw a small, pale blue velvet footstool and climbed on to it. Taking an arm each, they helped her up to the polished mahogany table top. She felt the one on her left pat her bottom.

'Nice arse there my dear,' he drawled through teeth clenched round a fat cigar, 'shall look forward to a bit of that!'

Standing barefoot on the table, she was hot from the chandelier inches above her. Totally lost and unsure what to do next, she looked down towards Douglas for guidance.

'Well, that's a gorgeous bit of lingerie you're displaying, but I think we're all waiting to see what's underneath it!' he suggested, his face sterner.

The burble of approving conversation ceased or was drowned out beneath the thumping and tapping of fists, or large black and gold fountain pens, growing louder and louder in her ears. Then the cries began.

'OFF! OFF! OFF! OFF!'

She looked down at the sea of faces below her, their mouths opening and shutting as they shouted, at the blur of white shirts and striped ties. Large, beefy fists were beating faster and faster, as she reached for the fastening of the gown and began to undo it. Undone, she held the edges of it, her groin and under her arms prickling, the noise of twenty excited men reaching a crescendo.

She let it fall, her face pale in the bright lights. Suddenly, loud and insistent, was the sharp knocking sound of wood on wood rising above the din of the shouting, petering out as attention was won. Douglas lay down the gavel and addressed the meeting once more.

'Gentlemen please, if I could beg your forbearance again for a moment?' He acknowledged the heated audience. 'We're very lucky today to have Stella who, I'm sure, will know each one of us intimately before the time's out this afternoon.' He grinned round roguishly and cleared his throat. 'It is indeed her fantasy, to present herself to each of you,' he continued, 'above the table at first, to enable you to get to know her. Please,' he lifted his hand, 'be my guest. Feel free to investigate her everywhere. Her hair, her certainly *far* from unattractive breasts, her buttocks her...' His eyes were glued now to her face, his brow creased. 'Her, oh what's the word, her...?' He waited.

'Tell them Stella,' he growled, 'that space between your buttocks, what do we call it? Tell me!'

She was defiant.

'You mean my arsehole?'

He went pale with anger.

'No, you *know* it isn't. That's not what we call it, is it?'

The man to his right interrupted, fed up.

'Yes it is, just get on with it, Spencer, we're waiting here, there's a good chap!'

Sniggers at this were audible from the far end. Stella grinned impishly, as Douglas's eyes glinted dangerously and his lips narrowed.

'Very well.' his voice low. 'Use her then, gentlemen, however you see fit, whatever you wish to do.'

Then he addressed her once more, 'Kneel down, Stella, and begin.'

Almost jauntily, she knelt down, shutting her eyes as a sea of hands stretched towards her, grabbing her, fondling and squeezing her, but nothing from behind. Where Douglas was sitting....

Endlessly it continued, fingers in her mouth, through her hair, tugging at her or stroking her, feeling her as she stretched out to full length, with her arms out in front. She rolled over on to her left side and met the gaze of Bill Johnson head on.

'Well, Stella, we meet in the strangest of places now, don't we? A pretty wee girl you are! So will you be giving me a kiss now, or shall your friend Clive be finding out what you get up to on your trips away? Assuming of course you haven't already told him!'

His face loomed closer and his lips opened wide. His tongue was soft and eel like in its slipperiness, it burrowed into every corner of her mouth. She felt fingers pinching her nipples but didn't know if they were his or not. She was being filled by fingers or tongues everywhere until she felt she could hardly breathe. Then the same voice which had interrupted Douglas.

'Time you were attending to this end of the table again, m'dear, come along, we haven't got all day waiting for your Mother Brown.'

This brought forth a roar of laughter and loud chanting cries, *'Under the table you must go!'*

She tried to turn but skidded on the polish, her ankles held firmly by the man with the fat cigar, who dragged her towards him.

'Not so fast, young lady!'

His hands were pinching lumps of buttock, bruising her; his stubby fingers prising her sore skin. She looked straight ahead, catching sight of Douglas, who sat very still, his eyes dark. He was leaning back in his chair surveying her, still unsmiling.

She lunged forwards, away from the painful probing, past the Colonel again, towards Douglas.

'Kiss me!' he said, pulling her face with both hands. He sucked her tongue until he could taste the blood where her small tendon had torn. Then he pushed her away.

The man who'd interrupted him was carefully licking his finger, his eyes bright. She closed hers quickly. Then felt a tight grip on her thin strip of pubic hair and was pulled away with a sharp yank. She heard Douglas's voice, deep below the noise.

'I haven't finished with you yet, next time you won't be so lucky. *Rose!*'

Her eyes watered with the pain as he let go and smiled a charming, warm smile.

'Well, gentlemen, are we ready for the ministrations of Madam Brown *under* the table now?' He gave her a prompting nod.

Stella turned to face the company again. Most of them had eased their chairs back in anticipation. The temperature rose and there was an odour in the air; the heavy, sickly smell of cigars and something else.

'*Under the table you must go e-i-e-i-e-i-o! If we catch you bending...*' they chanted, banging the table with their fists.

The man with the cigar yelled, 'Stool's this end, sweetie! Me first now! Get your north and south down here quick.'

Stella walked to the end of the table amid shouts and cheers. Her stomach churned as she carefully climbed down and squatted under its heavy, solid weight. It was dim and difficult to see. Twenty pairs of legs and barely any headroom. Her shoulders were suddenly tight in the grip of the man with the cigar. His penis was erect and smelled of stale sweat. She moved from left to right down the table, until her eyes stung and her hair was sticky and matted. The men above exchanged blue jokes as she worked, clinked ice into their glasses, popped the corks of their bottles of champagne.

She ran her tongue over her lips and continued to wait. Douglas, scraping his chair back, leant down towards her and beckoned, his eyes shining, a lock of hair falling forward. She crawled towards him and he grabbed her hair, coiling it around his fingers as he lowered his fly with his other hand. He wasn't wearing any underpants, she noticed absently.

'Open wide darling, don't be a naughty Rose, come along, last dose now, then you're all done, aren't you?'

She thought she was going to choke. Then his fingers were pinching her nose.

'Swallow now, Rose!' he whispered, *'Swallow it down, it's good for you! Good girl, that's very good, Jed will be so pleased at your performance today. I think everyone here's enjoyed it. I know I have – now!'*

She couldn't move. He was continuing.

'I think best stay where you are until we've all gone, then you can clean yourself up a bit and have a rest before dinner tonight. Seven thirty as usual. I'll see you later.'

He released her and she sat on the polished floor, waiting for the men to go and the place to be still, before venturing out. But she'd done it. And well; everyone seemed to be laughing and joking from what she could tell. She watched as the last man left the room. Then she felt tears falling – *it was my choice,* she thought. *I've got no comeback, but I'm finished with being Rose or anyone else. I want him to love me for being me now and I'll tell him tonight.*

Rhoda switched off the monitor with a satisfied smile. She hadn't emerged yet and must be exhausted. With any luck she'd be too tired for dinner, giving her and Douglas an evening to themselves before he went home. By the time *Stella* went home, she'd have had enough altogether. He'll soon find another little plaything *and I will have a nice fat cheque, not to mention the possibility of a few times with him before another little tart catches his eye.*

Reggie and Paula waited until it was empty. Screens around the gallery had depicted everything. Paula was amazed at the technology; nothing was left to the imagination.

She swivelled her gaze to Reggie and wondered what he was

thinking about. His knee had been resting against hers for most of the proceedings and once or twice she thought the pressure had increased. Her arms had rested between the seats but his had stayed within the parameters, his hands loosely clasped in his lap. She waved her hand in front of his face.

'Earth to Reggie; Earth to Reggie, come in please!'

He jumped. 'Aye pet, I was miles away then. We'd better find Jed I think.' He placed his hand on her knee. 'Get tomorrow sorted out. I don't want Stella facing another day of this.' He looked at her. 'Did you see his fingers, pinchin' her nose like? What a monster; to think our Helen *lived* with that and is off to visit him on Monday!' he exclaimed.

Paula rested her fist on his hand.

'Do you trust her with him? I mean I know she's going to tell him that you're getting married, but do you think that that will end the fascination she has for him or…?'

He withdrew his hand. '*Or*…do I think she'll still call him when she thinks I don't know?'

'Well?'

He shrugged his shoulders.

'Well it's up to her, pet, really. Not a lot I can do about it and I'm not goin' to let it wind me up like. It's her life, but I think she'll be happier with me, which reminds me, I'd better give her a call this evenin'.'

He stood up. 'Cheer up pet! It might never happen, come on.' He patted her shoulder.

As she rose, more suddenly than intended, the seat crashed backwards. A pang of jealousy over Helen felt like water boiling over a saucepan. She had to keep the lid on firmly, or turn the gas down – this place was getting to her. She headed towards the exit.

Jed was waiting in his office for them, tapping on his computer, his office phone under his chin. He motioned them towards two chairs.

'I don't care who 'e is, or says 'e is, Glo, the twenty for tomorrow are all booked and that's final. If he won't accept a seat in the gallery, at half price now tell 'im, then 'e can go to the brothel in the mornin' and wherever e' wants in the afternoon for free, plus a month's free membership, tell 'im.'

He rolled his eyes at Reggie and Paula and tapped his pen on the desk, waiting. 'Great, thanks Glo, that's great. Well done, see you later!'

He replaced the phone and swung round on his chair, holding the pen between both hands.

'Well then, guys! What did you reckon to that this afternoon? Word on the grapevine is it was a big success. I haven't seen Stella, but I think my hunch is still right that she won't be up for it tomorrow afternoon, so I left it with Piers to sort out a substitute. The only problem as I see it, is swinging it past Douglas, yeah? He seems determined to flog this one – '

'I said I could help and I think that's still possible.' Reggie came in, 'Do you know for certain though, where Rhoda fits in all this? Is she gettin' a piece of the action like, where Doug is concerned?'

'Difficult to say, Reggie. I know she winds him up, I told you, didn't I? She don't always know when to keep 'er trap shut and that really sets him off, but she holds the secret as far as his first wife Valerie's concerned and I'm certain of *that*.'

Reggie was enjoying this. Getting Stella away would be easy, if he could find out about Valerie that would really be the icing on the cake. 'You don't know *that* one then Jed?'

'No I don't, but I'd love to. Rhoda won't spill on that, I've tried and tried but no go,' the internal phone rang. 'Bear with me one second, Reg…Hello? Yeah, no worries…tomorrow mornin's in the Victorian brothel…well it's in discussion now actually.' He winked at Reggie. '…that's right I know, fantastic, back to normal on Monday, Glo! Will do, see you later.' He replaced the receiver.

'That was Gloria. She's done the receipts for today to go in the safe and wanted to check that was okay or to give them to Douglas. After droppin' the clanger over you and Paula, she wanted to be sure. Made nearly enough today to *buy* a racehorse for Goodwood, let alone bet on one, if there's a "Stella's" anything running next Saturday when we go, I'll do it,' He chose a winner there all right, but I'm not so happy about tomorrow, so what are you sayin' exactly, Reg?'

'Well I'm sayin' that if I play me cards right, I'll have Stella away safe *and* find out how Valerie died, without either Rhoda or our Dougie realising a thing.' He leaned forward in his chair.

'All I need is for you to find someone else to take Stella's place at the brothel in the morning, and keep Rhoda away from it. It wasn't the main event was it? Presumably that's the table-do in the afternoon again, which you'd got sorted, like?'

'It *was* sorted, yeah, so can we swap and one of the club girls goes there in the mornin, and one of your girls there instead in the afternoon? Douglas won't be goin' as he went today.'

Reggie looked at Paula. 'What do you reckon pet, Tracy or Mandy? We need to catch the eight fifty at the very *latest*. If the worst comes to the worst Paula, Stella and I can leave on the earlier train and the others can come home later. I'll be callin' Helen to expect me tonight and we'll take Stella along too. I'll get her home in one piece.'

Paula fought another stab of jealousy. *I must keep this under control,* she thought, *if it's like this now, what'll it be like when he's married?*

Jed's phone rang again – his mobile, he pressed busy. Then the other one rang, he picked it up and covered the receiver with his hand. Reggie and Paula stood up to leave.

'Give me a buzz later on this, Reggie.' He scribbled a number down on a piece of paper and pushed it across the desk. 'Sorry, have a good evening.'

Paula took Reggie's arm uneasily as they left Jed's office.

'We don't know where Douglas is at the moment, do we, so we'd better be careful. He looked pretty angry earlier on there, didn't you think? She didn't give the right answer when he wanted it, obviously.'

They worked their way back to the door with the entry system, into Raglan Mews. Reggie looked round for Rosie's Bar, its frontage almost groaning with the weight of dripping hanging baskets displaying a profusion of colourful flowers.

He smiled cheerfully. 'Do you fancy a meal there again this evening pet, without the other girls like?'

She squeezed his arm and gave a playful grin.

'Just you and me, Reggie,' she teased, 'are you sure that's safe?'

'No, I'm not, Paula,' he winked, 'it's why I'm askin'!'

She gave a little wiggle.

'Ooh, okay,' she said quickly, 'meet you about eight?'

'Sounds about right,' he said, looking at his watch. 'I'll go back now and call Helen.' He squeezed her hand and unhooked it from his arm. 'See you here at eight o'clock then.'

Paula turned into the underground hall and fumbled in her purse for change.

'Okay Reg, see you later.' and she waved. She studied the adverts on the escalator. The men or women on the posters all seemed to be giving her knowing smiles; then she caught sight of her reflection in the carriage window as they disappeared into a tunnel and she was grinning from ear to ear.

29

Douglas caught Gloria by surprise, on her way to the safe.

'Can I take those for you?'

He indicated the green cotton bag containing money and cheques from the till.

'Ooh, Douglas, you gave me a fright! I just called Jed to say they was going into the safe. There's cheques here and everything – '

'Then *I'll* tell him Gloria,' he murmured seductively 'that you gave them to *me*. Don't worry about Jed. I'll make sure everything's all right there, so run along!'

Back at the hotel, he opened the bag and counted out its contents, then looked at the cheques. Before he left London tomorrow he'd slip along to the Piccadilly branch of the Bank, put the cash in an envelope and pay it into his new business account, then have words with the Business Manager after he got home again. He was the new chairman of the Sirens Club. The share certificates to authenticate this were held at High Holborn branch, it was all in order. He had a look at his dates for July – Saturday 31st Goodwood, a reserved seat, tea, the lot, but he'd need an escort. He chuckled softly, wickedly…he knew just the lady. He was unassailable now. It was just four thirty, he took out his mobile and called her number.

'Hello,' he said, 'what are you wearing now? *Are* you darling, how wonderful! It's a lovely evening. I'll be waiting just beyond Peter Pan. I want to be back by six thirty, but it will give us a little while. Can you be free on Saturday the thirty first? Best frock and a pretty hat? I'll tell you more about it later,' he added mysteriously, 'I'm on my way.'

Stella stood for ages in the shower at the club: shampoo, soap and gel to make sure she felt squeaky clean. Repeating and repeating. She pulled a clean towel from a rack and wrapped it round tightly, then another one for her hair, before poking in her handbag for a key to open the locker that held her clothes from first thing.

The changing area smelled of musky perfume, not unpleasant. She assumed the other girls working that day had all gone home. All the other lockers were swinging open. She'd get back to the hotel, then later, tell Douglas she'd had enough of being Rose or anyone else. She was Stella Maitland and he could love her like that or not at all.

With an almost physical thud, she worried how to relay all this to Cindy. What if he didn't love her after all? With that same certainty that told her God made little green apples, in her heart she knew the truth, but miracles happened and she couldn't accept that; not yet. She'd performed well, she knew she had. He'd forgive her deliberate obtuseness in not saying *that word* again. He'd admired her for saying what she thought, hadn't he? Tonight she'd win his love. Zena would eat alone. She'd arrange room service to deliver a meal to their room – champagne, the lot – and they could revel in one last night of passion before Helen arrived. She clanged shut the locker door. What did *she* want anyway? Well, she smiled, serenely; she'd have to get past *her* first. After tonight Douglas would be occupied elsewhere.

* * *

Rhoda shut her bedroom door, tipping the dress from its bag on to her bed. She tugged at the dangling labels and held it up against her. It had been on the rail nearest the door of a small boutique in its mid-season sale and irresistible. It was a sleeveless shift in white silk with a low scooped neckline. Around the hem was a zebra style black and white design that faded as it reached upwards.

It flattered her figure, if anything it was slightly too big, but she'd bought it and intended wearing it for dinner *a deux*. In a case in the lobby, she'd noticed a necklace and bracelet that would go with it, but she hadn't studied the price. She slipped her clothes off and jumped in the shower. She'd get ready then nip down to have another look at them.

* * *

Paula explained she was going back to have a meal with Reggie later. Tamsin and Tracy were happy to hit the West End on this beautiful warm evening and compare notes later. Mandy was more curious, though, and back in their room she demanded more information.

'Is this a hush-hush meal for two or what then, Paula? Do you think you'll go back to his hotel after, for a bit of…?' She winked and nudged her elbow. 'I know you fancy him *really*, you were grinning all over your face a moment ago. Has he hinted at all? You can tell *me*.'

Paula was straightforward. 'We're going back to Rosie's. I don't suppose there'll be any time afterwards for what you're implying.'

She smiled saucily over her shoulder while sorting through the wardrobe. '…If you'll be happy clubbing or whatever without me for an hour or two? I expect I'll be back before you, so I'll leave the door on the latch if I'm already in bed.'

She removed a summery pastel top and a pale denim skirt, spreading them out on the bed.

'But please let me grab a shower first then I'll go and sit in the gardens for a while across the road and be out of your way.'

She crossed the road from the hotel and walked through Lancaster Gate into Kensington Gardens. It was so warm. They could sit outside. She looked at the fountains for a moment and felt the cool spray before wandering down towards Peter Pan's statue. She checked her watch and calculated. There was only one change to the Bakerloo line for Piccadilly Circus, then a short stroll from there, not long.

Finding a bench by the statue, she contemplated the meal. Nothing had been said, but there was a frisson that made it exciting. She'd read any signs and respond accordingly, or should that be *appropriately?* What *was* appropriately? She watched a pair of ducks land in the canal and swim round in circles before hopping out and preening themselves.

Musing, she noticed a woman approaching the statue from the opposite direction she had taken. Appearing at first glance to be casually dressed, on closer inspection she was wearing a fortune. She was blonde and stunning. She glanced around, but seemed jumpy. Scanning again the path she'd just taken. Then in the distance, strolling her way came a man. Shading her eyes, she set off at speed towards him. Paula, idly watching, saw it was Douglas. Having caught up with each other, they continued in the direction of the bridge.

She wondered who the girl was – was it a tryst? She'd looked so glamorous, the sort of looks that once seen were never forgotten. She'd tell Reggie. She glanced at her watch again: a quarter to six. She headed for the underground. Still unresolved was the question of Reggie – go with the flow, she decided as she sat in a carriage speeding through a tunnel towards Oxford Circus, go with the flow.

* * *

'The champagne you want on ice?' Room service wanted to be sure.

'Yes please, seven forty-five to room three-four-three.'

Stella replaced the receiver: oysters, steak and salad, and strawberries with lashings of cream and lots of chilled champagne. The digital clock beside the bed glowed six forty five. She'd tell Rhoda that Douglas would be dining with *her* in their room, so *she* would be dining alone. She could smell his aftershave, *Jacomo*, in the bathroom, but there was no sign of him yet. She must have just missed him.

She called Rhoda's room, but no reply. Going to the desk, she tore a sheet from the hotel notepad and wrote a message. She tried the phone once more, but still no reply. Wrapping herself in her fluffy white hotel bathrobe, she took the message and her key and set off. She'd employ a little authority this time. As she began to slide the note under the door, it opened. She stood up quickly, but the room was empty. On the small double bed lay a beautiful dress.

Curiosity lured her further into the room. She placed the note on to the bed where it would be seen – she could try and pull someone at the bar or something, a lone male might buy her a drink. The room was similar to their own, but on a smaller scale. In a corner near the window sat a large chocolate brown leather arm chair, with a mint green cushion. The decor was cream, mint green and chocolate brown. Suddenly, she heard voices. Douglas and Rhoda were in the corridor. In a silly, blind panic, she stared wildly round the room for somewhere to hide. They were getting nearer. Swiftly she dodged behind the large leather armchair wedged in the corner, out of sight.

'You'd left your door open, which isn't very safe, did you know?' Douglas rebuked, slightly alarmed.

'I was only going to be a minute. I thought I'd pulled it to, actually. I wanted to look at the jewellery in the case downstairs, but it was Boucheron and a bit beyond me. I watched this afternoon's event on CCTV.'

She draped her arms around Douglas' neck, but he was unresponsive and wooden. Clinging more tightly, she murmured,

'I'm sure Stella's in love with you, you know.' She looked down at his shoes, they were dusty. 'Do you love *her*, Douglas?'

He put his hands on her waist, more to push her slightly away than embrace her.

'I *don't* love Stella and I've never told her that I *did*,' he said straightforwardly, 'we have sex and her company's enjoyable, but that's as far as it goes.'

She stepped back from him. Slipping a hand into his trouser pocket, absently scratching his ear with the other he continued, 'It was all her idea originally to be an escort, entirely her idea you know. I merely availed myself of her talent,' he added dryly, rocking gently on his heels. 'A talent crying out for exploitation and which,' he confessed, 'has proved highly profitable.'

'You mean as a very beneficial commodity then, in fact!' Rhoda concluded.

'Yes absolutely!' He was wide eyed with conviction, 'Very much so, yes, but returning to your question, do I feel anything more for her other than being a satisfying *lay* occasionally. Do I *love* her?' he exclaimed, 'I can assure you the answer most categorically is, no I *don't*.

'Now then,' he said, changing his tone, dismissing Stella and looking at the dress lying on the bed, 'is this for this evening? I like it. It should look very good…wait a minute, what have we here? Well, well; a note…'

He picked it up, read it and folded it in two.

'It's from Stella, for you,' he grinned. 'Apparently you're dining on your *own* this evening! I'm having dinner in our room!' His tone was one of exaggerated mock surprise.

Rhoda smiled. '*Well*,' she asked coyly, '*are* you?'

'Good heavens, certainly *not*,' he laughed, 'and if you were to put that dress on this evening,' he drawled roguishly, 'I may even be tempted to return to your room and ravish you here afterwards.'

He sat on the bed. Stella hunched down as far as she could in the corner, every word a painful wound, cutting her.

Rhoda moved the dress and sat next to him.

'Poor Stella though, now *she'll* be all alone. That's cruel, you're horrible!' He kissed her warmly and replied, tritely, 'Well I'm cruel then, there we are, a pity. So,' he stood up, 'dinner at seven thirty? Wearing that sumptuous dress?' He opened the door to leave.

'And Stella?' she repeated anxiously.

'Well,' he replied, 'you heard what the note said, I'm dining with her. Now she'll have to dine on whatever she's ordered alone!' He put his head round the door, winking before closing it. 'See you downstairs at seven thirty in the bar.'

Stella sat still, hardly daring to breathe, listening to Rhoda muttering and moving round the room before disappearing in to the bathroom, locking the door behind her.

Stella waited a few seconds, heart pounding, before carefully easing the chair forward sufficiently to squeeze out before nipping across to the door, carefully closing it behind her. She looked up and down the corridor then climbed the stairs back to their floor.

Her heart was still thumping as she slipped the card in the lock. There was no sound and cautiously she stepped in. It was empty – no sign he'd come back yet, but the wardrobe door was open. She looked in and saw the safe, which she hadn't really noticed before, possibly because his clothes had been obstructing it. She tugged. It had a powerful magnetic catch, opened with a number combination on a pad on the door. It was firmly locked. She shrugged. He must have put something in it.

She flopped on the bed, his words and their implication dulled for a moment in the relief she'd escaped undetected. She picked up the phone and dialled room service.

'Hello, room three-four-three here. I wonder if I can change the menu for this evening to a beef salad and some fresh fruit with ice cream…No, cancel the champagne, just a salad…a large white wine and soda water with ice then thank you….the same time will be fine…yes, on the room please, thank you.'

As she replaced the receiver and stared at the closed door to their room, his conversation rebounded as powerfully as a demolition ball. She slid down off the bed to the floor. Tipping her head back, she howled louder, great rasping sobs.

'No, no, no, NO…NO!'

Rolling over, she clawed at the carpet, gasping for air. Her nose running and her face wet with tears. Crawling to the bathroom, she grabbed at the container holding tissues, tearing out a handful and blowing her nose. Suddenly she heard her mobile. She went to find it.

'Cindy?'

'Hello, Stella, how are you? Are you getting ready for dinner or anything? How's it all going? Is Douglas with you now?'

Stifling the sobs, she sniffed and rubbed her eyes.

'I'm fine, I'm having dinner…' She paused and thought swiftly. 'I'm having dinner later, Douglas is downstairs at the moment, how're you?'

'I'm well,' Cindy said softly, 'but worried about *you*. I thought you were going to keep in touch this weekend,' she chided gently, 'I've hardly heard anything and Clive's very anxious.' She persisted, 'He cares so much about you Stella, and I really think he loves you very much. I hope you're not going to hurt him.'

She curled into a ball and clutched the phone. Her throat hurt.

'Cindy,' she sounded hoarse, 'Cindy, Douglas doesn't love me. I don't think he ever really did.'

Despite the obvious upset, Cindy was annoyed, annoyed with Stella and sorry for Clive.

'So,' she snapped, 'despite all the times he told you repeatedly that he *did* then, you've finally decided that he doesn't after all. Well, are you there?'

Stella swallowed and shut her eyes.

'I'm here,' she said mournfully, 'I'm sorry Cindy, I'm sorry. I made a silly mistake, didn't I?' She cried softly.

She could say that again! 'You did, yes, but never mind, we all make mistakes. I just hope he hasn't really hurt you, physically I mean. He hasn't hit you or anything like that has he?' she asked anxiously.

'No, he hasn't hit me, but I – I've been so *stupid!*' she wailed, '*so stupid!*'

'Blow your nose, Stella. Now, what time are you coming home tomorrow?' Cindy was practical.

'I'm not sure, late evening by the time I actually get in. Shall I call you when I get there?'

Cindy pondered. 'Call me as soon as you get home, yes. Have you thought about letting Cathy know? She's got Jeeves with her now, he was upsetting next door's cat so I had to pass him over. Shall I say you'll collect him on Monday morning, would that be better?'

The thought of Jeeves had her weeping again. This whole weekend had been one huge, gigantic mistake.

She walked back to the bathroom and grabbed some more tissues, dropping the soggy ones in the bin.

'That sounds great, I can't wait to see him again, I wonder how he's – '

'And what about Clive, when had you thought of telling *him* anything?' Her voice was tart. 'He told me he'd called you and you'd pressed "busy". I had him in the shop this morning, nearly blowing his top.' She sighed in irritation. 'You put me in a very difficult position there, Stella! He's not stupid, you know.'

She cringed. There was a knock on the door and a muffled voice calling. Stella went to open it. The steward carried in a magnificent beef salad with all the trimmings and a glass bowl of fresh fruit salad and ice cream, placing it on the table. She thanked him, realising she must look a mess, but he took no notice.

Cindy was calling, wondering what was going on.

'Hello, *hello?* Are you still there Stella?'

She answered distractedly, 'Yes, sorry, that was my supper – '

'Did you say *supper?*' Cindy queried, 'but I thought you said you were going down for dinner later?'

'Well I'm not now, Douglas is eating with Zena this evening and I'm having supper up here in our room. I'll explain when I see you tomorrow, or talk to you, whichever.'

Cindy wondered whatever was going on exactly. She'd find out in time.

'Well, I'll let you get on with it then, cheer up! It's not the end of the world, life's going on here just the same and the sale's doing really well,' she enthused, 'just mind what you're up to the rest of the weekend, oh and I'd give Clive a call soon if I were you, otherwise he'll be calling me tomorrow as well.'

'I will, I'll call him,' she promised, 'Thanks for having Jeeves and getting him sorted. I'm sorry about the cat, he doesn't like cats. I'll call you tomorrow, bye now!'

'Bye Stella, take care and see you soon,'

Cindy ended the call, puzzled. At this rate, she'd never meet Douglas at all. She could tell Stella was more than upset. What exactly had been going on, she wondered.

30

Paula wandered down Piccadilly as far as Fortnum and Mason's on the other side of the road. Who was it she'd seen with Douglas? She certainly hadn't looked like a club employee, although some of them probably got paid enough to afford the clothes she was wearing. He was a very busy man that was for sure, talk about safety in numbers! She ambled down the Burlington Arcade, looking in all the shop windows, down one side and back up the other.

Crossing over, she continued down the Piccadilly Arcade, avoiding stepping out to Jermyn Street at the other end and confronting the tempting display of shirts she loved. Back at the entrance she turned right and continued on towards Eros.

Reggie had called Helen, who'd told him it was pouring with rain at home, a heavy thundery shower.

'What are you doing now?' she asked brightly as he stood naked, about to take a shower.

'Headin' for the shower, pet, then I'll go and look for some supper.'

'Eating out then?' she hinted.

'Aye could be, it's a beautiful evening here,' he replied.

'Don't get up to anything I wouldn't do,' she teased, 'I'll see you tomorrow, darling.'

'Aye, see you tomorrow, have a good night, pet, lots of love.'

He ended the call and stepped into the bathroom, whistling and singing.

He reached Raglan Mews at eight o'clock, as the shadows were lengthening. Paula was waiting for him, looking radiant and excited about something.

'Evening Paula, you're lookin' bonny!'

'You too, Reggie!' she beamed, 'Guess who I saw this evening?'

He considered for a few seconds, pulling open the door to the bar.

'Nah, give up. Who did you see then, surprise me!'

'Well, Douglas....' He rolled his eyes. 'No, wait a minute.' She clutched him, excited. 'Douglas *and* a strange woman!' she ended with triumph. 'A real stunner and possibly not English either. She seemed all nervous and jumpy.'

'Aye well, reckon she *should* be meetin' him! Need 'er head testin' otherwise!' He glanced round the bar. 'Now what is it you fancy kiddo, shall we have a look?'

They sat in the small courtyard beer garden with their respective plates piled high; Reggie was in a jokey mood.

'*So,*' he tried Paula again, '*so;* who did the monkey say was drivin'? Who was turnin' the wheel man?'

Paula thought she'd misheard.

'A *Monkey?* I'm sorry; a *monkey!*' she responded, more confused than ever.

'Aye man, reet answer! The monkey was – '

Paula put down her knife and fork and held Reggie's wrist.

'I'm sorry Reg,' she conceded, 'but I'm totally lost; the monkey was what? The monkey was doing *what?*'

'Driving! While the others were playing cards and stuff, the monkey was turnin' the wheel like!'

Paula smiled, regarding him.

'You are utterly ridiculous. You know that don't you?'

'If you say so, pet, I must be. But I don't think you heard a word of what I was sayin' did you?' He groaned in mock despair. 'And that was one of me best ones!'

Paula laughed. 'Poor Reggie, I'm sorry. I was thinking about that woman I saw with Douglas. 'If you'd seen her, you'd know what I meant; she was amazing looking; *more* than amazing.' Her expression was dreamy now.

'She put every woman we've seen in the club up to now in the shade and I'm wondering,' she continued, 'where he's found a woman like that? Seriously, I'd love to know.'

He looked up from his meal. 'It's really bugged you, hasn't it?' He pushed another forkful of fried chicken in his mouth, then two golden chips, considering this question while chewing.

'I've no doubt he plays a lot of cards close to his chest, Paula. After tomorrow, when I've had a chat with Zena or Rhoda whatever her name is, I'll find out what I can and tell you.'

He looked around the courtyard, where miniature lanterns were twinkling, strung around the walls. All the tables were taken with customers eating, drinking and laughing; a cheerful, jolly atmosphere. He swung his knife over his tomato sauce topped chips, fending a hovering wasp. Another was circling his head.

'Bloody things, aren't they?' he cursed 'The only things that spoil a lovely evening eating out – PISS OFF!' he shouted and several heads turned to stare at him, curious. He glanced round. 'It's all right,' he joked, 'I was talking to me wife not the wasp!' and grinned. Several other people were also defending their meals or drinks against the pestering insects and smiled at him.

'They'll go soon, it's getting dark. Back to their nests or wherever they live. Do you want another drink, Paula, same again or something else?'

'Oh, I fancy a Jack Daniels I think, a single on the rocks, thanks.'

Paula watched him go back to the bar. Music was thumping from something inside; she could hear the base and a faint sound of singing, wafting out. A slight breeze lifted her hair. The bar was packed, but she wasn't in a hurry. Just then a latch clicked open behind her and she turned round. A woman entered, ignoring the full tables, seeking an empty one. She quickly dismissed the spare chair opposite Paula. She was the woman from Kensington Gardens; she had turned and was addressing someone out of view. 'They're all taken I think, it looks very full inside. Shall we try somewhere else, a bit more private?'

Paula was quick. 'You can come here if you like, we're only having a drink now and I can go inside if this is any good to you?'

The gate was closing; the woman disappearing. 'Thank you very much, but we'll go somewhere else. Thank you.' And she shut the gate.

Paula rushed to find Reggie, who was paying for two Jack Daniels. He put the change in his back pocket and picked up the glasses.

'Whoa, slow down, pet; what's the matter?'

'I've just *seen her*,' she hissed, 'they're out there, that woman I said about and Douglas. She came in to look for a space and then left. I'll take these,' she grabbed both the glasses, 'go and have a look. See if you can see Douglas, then you'll see *her. Quick!*' she urged.

He went to the door and looked into the mews, both ways. Then he saw Jed and called. He turned and waved.

'See you tomorrow Reg, I'll give you a buzz. Off home now, catch you later!'

Then he was gone. There was no sign of any woman, or Douglas Spencer. He went back to find Paula waiting back at their table, alert.

'Did you see her? Did you see who I meant? She had long blonde hair, very attractive.'

Reggie picked up his glass and took a gulp, crunching a lump of ice.

'I *do* wish you wouldn't do that!' she complained 'It sets my teeth on edge. Did you *see* her, well?'

'Nah, don't think so. No sign of any woman like you were sayin'.' He had another sip. 'Saw Jed though an' I think he was on his own.'

Paula was resolute. 'That was her and Douglas, I'm sure it was. Oh what a nuisance!' She sipped her drink, agitated. 'Well, I'm sure we'll see them again. You can't miss a woman like that!'

'Looks like you then, Paula!' He tipped his glass towards her.

'Reg, please don't tease me,' she said quietly, 'I know you don't mean it!'

She sipped her drink and peered up at him from below her lashes, her head on one side; her auburn hair falling in curls over one shoulder.

He drained the last drop from the glass and set it down on the table.

'An' how do you work that one out then Paula, *ye dee yersel' doon, lass.*'

'I love it when you bring your Geordie out, Reg–'

'Do ye now, 'he said, with a wicked twinkle in his eye, *'when were ye peepin'?'*

Paula was glad it was shadowy. She could feel her cheeks were hot. The ice had melted and she sipped the last drop of water then put her glass down. Avoiding his gaze she asked, deliberately ambiguously:

'What do we do now? Where do you fancy going?'

'Well, there's a question for me! *Wad ye leik, some more Geordie, lass?*' After a lager and two whiskeys, he was native and restless.

'Yes please, Reggie! The girls have gone clubbing in the West End, I said I'd leave the door on the latch for Mandy – '

He stood and rolled his cuffs back. She rose unsteadily, touching the table for support and moved round towards the gate to the street. He took her elbow outside.

'Well,' he whispered, 'it looks like we're *gannin back te me hotel then, okay?*'

Paula tipped the elbow back he was clasping and slipped her arm around his waist. With his arm around her shoulder they moved out from the mews into Brewer Street, further on to Glasshouse Street, towards the hotel.

31

Stella picked at her salad, fretting, recalling what she'd heard. One moment she believed Douglas had said what he'd said to reassure Zena in some way, he hadn't *meant* he didn't love her! The next moment that he'd meant every word. He was using her, cared nothing for her at all and never had done.

She hugged her knees, rocking to and fro. That was just too much to take on board. If it *was* the case, as she'd told Cindy, then nothing was real at all and their whole relationship was nothing but…*what?* Oh God! Just *nothing!*

She'd just have to wait until he came back then have it out, realising with a start that was impossible – how did she *know* what he'd said? He'd talked of ravishing Zena in her room if she wore that dress. The remembrance of him picking up her note and reading it made her cringe. She took a piece of lettuce and held it.

She felt hungry and sick at the same time. The dining room was out – they were down there, she couldn't face that. No, he'd come back; where was he supposed to be? When he did, she'd still tell him she loved him, and see what happened. She thought back to their dates at home. All the praise he'd given her – *no*, it wasn't over; it couldn't be. She'd done nothing wrong, quite the opposite. He should be pleased with her performance. All that talk was just a sop to Zena. He was just a flirt – a very *sexy* but dreadful flirt.

After the spritzer she had another white wine from the mini-bar. Now she was tipsy and dreamy: Douglas would have a little fun with Zena *first,* as a sexual aperitif, before returning for the main course. They understood each other, didn't they?

In bed very soon, they'd review the weekend, enjoying a last night together. She felt hot with panic: this *was* their last night!

Tomorrow they'd be home. Helen was due, keeping her even *more* at arm's length. He'd *got* to come back or it signalled the end of everything – she heard a faint noise in the passage outside the door, then a card in the lock and smiled; he couldn't resist her really! She curled provocatively, naked on the large bed.

He looked surprised. Where else was she supposed to be at this time? She had no idea. It was a quarter to ten. Perhaps it was the fact she was naked, well she'd surprise him with her stamina.

'Oh hello,' he said politely, 'I won't be long! Did you enjoy your supper?' He reached under the pillow and removed his pyjamas, watching the colour drain from her face with obvious relish.

'I-I-I thought; I – are you not *staying* Douglas? It's our last *night TOGETHER!*' Shock was making her voice shrill.

She snatched up a pillow, wishing she was dressed; feeling vulnerable and foolish. He was the sophisticated adult to whom she could never aspire, she the whining child. Everything was disintegrating – she was adrift on the bed and he was floating happily away from her towards the door. It wasn't a case either of his mistaking her drowning for waving, he *knew* she was drowning; was quite happy to watch her and wave back, holding his pyjamas in one hand and a retrieved toothbrush in the other. He slipped it, like a fountain pen, into the inside pocket of his coat and gave it a little pat, grinning.

'Where are you going?' she demanded, 'Are you sleeping with Zena? I thought you wanted *me?*'

As soon as she'd said it she cursed herself, but it was too late.

'Ah well, you see in reverse order, that's where you're wrong, isn't it, darling? I *did* want you! Am I sleeping with Zena? – If I were, it's no concern of *yours* and as to "where am I *going…*"

His hand was on the door, his eyes popping and eyebrows rising in that condescending way he had.

'I *think*, Stella or *Rose*, I get confused with all these names, that's really for me to know and whoever I'm with to find out. Have a good night, Zena will escort you to the club in the morning although I'm forgetting, you're well versed in escort work by now and if you're *not* you certainly should be, goodnight – '

'DOUGLAS! – '

'What? '

'I thought; you told me that you…' She stood up from the bed trembling and clutching the pillow, raking her memory for something positive he'd said. Then it came to her, her eyes wide in fear of his leaving.

'You said that I "*had you*" you *did;* you told me that I *had* you!'

He feigned confusion, touching his brow and frowning before glancing up again, looking straight at her.

'I'm sorry, you've lost me, when was that?'

'When I whispered that I loved you one evening,' she blurted, 'I said I loved you and wanted you and *you said* that I *had you!*'

'Aaaah! A mere technicality I think!' He laughed and continued with his lop-sided grin. 'It's the difference between loving and *wanting*. As far as *sex* was concerned you had me, yes, although looking as you do now, all runny-nosed; well really, you certainly don't do much for me *now*, but although you professed love for *me* I have never at all *at any time,* said that I loved *you*! The affair is *over*, Stella – '

'NO! You called me darling, you *knew* I loved you; you let me show I loved you. You made me feel I was special, that you really wanted to make me happy. You *did*! '

'Well of *course I did!* It was a technique and it worked, didn't it? We had sex, Stella, and that was all it was – sex, pure and simple. It was all I wanted, I seduced you although you were willing and now it's over; finished! It's time to move on I think now. I'd never trust you – far too emotional and dramatic to cope with apart from anything else –'

'But that's cruel, you're just cruel…'

'Well all right then, I'm cruel, but you have Clive for all that lovey-dovey nonsense. He called you, so *presumably* he wants you, but I must go.' He looked at his watch.

'Goodnight!'

He shut the door.

It was more effective than physical violence. Stella couldn't move or think, just breathe. Her friends: Cindy, Cathy, Jo, Lydia, Clive were swirling around her in the way a film cameraman sits on a roundabout, filming a scene – round and round and round. She shut her eyes and felt for the bed, falling on it and keeping her eyes shut, trying to halt the carousel that was her mind. She couldn't; it wouldn't stop.

All of them had warned her, hadn't they, except for Jo; Jo had said how nice she looked on the morning of the lunch. She hadn't spoken to her since; could Jo help her?

She opened her eyes and clung on to the duvet for a moment as everything continued to spin. Then she ferreted for her mobile. The small screen was too blurry and she couldn't focus sufficiently to key in the number, so scrabbling to the end of the bed, she picked up the phone and dialled 9 for an outside line. Then called Jo's number and waited.

'He-e-llo?' It was Geoff, Jo's husband. 'Hello – anyone there?'

Stella swallowed with difficulty.

'Hello Geoff, it's Stella,' she croaked, 'Is Jo there?'

He sounded apologetic. 'I'm afraid not, no. She's babysitting William. She won't be back tonight. Have you got a cold?' he asked. 'You sound terrible!'

She felt the tears begin to prick her eyes again, and shut them; she was alone now, completely.

'No, no I haven't got a cold. Don't worry. I'll speak to her another time. Thanks Geoff, 'bye!'

'Bye then Stella. Take care.' He was worried. She sounded very distressed about something. 'Shall I tell her you called? Are you sure you're okay, where are you?'

Geoff sounded so kind and concerned; Jo was lucky.

'I'm in London actually, coming home tomorrow.' She didn't

want to say any more to him. 'I'm fine really, just a bit tired perhaps. I'll call her next week it's okay really, 'bye now!'

'Well as long as you're sure.' He didn't feel very convinced; he'd call Jo on her mobile. Stella could be a bit impetuous at times, what had she got up to now? 'Have a good night, safe journey home too, 'bye.'

'Goodnight, Geoff, thanks.'

She replaced the receiver and looked around, her head splitting. She'd find her sleeping tablets that she'd brought with her; take a couple and something for her head.

Looking in her drawer, she heard the door open again. He was coming back! He strode in, took one look at her stricken face stained with tears and makeup and went to the safe in the wardrobe, opening the door. Stella watched aghast as he removed a green cotton bag and a folded brown envelope. He'd removed his tie, his collar sitting open and she could smell his aftershave still. He didn't turn towards her. Closing the safe he shut the wardrobe and walked back towards the bedroom door, then stopped. Stella, her head pounding, flew off the bed and grabbed his arm.

'Where are you *going*, Douglas? I don't understand, I thought you wanted me, I – '

Douglas was quick, unhooking her from his arm as he replied in a reasonable tone,

'I think we've just said all this, haven't we? You've a satisfying, oh, *some*thing about you and you were available, but all good things as they say!'

He looked at her face with mock alarm. 'Oh *don't* look like *that*, sweetie!' He raised a finger. 'You *started* all these games: Madam Dubois, Rose, didn't you, Mmmm? Not me! I'm off to Zena. I'll pack the rest of my things in the morning before leaving.' He went to the door and leaned against it. 'You still have work to do, don't forget! Zena will catch the train with you; see you!' He closed the door.

Stella half ran and tugged it open. '*Douglas,*' she called, '*please; p-l-e-a-s-e!* – '

He turned. 'Please what? *Fuck* you? Stella, go and have a bath and get to bed, you've got a busy day tomorrow. Go on, goodnight.'

He waved her off and swung through the fire door, letting it shut behind him.

Stella reached the bathroom just in time. She fell to her knees and heaved, feeling blindly for the flush. It was all up her nose, then her stomach pushed again and she clung to the bowl, spluttering and coughing into the gushing water....

She was walking Jeeves somewhere and the sun was shining, she could hear a little stream somewhere too. She knelt down to find his ball. The ground was so hard under her knees. She scrabbled at the ground but it was cold and hard, then she was floating down a tunnel...

She peered up at the edge of the lavatory bowl and felt the heat from the bright bulbs above the washbasins, shining down on her. Suddenly, the flood gates opened and it all came surging back. She sat up carefully and reached for some toilet tissues, blew her nose and wiped her eyes, then slowly standing, filled a glass with cold water and rinsed her mouth out. Taking a few more sips, she caught sight of her face in the huge mirror. She was ghostly pale, almost grey, with dark stains under her eyes.

She scrubbed her teeth and finished in the bathroom then walked slowly back towards the bed. She had an empty stomach, so her tablets should work quickly. Tomorrow would take care of itself, she couldn't think about tomorrow now.

32

Rhoda had taken the opportunity to nip smartly through the bathroom while Douglas had popped back upstairs a second time. Butterflies were swirling inside her. She'd hardly been able to subdue her excitement at the prospect of sharing her bed with him for the night.

She fingered the necklace that he'd bought from the case in the hotel foyer; the one she'd so admired. She gave a quick squirt of *Red Door* eau de parfum before slipping into a pale pink baby-doll nightdress that complemented her blonde hair, tossing the dark wig on to a chair, fed up with it. She was looking forward to resuming a normal existence again. A quick rap at the door signalled his return, she'd never felt so excited – it was silly really, Helen was the only woman he loved, but they still had tonight.

'Rhoda dear, you smell *wond*erful you really do, *Mmmm!*' He sniffed her neck. 'Are you going to let me in so we can close the door?'

He squeezed through the gap, pushing the door shut with his foot then sliding his hand across her breasts under the pink frilled nylon as she clung to his shoulders, nuzzling his neck frantically, desperately.

'Oh God, Douglas, I know this sounds stupid, but I want you *so much!* I just can't *wait* to feel you in me! *Everywhere* – I want you in me *everywhere!*' She curled a leg around him, clinging as hard as she could.

Douglas grinned, enjoying himself. This was much better than the snivelling, hysterical wreck upstairs. Rhoda would look after it tomorrow, she could be a loose cannon and he didn't really want that.

'Steady on, darling; just let me put this down.'

He placed the bag and envelope on the desk. She was nearly over backwards. Sliding both hands under her buttocks, he lifted her on to the bed.

She watched him as he removed his coat and began to undo his trousers. He sat in the brown leather armchair in his shirt and shorts, relaxed. One arm flung behind his head, the fingers of his other hand tapping the arm of the chair, staring absently out of the window.

'Stella's a bit of a mess, Rhoda, I'm afraid. I don't want to dampen our proceedings; she looked damp enough already when I left her just now, hysterical…'

He turned to face her, watching as she rubbed her fingers over her breasts and pinched her nipples, playing with them idly while listening to him calmly.

'She was getting too emotionally involved and I couldn't trust her,' he continued, 'so I had to put an end to it. She isn't very happy at *all*!'

Giggles, like small champagne bubbles, danced in lines up inside her; she smiled with glee.

'She hasn't learned has she, Douglas, that life's a "Cabaret"? She takes everything much too seriously; I knew she would. But she was the right girl for the job I think, don't you? I mean, she gave it to you served up on a plate from what you told me.'

She studied her perfectly manicured toenails. 'She can't go all soppy now, after playing the little whore as hard as she could. *Huh!* What does she *expect* after all? What did she think the Club *was* for starters?' She looked at him, 'A Sunday school or something?'

Her fingers were lightly walking up and down the sheet on the bed, with the casual air of a cat observing a bird. Douglas wasn't fooled.

'Stella isn't an unintelligent woman, Rhoda. You'd do well to remember it. You've been exemplary so far, but don't let our one night of sex fuddle your brain so much you slip up on the way home now, will you?'

She smiled at him but he didn't return it. She felt like a small girl trying to distract an adult from admonishing them by flirting unashamedly.

'Oh come on Douglas!' she purred, pouting her lips, *'Don't be such a grumpy-grouch! Come and give me a little kissie-kissie.'* She eased the top of her frilly nightdress to just above her hips, 'Don't you want to see what a busy girl I've been?' She inched it down further, revealing smooth, soft skin.

Suddenly, another fair haired beauty superimposed itself in Douglas's brain: the unbelievably sexy image of the woman he'd be escorting the following Saturday – a juicy fruit so exciting even he could lose control, such was the danger and thrill. The effect was immediate – an erection like reinforced steel. Pulling his shirt off, he stumbled out of his shorts towards the bed. Rhoda's eyes lit up; grabbing hold of it with a lunge, grunting and squealing with pleasure.

* * *

Awaking later, she looked drowsily at Douglas by the dim light that seeped through the curtains. He was lying on his back, eyes open, staring at the ceiling.

'Are you awake?' she whispered.

'Yes, are you?' he whispered back, peering down with a grin.

'What's in the bag and envelope I saw on the desk?' She'd seen them in the gloom getting up to go to the loo earlier and wondered what was in them.

Turning his head, he lifted his arm up and cradled her next to him, gently stroking her with his other hand.

'In the green bag,' he said, 'is all the money so far from the weekend's entertainment.' He squeezed her. 'And in the envelope…' He slid a finger and thumb between her legs, tweaking her teasingly. 'In the envelope are the means to prove me overall controller of the Sirens Club.' The certificates were safely stashed away, 'How do you fancy a spot of promotion and instead of representing members *to* the board, you sat on the board *in your own right?'*

Rhoda wondered if she was dreaming and shifted to face him. 'Say that again?'

Flicking his finger faster, he heard her breathing quicken.

'I *said* how would you like to be promoted and sit on the board in your own right, as a director?'

She wriggled, trying to manoeuvre him on top of her again.

'If you're serious, if you mean it, that I can be a director, I'd *love* it Douglas!' She kissed hungrily, rubbing her hands up and down his back. 'But when could you do that? I mean, won't you have to call a meeting first?' Then a thought struck her. 'Does Jed know?'

He lay still for a moment. 'No he doesn't, not yet. You're the first, so don't mention anything until I've seen my solicitor. I'm serious, Rhoda, not one word to anybody. I'll call a meeting soon and form a new board – '

'You're not going to sack Jed, are you?'

She could still hardly believe this was happening. It was surreal.

Thrusting slowly, contemplatively, he continued. 'I shan't sack him, no, if he decides to leave it's up to him, but it'll be rather fun to call the shots. I'm looking forward to developing the club in a new direction. I have a few ideas, a little more soundproofing for a start in the private accommodation.'

He was shoving hard and Rhoda cried out in surprise and pain, snatching her hands away and trying to move. Placing his mouth over hers to muffle any further cries and pinning her down, he continued with some force, to push.

33

Reggie got Jed on his mobile the next morning.

'Have you heard what's happening yet? I'll come over the same way and head straight for the Victorian brothel. I suppose Stella will be along with Rhoda?'

Jed felt stroppy after a silly row with Erika the night before over the coming weekend. She'd been 'off' all night, sleeping with her back to him for most of it and he was browned off. Reggie was okay, but if Douglas tried to lord it he'd be after him.

'She should be, yeah. I'll put Stella upstairs in one of the empty rooms while you talk to Rhoda, then she can go on the door and Stella comes down to you in the brothel. You can explain about taking her home.'

He ran his hand over his gelled hair, wiped it on his trousers then cursed. This was too much like hard work. The sooner they went and left him to it, the better. He hoped Reggie would become a full member – Douglas being there had cancelled out publicising this fact, but then without Douglas there'd have been no Stella, who had certainly pulled the punters…

'That's fine Jed, then what?'

'What?'

Reggie sensed Jed had a problem that morning, perhaps he'd had a bad night, unlike him. He twirled the earring around that Paula had left behind, dropping it in his pocket.

'What time's Douglas leaving?'

Jed's other phone was ringing now – the desk light was flashing.

'God knows; he still hasn't given me the money and has the lot at the moment – look Reg, the other line's going, just come over to me with the girls as yesterday, the door number's the same, see you later, I gotta go – '

'Understand, Jed; catch you later.'

He flicked the switch on his desk and picked up the phone.

'He's *what?* He can't do that. What the hell's 'e think he's doin'? A good cut of that money's mine! He said *what!* A solicitor will? Who the fuck does 'e think 'e is? *No,* Gloria, it's not *your* fault. I'm just havin' a crap day today and he's just made it worse that's all… no, don't worry.'

It was only a slight detour to save time. Reggie went along Piccadilly towards the bank and the hole in the wall then stopped short. Just ahead of him was Douglas Spencer and walking beside him was a tall, extremely slim woman with long, shiny blonde hair. He turned, pretending to browse in one of the shop windows, as they reached the bank and stopped. She turned as Douglas slipped in his card and he saw her face. She was the most beautiful woman he'd ever seen, possibly a model or a film actress. She must be the woman Paula was on about. Now he could understand why. How the hell had Douglas pulled *that* one? He certainly was one dark horse and no mistake, he'd remember that face anywhere.

A slight breeze blew a strand of hair across her face and she reached up to brush it back with a long fingered, elegant hand. He couldn't pull his eyes away, she oozed sex-appeal. The hairs stood up on his arms like metal filings on a magnet. Douglas collected his money, looked up and down the road anxiously and they kissed briefly. He squeezed her shoulders then carried on in the direction of Green Park.

She was walking towards him; he stuck his hands in his pockets and stood idly as she breezed past: *The Girl from Ipanema,* he thought, as he continued to the cash machine then headed back towards the club. Paula and the girls were waiting for him on the corner of Raglan Mews. He was too dazed to notice the looks from the others, who suspected his dreaminess was connected to Paula's late night or early morning, depending on how you chose to look at it. They entered the security number and Mandy waved her hand across his face in jest.

'Hey come on, wakey-wakey, Reggie! We'll see you later possibly, but if not, we've really enjoyed the weekend, it's been great. Thanks for asking us, Paula, it's certainly different!'

She laughed. 'I'm glad you all liked it, and just take care now, you guys; and Tamsin – '

'What?'

Paula joked, 'If Douglas Spencer calls it's your turn next, I think!'

'Oh *yuck,*' she shrieked, 'No *way,* Paula! There's just *no way!*'

'Now who's doing what this morning?' asked Tracy.

Reggie cut in. 'I've just spoken to Jed and he was in a dream. It's Stella who needs a break and I think he's puttin' her upstairs. I want to speak to Rhoda, so – '

'Let's just see what he says first, I think, Reg,' suggested Paula. 'Would you be happy to go anywhere you were needed, girls?'

They looked at each other; Tracy spoke, 'Yeah I think so wouldn't we? I think this place is great and I got some fantastic tips. That hospital-mode is brilliant.'

Paula tapped on the door of Jed's office and opened it. He was at his desk looking furious, his large fist clenched and resting on a pile of papers.

'Yeah come in!' he waved, 'Gloria's just called me, Douglas soddin' Spencer's cleared off with all the money from this weekend and not only that,' he declared angrily, 'I've heard *I'm* to get a letter from his solicitor tellin' me about some re-structurin' of personnel here now he owns over half the soddin' shares.' He slammed his fist on his desk, making it shake. 'I don't believe it. I mean, I'm only the bloody manager here and do most of the organisin', and what does he do? Ponce around with his stupid upper-class accent enjoyin' hisself and doin' sod all!' He glared round at the surprised faces, daring any of them to speak. 'I'm tellin' you, if I hear one more thing about Spencer this mornin' I'll...what?'

Reggie was staring at a photograph frame on Jed's desk, a picture of a woman. It had tipped over when he'd thumped. It was the same woman he'd just seen kissing Douglas outside the bank. He had an awful feeling Jed's day was going to get one hell of a lot worse – possibly to the point of no return.

He wouldn't say anything for a moment. 'It's nothing really...'

There was an awkward pause; he had to say *something*.

'Pretty woman there, Jed, is she from here?'

Instantly he saw Jed's face he knew she wasn't.

'No she ain't; she's not club property, you won't see her around here – she's my girlfriend, Erika.' Then he gave a derisive snort. 'At least she was before last night. We had a stupid row about this weekend comin' and then she ignored me all night, cleared off this mornin' without even speakin' to me.' He gave a wry grin. 'Just not my bloody day, is it Reg?'

Oh bloody hell, Reggie thought, *no it isn't!* 'Aye man, you get days like that sometimes, don't you just?' *But not usually all on the same day....*

Paula, ever practical, made a suggestion. She'd seen the photo and immediately recognised it. She wanted to get today's show on the road.

'How about if Tamsin and you, Mandy, go to the Victorian brothel with corsets and stuff, then Tracy you go to the hospital-mode again, yeah? You said you liked that, didn't you?'

Jed sat back and swung his chair back and forth restlessly.

'We've got the whole works at the brothel, love – sounds, smells, and lighting – all authentic Victoriana. Brass bedsteads, flowery china piss-pots; you name it, we've got it. Have fun, and thanks for comin'. Hope we see you again...unless Spencer has other ideas of course. But no, thanks for comin' and makin' it a good weekend, cheers girls!'

As they opened the door to leave, Rhoda breezed in, and on seeing Reggie and Paula she gave a little shimmy; like the cat that had swallowed the canary.

'Oh I don't think we've met, have we?' she asked, grinning at Reggie and ignoring Paula. 'I'm Rhoda, although for the purposes of this weekend I've been Zena, pleased to meet you!' She leaned forwards and touched his arm.

Paula, towering above her, folded hers.

'Have I seen you looking after Stella this weekend? Travelled up with Douglas Spencer?'

Rhoda was so exhilarated, she was in rapture.

'Yes, that's right, I did. Stella's waiting at the brothel, I just left her there. She's not too bright this morning. How she'll manage this afternoon I don't know, Douglas intended she should do another table scene, he – '

Paula interrupted.

'I'll go and fetch her shall I, Jed? Take her upstairs, yeah?'

Rhoda was assertive.

'Well I don't know about that dear, *Douglas* said –'

Jed cut her off, fed up with all this.

'But he ain't here now, is 'e? He's buggered off home and until I receive his so-called *letter*, *I'll* say what's what.' He turned to Paula. 'Thanks Paula, if you could take her up to Melissa's room on the second floor, she's off today. Here's the key.' He fished a key out from his drawer and passed it to her. 'Thanks see you later.'

Paula winked quickly at Reggie and left the room.

Jed swung his arm out. 'Take a seat Rhoda, Reg, would you like some coffee?' He went over to a filter machine in the corner of the office.

'Thanks Jed,' he replied, 'black for me and two sugars. Rhoda?'

Rhoda, next to Reggie, crossed her legs, tugged down her skirt and patted the confounded wig.

'White, please and one sugar, thank you.' Turning, she

addressed him in a superior conversational tone which he found intensely irritating.

'Did Jed say you were *Reggie,* did I hear?'

'Aye he did that; Reggie Crifton, minor celebrity more I think now!'

'I *thought* I recognised you! Well! I think Douglas *has* mentioned you once or twice…thank you Jed.' She accepted the coffee, giving it a stir and looking around imperiously for somewhere to put the spoon.

'Give it here, pet!' He took it, placing his and hers in his top pocket. 'I thought you and I could have a little chat and an early lunch maybe? Douglas has gone home now, hasn't he, so perhaps you'd like some lunch?'

Rhoda was thrilled; she was living the high life already.

'That would be lovely, yes. Douglas is very busy, he's got Helen coming tomorrow and off to Goodwood at the weekend. '

Jed shot round; it was what his row with Erika had been about. They *always* went to it every year, but this year she couldn't make it – some conference in Barcelona or something, she'd been very vague. So Douglas was going as well – *he would,* he thought angrily.

Rhoda continued airily, 'I'd hoped he'd take me, but I think it might be Helen, seeing as she's around then.'

Reggie raised an eyebrow but kept quiet; he'd seen Jed's expression and was rapidly putting two and two together. He knew for certain it wasn't Helen and unless he'd got the wrong end of the stick completely, he had a very good idea who it might be.

'I'm not a bettin' man myself,' he said, 'but I think if it's live, horseracing has lots of atmosphere, especially if your horse is leading to the winning post!' He shot his arm out straight. 'But it's a mugs game really unless you study form and know what you're doin' like, and I can't be bothered with all that.'

Jed gulped the rest of his coffee down and set the mug down on his desk determinedly.

'We *always* go, Erika and me.' He stood the frame back up on his desk. 'But this year she's on about some conference in Barcelona or somethin', I don't know. I'd bought her a new dress and hat and now she says she won't go – '

Rhoda butted in. 'Barcelona did you say? *Well*; I think *I'd* rather go to Barcelona actually – '

Seeing Jed's pained expression, Reggie took her mug.

'How about you go to the lounge here for a moment pet; I just want to have a word with Jed in private, then we'll go and find somewhere for lunch, shall we?'

He thought quickly, tying up loose ends. 'I shouldn't worry about Stella and Paula either, they'll be okay. I'll see you in about oh,' flicking his wrist for his watch, 'twenty minutes? Eleven o'clock?'

Rhoda glanced swiftly at each man, wondering what was coming. Had she said something she shouldn't? She felt so excited; it was easy to get carried away. She coughed, embarrassed. Reggie opened the door for her and she nipped out, giving him a quick smile. He felt he was wearing lead divers' boots. He didn't want to turn round but he had to. Paula had seen the photograph and he knew that she knew too…

Jed kicked off.

'Well Reggie, what do you want to tell me? I could sure do with some good news.' He laughed hollowly. 'You know, there are crap days and crap days, aren't there, and today, so far, it's been top grade crap. So come on, make my day. It can't get any worse than it already is!'

Seeing his expression, he sensed something was wrong and sat up from sprawling and twisting in his leather-recliner, alarmed

'Can it? What is it, Reg?'

Reggie reached for the photograph frame and studied the picture closely. It was a good likeness. There was no mistaking it. His mouth felt dry; he really didn't want to do this but there was no choice now, Jed would know sooner or later. He could smell

Jed's perspiration; it was the smell of fear. He looked up from the photo and caught his eye.

'Do you know something about Erika?' Jed's lips were a tight vivid line in a shiny face. 'If you know something about Erika, tell me. She's the only woman I really care about. I mean, you know,' Tongue tied now with embarrassment and unused to this sort of conversation, he didn't know what to say or how to say it. 'I mean like, I love her, Reg. I fool around maybe, but I love her and if anything happened, if she...'

He didn't know how to finish. The pit of his stomach felt like it contained two feet deep of hard core.

Reggie smiled faintly then rubbed his face with his hand and took a deep breath.

'You said Erika wasn't club property, didn't you? '

'That's right, she isn't. She's *my* property!'

He spoke quietly and carefully, 'She *might* be your property Jed, but she's someone else's as well I'm sorry to say and Paula and I have both seen it, man.'

Jed swallowed; *no* it couldn't be! *Surely to God it couldn't be... could it?*

His voice was a growl, so low it was almost inaudible.

'Please don't tell me it's that shit bastard *Spencer*.'

Reggie said nothing, he didn't need to, Jed knew. He watched anger creep across his pale features as if with an artist's brush. His eyes were small, brilliant black stones, his fist clenched like a huge ham. He let go of his foot, placing both of them on the floor.

'If he's fuckin' touched her I'll *kill him!* I *will*,' he vowed, 'I'll bloody *kill him!*'

Reggie's eyes scanned the ceiling, then flew down again, avoiding Jed's gaze.

'Man, I really didn't want to tell you, but I'd say there's a fair chance, knowing him, that's the very *least* he's done.'

He watched Jed teeter on the brink between calm and fury, settling on calm. He picked up a pile of scattered papers and straightened them, tidying everything on his desk with precision, a determined look on his face. More than determined, it was the unclouded look of a man who had, in an instant, made all the necessary decisions and was completely at peace with the world. It was too quick, though. This new mood was dangerous; Reggie waited.

'Thanks for telling me, Reg; I'll deal with it,' he said pleasantly. 'Was there anything else? I'd like to invite you to full membership, but the business is in abeyance at the moment!' He smiled a crooked smile before continuing, 'I hope we can keep in touch though? You have my mobile number, don't you?'

He paused. 'Apart from you and Paula, is there anyone else you're aware of who knows about…Erika and…?' He waved his hand in query.

'No Jed, nobody that I know of, no. Paula saw them in Kensington Gardens, I think, she –'

'When was that?' he demanded.

'Yesterday, late yesterday afternoon – '

'*Yesterday!*' he shouted, then remembered himself and resumed his calm. 'Yesterday evening we went out for a drink. I saw you at Rosie's, said I'd call you. It was after that she turned all, all…' He couldn't find the word he wanted. '*Funny*, I suppose, different. She cut herself off from me. D'ya know what I mean?' he appealed.

'Aye, I know what you mean, but no. No one else knows as far as I know man, but now what's up? What's happened?'

Jed was restless, distracted, his brain in turmoil suddenly. He yanked open a drawer and sorted through it, looking for something and then looked up.

'Do you think she's going with him to Goodwood and not Barcelona at all? I mean, where did Barcelona come from all of a sudden?' He shut the drawer. 'Look, I'll get this sorted, go and find Rhoda and have fun. She seems on heat or somethin' this morning, and take care of Stella for me; she doesn't need a wanker like Spencer either, does she? I'll catch you later, yeah?' He was dismissed.

'I'll give you a call, aye; take care Jed.'

He left and headed for the lounge area and Rhoda.

Jed opened the brochure from Goodwood, called the Members enquiry number and waited.

'Hi, Jed Zeitermann here, just a quickie, I've got tickets for this Saturday and hear Douglas Spencer's going, can you tell me, does he have a companion with him at all? I thought if he did we could all sit at the same table for lunch, can you have a look?' He waited as the line went on hold for a moment. A few seconds later they were back. 'He does? Thanks, would that be Erika?' He held his breath. '…A Ms. E. Helshonn, great, thanks very much. Pardon? Er, yes if you could which enclosure are they in then; the Gordon? Yup, seats seven and eight? Fantastic, thanks very much…We will, yeah; lookin' forward to it. Thanks, 'bye.'

Jed looked at the clock then scrolled his mobile for contacts and hoped the number was still the same. He drummed his fingers on the desk anxiously. It had rung six times, then an answer.

'Hi is that Razz?' He let out his breath, unaware he'd been holding it. 'Yeah, it's Jed. Can you meet me this lunchtime? I've a problem that needs urgent attention…yeah that's right…yeah… dead man walking…this Saturday, Goodwood; I've got all the gen…Fancy a Chinese? Just round the corner, Foo Wah Sing's good…one fifteen's great. See you there, cheers, mate.'

34

He found Rhoda waiting for him in the lounge, inspecting the wallpaper behind one of the banquettes where it was beginning to peel. She turned and smiled confidently.

'Hi Reggie, I was just looking at the state of the decoration in here. It needs a bit of refurbishing, I think.' She fluttered her eyelashes and simpered. 'Once Douglas has me on the board I'll make a few suggestions about decorating – '

Her hand shot to her mouth in real panic: *I mean it Rhoda, not one word to anybody. I'll call a meeting soon and form a new board.* What had she done? She felt her face flush and her knees went wobbly. She sat down quickly; how *stupid* could she be? She hadn't meant to say anything.

Reggie was gallant, laughing an easy laugh. He plonked himself down next to her and raised a hand to a waiter.

'Don't worry, Rhoda. What'll you have to drink?'

She smiled gratefully; he was quite charming.

'I'll have a gin and tonic please, I think.'

Once settled with their drinks, he reassured Rhoda she'd said nothing wrong. The superior manner from Jed's office had disappeared now as she quietly sipped her gin, more subdued.

'I thought we could find a little restaurant near here and go for some lunch later.' He winked. 'Relax and let the gin take over, Rhoda! There isn't a lot you can tell me about Douglas I don't already know, you know. I wound him up something wicked every time I rang Helen and I can tell *you* a secret,' he continued smoothly.

'Really? What's that then?' Rhoda waited, all agog.

'Well, you know she's goin' to *stay* there tomorrow? What you *don't* know is she's going to tell him she's marryin' me!'

He watched with enjoyment as her eyes stared in amazement.

'*Marry* you, when?' She set her drink down in surprise, feeling slightly unsteady as the room swam with her.

Reggie was vague and non-committal.

'*Oooh* this year I hope. We haven't set the date yet, but he needs to know. She's going down on Monday and looking up a few friends while she's down there and then coming back Friday I think, or maybe sooner if he doesn't like the news, which I suspect he won't, but that's too bad.'

Rhoda digested this, taking more sips from her drink and adding a little more tonic. Helen was the one woman he loved most in the world. Stella was history; that left...her hand went to the necklace round her neck that he had bought her from Boucheron. She would watch her step there for a while and maybe....

Reggie studied her as this information sank in; she didn't know the gin was a double. Hadn't noticed him signal to the waiter – it would work in a minute.

'There's one thing I *don't* know about Douglas though, that *you* might Rhoda,' he crooned softly in her ear.

Rhoda had another sip; she was enjoying this. He was very nice.

'What's that then, Reggie?'

'Well...' he began, carefully edging closer to her on the seat, 'I never heard properly what happened to Valerie, his first wife. Except I know he holds a *very* high opinion of you where that's concerned,' he said, '*very*. Do you know what happened? How did you help him? I know it was a long time ago now and you needn't tell me if you don't want to, but I'll never repeat what you say. Was it...dangerous?'

Rhoda wasn't sure what he meant. '*Dangerous?*' she repeated, confused.

'Did you have to try to rescue her *together*?'

'Oh no, not at all, it was too late for that she was already dead, but,' she looked slightly squiffy he thought.

'Well…they'd been playing games I think, that went a bit wrong. He'd had this clingfilm out and wrapped her up in it, you know.' She leaned towards him and whispered, '*naked*…but that wasn't what killed her…' She felt very dizzy now and her stomach suddenly rumbled. Perhaps she should eat a few more nuts; she grabbed a handful.

Deciding this conversation would go nicely with lunch, he tipped the last of the tonic into her glass and offered it to her.

'Finish this up and let's go and find somewhere nice to eat, then you can tell me the rest, pet, this sounds interesting.'

With the careful seriousness of inebriation, Rhoda continued.

'Oh it *is* Reggie. It's *very* interesting *indeed*. Yes, let's go for lunch, shall we? Somewhere very, very, very nice and I'll tell you *all* about it. I think actually,' She prodded his thigh to make the point, 'they were very, *very* naughty….'

Reggie helped her up and took her arm firmly, leading her towards the door. Her head was itching madly. She stopped and tapped his arm.

'Just a minute can you, I want to go to the Ladies. I need to do something.'

He watched as she tripped unsteadily into the cloakroom. She looked around hazily, no one else was there. She reached up and whipped the wig off, stuffing it into her handbag after hooking out a hairbrush and her lipstick. She teased out her blonde hair, tutting at the dark roots, applied the lipstick and tottered out again to a surprised Reggie.

'Sorry about that, I hate the bloody thing. I have to wear it for Zena and Stella you see, but it's so itchy.' She took his arm again. 'Shall we go and I'll tell you the rest, shall I?'

* * *

Paula had given Stella all the tissues she could find in Melissa's room and returned with wreaths of toilet paper from the Ladies outside.

'Here you are. Look, why don't you call Doctor Carroll and ask if he can refer you to someone for counselling? I think you need someone to talk to who can help and understand you, yeah?'

Stella was grateful to Paula. The news that she was going home with Reggie and the girls was wonderful.

'Shall I find us some sandwiches or do you want to go and get a bit of fresh air and find a snack bar or something, what do you fancy?'

She peered in the mirror and fussed with her hair; her eyes were red and she looked so tired. Paula unzipped her handbag.

'Look, here you are,' handing her a brush, 'do your hair and put some of this on.' She gave her some blusher and lip gloss. 'You'll look a whole lot better and then we'll go and find a burger, yeah?'

* * *

Douglas sipped an Americano coffee as the train eased out of Euston station. It had been a long weekend. The ground covered, the deals clinched. All it left now was to decide who to have as new directors.

Rhoda for one, he decided; *keep your enemies close*. She was a liability at times. Bill Johnson perhaps, the Colonel. An Irishman on the board would be fun and he might also bring fresh ideas, he'd said something about better facilities for those who just liked to watch privately...he wasn't quite sure how that could be incorporated, but the club was his; he was open to any sensible suggestions – then he remembered Stella. He shook open his paper with a crack and put his glasses on, staring out of the window again for a moment. She was a mere inconvenience now, she *might* cause a problem, but he doubted it. Too much mud would be left sticking to her if she did – working at a sex club in Soho. That wouldn't go down well with the good citizens of Little Denton, her reputation would be finished. He'd get home and call Helen to finalise tomorrow, then a lovely wallow.

35

Jed left the club at ten to one and wandered up towards Chinatown. It was a breezy day, not as hot as it had been. He'd been cogitating over Erika. If his plan worked, she was in for a very nasty shock at the weekend: then the boot would be on the other foot – she'd be worrying what to tell *him*. How long had this been going on he wondered? So many songs had been written about what he was pondering now and then he laughed out loud; her favourite song was 'I heard it through the Grapevine.' He would play that this evening and see what happened.

He'd reached the top of Gerrard Street and turned right into Newport Place. Razz, a five foot five, thin streak of nothing, was leaning against the bollard at the beginning of Cowland Court, smoking a small rolled up cigarette. It looked suspiciously like a spliff. He wore skinny black jeans and a zipped grubby leather biker jacket. His thinning, wispy hair was blowing around in the breeze and aviator reflective sunglasses made it impossible to tell whether he'd seen Jed approaching or not. A lift of his right hand in his direction indicated he had. Taking one last drag from the thin smoking rollup, he carefully extinguished it against the bollard and slipped it back into a pocket in his jacket.

'Jed, mate, how're you doin'?'

'Not so bad until today! Shall we go and eat? I'll tell you all about it.'

The Foo Wah Sing wasn't packed but busy enough. A smiling waiter was quick to take the orders; he smiled and nodded at Jed's companion and waited. With a cursory glance across the wide laminated card, Razz ordered king prawn chow mein and beef in black bean sauce. Jed chose chicken sweet and sour with fried rice and special bean sprouts, with a wink to the waiter, who was grinning fit to burst.

'What's with the special bean sprouts then Jed?' Razz was curious. 'Do they put something in 'em? '

'I don't ask mate,' Jed replied, 'all I know is they're the best sprouts anywhere I've had. They always look innocuous, but it's the sauce they come in, it's well…pretty good! Whatever it is, I could do with it today!'

Resting one hand on his thigh, he put his other elbow on the table. He waited while another waiter lit the dish warmers and asked if they wanted a drink. They ordered two beers. The food arrived steaming hot and drinks ice cold. Razz looked at the bean sprouts.

'Help yourself, Razz,' Jed offered, 'I'm hoping you're going to be able to help me.'

Razz removed his sunglasses, tried a few and nodded in approval. He felt in a pocket and removed a pen and a small, scruffy pad of paper.

'Okay then,' he said, testing the pen, 'so tell me exactly what you're lookin' for. I'm guessing you want a quick contract shoot job, yeah?'

Jed leaned forward over his food and kept his voice low.

'Yeah, male target, sittin' in either seat seven or eight of the Gordon Enclosure – '

'In *either* seat seven or eight?' He glanced around quickly. 'It could make a hell of a lot of difference, Jed!'

Jed screwed his face up angrily.

'His companion in the other seat is Ms. Erika Helshonn. I don't think she could be mistaken for a male!' He shovelled in a forkful of shoots, sauce dribbling down his chin and glared at Razz.

'*No*, what *your* Erika you mean?'

Jed wiped his mouth roughly with his hand. 'I do yup, *my* Erika! Least she *was* until I found out this morning. I've turned it over in my mind though and decided I'll do nothing, say nothin', seein' as she won't have him sniffin' around for long.'

He chewed some more chicken sweet and sour and had a gulp of beer before continuing, 'She's the one who'll have to do some explainin''

He shot Razz a wry grin and waved his fork. 'Told me she was goin' to Barcelona on a fuckin' conference. Load of bloody bollocks! She's goin' to Goodwood races with this guy Spencer who's not just satisfied with nickin' my woman, but who's also cleared off with all the takings for this weekend *plus*,' he spluttered angrily, 'he's bought the club with shares from four bastards who sold out to 'im and is sendin' me a soddin' letter to say so!' The table was shaking from the weight of Jed's fury.

Razz leaned forward and spoke calmly.

'Look mate, I understand and there won't be a problem. It's brilliant you know where he's sitting. Saves watching the car parks.' He looked down at his piece of paper. 'I think I've got that, just a quick check okay? Saturday thirty-first July, Goodwood racecourse in the *Gordon* Enclosure, not the Lennox? Are you sure of that?'

Jed nodded. 'Yeah, it's the Gordon all right.'

'Okay then, Gordon Enclosure, seats seven or eight, whichever is the male. I don't give any names and I leave it to the experts when to do the job. He'll judge it best, but in five days' time...' He sucked his teeth and drew a mobile phone from another pocket. 'It's gonna cost you, Jed!'

Jed drained his beer and signalled for another.

'I don't care, Razz, I just want the bloke dead, he's just a fucking pig – '

'Yeah, yeah, I understand. He's a fuckin' pig. Now look, here's a number to call to confirm arrangements. On Wednesday you put fifty grand into this account.' He indicated a row of numbers under a phone number, a sort code and account number. 'You get your bank to do a credit transfer to it and then the following Wednesday, the fourth of August, you pay the balance of another fifty grand into the same account, okay?'

Jed peered at the piece of paper. He didn't recognise the dialling code for the phone number. He took out his wallet and slipped the paper inside. Razz continued.

'Now; just hang on to that number because I won't have a record of it and after Saturday this account will be closed to me, so it's up to you after I've arranged this today, but don't worry, you can just forget about him now. It's all done.'

Jed swilled down another mouthful of ice cold beer.

'Cheers mate, I owe you one! Any time you want special service at the club, just give me a bell first, yeah, and I'll sort it for you.'

* * *

Sitting upstairs in a Prêt-a-Manger and tucking into a spicy chicken burger, Paula heard her mobile and reached for it.

'Hi Reggie, yeah, we're not far from Trafalgar Square…burgers and coke…okay…what are you doing with Rhoda or Zena, whatever her name is? Oh yeah fine, what? Are you *serious?* No wonder Helen left then…oh God…does she? I think she gave Stella a bit of a rough ride, but then what goes around. I expect he'll drop her too and anyway he'll have his hands full of someone else on Saturday, won't he, according to your text! How did he take it…I don't suppose he was, see you later yeah, at the hotel… will do…see you then, 'bye.'

Paula placed the phone back in her bag and smiled at Stella.

'Reggie's with Rhoda, only *you* know her as Zena.'

She bit a mouthful of burger, her eyes bridging the gap in conversation while she chewed. Stella waited.

'Rhoda and Douglas had it planned. She was wearing a wig all the time you saw her, her hair's blonde really. What's up, Stella?'

Stella had turned pale and was gripping the table.

'Here have some of this.' She picked up Stella's coke. 'It's okay; we're going to think positive aren't we, yeah? You don't have to see him anymore. I'm sure Clive will understand if you tell him,'

A *bit* optimistic, she thought. How do you tell someone you're sorry, but you've been working in a sex club without knowing what it involved? It was stretching it. *Maybe he'd forgive her.*

'That was Jed; I know it was,' she said aloud, 'the man at Maple's Farm was Jed.' She looked at Paula. 'It all makes sense now. So who *is* she then, apart from being Rhoda and not Zena, does he know?'

Paula finished her bun and swallowed the rest of her coke. 'Reggie knows all the gossip and I'm sure he'll tell you on the way home, we've got to get back to Bayswater from here to pick up my stuff and then go back to your hotel and off to the station.'

Stella swallowed a mouthful and ran her hand through her hair, feeling idiotic. She couldn't tell Clive or anyone. She was going mad. She'd see Doctor Carroll and get some counselling like Paula suggested. She took another mouthful but felt sick looking round at the other people in the cafe; did they know what she'd done? She felt raped, *defiled*; had loved Douglas so much, so *much*...

'Come on, sweets, let's go yeah? Look, don't look so worried it's not the end of the world and you're not a kid anymore, so don't waste tears over crap like him. You'll find someone better than that. He's just a bastard, so come on.'

* * *

Apart from some bits of junk mail and a couple of letters that were lying on the mat and the answer phone light flashing madly, there were no other signs he'd been away. Everything in the cottage looked the same; comfortingly the same. Douglas carried his case upstairs and checked the sheets on the bed in the room Helen would have. Everything was fine, there was nothing left to do except call her to check the time of her train. He went down and put the kettle on. His cleaner had left some fresh milk. In his study he unzipped his document case and pulled out the envelope containing the share certificate receipts. He'd have to get those to the bank tomorrow. There was so much to do.

He tried his messages; nothing of any great import – one from the Aston Martin garage to say it was time for his annual service and a couple from personal friends, then there was a pause as the machine skipped one that had been silent, finally one in a voice that sent a tingle down his spine.

'Hello Douglas, Erika. Just to say I have a dress and hat for Saturday. I shall be at the Services at Junction ten of the M25, as you suggested, by ten o'clock, which will leave time in case you are early. I shall be waiting by the entrance to the Little Chef. Call my mobile if you have difficulty with this. I am so looking forward to this weekend and to stay in Chichester will be much nicer than Barcelona. Jed is thinking I shall be in Barcelona and is taking me to Heathrow now, then I –' the message shut off, then came on again. 'I'm sorry for this, the tape ran out. I have a car waiting for me at Heathrow which I shall drive to meet you and leave at the Services. We mustn't forget to take the car back to Heathrow. Call my mobile, Douglas, or leave message you are home, 'bye.'

He pulled the road atlas down from the shelf in his study and checked the route: easy, except traffic would be heavy on the M25. He'd be up early in order to get there in time for the first race. He opened the brochure on his desk containing the tickets: Gordon Enclosure, seats 7 and 8; @ £32 each inc. Members Discount. He would look out his Panama hat and club tie and check his linen suit, plenty of time yet. There was Helen first. He sipped his tea, savouring it. Everything was wonderful.

* * *

Jed picked up the receiver in his office and then replaced it. He took two deep breaths and tried again, keying in 141 before the number, wondering if the call could still be traced. The ringing tone was different. It sounded muffled somehow. After a moment, several rings, it was answered by a rich, deep, cultured male voice. Jed wondered if this was the right number. He visualised a man as different from Razz as it was possible to get. It made him even more jumpy.

'Oh hi, yeah, hello, I'm calling this number.' He repeated it. 'Is this you?'

'That's correct, yes. Don't worry, everything's in hand. We're talking about Saturday now aren't we, this coming Saturday?'

'Yes, that's right. Just to say I've got all the information and I'll have the money in the account on Wednesday, by direct transfer –'

'Splendid. Did you wish to give me any special instructions at all? Was there anything you wanted to say, as now's your chance?'

'Yeah, well I want him dead for a start, but then I suppose you'll manage that.'

The line was very quiet; he was sweating hard. If anyone walked in now! He'd better be quick.

'And, well, I think maximum pain, minimum impact. Could they be dum-dum bullets perhaps?' There was no sound and Jed wondered if anyone was still there. 'Hello?' Pause.

'Don't worry; it's taken care of!' returned the voice, then the line was dead. Jed quickly redialled, he'd thought of something else. 'The number you've dialled has not been recognised, please hang up and try again…The number you've dialled has not been recognised, please hang up and try again…'

He did; still nothing – he hung up. He'd just have to wait.

* * *

'Helen? It's Douglas. Hello, just a quick call to check what time I'm meeting you tomorrow evening…right…that's splendid…oh yes thank you, very nice, very nice indeed. Look, I'll be popping back to town again on Wednesday…yes…an important meeting in the afternoon…I *shall,* yes. On ice all waiting for you. Bye now, bye.'

After a quick tidy round, Douglas turned off all the downstairs lights and climbed the stairs, walking into his bedroom on the first night of the last week of his life.

36

Stella paid the mini-cab driver, took her bags up to the front door and searched for her key. Her neighbour Jim was mowing his front lawn while his wife Donna was busy weeding. She looked up as Stella was fiddling for the key.

'Hi Stella, have you been far this weekend? It's been lovely weather apart from a storm we had the other evening.'

She sounded so *normal*, thought Stella.

'I've been up to London.' She found her key and opened the door, it all smelled clean and fresh. 'I've just got back. Yes, the weather has been warm.'

Donna was interested, curious really. She'd seen a flashy Aston Martin outside a few times recently. Stella was an attractive woman living alone and kept herself to herself often, there must be a man involved *somewhere*…

'Was it a shopping trip or did you see a show?'

She put down her trowel and walked round to Stella's driveway, arms folded and waiting.

'No nothing like that, I…' she thought, stumped, 'I stayed with some friends at a hotel.' She wished the woman would just go away. 'I suppose it was a business trip really, they own a business in the West End and I went to see it.' She stepped into the porch, perturbed to turn and see Donna ambling further up her driveway.

'Oooh, what sort of business is that then? Whereabouts in the West End do you mean? I used to work in Regent Street for an insurance company.'

Stella was looking embarrassed, shifty almost. There was something interesting going on here, she thought.

Annoyed by this inquisition, she didn't want to be rude. She turned in the porch, one hand on the front door.

'Oh it's a club, a private club.' Donna's eyes were on stalks now, her hands on her hips. 'I just went to have a look and meet some of the members. Anyway, I'm sorry, but I'm rather tired now after the trip and I have to phone my friend Cindy, so…'

That was that, thought Donna, but she'd keep her eyes open.

'Well if you want to pop over for a coffee any time, you're welcome. Come over for a chat?' She returned to finish her gardening.

'Thanks; I'll see how things go, 'bye!'

She sank down behind the closed front door, relieved to be back in her own place again, imagining how Donna would have stared if she'd allowed either Paula or Reggie to drop her back, she was obviously curious. Carting the bags up to her bedroom, tiredness hit her like a truck. She flopped on to her bed where within seconds it hit her: no more Douglas, it was finished.

The telephone rang through her howling; her pillow wet and slippery, black mascara circles on it from her eyes. She fumbled for the receiver, reaching under her pillow for a tissue to wipe her face and nose.

'Hello? *Hello?* Is anyone there?'

'Hello, it's me…'

It was Clive. It felt like a slap in the face.

'Oh hello Clive, I'm, I'm home!'

'So I hear; I couldn't get you on your mobile.'

He was breathing angrily, Martha had gone out somewhere. He didn't know where and didn't care either. He just wanted to know what had been going on.

'So when am *I* going to hear all about this little trip then? You'd told Cindy a bit more than you'd told *me!*'

Stella shut her eyes. Her head pounding with tiredness and emotion and she felt ripped to shreds on all sides.

'I, I, I'm getting Jeeves back in the morning and I need to see Doctor Carroll –'

'You will by the time I've finished with you, you bloody lying *bitch!*' he yelled, holding the receiver tightly. It was making his ear hot. 'You never went to Dreighton with *Cindy! Did you*? You went with *Douglas!* I know, because I went to town to meet Bill. I passed the shop and saw Cindy in the window. I'm not completely stupid you know.' Then he laughed in derision. 'Unless loving you *qualifies* me for being stupid, in which case, but before I realised I was standing in a bloody *queue.*' He snorted contemptuously. 'I probably *was* stupid.'

The mention of the Colonel scared Stella, would he say anything to Clive? That he'd seen her at the club – did men talk about that sort of thing? The vision of them all sitting round the table, of Bill's remark to her before he kissed her made her feel ill.

'Well! Hello? Are you still there?' Was she alone or was that bloody man with her. His anger fuelled by jealousy and anxiety. Despite this, he didn't want to lose her unless he already had…

'If that bloody man's round there with you I'll –'

He didn't know. Everything was so bloody.

'HE'S *NOT! He's not!* He was just using me, he didn't –' she was hysterical.

'*Using you?* What do you mean *using you*! Taking you out for lunch, because that's all he was doing according to *you*, wasn't it? Except there's no such thing as a free one! If he'd been *sleeping* with you, *screwing* you, that's *using* in my book, if he didn't love you. But you said you *weren't* sleeping with him, didn't you?' he shouted bitterly, 'You told me you weren't having sex with him and like an idiot I believed you –'

Martha had come back. He heard her shut the front door and go in the kitchen. He lowered his voice.

'Martha's back. I'll call you tomorrow.' He put the phone down, frustrated. He kicked the base of the bed with his heel hard and rubbed his face.

'Whatever's the matter, Clive?'

Martha had climbed soundlessly up the stairs, a look of

suspicious surprise on her face. Clive looked up and saw just the hint of a smirk appear, like an anxious actor, waiting in the wings for his cue.

'What? Oh nothing. It's nothing! ' He couldn't think what to say that would sound plausible. 'Nothing to worry about anyway –'

Martha wasn't going to give up easily.

'Well it didn't sound like nothing and why my coming back stopped you from finishing the conversation, I can't imagine. So you'll call them back tomorrow will you? Whoever it was I'm not to worry about?'

The actor had heard his cue and was playing to the gallery now, hamming it up for all he was worth with a show stopping smirk.

Clive thought: *the first line of defence is attack…*

'Well if you heard me say that, why ask? If you *must* know it's just a simple matter between me and Bill Johnson, that's all. It doesn't concern you. I'm speaking to him tomorrow.' He stood up and looked down at her. 'And where were you then this evening since…' He scanned his watch, 'since five o'clock?'

Suddenly the actor's lines had dried up and there was no prompt, leaving nothing except to ad lib.

'I'd arranged to meet Davina from Pilates –'

'Not going tomorrow then? Or is *Davina* not going? Funny evening to go out, a Sunday, when you'll be seeing her tomorrow anyway isn't it?'

Pushing past her he stomped downstairs and grabbed the paper.

'I'm going out in the garden, get a bit of fresh air!'

Martha heard the conservatory door shut with a click. At least he had fixed that. She picked up the receiver and pressed redial quickly.

Stella had just finished speaking to Cindy and as the phone rang again, she picked it up.

'Hello? *Hello?*' No answer, but the line was open, then it went dead.

She tried 1471 and listened: it was Clive's number, but Martha had just come back, hadn't she? She replaced the receiver carefully; it didn't ring again.

* * *

Helen had just finished packing her case upstairs as the door opened.

'Oh Reggie, I didn't hear you come in. Did you have a good time? Manage to find anything nice while you were up there?'

For a moment he had to think what she was talking about, before remembering he'd said he was going shopping.

'Aye well I had a good look round.' He paused and sat down on the bed, tilted his head and gave her a cheeky look. 'I also looked up Jed Zeitermann while I was there, at the club I showed you about in the paper.'

He waited to see the effect. She was bent over an open drawer from a chest of drawers with her back to him. Stiffening, she stood up, pushed her hand into the small of her back, stretched and turned to face him, her expression one of annoyance.

'Oh yes, and what did you find out then?'

Reggie met her gaze. 'I asked him what he knew about the connection between the people we'd read about in the magazine and Douglas Spencer, that's all.'

Leaning against the chest of drawers, her face straight, she looked rather tired.

'And what did he say to that? I didn't really want you to pursue that one, Reg. It's history now, Rhoda, Douglas and so on, but what did he say?'

'He said that Rhoda was still involved in the club and that Douglas visited from time to time.' He took a chance. 'He's on the board of directors actually, a significant shareholder.'

Her eyes widened in disbelief.

'A significant *shareholder*! *Douglas* is?'

Catching a sneeze, he stood and pulled a handkerchief from his pocket. 'That's what he told me, aye. I asked if he was very...' He paused as if considering his words carefully. 'Very *active* on his visits, but that sort of information was confidential and he didn't want to speak out of turn, but he hinted that there was plenty of life left in him yet, so there we are. Bit of a dark horse our Dougie, as I suspected.'

Helen said nothing and walked downstairs. He heard her emptying the dishwasher and putting things away. He felt a bit edgy, guilt making him prickly. Had Helen managed to eradicate all her emotional attachments to Douglas? Then a thought struck him, maybe she thought he'd brought her something back. Curious why he'd wanted four days up there to begin with. She didn't know about Paula either, believing he was on his own. He kicked himself: he *should* have bought her something, but he'd been so caught up with the club – and Paula, he realised guiltily, it hadn't even occurred to him.

He followed her downstairs, going to the fridge and pulling out a bottle of sparkling white wine.

'Did you fancy a drink, an early night, or both? I missed you, pet!'

Turning from what she was doing she studied him, her expression unreadable.

'Were you alone up in London, Reg?'

He swallowed nervously,

'London's a very busy place, pet! A lot of people –'

'You know what I mean!'

'Why do you ask?'

'I want to know, that's why; did you take anyone with you?'

He couldn't take the chance, the back of his neck prickled.

'Paula got on to the train later and we travelled up together, she stayed in Bayswater and I was near the Strand. We met up a couple of times like; did you know, then?'

Helen smiled and stood in front of him. Slipping her arms around his waist she rubbed his back.

'I had no idea, no, but I hoped you'd tell me the truth one way or another and you have.' She pressed her cheek against his chest and felt him breathe a sigh. 'What was that for Reggie, relief?'

He kissed the top of her head. 'Glad to be home I think. Tomorrow you're off to see him! Has he *phoned* you? Is he *meetin'* you?'

Helen peered up and grinned. 'Yes to both of those and yes, I'd like a drink – in bed I think, come on let's go.' She took his hand and picked up the bottle of wine.

He patted her bottom. 'You take that up. I'll bring a couple of glasses. Where's Buster?'

Helen started up the stairs. 'Out in the garden I think, give him a call, but don't be long. I'll be waiting for you!'

He opened the back door and whistled. Buster came charging in wagging his tail and jumping up. He played with him for a few minutes before the dog went charging round in circles and settled down with a bone.

Walking into the bedroom, she turned on the bedside lamp and something sparkling on the carpet caught her eye. She picked it up and peered at it – it was a sparkly earring, not one of hers. She heard him talking to Buster and then climbing the stairs. She sighed and waited. He was whistling tunefully as he pushed the door open, stopping abruptly as she dangled it between finger and thumb.

'This must be one of yours, Reggie. It certainly isn't one of mine!' She looked at his stricken face for what seemed like an age before breaking into a smile.

'You're incorrigible, did you know that?'

She drank in the relief in his eyes and hugged him, letting sleeping dogs lie – for now.

37

Monday 26th July

The alarm was ringing; the inside of her head felt like one of those snow shakers in a little Perspex dome. Gradually it began to settle and clarify – at eight thirty she had to call the surgery. Like a freezer burn, the pain of Douglas's words and his cruel manner stung her. In panic she realised she would probably bump into him at some stage. Her alarm, on snooze, jangled; she reached for the phone and dialled.

'You're through to Great Denton Medical Centre. Your call is moving up the queue and is important to us, please continue to hold and – good morning Great Denton Medical Centre,' Stella swallowed before replying. 'Oh good morning, I wonder if I can have an appointment with Doctor Carroll, this afternoon if I could.' She had to collect Jeeves and call Clive, she remembered.

'Three fifty, ten to four?'

'Thank you, yes that will be fine. Ten to four, thank you.' She clung on to the receiver as if it were a lifebelt.

'And your name is?'

She swallowed, feeling that as soon as she said it, this woman would know all about the weekend, 'Stella, Stella Maitland.' She waited. 'Little Denton?' *Was her tone curious?* 'Yes, that's right.' A slight pause. 'Three fifty then.' And the line went dead. Tentatively she reached for her mobile and found Clive's number, she hesitated and then pressed it – it was ringing.

Clive was in his car, having collected the paper. He saw her name and pressed answer.

'Hello, I wondered if you'd call, I want to see you. I think we've got a few things to sort out,' Glancing out of the window he saw one of his neighbours walking her dog. He slouched down in his seat and turned away. 'Martha's going into Dreighton this morning and staying for lunch. I could come round about half eleven?'

Stella thought quickly, she could collect Jeeves and be back in time for that.

'That's fine, Clive. I'll see you then. I'm going to see Doctor Carroll – hello?' He'd gone.

* * *

Douglas wiped up his breakfast things and picked up his document case containing all the necessary paperwork. He nosed the car carefully round the corner and headed for Dreighton and his solicitor, Howard Gregory, of Gregory, Marshall and Sterne Solicitors. The journey was uneventful, but everything seemed brighter, more vibrant somehow, excitement fermenting inside him like distilling homemade wine.

The offices were in an attractive Georgian building opposite the War Memorial near George Row. He took a space in front of an Estate Agent, which gave him an hour, crossed over the road and up three front steps, pushing open an imposing dark green painted door flanked by gleaming brass plates resting on sandy coloured stone.

Inside it was hushed and dim in the hall. A magnificent Georgian staircase was in front of him, rising to Howard's office situated on the first floor. Nestled in the corner stood an imposing Grandfather clock. The receptionist, an attractive strawberry blonde in a smart fawn suit and ivory silk shirt, smiled an enquiring smile, called Howard's number and invited Douglas to continue on up to his office. He breathed in her perfume, which smelled clean and fresh, inclined his head and wished her good morning, then climbed the stairs.

Howard Gregory was waiting in a formal charcoal pinstriped suit, white shirt and sober silk tie. He was heavily built with a shock of white hair and an avuncular, easy manner. He wore a gold crested signet ring on the little finger of his left hand, and a pair of tortoiseshell rimmed reading glasses. He beamed a wide smile and ushered him in, closing the door behind him; indicating a chair in front of his desk, covered in well-worn green studded leather.

Peering over the glasses, he grinned but his eyes were sharp and professional.

'Good morning, Douglas, I'm glad I could meet you, your message sounded fairly urgent the other day. So how exactly can I help you?'

Unzipping the case on his lap, Douglas removed the share certificates, placing them on the desk in front of him.

'I'd like you to send a letter to Mr. Jed Zeitermann today, first class. Informing him I intend to call an extraordinary board meeting on the twenty eighth of July; this Wednesday. I'll be announcing the new directors to the board and taking over from him in the chair.' He paused to allow this to sink in. Mr. Gregory's expression remained unchanged so he resumed. 'Jed has been company secretary and acting CEO for some years (*ever since I can remember, but all's fair…*) holding the position with the agreement of the other directors. Four have now sold their shares to me, resigned from the board, leaving me the majority shareholder. I intend to take control of the running of the business and have some names I would wish to see as new directors.'

Howard opened his mouth slightly and scratched his cheek, pondering this. He eased his chair back from his desk and crossed his legs.

'I see,' he said slowly, making a steeple with his hands and gently tapping his fingertips. 'So have you in*formed* Mr. *Zeitermann*, did you say?' He nodded. '…about this new arrangement?' Douglas was wary, on his guard. Howard smiled blandly. 'I only *ask* because

Wednesday's the day after tomorrow and normally this sort of thing would take a *little* longer.' He rubbed his nose and sat forward. 'When did you acquire the share certificates?'

Douglas's chair was sat lower than the desk, and he pushed on the arm of it and propped himself up a bit.

'They were transferred to me at a meeting in High Holborn last Friday.' Mr. Gregory looked surprised, but Douglas continued. 'I had contacted them prior to this, obviously, but it was arranged that I would be up there this weekend just gone and it was convenient to receive them then. I can assure you everything's in order and Mr. Zeitermann's aware of the impending changes – he'll be expecting the letter. I intend to invite him to remain on the board, but whether he *will* of course, is another matter.'

Howard removed his glasses and polished them with a small cloth before replacing them and running his hand through his barbered, but rebellious hair.

'Quite; well I get the picture and I'll send a letter to Mr. Zeitermann. Might I enquire as to the correct address?'

Douglas cleared his throat discreetly. 'If you could mark it for his personal attention and send it to the Sirens Club Limited, number fourteen to eighteen Raglan Mews, off Brewer Street, London, West one.' He watched for hesitancy as Howard copied down the address but couldn't detect any.

Howard put down his pen, drawing on an expression he used when dealing with a potentially sensitive issue – Douglas Spencer was a good client.

'It may seem a little intrusive, but as your solicitor and instructed by you to deal with this important matter, I wonder if I might ask as to the *nature* of the business we're talking about here, that you'll in future be Chief Executive of?' He noticed adroitly and with interest, that Douglas fought shy of his direct gaze as he replied.

'The club was established in nineteen fifty-nine as an adult licensed club, for the purposes of adult entertainment. It's quite a thriving concern now with an annual turnover of just less than ten million pounds. I have a number of new ideas and hope to see some developments and profits continuing well into the twenty-first century.'

He stared fixedly at a point above and slightly to the right of Howard's head and paused, waiting for a response. There was silence except for the sudden booming of a car radio below, which cut off abruptly as the car stopped.

Howard Gregory continued to peer over his glasses. A nerve was twitching near his left cheekbone. He scribbled some additional notes on a pad.

'.And the name of the club, the,' he glanced down, 'the Sirens club. This was chosen because?' Douglas was still evading his eye, he noticed. 'Because? It's a rather unusual name I'd have thought?'

Douglas shifted his position in the chair and stared full-on, slightly rattled. 'The letters are an abbreviation, quite clever really from a publicity and advertising point of view.'

Howard relaxed in his chair and smiled. 'You have the advantage of me there Douglas, I obviously don't get out enough, so, indulge me.' He cocked his head to one side and removed his glasses, a twinkle now in his eye.

Without demur Douglas replied, 'It stands for sexual and rather daring intimate new experiences. It's a club, a private members club and not a brothel.'

Howard dangled the arm of his reading glasses, then lightly sucked the end and surveyed Douglas with amusement.

'My dear chap, I didn't think for one moment it was, but thank you for the clarification. I shall attend to the letter right away and open a new file. If there should be anything else you need, please don't hesitate to contact me.' He leaned forward. The interview was over.

Retrieving the share certificates, Douglas filed them back in his document case, adjusted his tie and rose. Howard Gregory opened the door and extended his hand.

'Good to see you again then Douglas and I wish you good luck with your new…venture, from Wednesday!' He smiled as Douglas shook his hand then turned towards the staircase.

'Thank you Howard, good morning to you, I'll keep in touch!'

He flapped a small wave on his way down. He checked his watch, looking for any parking wardens, before crossing again to the bank on the corner. He deposited the envelope containing the certificates then walked back to the car and drove home, leaving it out ready to collect Helen later.

38

Jeeves was ecstatic to see Stella again as she picked him up and hugged him so tightly he gave a strangled swallow and tried to wriggle backwards, scrabbling back down. Cathy finished drying her washing-up and putting things away, she was brisk.

'He's been a good boy, I've packed up his bed and bits and pieces they're by the front door. So how did you get on up in London then?' Bending, she put a bowl away in a cupboard. 'Cindy said you'd called her and that you were a bit upset.' She took a cloth and rubbed the draining board down vigorously, before wringing it out and hanging it over the tap. She leaned against the sink, waiting expectantly.

Picking Jeeves up again, Stella buried her face in his hair. 'I was upset when I called her; Douglas has…' Jeeves did not want to be a shield between Stella and Cathy; he sensed all was not well and wanted all four paws on the ground. Stella released him, not sure then where to put her arms. She hugged herself and continued. 'He's *dumped* me, I suppose. I – I'm seeing Doctor Carroll this afternoon, to try and arrange some counselling.' She stared at the floor, feeling uncomfortable.

'I did try to warn you, didn't I? We all did.' Cathy rubbed her fringe back then picked at a bit of fluff on her cropped jeans. 'We told you what we thought about him but you wouldn't listen. Cindy had Clive round to the shop. When are you going to see *him*? He must be pretty fed up, Stella.'

She looked for Jeeves's lead and clipped it to him.

'He's coming round at half past eleven. Look, thanks ever so much for having Jeeves, I'm really grateful.'

Cathy followed her to the door.

'That's all right, I'm just glad you're back in one piece! I'll come round as usual next Tuesday if that's okay? Unless you want me tomorrow? Hang on I'll help you with this lot out to the car...'

Stella opened the boot and the doors and Jeeves jumped in.

'Next Tuesday's fine, thanks. I hope I'll be back at the shop then.' She turned and gave her a hug, 'Thanks for everything, Cathy, I... ' She felt choked.

'Hey, come on Stella! What are friends for?' She squeezed her shoulders, pushing her away gently. 'Go on, off you go, don't get upset, it's all over now. I'll see you next week, take care!'

She waved her off, wondering what the full story was, no doubt she'd find out.

* * *

Once home, Stella flitted from one job to another, feeling jittery, shouting at Jeeves, who raced upstairs and curled up on the landing out of the way. Opening a cupboard to reach for a coffee mug she knocked it clumsily. It fell, bounced off the worktop and smashed on the floor. The kettle boiled then the telephone rang. Standing in the kitchen she bent her head, pushing her fingers through her hair and winding it round, covering her ears until it stopped. She began to sob then stopped, grabbing a sheet of kitchen paper to blow her nose. She steadied herself against the sink, pulling herself together. This would be no good when Clive arrived, she'd got to get on with it, be adult.

The clock said ten to eleven. Upstairs, she sorted through her wardrobe and found a dress from Laura Ashley: a safe choice to wear. She studied her reflection, then reached up and fastened her hair with a gold clip. She looked drawn still, gaunt. She'd no idea what she was going to say and couldn't get her head round what the weekend had all been about: sex. She'd been used by Douglas and that woman Rhoda, whoever *she* was; had fallen for Douglas completely. Now she had to think. It was twenty five past eleven, she went to the bathroom, removing Clive's bottle of *Halston* and put some on, patted a trembling Jeeves, and then went downstairs to wait.

Clive parked round the corner, putting the key in his pocket. Anger was spurting and erupting like geysers in a hot spring. Uncontrollable bursts of fury interspersed with confusion and frustration at his situation with Martha. He strode grimly up her drive where that *man* had parked his Aston Martin. He looked up and saw her standing at the front door wearing a dress too good to be true; who was *she* trying to kid?

'Do you want a cup of coffee, Clive, I've –'

His expression stopped her. She moved out of the way as he stormed past without a word into the kitchen where he waited for her, quietly menacing.

'I don't want coffee, Stella. I want explanations – right from the beginning when you went there for lunch.'

She took a sip of steaming coffee, nervous giggles threatening to erupt at any moment.

'*Where* for lunch?' she challenged. It was the wrong question.

'Don't you play silly-beggars with *me!*' he said, speaking so quietly the giggles were stopped in their tracks. 'I want to know to the very last detail what happened when you went round for lunch to Douglas Spencer, and we'll start with your underwear.' He was glad to note the alarm in her eyes, he'd caught her off guard; she wasn't expecting that. 'If you wore any at all that is?'

Stella swallowed, deliberating; then felt more confident.

'I did actually; that mint green Agent Provocateur set. I was only going to wear the bra first then – no *wait!*' She saw his lip curl in disgust. 'I don't mean I wasn't going to wear *any* pants, I, I meant I was going to wear different pants under the skirt, but then changed my mind. I…'

She felt flustered and panicky, his expression and quiet tone getting to her. Walking into the sitting room, he sat in an armchair. Stella knelt quickly, trying to diffuse the situation.

His face contorted in anger.

'Why bother to wear it all if you weren't expecting to show it all? And you *were, weren't you, Stella?*'

She tried, but her hysterical giggles were as uncontrollable as excited small children waiting for Father Christmas. Giggles would provoke him, make him violent. Her knees had gone to sleep so she shifted. Grabbing a handful of hair, he pulled roughly.

'*Get up! Get up!* Carry on, I'm waiting!' Letting go, he sat back in the chair, glaring.

'I suppose you doused yourself with perfume like you did for me?'

'I wasn't going to. Then I changed my mind. I put some there on impulse –'

Clive snorted in disbelief. 'You put it there *"on impulse?"* Like hell you did, you *tart!* You are; you're a bloody WHORE!'

Incensed, he grabbed the bottle of *Halston* from his pocket and smashed it against the tiles round the fireplace, filling the room with the reek of it. Stella trembled, rocking on her knees.

'It was! It was!'

'Go on, go on!'

'What's the point? You won't believe anything I say!'

'Try me.' He was quiet again. 'Just try me darling, or was it *"sweetie"?*'

'Okay, okay.' She turned both hands out, placating. 'Look, I just wanted to look and smell nice. I'd want to do that if I was going *anywhere* not just round to Douglas. When he tried it on, I *told* him I wasn't a tart. I said just that; that I wasn't a tart.'

Clive was cynical. 'Oh, you did yeah? And what did he say to *that* then?'

Stella was positive. 'I can remember, he said of course I wasn't a tart and what a thing to say!'

Clive continued pedantically. 'Right, so you told him you weren't a tart and he believed you and you haven't had sex with him because all he wanted to do...' He sat back in the chair and stared at her, his eyes and tone full of sarcasm. 'All he wanted to do was take you out for lunch and treat you like a lady, right?' He shot forward, his face up close to hers. '*Right?*' she felt his saliva on her cheek. 'Am I *right?*'

'I don't know, I don't –' she was distraught now.

'You don't *know?* What d'ya mean *you don't know?* You've just got back from London after four nights. What was it then?' He leaned forward again. '*Single beds?*'

She looked down. He struck her hard. She sprawled on the floor and lay there. He waited, watching her. Her face crumpled and she reached up to rub it.

'Why, Stella?' he asked quietly.

She looked up and he gave his cynical half-smile.

'How on earth did you let it get to this, *Mmmm?*'

He rose from the chair and sat down beside her, hands dangling between his raised knees.

'What did you think you were going to gain? I mean…' He was calmer. 'I know I can't offer you very much *really* but what was it all in aid of? I don't understand what made you do it. Whatever it was you actually *did* – did you…' He tried to find the right words. He couldn't get to grips with it. 'Did you go along to wherever it was, with, with…Douglas,' he clenched his jaw, 'and his colleagues? What about this woman, Zena? What was it all about really, this trip I mean?'

He rubbed a hand across his face and through his hair, resigned, like a patient in the dentist's chair awaiting the drill.

'I assume you slept with him. I can't believe he took you to a posh hotel and didn't, but what sort of occasion was it? Where were these colleagues from, that he'd gone to see?'

He was calm and reasonable. If she was careful she *might* be okay.

'I didn't get *very* involved,' she said, biting her lip. 'He knew someone called Jed Zeitermann, he has a club in, well *near*, Piccadilly.'

Clive was surprised and curious, faintly suspicious.

'A *club*, what sort of club? Do you mean a Gentlemen's Club?'

Stella felt her cheeks redden and she avoided his eye.

'It was mainly for men, mainly men went there…'

Thoughts like darts of flame came slipping into his mind under and around a closed door, a door he didn't want to open in case it all got out of control. 'Go on…went there for – what?'

Tucking stray strands of hair back behind her ears, she held her breath. 'Well I think it was or *seemed* to be from what I could tell, a rather upmarket sex club,' she ended lamely, '*sort of.*'

'A *what?* It was a sort of *sex club!!*' he yelled, the enveloping flames leaping now. He was on his feet. The reek of perfume making him want to be sick; back in the kitchen he didn't know what to say. He wanted to kill her.

She scrabbled up, running to him. He gripped the sink, his knuckles white with the effort of keeping them there and not hitting her again.

'I didn't get involved, Clive, honestly. Zena…' *Keep it simple,* she thought, *don't say she was Rhoda.* 'Zena told me what it was all about.' She moved closer but he shot back. 'We had a look round London, I met another girl too: Paula, she was great fun. We just let the men get on with it – like I say, it was really a man's thing and I didn't have anything to do with what went on.'

His expression was full of contempt. She folded her arms and stared at the floor a moment.

'Okay I admit, yes, I did sleep with him and for that I'm saying sorry. I'm really sorry, Clive. But I didn't have anything to do with their activities and that's the truth. To be perfectly honest, I didn't want to know what he *did* get up to really, I *didn't.*' Well *that* was true enough she realised. 'He spent a lot of time there and I went out with Paula and Zena during the day and – where are you going?'

Clive stared vacantly. 'Where am I going? Home I suppose. You don't need me, not now you've had *him*. Not much point in hanging around here, I might as well go.' Misery was replacing the flames, extinguishing them, his mind charred and empty. The future was stretching ahead, uncertain, ruined.

'Please don't go Clive!' Propelled into action, launching at him she clung to his comforting bulk, now motionless and rigid beneath her grip. 'I'm so sorry Clive, there isn't any Douglas now. He doesn't want me, so please don't go –'

'Do you want me instead then?' he asked glumly.

Releasing him, she stepped back. 'Yes please, I would like you if you could, if you think, if you want to?'

He stared down at something on the kitchen floor; what was it? He bent and picked it up, the head of a spring onion with small trailing roots. He dropped it on the draining board and sighed. Putting his hands in his pockets, he shrugged his shoulders.

'Well, I don't know *what* to say.'

He gave a hopeless grin and stared out of the window at the brilliant blue sky. Across the road a small girl was trying to skip with a rope which was a fraction too long for her, while next door to that a woman was busy cleaning a car, hosing all the suds off. Martha would never ever do that, he thought cynically, emitting a small grunt.

'Well, let's just cool it for a while and see how we go then? If you're *sure* you didn't have anything to do with this…' he couldn't say" sex" '…this *club* place then?'

Relief flooded through her, like rain on parched soil.

'No, no I promise. I slept with him and it was a stupid, idiotic mistake. He was using me, he deliberately seduced me and now it's over.' She twisted her fingers together and chewed her bottom lip. 'I understand you want some space,' she said quietly, 'I won't pester you, just get in touch when you want to and I'll be very happy.'

'Really?' He tipped her chin up to look in her eyes.

'Yes, really.'

She looked so relieved, he thought. He turned and opened the door.

She watched as he walked down her drive and back towards his car. In that instant she knew that Douglas Spencer was like morphine in her veins, as Nicki had said. She was addicted to him. A junkie; and cold turkey was coming. She climbed the stairs, dragging each step, to her bedroom. Flopping on the bed she sobbed silently into the duvet as if the end of the world had come.

* * *

Doctor Carroll switched screens and saw Stella had arrived for her appointment fifteen minutes early. Running a comb through his unruly light brown hair, he smoothed down his crumpled jacket, straightened his tie and went to the door.

She looked awful; he called her.

'Hello!' he said.

She wondered how he managed to imbue so much expression into 'hello'.

'Hello Doctor Carroll.' She hesitated. Where would she begin? 'I, I was wondering if, I don't know if you could, it's rather urgent really, if you –'

'Come on Stella, what's it this time? You can call me Martin you know…' he added.

'Well, Martin.' She darted a quick glance at him. 'I'm hoping you can arrange counselling for me. I need to talk to someone as soon as possible really….'

'*Ye-e-e-e-s*, nothing I could help with?' He smiled encouragingly.

'Well I don't think so, not really. It's so, so *complicated* –'

'Nothing new there then, I'm glad to hear!' he joked and leaned back in his chair before swivelling it across from behind his desk.

'Hey, what is it Stella?' Her face was strained, she really looked worn out. 'What's the matter?'

'I've been to London. I went with a man,' she looked up quickly, 'not Clive. Douglas, Douglas Spencer.'

'*Right* and who's Douglas Spencer then?' He was serious.

'He's, he's single, I asked him round to my place for supper back in May and then he invited me –'

'You invited him round in May and then he asked you....?'

'He asked me back to *his* place, to thank me for the invitation he *said.*' Digging her nails into the palm of her other hand and twisting her thumb. 'But I found out this weekend it was all a set-up really, to get me up to a sex club in London.'

Martin tried to stifle a look of horror.

'A *sex* club! He in*vited* you to a sex club? What *sort* of sex club? Stella! What are you up to now?'

'Martin, I'm in a mess and need to talk to somebody urgently, I don't think you can help me really, not this time. I didn't want him in the first place, but he encouraged me, made me feel very special. Wanted to make me happy, so he said.'

'He deliberately seduced you. That's what it boils down to isn't it?' Doctor Carroll was sympathetic.

'Yes; everything's a disaster, I've really screwed up. I can't believe what I've done with men *and* women. I was stupid. I really thought he loved me. It was how he made me feel.'

'He knew what he was up to; he just played on your weaknesses. Hang on a minute.' He picked the phone up again and made a call. 'Hi, yeah, Martin Carroll here, have you got an appointment with Emma as soon as possible? Yeah sure....'

He turned to her. 'There's an appointment here on this Friday at eleven o'clock with Emma Calvert, a cancellation. Would you like it?' Stella nodded. 'Friday's fine. It's for Stella Maitland. Great, thanks, bye!'

She smiled, relieved. 'Thanks Martin, thank you. How long is it for, do you know?'

He rose from his chair and moved nearer. 'It's usually an hour. She'll offer you a follow up appointment to carry on as long as you need her, but not normally for longer than ten weeks.' He smiled and put his arms out towards her, offering a hug, 'Come here you silly thing, honestly Stella, what *are* we going to do with you, hey?'

He squeezed her tightly and rubbed her hair. 'You do get yourself into some problems, don't you? I wish you could just be happy, I really do!'

'Do you Martin?' She nuzzled his chest, his shirt and tie felt soft to her face and she could feel his body through the shirt, his heart beating rapidly. She whispered to him, keeping her face against him. '*I want you…*'

He spoke softly.

'I want you too, Stella, but we've been here before, I think. Look.' He cupped her face in his hands. 'Come and see me next week, after your session and tell me how you got on.' He squeezed her shoulders then released her, ushering her towards the door. 'Make an appointment next week to see me?'

He smiled and returned to his desk.

39

Helen sucked the end of her pen, stuck on a Mediterranean dish. Ten letters, 'A' something 'L' something-something 'E' something-something something 'O'. She stared out of the window. It was difficult to know what speed the train was travelling. She mulled over how she'd tell Douglas that within the next couple of months she'd be Mrs Reggie Crifton. A rattle just behind her was the steward with a refreshment trolley. Ordering a coffee and a packet of shortbread, she sorted out some change.

She watched as the front of the train curved round, heading towards a tunnel. *Later she wouldn't remember if she'd taken a sip from the coffee or not, but she remembered that the dish was Aglio e Olio.* Then in slow motion the darkness of the tunnel engulfed her, as all the carriage lights went out. A terrible roar and the screech of scraped and mangled metal shattered her consciousness and scalding coffee poured on her lap. She screamed, but as in a bad dream, was unsure if any sound came out.

The smell was overwhelming; an acrid, burning smell of soot and rubber, then panic. Subduing the desperate desire to run blindly, she scrabbled around for her handbag which she knew had her phone. Once located, she clutched it tightly in one hand, sobbing from the pain of the scalding coffee, easing herself out of the seat and back towards the door.

An eerie silence fell in her carriage as five shapes became discernible; fellow passengers who, soundlessly, were following her towards the exit. It was impossible in the darkness to recognise them as men or women. Incongruous now, the orange lights on the door-open button glowed, the internal doors stuck at open; the door to the carriage remaining firmly shut. A dim but welcome shaft of daylight was visible beyond the final carriage as silhouettes of people moved towards it. Smoke was drifting towards the carriage like grey cumulus nimbus clouds. She could feel the heat.

She didn't recognise the voice as her own, but it was.

'We've got to get through to the end carriage, so just follow me. People are getting out, getting out from the last carriage. I can see them.'

* * *

Reggie was surprised as 'Helen' came up on his ringing mobile and wondered if she'd forgotten something.

'Hello, pet? Oh God, are you okay, where are you now?'

Sitting on the side of the track, Helen watched as more coughing passengers, some bleeding, stumbled into the daylight, the shock on their faces looking both comical and macabre. In the distance she heard the wail of sirens coming along the road running parallel to the track.

'I'm out and just a bit shaken. I've scalded my legs with hot coffee, but up my end we're all fine. I don't know how it happened _'

'I'm coming to get you,' he said, 'which stations are you between, do you know?'

'There's a s-s-sewage place right opposite me and a sign that says Wheat something.'

'...hampstead? Does it say Wheathampstead?'

His voice was so comforting and strong, it made her want to cry.

'Yes, yes it is. It *is.*' She clutched the phone in both hands.

The area was crawling now with the emergency services. A fire engine had raced over the hill to the other end of the tunnel, two police cars in its wake.

'Helen, please stay where you are. I can find you, it won't take me long. I'm on my way. Do you need to go to hospital do you think? Hello?'

She was trying to speak to both an ambulance man and Reggie. Signalling she was okay, he moved to a woman who seemed to have fainted, another man holding her hand.

'Hello I'm all right. I'll *g-g*-go up to the track. There's probably a lay-by there or something. I'll wait for you and I'll call *D*-douglas as well, tell him I won't be *c-c*-coming.'

'You sound cold, pet, take a blanket if they offer you one and keep warm. I love you Helen, I'll be there as soon as I can.'

She laughed. '*D-d*-don't you go too fast, darling! I'll see you soon and love you *t-t*-too.'

* * *

Douglas had finished mopping up a spill from the vase of flowers he'd put in her room when the phone rang.

'Hello?'

'Hello; Douglas it's me. I, I, we've, *h-h*-had a train crash.' She clenched her teeth. 'I'm safe, but I won't be *c-c*-coming to stay now I'm afraid. Reggie's coming to fetch me. He's on his way now. I'll give you another call when I get back home –' A woolly blanket was warming her up.

Concern, fear and jealousy gripped him. He clutched the receiver, helpless and useless.

'Helen; Helen, are you sure you're all right? What happened, where are you, darling?'

'I'm near Wheathampstead. The front carriages suffered the worst. It'll probably be on the news. I'll call you when I get back.'

Stricken, he stared stupidly at the flowers. 'Helen, if there's *anything* I can do please let me know.' He paused; tense, unwilling to end the conversation. 'I love you very much darling –'

'I *know* you do, Douglas. I'll call you later. Bye now.'

She ended the call quickly, watching the road for Reggie's car.

40

Tuesday 27th July

Jed sifted through his post and saw the letter from Gregory, Marshall and Sterne Solicitors, marked private and confidential. He opened it, pulling out a thick folded sheet of ivory vellum:

> Mr. Zeitermann,
> The Sirens Club,
> 14-18 Raglan Mews, off Brewer Street
> Soho,
> London W1

Dear Sir,

Please accept this letter as formal notification, that from Wednesday, 28th July 1994, the chairmanship of the Sirens Club, occupying the address 14 – 18 Raglan Mews, off Brewer Street, Soho, London W1, will hereinafter be assigned and entitled to Mr. Douglas Spencer of Watermead, Little Denton, Dreightonshire, DR10 4NG as the majority shareholder. Mr Spencer will be holding an extraordinary General Meeting on this date and shall review and appoint directorships. Four current directors have resigned and their letters of resignation will be sent to you. Mr Spencer intends to propose developments to the club which will be put to the board following the new appointments. You are invited to attend the meeting which will be held at 3.00 pm in the boardroom of the Club.

Yours faithfully,
H.F. Gregory
For Gregory, Marshall and Sterne Solicitors

A smile, like the rising of the sun on a beautiful summer day, crept across the features of his face, spreading its warm rays through his whole body. Mr Spencer was welcome to do and appoint whomsoever he wished. He would raise no objection; he'd sit back and enjoy the show!

He dialled his bank, checking to confirm fifty thousand pounds would be transferred to the numbered account he read out once more to the clerk. She assured him it would. He felt as he'd never felt in his life before – an odd mix of excitement and nervousness. He held the future *or rather the end he realised,* of the self-appointed chairman in his hand.

This feeling of power almost countered the feelings of anger and revulsion he was nursing against Erika and her coming weekend trip to 'Barcelona'. That would come to a sorry end too, he was glad to say. He felt a twinge suddenly and grinned, unable to perform with her last night, that wasn't a problem now – quite the opposite! He dialled three numbers on the internal line. Miranda was available, ready and willing – good, he'd be over straight away.

* * *

Helen turned to find Reggie eyeing her tenderly and intensely. She reached out, pulled his arm over and kissed him. She still felt so tired and her thighs were sore and red.

'What time is it, darling?'

'Just coming up to quarter to nine, but that makes no difference to you, seeing as you're not going anywhere today.'

He kissed her again. She didn't protest. She looked tired and pale.

'I need to get Douglas and bring him up to date.' She pushed his hair back, hugging his neck. 'I think the sooner I tell him I'm going to marry you, the better.'

He wriggled, making himself comfortable on top of her.

'Well there's no rush, in fact how about leaving it and telling him…' kissing her eyes very gently, '*after* you're Mrs. Crifton? He doesn't *know* that was what you were *going* to tell him. You could be telling him anything at all, like for instance "please could you leave me all your money when you die?"'

'*Reggie*, that's *terrible*! You're a naughty *boy!*' She giggled and beamed at him, then quizzed him, uncertain if she'd heard correctly. 'Did you say *after* I'm Mrs. Crifton?' She winced suddenly as his legs rubbed her sore, scalded flesh. 'Ow! Careful darling, the coffee was black and very hot.'

'Sorry!' he apologised, 'I'll slide down carefully and kiss it all better in a moment, but first I *did* say *after* you were Mrs. Crifton, if you want to marry me very soon and without too much fuss. I was thinking of the Registry Room at the Chelsea Old Town Hall in the King's Road, just…' He kissed each cheek, 'Two witnesses and us – Mrs. Crifton in thirty minutes on a Tuesday, Wednesday or Thursday afternoon. Then later, when you're feeling better, we can have a big party. What do you say?'

Suddenly emotional, she swallowed. 'I think that'd be very nice, very nice indeed. A Thursday afternoon perhaps?'

'Your wish is my command, pet, leave it with me, we can have two witnesses so you can be thinking who to choose while I kiss your sore spots better and then bring you up some breakfast in bed…'

* * *

The crash had Douglas stumped. Being unable to control a situation threw him completely; *just focus on the meeting tomorrow in London*. David and Piers would make four directors, plus Jed. Jed. All was not lost, he had Jed well and truly nailed: Erika… suddenly this present cloud showed its glittering silver lining and with it, a return of equilibrium. He went through to the study and rummaged for Bill Johnson's number and called him. No answer, so he left a message. Then he tried Rhoda, who answered on the third ring.

'Hello?'

'Hello, Rhoda, I hoped I might catch you. Shall I pick you up tomorrow morning at nine thirty? The meeting's at three. I take it you're still in favour of joining the board?' *Can a duck swim?*

Rhoda tried to temper her enthusiasm, be professional.

'That'd be fine, Douglas. I'll be ready.' Then as an afterthought: 'I saw the news late yesterday and caught the train crash in the tunnel. Terrible; no survivors from the front carriage at all! They think it's probably vandals, but not much information at the moment' She paused, unsure. 'I wondered if it was the train that Helen was on, I assume it wasn't?' The ensuing silence struck a chill of alarm. 'Is she with you?'

'She's not, no.' He scratched his brow distractedly. 'It *was* her train but she was near the rear, in the last but one carriage apparently, quite safe I believe.' She could sense the irritation and frustration in his voice. 'She called me just after it had happened and said Reggie was going to collect her, she wouldn't be coming. I'm still waiting for any further news.'

Rhoda's brain was in top gear. 'Oh Douglas, I'm so sorry to hear that, I expect that's spoilt your plans for Goodwood –'

'How did you know that? That I was going to Goodwood?' He was riled now, his irritation at full steam.

Rhoda bit her tongue, she'd done it again, but he'd *told* her.

'You *told* me, or…' Doubt crept in, had it been Stella who'd told her? She couldn't be sure. *Somebody* had. '*Someone* did.' Her cheeks were burning, remembering when she'd been in the office with Jed, Reggie and Paula, then she'd got rather tiddly: *oh Hell*. She'd wanted to be his escort. Why couldn't she keep her big mouth shut? Just back pedal fast. 'I'll be ready and waiting for you tomorrow at nine thirty, shall I need to bring anything particular?' *Bar my brain,* she thought, kicking herself.

'Not really, except your diary. I'll see you in the morning then, goodbye!'

'See you tomorrow. Bye-e-e!'

She replaced the handset quickly, furious. How *could* she have been so stupid? Gloria was right. He had this effect, sending common sense right out of the window. She hoped Gloria would be there tomorrow, she felt an affinity there now.

Douglas put down the phone, pondering how she knew he was going to Goodwood. He *might* have told her of course, but he couldn't recall *when* exactly. He felt a chill: someone had walked over his grave.

* * *

'*Clive!* Clive, where are you?' Martha yelled from the hall. 'You put the wash on sixty degrees. You couldn't wait, could you? You're stupid.'

The silence infuriated her even more. She stormed up the stairs to find him at the computer, intent on the screen. She stood exasperated, her arms out from her sides like taut guy ropes on a tent, her fingers out like claws.

'Didn't you hear me yelling at you? What on earth were you doing! You tipped the whole wash in, everything, at near boiling. *You're mad.*' The tendons on her neck were sticking out in fury. '*Say something then!* What's the matter with you?'

Clive minimised the screen he was looking at unhurriedly and turned. 'Yup,' he said, acknowledging her now.

'What do you mean; "yup"?'

'I mean yup, I'm mad. Fed up, pissed off, whatever and as far as the washing goes, I don't give a fuck!' He enjoyed her shocked expression. 'Just turn it off or something I don't care, just deal with it and then go and moan to your friend Davina, or whoever he is –'

'*She* is, you mean,' blanching, 'Davina's a *she*!'

'I meant "she". Just go and deal with it and sort it out, I'm busy....'

Martha stood glued to the spot; she took a breath to say

something else but Clive was there first. He wanted to get back to what he'd found.

Standing up he turned on her. 'Look, just *clear off can't you?* I'm sorry. It was a mistake. Just switch the bloody thing off, it's not the end of the world! Most of it seemed to be cotton anyway.' He hurried her.

Well, go *on* then! Go and *stop* it.'

He sat back down then heard the kitchen door slam. Raising the site he continued reading:

The S.I.R.E.N.S. Club, it said.

He looked at the black and red images of men and women moving on the screen in suggestive poses. This was the Home Page. Scrolling down he found 'Contact Us' and clicked on it, staring at the names: Jed Zeitermann, Douglas Spencer – he didn't recognise the others. This must have been the club Stella had been on about. He scrolled back and clicked on 'Events'

Weekend Spectacular with Guest Star 'Stella' July 17th – 18th SOLD OUT

Ladies Night: with Sherrie and Girls Tuesday August 3rd – Tickets available

Hospital Event: Members Evening with Miranda and her Staff Friday August 13th – Tickets available – Lucky for some!!

Why not join and become a member – receive a newsletter and invitations to special events. Go to our Membership Page for details of membership fees.

Clive returned to 'Contact Us' and saw an email address and two telephone numbers, one an 0845 number charging calls at local rate. He listened: Martha was chuntering loudly and still banging doors about, the washing machine was now silent.

She came to the foot of the stairs.

'I'm going out in the garden. I've turned the machine off. Just leave it as it is and I'll sort it out later.'

Opening the kitchen door, she then closed it, remaining very quietly where she was. She could hear herself breathing, feel her heart beating. The last time she'd pressed redial it was Stella. She waited a few moments...'beep –'; the extension upstairs was in use. Very carefully she lifted the receiver from the wall-phone and listened....

He dialled the 0845 number, the dialling tone sounding hollow. 'Hello, you're through to the Sirens Club, London's premier sex club, bar and restaurant.' Then a series of options....

Clive hesitated over what to do and his hand felt clammy. The automated voice came on again: 'If you wish to speak to a receptionist please hold and your call will be answered shortly, if you wish to return to the options menu, to hear the options again, please press the hash key now.' He decided to hold and take his luck with a receptionist. Donna Summer's rendition of *Hot Stuff* was playing loudly and making him feel edgy. He looked out of the window but couldn't see Martha, maybe she was in the front. He held on through two more recordings, interspersed with assurances that his call was moving up the queue and would be answered shortly.

Downstairs, Martha was holding her breath and the phone slightly away from her ear. She loathed this song. She was desperate to hear what Clive had to say. Maybe this was to be her chance. David was incredibly patient, but wouldn't wait forever and *she* didn't want to wait much longer, she was sick to death of Clive. Voices were on the line again, she listened.

'....no that was sold out and was last weekend. Did I what?'

Gloria sensed she had a right one here, the sort that once upon a time would have come out of the chemist with a toothbrush instead of a packet of condoms. He sounded very nervous and the line wasn't good.

Clive was sweating now. It was running down his back.

'Do you know who the 'Stella' was? Who it says was the star of the weekend? Was that her real name, do you know what her name was, please?'

The console was telling Gloria that there were other calls waiting in a queue. This guy, whoever he was, sounded like a timewaster or a trouble maker and no way was she going to get herself into another Paula and *Peggy* situation.

'I'm sorry, darlin,' but unless you're a member I can't give out information like that, but I can tell you honest that most girls workin' here don't use their own names, they usually have a stage name if that's any help. Now is there anything else I can help you with today?'

Clive thought. 'Yes, one more thing. What position does Douglas Spencer hold there, can you tell me that…hello?'

Downstairs, Martha nearly dropped the phone in surprise. Douglas *Spencer*! Belonging to a *sex club?* Surely not!

Gloria was on her mettle now. This man might be daft, but certainly not stupid. She'd be formal.

'*Are* you a member here?'

'I'm not a member, no. I just wanted to know what position, if any, Douglas Spencer held there, does he work there?'

That was a moot point, thought Gloria. Depends what you class as work really – if it was getting your leg over as many times in a day as you could, then yes, he did work, *very hard!* And as far as 'what position' did he hold? She had a little snigger. She wouldn't mind finding out, but a fat chance of that!

'Have you looked at our website, love, if you do you'll see that it says he works here but more than that I can't tell you; it's the rules you see.'

Clive felt there was more to this but he'd give Stella the benefit of the doubt. It was a coincidence, but she *might* just have told the truth and he wasn't going to get any further here today.

'Okay, thank you for that, I understand, of course. Thank you, Bye.'

He put the receiver down and sat heavily on the chair in front of the computer, feeling very depressed.

Martha replaced the handset and crept to the door to the

garden, opening it carefully then closing it quietly behind her. She needed to sit outside and collect her thoughts. See David as well, as soon as she could.

* * *

Helen opened her eyes and stared around. Feeling a little more comfortable and relaxed, she turned over. Next to the bed, on a small table, were the remains of her breakfast. Her mind was all fuzzy, she recalled something about getting married at a registry office in Chelsea, but the memory kept evaporating; it must have been a dream. Rolling on to her back again she tried to work it out. Just as she was about to call out, the front door opened and with a scampering of paws up the stairs, Buster was panting fiercely and yapping with excitement, pawing at the side of the bed. She put a hand down to him and called.

'Are you there, Reggie?'

'Coming, pet!'

He was climbing the stairs, strolling in with Buster's lead and looking relaxed in jeans and a faded checked shirt. 'You've woken up then,' he grinned, 'you look much better, how do you feel?'

He picked Buster up, who now turned and licked his face with enthusiasm. Helen laughed.

'I feel fine, much better, but surely it isn't four o'clock? Have I been asleep all day?'

'Near enough.' He lowered Buster, who looked hurriedly around for something to chew, couldn't find anything, so curled up and promptly went to sleep. Reggie sat on the bed. 'I gave you a temazepam; I thought it would do you good to have a good rest today.' He brushed her cheek. 'You've got some colour back now, are you peckish at all, anything you fancy?'

Helen thought. 'I had a rather odd dream. We were going to get married soon in a registry office. I think it was Chelsea, it was very real –'

'Not a dream, darling.' He bent over and kissed her. 'You agreed we'd get married on a Thursday afternoon there, I sent them an email for the soonest Thursday available, so you'd better find something to wear quickly!'

She struggled to sit up and he propped some pillows behind her. Reaching out, she hugged him.

'Reg, that's wonderful, but I'd better call Douglas, he must be wondering what's happened –' She saw his face. 'Has he called?'

'Aye, he called about midday. I said you were fast asleep and I wasn't going to wake you, you'd call him when you woke up. You'd had a good night, but you were still very tired.'

'Oh darling, I'd better phone him, can you pass it to me?'

Douglas had been in a quandary all afternoon. He'd begun planting some bedding plants but couldn't settle. Jumping up each time he thought the phone was ringing. He was sitting at his desk, sorting papers for the next day's meeting, when it did.

'Hello?' He was anxious.

'Hello Douglas, I've only just woken up. Reggie said you'd called, but I was fast asleep.' She was playing for time, prevaricating – he knew all that. 'How are you?'

'I'm fine. Now what happened to *you* darling, tell me!'

'Well I –' Reggie, having leaped up the stairs two at a time, was signalling to her. She placed her hand over the receiver. 'What?'

He whispered urgently. *'Don't tell him about the plans yet, not 'til afterwards, okay?'*

She nodded. 'Sorry about that.' She tried to think now what she *could* tell him and then had an idea. 'Douglas, I'd got some news to tell you and after what happened on the train, I shall enjoy it even more. We're planning to go away for a few weeks –'

'Oh yes.' He didn't sound very thrilled.

'Yes, Reggie's been offered some work in Spain, singing in a hotel in Valencia, we're off in August, not long. I'll give you a ring before we go, we could be there until the end of September.'

'Oh, it could be as long as *that!* I see, well...' He tried to collect his thoughts, doodling with his pen. 'Look; *do* that and then when you get back, perhaps you could come and stay then. Before the winter sets in again anyway, do you think?'

She'd cross that bridge when she got there, as Mrs. Reggie Crifton.

'Well we'll see, Douglas. I'll give you a call –'

'Yes; what date did you say?' He didn't think she had; he was poised with his pen.

'I *think* he said it was the fifteenth, I'm not terribly wide awake today. I'll let you know.'

'Well if you *could* then, that would be splendid. I've sent you a little something. I hope it will speed your recovery. Well, all the best then and lots of love, darling, take it easy. I'll wait to hear from you.' His doodles were tearing through the paper in long furrows.

'I will, and you, speak soon. Bye now.'

'Goodbye, darling; I love –' But she'd gone.

41

Wednesday 28th July

Jed wondered if he could keep his cool. Erika was keeping hers, no sign at all of duplicity, yet he'd heard her talking to someone on her mobile late last night (he'd assumed it was Spencer) while she'd been in the bath. He'd listened outside the door to her splashing softly and giggling seductively, murmuring words he'd strained to hear but couldn't. Once she'd laughed out loud and the echoing sound had made him jump.

The thought of it now, as he sat waiting in the boardroom for Spencer to show his face, had him screwing his fists up in anger. How he'd got through the night he didn't know. She'd been as randy as hell when she'd climbed later into bed. He'd read somewhere, on the net possibly, that spouses or partners would have a rush of the pleasure hormone when anticipating (or often immediately after) a liaison with a lover, which would make them overwhelmingly sexual towards their legitimate partner for a while, before the effect wore off. They would then feel distanced… then guilty. It made men buy flowers or women cook exotic meals: guilt.

Well, he'd wait and see what was cooking this evening! This morning she'd barely uttered two syllables to him, she seemed so tense. The only thing keeping him going was the knowledge that come Saturday night, she'd be wondering what the hell had happened and how she was going to get out of this one. He looked up at the clock. Where was he – the condemned man? It was nearly ten past three and so far, he was sitting in the room on his own. Well if *this* was how he thought you ran a business….

The double doors snapped open and in walked Douglas Spencer, Piers Falby and David Thorpe, followed by Rhoda Chambers, who was nearly wearing a very expensive looking dress, he noticed. His eyes were locked to her chest; he hadn't realised how big it was. Spencer, he observed wryly, had splashed out on a new, discreetly gleaming, lightweight cashmere suit. *You won't get much wear out of that,* he thought, *hardly worth buying, but then you're not to know.*

'Good evenin', Spencer,' he drawled arrogantly with a smirk, glad to see a spark of irritation in the man's eyes. He was going to enjoy this, wind him up a bit. If it got him kicked off, well, so what? He slouched in his chair and checked his mobile: an alert had told him earlier that fifty thousand pounds had left his gold reserve account – he just wanted to look at it again. What was the man saying now?

With a pained look of disdain mixed with disapproval, Douglas Spencer closed the doors behind him and glared at Jed, who was slouched checking his mobile phone.

'Mr Zeitermann; glad you could make it! I take it you received the letter from my solicitor and the letters of resignation from the four no longer with us?'

Jed sat up, acknowledging the other three with a nod and a blatant wink to Rhoda, whose cheeks coloured as if he'd paint-balled them.

'Yeah got all that, been sittin' here waitin' for ten minutes.' He folded his arms across his chest, the shoulder seams of his suit straining, his Rolex and a gold bracelet gleaming.

Ignoring this, Douglas sat down at the head of the table.

'Well then gentlemen – and *Rhoda*!' he sang unctuously. 'This shouldn't take long, I want to establish the new board here and briefly run through some proposals I have in m*ind*.' He looked around the table with authority. 'To increase interest and raise our pro*file* well into the twenty-first *cen*tury.'

'Well done, Spencer, congratulations!'

Stella was quite right, Jed thought, he did have a silly way of speaking.

Douglas looked at Jed, whose eyes were twinkling beads of jet, his arms still folded across his chest.

Jed noticed his expression change slightly, clouding over, tinged with fear almost. Like someone confronted by a dangerous looking yob. *Good,* he thought, *bring it on, make my day!*

Douglas continued, regardless. It was natural Jed should feel bitter; his nose was out of joint.

'First then, if we can, to the new appointments and for that I must announce an apology from Colonel Johnson, David and Piers are continuing as I presume *you* are?' He eyed Jed somewhat less warily now, he could like it or lump it; he was calling the tune.

'I'll continue,' Jed said, adding belligerently, 'In what position though, exactly?'

Douglas was magnanimous.

'In the position you are now Jed, if that is agreeable?'

'...but what about all the money from the weekend spectacular that you cleared off with then?' He looked across the table – the two other men looked slightly uncomfortable, rustling and sorting their papers and Rhoda appeared like a woman whose child you'd just insulted.

'Are we going to see any of that, then?'

Douglas put his forearms on the table, inter-locking his fingers.

'Bonuses will be paid each Christmas; your entitlement will be added th*en*.'

And yours is arriving this weekend, mate!

'Okay; yeah, that's fine.' He smiled and nodded once, looking affable now, which – if it unnerved Douglas – then good!

Frowning slightly, Douglas winced and carried on.

'Good then, so now that leaves Rhoda, who's here and happy to join us and continue representing the women employ*ees*.'

The look of supreme favour he bestowed made Jed want to be ill; Rhoda was positively oozing admiration.

Jed wondered how often he'd screwed *her* and doubted she knew where he was proposing to dip it *this* weekend. He liked everything in tidy, watertight compartments, except one of them had leaked. He was getting too big for his boots by half, but no worries, he thought to himself, just three more days....

42

Thursday 29th July

Erika pondered, was it wise to accept Jed's lift? It was the first time she'd cheated on him for a weekend and as it drew nearer she was finding it harder to deal with. He was so possessive sometimes, or did it just seem that way ever since she'd taken up with Douglas, nearly a year ago? He'd told her it was all in the build-up; now, at last, he'd decided it was time to crank things up a notch and spend a few nights together, the races first and then three nights in a smart hotel in Chichester.

That hadn't presented a problem: she was packing easily and casually for a trip to Barcelona, there was a flight departing at the right time and a car waiting for her to drive to the pick-up point. However, a feeling of uneasiness wouldn't go away.

Perhaps she'd cook something special this evening, paella and some Sangria; that seemed a good idea, something to get in the mood for Spain. She could always say that while in Barcelona she'd received a call from the office to fly somewhere else if she couldn't face coming home immediately, just play it by ear, but first go and get some ingredients for her meal tonight.

* * *

Stella was busy in the shop and thinking about her visit to Emma that coming Friday. She needed someone who was neither Douglas nor Clive and as she sat with her head down between her knees, trying to make the dizziness go away, she realised who that was....

Linda, Doctor Carroll's wife, had had just about had all she could take and the girls were sensing the strain. Just entering their teens, they were sophisticated in their view and driving her mad. Divorce was the elephant in the front room but such a big step; the legal ramifications – sorting out the house and custody of the girls, who also stayed out as long as they dared: expert at playing one parent off against the other. Should they just battle on and make the best of it? Do you just stay with someone when you don't love them anymore, and they don't love you either? Wasn't life too short for that? It was time she took the bull by the horns and had it out with Martin; suggest separation as the first step.

43

Friday 30th July

Douglas woke suddenly and looked at the clock – eight thirty: he'd overslept. He was chary of phoning Helen again; she'd been quite specific in her plans: a trip to Valencia, very warm at this time of year. The gap through the curtains was a brilliant blue; with any luck it would hold all weekend. His irritation evaporated as he planned. The tickets were all ready and lunch and tea booked at the Double Trigger. He was looking forward to squiring Erika round the parade ring. There was something erotic almost, watching the horses parade and strut their stuff with flanks gleaming and everything immaculate. Some keen to get going – pulling and tossing, getting excited while the grooms paced round with deadpan faces.

The meeting had gone well at the club, Jed surprisingly subdued. He'd been expecting confrontation but hadn't met it, so why had he woken so irritable? His sleep had been disturbed by dreaming he was falling into blackness, waking with a jump before dozing off only to find the same thing happening again moments later, leaving him bleary eyed. Erika had sounded seductive on the phone, tantalising him with what she was doing in the bath and what they'd do at the hotel.

They'd meet tomorrow at the Services as arranged and take it from there. Stepping out of bed he trod on something sharp and bent to have a look – it was a bit of decoration from a fancy piece of lingerie Stella had worn to turn him on. A red see-through concoction decorated with red and gold sparkly stones. He glanced at it for a moment before tossing it into the waste paper bin. She'd served her purpose; she certainly had talent. That was what had amazed him really, he decided, nothing else, but it was over and time to move on; she'd get over it.

* * *

In her dream a phone was ringing, but where from? She woke suddenly. Jeeves, disturbed by her cries and thrashing about, had jumped on the bed. She looked at the phone next to her and wondered. Picking it up, she dialled 1471; Clive had called at eight o'clock. She looked at her watch, it was eight twenty. Not really thinking, she called it back. Martha answered.

'Hello? Hello?'

She panicked. 'Oh I'm sorry. I think I have the wrong number, sorry to bother you!' She replaced the handset quickly, before realising Martha could (and probably would) do the same as she'd just done and recognise the number.

Her heart thudded; how stupid! Why not have just said it was her? She'd called the number by mistake. She waited to see if the phone rang again, but it didn't.

* * *

Martha stared at the receiver then dialled 1471. Sure enough, it was Stella. She went to the foot of the stairs.

'*Clive*...Are you up there?'

He'd tried Stella at eight o'clock from his mobile with no luck, so tried again from home but still no reply, he wondered what Martha wanted. What hadn't he done now?

'Yup,' he called, knowing this would irritate her.

Martha now allowed a smile, begging to be unleashed, to slip into place across her lips. She had him! 'Did you call Stella a moment ago?'

She waited for Clive to respond to this. It was a clever 'have you stopped beating your wife' question – he would know she knew already.

He took a deep breath. Martha must have traced the call from 1471 when the phone had rung again. His spirits rose slightly – she'd tried to call him back after all. He decided on bluff.

'I might've done – called it by mistake. I was trying to get Marker's Garage and must have pressed Maitland instead. Anyway, I've got to pop out for a moment to see about the car.'

Heading down the stairs, Martha blocked his path.

'Well I *was* surprised when Stella told me she had the wrong number, it all sounds pretty odd to me,' She picked up the handset. 'Do you want to speak to Stella now or shall I?' She watched as the blood drained from his face in fear.

'Just leave her alone, she's got enough problems as it is. I don't want you to call her, *leave it!!*' Grabbing the handset, he slammed it down.

'Clive, I've just about had enough of this. You must think I was born yesterday. Don't compound things by telling me you're *not* having an affair with Stella, but is it serious or just a fling?'

She shrugged her shoulders and flicked back her hair. 'Heaven knows, there's not much love lost between us, but I want to know what all this is about.'

He eased her out of his way, thinking desperately.

'I see her to help with her computer and with the accounts from the shop occasionally. I'm her *friend;* we're *not* having an affair, whatever you might think. Now I'm off to the garage.' He paused, sarcastic, 'Do you want to come with me? Make sure I don't make a detour?'

Martha was ready to play her ace. 'Like the one yesterday that took you to Stella instead of B&Q?' She'd scored a bull's-eye; he was stunned. 'Oh yes,' she said triumphantly, 'Angela was cleaning her car in the morning and we met later in town, she told me she'd seen you there.'

Clive remembered seeing a woman cleaning a car, but hadn't

recognised her. He wondered how Martha knew her, or she him for that matter.

Martha read the confusion in his eyes.

'Pilates, Clive; that's how we know each other. She's divorced I think...' She studied her nails then looked up. 'Anyway, you'd better get on, don't want to stop you.'

Clive didn't like the expression on Martha's face and felt trapped. He'd take the car to the garage and get back as soon as he could, to face whatever was coming: things were reaching a head.

As soon as the car had gone, Martha picked up the phone. Stella, searching for a pair of shoes to wear with her grey jacket, heard it.

'Hello? Hello?'

'Hello Stella, Martha; how long have you been playing around with Clive now?' coming straight to the point, her tone even. 'I don't mean when he comes to help you at the shop or with anything else, dear. I mean how long do you think you've been...' she considered, '...been an *item*, shall we say?'

Stella tried to swallow but her saliva had been removed.

'Martha, I, I –'

'Can I help you?' she suggested, 'Weeks, months? How often does he phone you? He does, doesn't he? How often would that be?'

'Every day; he calls me every day.' She wondered if Clive was there, unable to intervene.

'Every day...' Martha repeated this, her tone flat. 'Right, well, you're welcome to him from tomorrow, Saturday. He can pack and do a few more jobs for me today; we ought to discuss a few things too, then you can have him with pleasure. I've put up with enough. Goodbye!'

Ending the call, she immediately dialled David.

Putting down his paper, he went to fetch the phone. 'Hello, David Pearce?'

'David it's me, Clive's just gone to the garage with the car and when he gets back he's getting his marching orders –'

'Hang on, slow down dearest. Now, what's happened? Tell me slowly!'

* * *

Stella stared in horror at the phone, immobilized. She tried to call Clive but it was turned off, she guessed he'd gone out somewhere and would find out when he returned. Jeeves was campaigning for a walk. She'd do that and then go for her appointment.

* * *

Emma Calvert, psychologist, and member of the Kettering mental health team, breezed through the notes once more in Stella Maitland's file sent by Dr. Carroll, before calling her into the consulting room at Great Denton Health Centre.

She was vulnerable, that much Emma gathered straight away; smart, but all a veneer; as brittle as the caramel on a toffee-apple. As if aware of this, her expression was confrontational. Emma smiled. 'Relax, Stella! I'm Emma Calvert. You've been referred to me by your GP Doctor Carroll?' She was bright and breezy with the same voice air-hostesses use.

'Just relax and think what it is you want to tell me; what's on your mind and worrying you, and whatever it is, it won't go beyond this building, except to my colleagues at Kettering. The important thing is we want to *help* you, Stella.'

Two tears slid down in twin wet streaks. This woman probably meant well, but how could she possibly understand everything she'd been through?

'Would you like some water?' Emma held a plastic cup.

Stella nodded, taking a few sips before shutting her eyes and beginning.

'I've just come back from London, from a *club* in London.' She paused and then told the full story.

'I've come here because I don't understand myself, why I'm like I am.' She paused again, trying to control the emotions inside; it wasn't easy.

'I hate myself *and love* myself, if that's not silly. I love...' She tensed, correcting herself. 'I *loved* Douglas; he's single. Clive has a partner but loves *me*. Look this isn't making any sense at all. I'm not normally like this, really I'm not,' she added fervently, 'and I keep crying.' Emma nodded encouragement.

'I feel I'm wasting *your* time now as well and don't know how you can help me, only I can do that, can't I? I just don't know how to. Sorry.' *She'll never understand all this; never.* Stella waited for her response.

'What are you *sorry* for, Stella?' Emma was gentle. 'Do you feel you have to apologise for *everything*? That whatever happens generally, to you in particular, you have to a*pologise* for? Is that how you feel?'

She'd hit the nail on the head.

'Yes it *is*!' She grabbed Emma's hand; she understood, at last someone *understood!*

Emma watched her and saw desperation; she looked like someone who'd gone to see a clairvoyant and was hoping against hope that her hand or the crystal ball would foretell happier times ahead. That's what made her vulnerable, she decided. Her self esteem was so low that *anyone*, any circumstance, could manipulate her. She'd read the notes and Douglas had done that from the start; she hadn't known which way was up. She'd bend over backwards for *anyone* who was going to boost that esteem; a gift for those wishing to abuse her – a gift wrapped with a label attached: 'Please Use Me thank you/sorry.'

'Do you want to tell me the whole thing from the beginning? You don't have to apologise for anything here,' she explained kindly.

'Detach yourself from it if you can. Where did this nightmare start? Who did it start *with* perhaps? Does that help at all? Take your jacket off, relax and let's go, yeah?'

* * *

Erika was surprised to see Jed's car parked when she returned from the hairdressers, her nails and hair glinting and perfect. She pushed open the door, the sound system was on. Her favourite Marvin Gaye was sounding in every room it seemed!

'Hello!'

Erika jumped out of her skin, dropping her bag. Jed was in a cut away black t-shirt, muscles bulging and a pair of tight black jeans and bare feet, his hair gelled and spiky.

'Thought I'd come home early and give you a surprise, seein' as you're off in the mornin' early.' He grinned, chewing and stretching some gum, his jaws working hard. 'Eight o'clock was it you need to get to the airport?' Looking her straight in the eye, 'The flight's leavin' just after ten?'

She bent to retrieve her bag, trying hard to quell her nerves.

'Yes, ten o'clock take-off, I'll go straight through to the departure lounge.'

'Okey-doke, darlin''

He loomed over her in the living room doorway, arms raised, one hand on each jamb. The song continued – Marvin Gaye – singing her fate, 'Whatever you say. Like the music?' He jerked his head in the direction of the player. 'One of your favourites this, isn't it?'

She placed her hand on his chest and smiled. 'You know it is. I love it. So,' sliding both arms round him and smelling his body, his aftershave mixed with a faint tang of sweat – hoping he couldn't feel her heart thumping. 'What would you like to be doing this evening, for my surprise? I thought you'd be working late tonight.'

He lowered his arms, pulling the bag away, then took hold of the hem of her skirt, inching it up to her hips. She was wearing a blue lacy thong. He gazed at it, still chewing. She could smell the spearmint.

'Well I don't know about *you*, but *I* feel like a bit of rumpy-pumpy before you head for Spain.' He lifted her up, holding her against him, a hand under each buttock. 'So let's draw the blinds, get naked and start, yeah! Supper can wait a bit. I'm gettin' up this time. I must've been workin' too hard before, but it's growin' nice and big baby, just how you like it!' He carried her through to the bedroom. 'And I'm feelin' dominant, babe! I'll give you something to remember me by and take what I want to remember *you* by!'

He tipped her on to the bed and removing the gum, tossed it in the bin, then removed his shirt and unfastened his jeans.

* * *

The session with Emma had helped; she felt calm. Clive would be arriving tomorrow, she assumed. They'd just have to make the best of it. Her phone signalled a text: 'Don't call me. I shall be with you in the morning to stay. I love you my darling. Clive xxxx' she climbed the stairs and emptied some drawers out, making space in the wardrobe. She tried to convince herself it would all work out. Clive loved her. She flopped on the bed and lay there; he loved her. She hoped further sessions with Emma would help; she couldn't cry anymore, there were no tears left to cry.

44

Saturday 31st July

'Going: Good – good to firm in places, 1.55 first race' Douglas studied the paper whilst finishing a piece of toast and thick cut orange marmalade, his second cup of tea cooling. The sun was creeping round to the conservatory. It was going to be a very warm day. Mist was still curling like wispy dust covers above the fields. His rising excitement was under control: anticipation. The gleaming black Aston Martin was sitting waiting, the garage door raised, ready to go.

He'd been quick booking lunch at the Double Trigger, too quick possibly and he wondered if he should have prepared a picnic instead, but it was exclusive and smart there, they could see and be seen. He preferred the Gordon, which had a good view of the finishing post and was near the parade ring. His cream coat was on a hanger ready in the car, along with his club striped panama, his members badge visible on the windscreen.

Checking his watch, it was just coming up to eight fifteen; he was meeting Erika at ten o'clock at the junction ten Services. Lunch was booked for twelve thirty, so even allowing for traffic nearer the course they should be in excellent time. He paused by the garage, the palm he'd just noticed from the window wasn't just leaning – there was something wrong with it. He went to investigate. A frond came away in his hand; it was dead. He shivered in the heat then pulled himself together, it was nothing. He climbed in the car, bang on time.

* * *

Erika winced, climbing carefully into her small rented Fiat. She'd never known Jed as aroused and ardent as he'd been last night, she was aching and sore everywhere. Her case was wedged in the boot, her laptop bag resting on the back seat. She adjusted the driving position and mirror, put the paperwork with her clutch bag on the seat next to her and eased her way out from Heathrow and on to the motorway. As she approached junction ten of the M25, she saw the sign for the Services and pulled off up the slip road. She was early – just coming up to twenty past nine.

She found a parking place, took her bag from the boot and wheeled it towards the restaurant. The hat she'd wanted to wear wouldn't fit in the case and there was no reason for it in Barcelona; instead she'd packed a black and white feathered fascinator, the feathers set in a primrose yellow base, trimmed with a matching satin bow. She wanted to shake out her floaty chiffon and silk satin dress as soon as possible – she'd used a steamer at the club, hoping Jed wouldn't catch her.

Shown to a table, she ordered a coffee and took a couple of pain killers. She'd been scared to resist; there was urgency, an almost manic force behind Jed's passion that was unnerving. She dithered about calling him on her mobile. She'd be waiting to board now, if she'd still been at the airport, what if the flight was suddenly cancelled? Deciding against it, she finished the rest of her coffee and wheeled her bag through to the cloakrooms, squeezing into a cubicle and unzipping the case.

It was a bit of a struggle in the confined space, but she managed it. Folding her linen trousers and casual sweater in place of the dress, and stuffed them in. Emerging, she fitted the fascinator in place, checking everything in the full length mirror. She touched up her makeup and returned to the busy services foyer, attracting ogling glances from a couple of lorry drivers and gawps from a large unruly family in gaudy, shabby sportswear and trainers. She headed back to her car to wait for Douglas. It was just coming up to ten o'clock.

The journey was going like clockwork, the bulk of the traffic still to come. The car was a pleasant eighteen degrees, the outside temperature already creeping up into the high seventies with hardly a cloud in the sky. On pulling into the service station, Douglas saw her waiting for him, looking amazing. He swung the car round, stopped and got out to greet her.

'Erika, you look a picture!' He kissed her cheek, surveying her. 'Have you had a coffee or something, are you ready to go?'

All her worries were fading, he was dashing, sophisticated... virile. The pain killers were working, Jed forgotten now as she eased herself gingerly into the luxurious depth of truffle leather, strapping herself in as he closed her door.

'I've made it, Douglas. I can't wait for this weekend to begin, you are so smart and you smell delicious too!' She leaned over as he climbed in, brushing his cheek.

'And I'm looking forward to it *too*, darling, very much.'

His door closed with a subtle thud and they purred out on to the A3 Portsmouth Road.

By the time they reached Kennel Hill, the traffic was building up, the heat making drivers impatient. Erika glanced across to a car pulled up and waiting beside them and met the eyes of a fellow race-goer, staring at her. He stared until his passenger, a woman of considerably more years than Erika, leaned forwards to see what was attracting her husband's attention, whereupon his eyes immediately returned to the road and the car ahead. She smiled, placing her hand on Douglas's thigh as they edged slowly forwards, settling herself more comfortably. Douglas glanced across.

'Is everything all right, darling? We're nearly there; about another mile or so, this is the worst bit until we get to the car parks.'

'Well here we are, I think? Seats seven and eight...' He held her elbow. 'But we've plenty of time, let's wander and see what the runners are like, shall we?'

He raised his hat to a woman sitting in the row behind them, who smiled. His hand in the small of her back, they walked towards the parade ring, a programme tucked under his other arm.

'It's so as I imagined it would be, Douglas, all the crowds of people here.' She looked around at the milling throng of spectators: a sea of colour and style. Unlike the usual way of nature, where the male of the species is allowed the finery and show, here the ladies could parade in full regalia: hats, frocks, shoes and handbags, the exotic and the traditional, side by side.

Erika eyed the extravagant millinery with a pang of envy. Her dress had a fitted primrose satin bodice, with a softly flared skirt, surmounted by the sheerest white silk chiffon, ruched over the bodice and floating over the skirt, a black sash accentuating her waist. The wonderful brimmed hat that went with it she'd purchased from Fortnum's, after the fascinator, which had been buried in a drawer. It wasn't quite the same. She glanced up at Douglas, needing affirmation she was looking good, that he approved, and he encircled her waist.

'There are crowds of people here, but none of them look as beautiful as *you*, sweetie –'

'Do you mean that? This isn't the hat that goes with it normally. I couldn't fit it in the bag. I wanted to look wonderful for you –'

He squeezed her, lifting his hand to stroke her exposed shoulder blades. 'And you *do,* my darling I mean every word. I'm thrilled to have you with me, I'm sure we'll find occasions you can wear the other one, but what you have is *very* attractive on you; alluring. Don't worry, you look beautiful.' He patted her bottom. 'Now, come along and let's see what we think for the first race.'

Feeling happier, Erika continued as he steered her carefully through the throng. 'What time is that, the first race?'

'One fifty-five I think.' He opened a programme and handed it to her. 'Now, here we are; have a look and see what you think. I have lunch reserved at the Double Trigger for twelve thirty before that, so –'

'The Double Trigger, you say? Like a gun?' She glanced up. Douglas bent and kissed her ear.

'Yes darling, a gun has a trigger; but this name refers to a horse, a *stallion*.' He gently tickled her neck then whispered, 'A famous thoroughbred stud.' Nipping the bottom of her earlobe quickly, he shot a red hot spear of lust straight through her and she stumbled against him.

He chuckled wickedly. 'Steady on darling, concentrate! Here comes a lovely one, what do you think of him?'

Sipping her coffee, Erika marvelled at the sophisticated and stylish interior of the restaurant. Scents of fine cuisine and expensive perfume mingled in the warm but conditioned air.

'This is very smart. The pictures, are they of the horse? The Double Trigger?' She blushed attractively; Douglas softly giggled.

'Some of them are, darling, yes. Does that fascinate you then? The thought of a stud, do you like horses?'

'I like horses, yes. I can ride, Douglas. I enjoy riding...' She grasped her cup, trying to avoid his eye.

'I *know* you do sweetie, there'll be plenty of opportunity later for a little canter, *mmmm*? *Look* at me! You're very desirable when you blush, you know. Shall we make a move and find our seats?'

The gentleman in the last seat of the row stood and raised his hat to Erika, as she preceded him to their seats.

He studied Douglas as they sat, assessing him casually and acknowledging his smile.

'Wonderful weather today, they may change the going to firm later, do you think?'

'Very possibly, absol*ute*ly,' Douglas agreed pleasantly. 'Truly glorious, Goodwood, *isn*'t it?' He returned to studying the form.

Erika clutched her slip from the bookies, feeling excited. She'd picked the stand she liked the look of, not understanding the odds, choosing the horse she liked the sound of – 'So Be It', an each way bet.

'Have you chosen your horse, Douglas? You didn't go on the course with me.'

'I use the tote, darling –'

'What is your horse? I have "So Be It."'

He smiled. 'I'll tell you if it wins. They're getting ready now. You can borrow these when they're over the other side.' He lifted his binoculars then pointed. 'There's yours now, see? It's over by the rail in the pink, blue and white. You'll have to remove your sunglasses. They're very smart darling, were they expensive?'

Erika smiled. 'Yes they were; they're Gucci, can I have a look?'

He gave her the glasses, resting his hand on her shoulder.

She looked, it was frisky. This was going to be fun.

'Well done sweetie; beginners luck ind*eed*!'

Douglas grinned, the horse of the same name having just completed a row of four winners for Erika, who had excitedly put the money in her clutch bag, the bookie having paid out with a rueful grin and a wink.

'If I eat all this tea I'll get too fat, but I love this cream.' She spooned some more from the dish to her plate. 'I'm really enjoying myself and I love the atmosphere, it's wonderful. Thank you *so* much for bringing me here; we'll have a wonderful time together.'

She leaned across the table. 'I have some beautiful lingerie for you to see later, some very sexy. Just the way you like it!' She narrowed her eyes intensely. 'I'm looking forward to riding my own stud tonight! It will be fantastic!'

'It *will*, darling. I want to make it memorable, satisfy you completely.' He twitched a grin. 'In every w*a*y. You *must* tell me everything you want me to do.' He crinkled his eyes. '*Everything*. We'll have no holds barred, access to all areas! Wonderful, I hoped you'd blush again! You look delicious when you do. I shall eat you up later!'

He licked his lips. She was gorgeous.

'Are you ready for the final onslaught? The last race, the

Steward's Cup's the most exciting; it'll be very crowded then. Afterwards we can amble and take our time. It's not far to Chichester. I booked dinner for eight o'clock.' He stood up and offered his arm. 'Shall we go?'

They strolled to the betting then found their seats. The last chair was empty, the gentleman no longer around.

Erika stood close to Douglas; the horses were entering the final straight. Decorum had disappeared and she was jostled in the crowd. Turning, she thought she saw the man who'd been sitting at the end of their row, but he didn't return her smile, consulting with a woman standing next to him. They all looked the same, the men, in linen suits and cream panamas. A deafening roar went up and the horses thundered past; she hadn't been able to choose one in time. Now shouts, screams, and waving arms were all around her, jamming her, making her nervous in the crescendo.

Douglas turned smartly towards the winning post, for an instant facing the man who'd sat next to him during the first race. He sensed a rushing in his ears, blotting out the crowd. A slight thump once against his stomach brought with it an incredible, unbelievable pain. It was erupting like molten lava inside him and he gasped in surprise, gaping at the man as he clutched there in agony. He shut his eyes for a moment, gasping, and then opened them. Shooting out his hand, but the man had gone. Staggering backwards in the mêlée, he heard a curse from someone behind him who shoved him forward. His dream was recurring: he was falling, but this time in the most excruciating, burning pain. He felt the cloth of the coat of the man in front of him as he fell, then it all went black and he knew no more.

The noise subsided, the crowd surging and dividing. Someone had tripped slightly behind her and she turned to find Douglas on the ground, curled up as if asleep. His eyes were fixed wide open as was his mouth, as if he'd fallen down shouting. Erika stared, bewildered for a moment, then crouched and gently shook his arm. Blood, in a brilliant red stream, was oozing gently from between his fingers. She stared stupidly, her lips moving and working but no sound escaping. She looked up frantically; everything was in slow-motion. A few people were watching with mild concern and curiosity, stepping back, unwilling to get involved, some tripping over him. Turning him over, she couldn't find blood anywhere else, then she realised her hand had left the bloody stencil mark she saw on his coat: her palm and five fingers and she began to scream.

45

'Miss Helshonn? Erika Helshonn, is that your name, can you hear me?'

She knew the paramedic was speaking to her, but he looked miles away, from the wrong end of a telescope. She felt dizzy, her head numb and woolly, as if filled with padding and unable to function properly. Smelling antiseptic, she found her hands being wiped carefully by a woman in a green uniform with a badge, using a white cloth, kneeling next to a medical case, open and full of medical equipment.

Looking around, she saw she was within a sealed off area now. Posts with flapping tape between them were staked around her and police were everywhere. There was no sign of Douglas. In the distance, emergency service vehicles and police cars with blue flashing lights were parked. She tried speaking, but no sound would come. Everything was dissolving around her. There were pins and needles in her arms and her head felt so light. Pinpricks of light, like minute fireworks, were shooting in her eyes. She heard the man's voice again, speaking to the woman holding and wiping her fingers.

'I think she's going again, is there any more ID in her bag, a phone or something? Get it out and let's have a look.'

The woman opened Erika's clutch bag, drew out her mobile and addressed her clearly.

'We're going to call someone for you, sweetheart, okay!' She pressed the buttons, concentrating.

'Is there ice there, an emergency number? Who've you got? I'm going to wrap her in a blanket, she's a bit shivery.'

'I can't see an emergency number, there's "Jed" here – quick I think she's going….'

* * *

Jed had just opened his second bottle of ice cold beer when his mobile sounded, and he looked at the screen: 'Erika.' He checked his watch, it was six thirty. Cautiously, tension uncoiling like the tendrils of a burgeoning creeper, he pressed answer and waited.

'Hello, hello, is that Jed please?'

Who was it? 'Who's calling?' *Don't panic; whatever you do, don't panic.*

'This is the accident and emergency department at St. Richard's Hospital, Chichester; staff nurse here. Am I speaking, or can I speak to, Jed please? Hello?'

They must have Erika's phone, although *his* phone would have Jed on as well...so *now what? Just try not to panic; it's not the police – yet.*

'Jed Zeitermann here, yeah; can I help you?'

'I have the mobile phone here of Erika Helshonn. We have her in this department under sedation. It's not serious but she's suffering severe shock. Are you a friend or relative? We couldn't ascertain from her the best person to call. Can you tell me your relationship, please?'

The woman sounded calm and pleasant, no hint of anything else.

'She's my girlfriend.' *Act dumb; you don't know what all this is about.* 'What happened then? Is she there, can I speak to her?'

'Not at the moment, she's had an injection and is sleeping. We're keeping her in for observation tonight in the Emergency Medical Unit but tomorrow if the registrar clears her, she'll need to be collected.' The nurse bit her lip, she needed to be diplomatic. 'Miss Helshonn was brought here from Goodwood Racecourse. There's a police investigation in place and she may need to answer a few questions tomorrow if she's well enough....' Silence. She wondered what this was all about: a very attractive young woman in the company of a man old enough to be her father, who'd been shot.

'At Goodwood races, did you say Goodwood *races?*' He tried to sound confused. 'I thought she was going to Spain, to Barcelona. I dropped her off at the airport, at Heathrow this morning… Goodwood *racecourse!*'

He decided he'd take a chance and come clean. If he could get to Erika before she had a chance to say too much it could all work out. Nothing could connect him to the hit man. There was no evidence at all, with a million pound business you were moving money about all the while, all over the place.

'*Hang* on a minute,' he asked, 'was she with a colleague of mine, Douglas Spencer?' As if a penny was dropping somewhere. 'I called the racecourse, oh, last week some time I think, because I was *going* to go. I thought we might all be able to sit together but then Erika told me she was going to Barcelona, so I thought that was that. Is *he* there as well then? Obviously I must've got the wrong end of the stick. Is he there? Did he go or what?'

'I think it'll be better if you discuss all this tomorrow when the police are here. I *can* tell you Miss Helshonn was with Mr. Spencer, but towards the end of the final race he was shot by what they think was a hit man. An investigation's underway and an appeal and report should be on the news tonight.'

She hoped she hadn't spoken out of turn; he'd soon get to know. She'd try to be on duty when he arrived, curious now to see who this woman was two-timing.

'Can I take it then you'll come and collect her tomorrow? When you arrive, come to the A and E department and then follow the signs to the EMU.'

'Did you say Douglas Spencer *shot?*' He sounded incredulous. 'I can't *believe* it! Yeah I'll be there tomorrow, as soon as I can.' He had an afterthought, 'Tell her I'm comin' and everything's okay, can you? Tell 'er Jed says not to worry; bloody hell, she must've had a hell of a shock. I hope she has a good night, I'll be there around lunchtime tomorrow I should think, thanks for callin'. Bye now.'

'See you tomorrow then. I'm sure she'll be fine, goodbye.'

* * *

Stella watched as the car pulled into her drive, filled with cases and boxes. Clive climbed out carefully, holding a bouquet of flowers from the corner shop: a bright mixed bunch with a fern and a stick of greenery. *He loves you, Stella, a caring and loving man, who's come to look after you and be a good companion. That's what you need now, Stella, a good companion. Kindness and tenderness, you don't need passion, dear.*

Why wasn't she grateful, she wondered? She must pull herself together and be grateful, open the door and smile! This was faithful Clive, who she'd treated so badly; *so badly she should be ashamed, she reminded herself.*

'Hello Clive, come in, oh thank you for the lovely flowers, they're beautiful.' She took them and sniffed. 'Thank you very much, I'll put them in water straight away, come in.'

She held the door then saw Angela across the road, fiddling with her front gate it looked like, and gave her a wave.

'That's Angela, Clive.' She indicated the watchful woman. 'She's always out cleaning her car. She's very friendly, but Donna next door's a bit of a gossip and likes to know what's going on. I expect she'll make some comment. Anyway, come in and well, make yourself at home!' She waved her arms around and smiled at him, then hugged the flowers again. 'I'll go and find a vase, won't be a sec.'

Clive set down a holdall carried in with the flowers, and returned to the car to continue unloading. Pulling stuff from the boot, he saw a woman approaching from his right; he assumed this was Donna. One suitcase in each hand, he offered a brief smile and strode past her up the driveway, putting them down in the hall.

'I think Donna's spotted me already, she's out there now....'

'Is she?' Stella placed the flowers in the sitting room and peered through the window. 'Oh yes, that's her; just ignore her, she likes to be nosy. I thought we could go out for something to eat later perhaps, about six o'clock?'

'Where shall I take these cases? Upstairs okay?' He paused on the bottom step. 'And that sounds great, yes; we could find somewhere quiet to go.' He trudged up and Stella followed him. In her room they paused awkwardly; Clive put the bulging cases down and sat on the bed.

'I don't think this is going to be very easy for either of us really, Stella. So much has happened. I *know* you don't love me or think I'm in the same league as, as, that other man, but I *do* love and care about you. I'm sure we can be happy.

'We *used* to be happy didn't we, until *he* came along and spoilt it all?' He looked up with that lopsided grin he had. 'Sit down here and kiss me.'

He held his arms out. She tried, but couldn't stop her body tensing almost rigidly – she didn't want to do this, didn't want to be with him. She knew who she wanted.

* * *

'Shall we put the news on? It's nine o'clock, see what the headlines are?' Clive went towards the television. Back from a shopping trip and a meal at a Chinese afterwards, Stella felt exhausted with nervous strain. They couldn't go on like this: Mr and Mrs Nice Guys again, in their 'ideal world.' She would go mad.

'You look tired, my darling, we'll just watch this and then you can go to bed.' He sat next to her.

'…And the main headlines tonight: Police are investigating a murder at Goodwood Racecourse in Sussex earlier this evening, as the last race was finishing. The dead man has been identified as Mr Douglas Spencer, a former gynaecologist from Harley Street who was involved with a Club in London's Soho, the famous Sirens Club. The police have begun an investigation and are keen to speak to a Miss Erika Helshonn –'

Clive pressed the remote as Stella collapsed next to him, her whole body limp. He didn't know what to do. Hesitating, he lifted an arm, slipping it round her shoulders; she didn't seem to notice.

'Stella, are you all right? Who was Erika Helshonn? Was she at the club too? Hey, come on my darling, he's dead now; the bastard got what he deserved. You should be happy, don't you think?'

Shrugging his arm off, she rose unsteadily from the sofa.

'I'm going upstairs to bed now, Clive. I don't want to know any more. I don't know who Erika was, but Jed was the club manager. I expect it'll all be in the papers now as well. I'm sorry, but I just want to go up to bed.'

46

'Helen, *Helen!* Come here and see this, *quick!*' Reggie stared at the screen in disbelief.

Helen's muffled voice was agitated. 'What is it? I'm in the bath!'

'It's Douglas, pet; he's been shot at Goodwood races. It's on the news!'

Helen wondered if she'd heard correctly. Did he mean he'd been caught on camera? She hauled herself out of the bath, grabbed a towel and nipped to the bedroom.

'Did you say *shot?* What, *fired* at?'

'Aye, looks like it, he's dead, Helen. Police are looking into it. It looks like he went with Erika after all. She's at St Richard's Hospital in severe shock they said and you'll know who's at the bottom of this....'

Helen looked blank.

'No, no, Reggie, who is?'

'Jed Zeitermann, manager of the Sirens Club. Erika was his girlfriend, Paula and I caught them together, caught her with Douglas, I mean. I guess he wasn't too happy about it, like.'

Helen stared agog, her brain struggling to process this information. 'Douglas went to Goodwood races with this man's girlfriend? But how do you know?'

He explained again, gently. 'Because they've just said so darling, Erika Helshonn accompanied Douglas Spencer. He's dead, shot by a hit man they think and she's in St Richard's Hospital, Chichester, in shock, home tomorrow if the doctors are satisfied. The police are questioning her but so far they don't seem to have a lead – at the moment.'

'Are you going to say anything? Are you going to go to the police?' she asked anxiously.

He sat back, more relaxed. 'Not yet; I want to see how things develop. I'm not jumping in feet first and it's no use getting all het up either.' Seeing her expression, he added, 'let's just calm down and see what gives, shall we?'

'Okay,' she agreed reluctantly, 'but I think you'd better fill me in with a few more facts first.'

47

After a disturbed night, Jed woke and called Reggie at eight o'clock. Helen answered, annoyed at being disturbed at that time on a Sunday morning.

'Hello, Helen Colshall?'

'Oh hi it's Jed Zeitermann; sorry to disturb you, could I possibly speak to Reggie?'

She rolled over and passed the receiver. 'It's for you, it's Jed.'

He winked and settled down with it.

'Mornin' Jed, aye, I saw the news. I wondered if you might be ringin'. Are you goin' over to the hospital later?'

'I'm goin' as soon as I've finished talking to you. How much have you told Helen? I know she's right next to you, but if I hold the conversation this end, you can just say yes or no, okay?'

'Fire away Jed – I told her Erika was your girlfriend and Spencer had pinched her like and you weren't likely to be very happy about it but no more. I haven't heard from Paula, although she must know and so must Stella. Aye man, it's goin' to make headlines for a while seein' as he's dead, so go on – '

'I fixed the whole thing up with a mate of mine soon after you'd told me and he did the job. It was a contract. He disappears and I pay the balance on Wednesday….'

Reggie was waiting. 'Aye, I'm with you so far…'

'For God's sake, don't repeat any of this. I can trust you, can't I?'

He suddenly felt vulnerable and nervous. Reggie was the only one he'd tell. Concerns and worries were racing round his brain like a blurred fairground ride, spinning and spinning. He was dreading the police questions, he'd have to get to Erika before they did and make out he didn't care what the circumstances were, he was glad she was okay.

'I'll have to speak to the police at the hospital,' he continued, 'I'll say I dropped her off at Heathrow, thinking she was goin' to Barcelona. I'm not over the moon findin' she went to Goodwood with a bloke I work with, but under the circumstances I'm glad she's around. Anyway, seein' as he's dead, there's not a lot I can say to Spencer, is there? I reckon they'll see that.' He rubbed his hand through his hair. 'I mean, they'd understand that I'd be mad *now*, but not much I could do about it. It puts the Club in a bit of a state though. Do you think we should just sit it out and see what happens? Just play it as low key as possible, yeah?'

'Aye man, I think that's essential.' Helen rose, signalling she was going down to make some tea. He nodded, smiling. It wasn't returned. He waited a few moments.

'Are you still there?' Jed was anxious to wind this up and get moving.

'Aye, Helen's just gone down to make some tea and talking of over the moon, she certainly isn't as he was her heart-throb for so long. I won't tell anyone what you've told me, but keep your wits about you and your mouth shut when you can, or you're goin' to be in deep shit. You don't need me tellin' you that, man! If it was a professional job, nothing should trace back to you.'

'I will and thanks mate, I owe you one. Is there any chance you could come up the Club again soon? We'll have to discuss what we do now he's gone. If you're interested, I'd like to see you on the board when the dust has settled a bit. What would you say to that?'

'Aye, well I'll consider it, but like you say, I think one day at a time at the moment, Jed, be canny.' He listened. 'She's on her way back up now; good luck! Keep in touch.'

'Thanks mate, I will.'

Jed hung up and rooted through his wardrobe for the shirt and trousers that Erika liked on him, sloshed on some aftershave and set off for the hospital.

Erika had been moved to a private room. As the nurse admitted him, she was sitting looking out of the window, dressed in the sweater and linen trousers she'd worn when he'd dropped her off at the airport. Her face wan, she portrayed nothing as the nurse spoke to Jed before leaving, but as she closed the door behind her, she sank her head between both hands, her fingers scraping her scalp, her shoulders shuddering in silent sobs. He sat squarely on the edge of the bed, hands facing inward on each thigh.

'Cut the crap, Erika, and turn off the waterworks. Listen to me yeah. *Look* at me!'

He pushed a box of tissues from the bedside table at her and waited while she pulled one out. She flicked a glance at him nervously, fixing on his knees. His legs were apart and she tried not to look at his crotch. All her emotions had migrated to her extremities and were sitting there like lumps of lead, her head throbbing as if this process had ripped her brain to raw shreds. Attempting something close to a smile, she waited.

'Now look, I don't know if you've said anything to our boys in blue yet, but as far as *I'm* concerned I dropped you off at Heathrow, thinkin' you were on your way to a work do in Barcelona. I've just learned in the last twenty-four hours, that instead of *that* you was swannin' off to Goodwood races with Douglas fuckin' Spencer!!'

He waited while she took that in.

'I'm not exactly thrilled about it and they wouldn't expect me to be, but I'm not about to brain you either. What I *do* need to know is was you *really* plannin' to ditch me for that bastard? Look at me and tell me, do you love me or are you still screwed up with that scumbag? I need to know, Erika, and now would be good, yeah?'

Staring at him, desperation and confusion streamed from her eyes. He must be at the bottom of this somewhere, she thought and isolating that thought – that he was responsible for the death of Douglas – was chilling. He was waiting for an answer but she needed time and there wasn't any.

'Do you love *me* Jed? Even though you know what I was doing, do you still love *me?*'

'I've *always* loved you, Erika, more than any woman I've ever known and if it helps, yes, I still do. So come on, do you want to try again and make a go of this together or not?'

Standing up, she put her hands on his shoulders and took a deep breath.

'I'm very sorry, Jed. I've never cheated on you with anyone else and I do still love you. I want to make a try with this; if you'll have me back we can –'

There was a knock at the door and a policeman came in. Nodding briefly at Erika, he addressed Jed.

'Jed Zeitermann?'

'Yes, that's me.' He stood up.

'Mr. Zeitermann, you're aware now of events that have occurred recently, the death in suspicious circumstances of Mr. Douglas Spencer.'

It was a statement. Jed said nothing, waiting.

'It appears Mr. Spencer had just assumed the position of chairman at the Sirens Club.' He paused and Jed remained silent. 'I can tell you that, at the *moment,* you are not under caution. Were you up until last Wednesday, Chief Executive of this club, the Sirens Club?'

'That's correct, yes I was. Mr. Spencer had acquired sufficient shares to become Chairman. I had a letter from his solicitor telling me so. He then called a meetin' to announce it. I was retained as C.E.O.'

The policeman's face was reasonable, almost congenial, but Jed was wary; he'd answer what was asked, but no more.

'I wonder if you'd mind going to the station when you've finished your visit here with Miss Helshonn, to answer a few more questions. Assist us with our enquiries as they say.'

Jed didn't sense there was an alternative option here.

'Yeah I'll be right there. I need about half an hour?'

The policeman checked his watch.

'I was thinking more in the region of the next five minutes? My colleague's there waiting for you. Inspector Swift. I'll have a few words with Miss Helshonn here when you've gone.'

From his stance like the rock of Gibraltar, it was obvious he wasn't going anywhere.

Jed was calm he sat back on the bed. The policeman stood at a discreet distance by the door.

'I'll go to the station now and explain how I dropped you off at the airport, but look, I meant what I said. I love you and I'm sure we can sort this out. Just look after yourself and I'll see you back at home soon, yeah?'

Kissing her, he squeezed her shoulder before turning to the officer. 'I'm on me way – I take it you mean the station in the town here?' He put his hands in his pockets then took them out, unsure what to do with them.

'That's the one. Inspector Swift's waiting for you,' he said, opening the door.

Jed turned, waving quickly at Erika, who smiled, looking happier. He left to find his car and head for the police station.

48

Rhoda finished her third vodka, with a dash of tonic and no ice, without a clue what to do. She'd picked up the phone to call Douglas and even dialed his number before realising he'd never answer again. She'd call the club on Monday and try to speak to Gloria, find out what the situation was there, now he was no longer around. Would her position as a new director still be valid? How much would she be paid? No more cheques from him now! She sat in an armchair and stared out of the window.

Everything was so normal. It wasn't even the main story on the news anymore. She couldn't remember ever feeling at such a loose end. Most of her life, from the time she saved him after Valerie's death and guarded his reputation so carefully, had been spent living vicariously through him, clinging on to something that was never really there. He'd longed for the true love of Helen, but hadn't sat moping about it, getting on with his life in the meantime, but she, she realised now as the full weight of loneliness began to hit her, had completely let life pass her by emotionally. Now she had nothing.

Tears, like the large heavy blobs at the beginning of a summer storm, fell on her lap and increased in the deafening silence. She imagined Helen, happily settled with Reggie; Stella, presumably back with her friend Clive again, that Douglas had told her about, and Jed – his girlfriend would have some explaining to do, but nothing that they couldn't sort out in time.

Gloria owned a small Yorkshire terrier called Rascal that she'd seen a couple of times, a cute little thing with a red bow on its head; everyone seemed to have *someone* and she had no one left. Her nose began to run and drip with her tears; she reached over for a tissue from a box on the coffee table then succumbed to the heartrending sobs which felt they'd go on forever.

* * *

Erika paced the flat, trying not to nibble at her manicured fingernails. She never bit her nails, but she was so tense waiting for a phone call from Jed she couldn't keep her hand from her mouth.

She looked at her watch and stared at the phone, willing it to ring; it was getting on for midnight. The journey home from the hospital had been horrendous: a taxi all the way to the service station to collect her car, then returning it to Heathrow and then coming home by train and tube. She was exhausted. Jed had been at the police station for nearly eleven hours. Suddenly it rang and she grabbed at it.

'Hello? Jed?'

'Hi, is that Erika Helshonn?' It was a woman's voice. 'Yes, yes it is…' She held the receiver in both hands anxiously. 'Who's calling please?'

'Hi Erika, this is Virginia Sheldon from the *Daily Reader*; I know it's a bit late, but I wondered if you might like to give me your side of the story tomorrow.' She continued without taking a breath, determined to have her say. 'The events surrounding Douglas Spencer's death must have been very traumatic for you and the consequences far-reaching for the future of the Sirens Club in London. If you talk to me exclusively, we'd offer you a considerable payment; in fact for any information you gave me in an interview, plus the interest there's going to be in this story, you're in a position virtually to name your price, what do you say?'

'I, I know where you're from and I understand you are looking for a good story, but I think I could help you if I tell you of a woman who was closer than me to Mr. Spencer and who would know more about the effect on the club now and I'm sure would be willing, very much, to talk to you for some payment. I'm waiting here to get a call from my boyfriend and need to have the phone free.' Scrabbling for the telephone and address book she turned to the C page. 'I have it here; her name is Rhoda Chambers if you are interested, she was recently moved to the board by Douglas and will know a great deal about what you want to know, I think.'

'That's fantastic, Erika, thank you, I'd love her number.' Her pen was poised ready, next to the name she'd just noted. Carefully copying it down she repeated it.

'Yes that's correct; I'm sorry, but I really need the phone free now, thank you!' She pressed the button and ended the call. Almost immediately it rang again.

'Hello? Erika here –'

'Erika; Erika, I'll be home soon, are you okay?' Jed sounded elated but tired.

'Yes; yes I'm fine. Are they letting you go then now?' She frowned and cradled the phone carefully, as if it was very precious.

'Yeah, I'm free to go for now, no charges as they can't find nothin' and I'm knackered.' His head was thumping violently, the questions hadn't stopped, just a five minute break to go to the loo. He screwed his eyes up against the pain and felt sick. 'I'm going to go and find some twenty-four hour services and have a coffee and somethin' to eat. I can't say what time I'll get in, but I'll see you when I see you.'

The relief flooding her precipitated another wave of exhaustion.

'Fine, I think I'll go to bed. Wake me up when you get back and please drive carefully. I, I'll see you soon then, Jed.'

'Yeah, yeah babe, see you soon; yeah okay….'

He was so tired he couldn't think straight and ended the call. He'd deal properly with *her* in the morning. The greatest news was the bastard was dead: so far so good. The account number to deposit the balance was safe in his office; he'd send it on Wednesday. First, get out of here and hit the road. He set the SatNav for the first suitable service station, a Granada just over four miles away and not much traffic at this time of night – or morning, as he saw the digital clock on the dash. He checked his mirror and slowly drew away.

49

Rhoda woke from her dream with a start as the phone kept ringing. Slumped in the armchair, one empty bottle of vodka on the floor and a half empty one open on the coffee table, she felt dreadful, as if a layer of underlay had been put in her mouth before the carpet, and her skull used to tack it in place. She reached for the phone and let out a sound.

'Yeah?'

Virginia softened her voice. This yelled 'hangover' big time.

'Hi, I'm sorry to trouble you, disturb you, at this difficult time. I was offered your name and number as someone close to Douglas Spencer, who knew about his interest in the Sirens Club. Someone who *might* be interested in being paid for an exclusive interview with the *Daily Reader*, in fact if you're the person I was led to believe, you can name your price. My name's Virginia. Can I ask you, Rhoda, would you be interested at all? I'd love to hear your angle on this story. A little perhaps about Mr. Spencer's background in connection with the club? Was there anyone, apart from yourself, he was connected with perhaps, who worked at the club?' *Pause,* she thought, *let this soak through the alcohol.*

Through the jumbled aching mess that was her brain, Rhoda forced herself to think straight. This lady was from the newspapers and she was offering money. Whatever price she cared to name it seemed, for information on Douglas Spencer. Suddenly everything became clear: kill two birds with one stone! She snorted at this silly expression, holding her throbbing head for a moment. *Tell them all about Douglas and the weekend with Stella;* the little stuck up cow who'd usurped her, thought she was one better than her. Absolutely, what was she waiting for?

'Hello, yes; I'd love to talk to you. I can tell you quite a lot, especially about the weekend just gone and the star of that show, Stella, Stella Maitland actually, yes.' Nausea surged – she needed to lie down for a rest first, but *try and organise something, don't let her get away*. 'Can I get back to you at all? It's been a big shock for me you see; I was very close to Douglas before Stella came on the scene. She thought she was his sweetheart, but she was just another whore and –'

Virginia had struck gold. This was a good four or six page spread. 'Rhoda, if I could just stop you there. I totally understand you need to rest (*and sober up a bit*) so how about we make an appointment and I come round and see you when you've had time to recover from the terrible shock you've had, okay?'

Rhoda was glad; she sounded very understanding. She'd look forward to pouring this out – there was no harm, it would bring publicity to the club and get her own back against Stella.

'Thank you very much; I expect you'd like the news as soon as you can, so how about say four o'clock this afternoon? I can give you the address.'

Virginia checked her appointments, setting an hour for this. She would get the copy ready for the evening. It would come out fresh on Tuesday, just when the others had thought they'd got the lot.

'Four o'clock will be fine, if I could just take your address and before I do, check that the *Daily Reader* will have the exclusive rights to this story?'

Rhoda kicked her brain into gear; one last effort before hitting the sack for a few hours.

'For the right price you can, absolutely, all yours; shall we say…' She thought wildly for a few moments – pay the mortgage off, a little holiday somewhere nice…. '…How about one hundred and fifty thousand pounds, for every last detail? It was a big event, the Stella Weekend Spectacular.'

Virginia smiled; it was in the bag and for less than she would have offered. 'I don't see a problem at all with that, Rhoda. I can let you have a cheque later today if that's all right with you?'

Rhoda bit her lip hard to check she wasn't dreaming. All her money problems had been solved in one day.

'That's fine by me, Virginia; I look forward to seeing you later and my address is forty-two, Thirlstone Road, Little Denton, Dreightonshire, DR1 4BZ Thanks, I'll see you later then?'

'Fantastic; you will, I'll see you soon. You go and have a good rest now and take care!'

Rhoda stood carefully and headed upstairs to the bathroom and then bed for a few hours. She set the alarm to wake her at three; an hour to gather her thoughts.

50

As the first glimmers of light became visible under the curtains, Stella turned over and began to drift into sleep. She'd lain awake for most of the night, listening to Clive's loud snoring which stopped when he turned over, then half the duvet would go with him and the bed lurch. Now it all seemed peaceful. She wondered if it meant *he* was now lying awake, but as drowsiness enveloped her she welcomed it, a conversation now would rob her of any sleep at all.

Clive *was* awake; it was Tuesday, demons having plagued him all night with images of the woman sleeping beside him (looking beautiful now) flaunting and parading her body for the man now dead. She'd sworn nothing had gone any further. That she hadn't ventured into the club itself, but this was hard to believe.

That enough was punishment now, although he'd had a job dealing with it: listening to confessions about her feelings for Douglas twisted the knife. Her apparent unawareness of this – holding him and crying on his shoulder over the bloody man – was almost more than he could bear. He was glad he'd been shot. That was the *only* consolation; that someone had hated him enough to do that, or organise it, but it was still a bit of a mystery. The tabloids were having a field day.

He hadn't bought a paper since Saturday, but he'd fetch a *Daily Reader* from another newsagent. Word was spreading how he and Martha had split. He didn't want to face any gossip or knowing looks from Shirley at the corner shop, who seemed to know everything.

He could tell by her even breathing, she was fast asleep. He peered carefully at his watch: just after four o'clock, he'd doze and not disturb her if he could help it, she was his darling and he loved her so much.

* * *

At half past eight Rhoda called Gloria's mobile.

'Hi Rhoda, are you okay?' Gloria sounded full of beans. 'I've just been readin' the *Daily Reader*! Bloody hell girl, didn't leave much out, did you? We're expectin' a busy day today, Jed's here, lookin' a bit worn out but otherwise on form. We're all tryin' to keep out of his way, heads down and just get on with it. I think anyone askin' him *anythin'* today's askin' for trouble. I can't stay on this long, love, got to sort the till out for the first customers. Are you coming up here soon because we could do with the help?'

Rhoda felt so much better. What a difference a day made!

'I'll be up there as soon as I can. Probably not today, I'm still in a bit of a whirl and I've got some business to sort out –'

'I bet you have! How much did they pay you for that little lot, or aren't you tellin'?'

'Secret, Gloria, but I'm goin' to test my credit card, give it a bit of action I think, if you know what I mean.'

'You do that, girl, and then tell me about it.' Gloria laughed raucously and coughed. 'Got to go, there's a queue at the door; honestly, just got out of bed half of them and takin' their kit off again already, what a life! Anyway, it keeps us in business; 'bye love!'

* * *

Stella woke to a rose from the garden in a small vase and a little note: 'I love you' on her bedside table. She looked at the clock: eight thirty, he must have gone to fetch a paper. She rolled over and stretched, slightly more refreshed now for a few hours of undisturbed sleep. They'd have to have to sort this out, his snoring, tossing and turning were unendurable. She couldn't have another night like that. No way.

She stumbled down for some breakfast. Clive's mug and dish were draining by the sink. She turned the radio on and pottered around, Jeeves fussing for his breakfast too. It was Tuesday, she realised, Cathy would be around soon and there was the shop to go to. Try and establish some routine again.

Clive, having collected the paper, paused outside the shop to flick through it. He reached the Gents next to the shop just in time as all his breakfast came up. The lavatories were empty. He retched, coughed and spat down the reeking bowl, unable to stop. The story was unbelievable, with a few grainy photographs as well.

There was no mistaking it, the naked woman on the table was Stella – his Stella, the woman in whose house he was now staying. The same little lying slut he'd been sleeping with and had just left a note for – the lying, treacherous, scheming little whore that was Stella. His anger knew no bounds now, God help her, he thought as he clutched the bowl, God help her because he'd kill her, he'd go home and kill her. He slammed his fist against the wall of the cubicle, which shook violently. Another man coming in turned and nipped out again. Then two more appeared and one spoke.

'You all right, mate?'

Scrambling to his feet, Clive staggered to the basin. He looked ashen.

'Yeah, yeah I'm okay now, I'm okay.'

'Are you sure? You don't look it.' Bending, he picked up the paper. 'Is this yours? Just been readin' that, sounds some club this Sirens thing! Shame my missus wouldn't let me near a hundred yards of somethin' like that!'

Clive took it and lurched out to the street. He sat heavily on a seat near the bus stop, ramming the paper in the bin next to it before realising Stella would have no idea of this story. He'd go back, shove the paper at her *she deserved to read all of it*, then leave and think what to do next. Perhaps he could stay at Bill's, spend a few nights there to cool off a bit. Killing Stella wouldn't solve anything but he couldn't be near her at the moment. He'd got to get away.

Stella, up and dressed, was finishing putting some makeup on when she heard the back door open.

'Shan't be long, Cathy, just putting a spot of lippy on then I'm off to the shop. Clive will be back in a minute, I think he went to get a paper, although he's been gone some –'

She didn't get any further; his expression as he stood in the doorway stopped her. She'd never seen him look so angry. Traces of vomit stained the front of his shirt and she could smell it. His whole body was shaking with rage as he clutched his paper, the pages all loose and trembling in his hand. When he spoke she could hardly hear him.

'I went to fetch a paper and you're in it. You're the star of the whole show, Stella! Fame at last, go on take a look.' He waved the paper at her. 'Or shall I read you what it says?' He shook it open. 'It says, let's have a look, it says: "*Sensational Stella's a really good Suck!*" and a lovely picture of you lying on a table with nothing on, surrounded by men, some of whom have those little black rectangles over their faces, so you can't see who they are, but you can sure as hell see what they're doing, then the report fills you in on the rest, what happened under the table and where they got the headline from, I presume?' He looked up at her. 'Would I be right there?'

The room swam before her; she dropped her stick of lip gloss and clutched the chest of drawers. Her chest felt tight, as if it had been clamped, then she heard the back door open again. Jeeves was barking excitedly as Cathy breezed in, she said something to him then called out.

'Hi all; are you up there, Stella?'

'We're here, but I'm going in a minute – just having a word with

Stella. I won't be long. Well?' He looked at her again. 'Am I right or am I right?'

'Clive, oh Clive, I, I just, I don't know what to say to you; I, I'm, I'm so –'

'You're what, Stella...*hmmm?* Sorry? *Sorry?*'

He spat the word through clenched teeth, his voice low. He tried to control himself, hold himself in check. His jaw was rigid, his free hand clenching and unclenching. Cathy had turned the radio up a bit, singing along whilst bustling in the kitchen.

Tossing the paper on the bed he turned back towards the door.

'I'm going; I'm going to stay with Bill if he'll have me for a few days, to think things out. I've nowhere else to go now. I don't want to be with you at the moment, I can hardly look at you – how *could* you, Stella? How could you *do* something as, as vile as,' he stopped, lost for words, 'I can't even begin to describe it. You make me sick looking at you, you disgust me.' He rubbed his hand through his hair, bewildered, uncomprehending. 'Have you no respect for yourself anymore? You've obviously none for me, but can't you...'

Cathy was coming upstairs. He stood out of the way as she reached the landing.

'Hi Clive, are you...okay?' She saw the state of him and could smell the sour smell as he passed her.

'I'm fine Cathy, thank you. I'm off now. I'll collect some stuff later, when you're at the shop.'

He strode downstairs and straight out of the back door, slamming it. Cathy regarded Stella, who was curled up on the bed and staring straight ahead, her face white and drawn.

She pulled the sheets of newspaper towards her and began to read, her lips moving, face intent and her eyes wide. Jeeves, bounding up the stairs, jumped on the bed trampling the sheets. She pushed him off while continuing to read.

'Oh Stella, what have you done? What the hell were you thinking of? Have you read all this, all what this "spokesperson" has said, who works at the club? Do you know who it was who's said all this about you? Have you any idea who it might be? Stella? Speak to me?'

'It was Rhoda or Zena as she called herself. She met me there, but knew Douglas all the time. It was all a big game to them, just a game and making money –'

'But what are you going to do? I mean, this is disgusting and everyone's going to read this and know it's you! Whatever are you going to do?'

Taking a deep breath she sat up straight and reached for the phone.

'I'm going to call the surgery and speak to Martin.'

'Martin?' She looked worried. 'Who's Martin?'

'Doctor Carroll, my doctor; he'll understand and know what to do.'

She dialed the number and waited. Cathy took the paper and folded it up, waiting, unsure what to do next.

'Oh hello, can I speak to Doctor Carroll today please, can he call me back at all? Oh…oh yes of course, sorry; no, no there's no one else; thank you.'

Cathy was waiting. 'Well?'

Stella reached for her mobile. 'It's his day off. I'll call him on his mobile. I've got his number…'

Cathy grabbed Jeeves, mouthing she'd take him for a quick walk. Stella nodded.

'Hello, Martin Carroll?'

'Martin it's Stella. It's very urgent, have you seen the *Daily Reader* today?'

'No, but I suspect it has something to do with you, has it?'

'I must see you Martin. I'm leaving here today, right now. I need to see you really urgently, can we meet?'

'I don't know, Stella, things are a little awkward at home for me too at the moment. Where are you going? Keep in touch, I want to help you whatever you've done, it won't be *that* bad you know! It'll all die down and people forget.'

This sounded encouraging. 'I'm going to try to get in at the Fish and Fly Hotel, go and see Mick and Trina. They're always pleased to see me. Clive's gone away for a while because he can't stand the sight of me, I disgust him. I'm disgusting, Martin, aren't I?'

'No you're not, Stella, you know you're not. You're worth so much more than you think you are, you know. We could pop over to Lower End, go to Sara's Coffee Shop and have a coffee if you wanted? You could catch the train from there to Aldbury. Shall we do that? I could meet you there at say between half ten and eleven?'

She looked round her bedroom. There were just a few things to pack. Martin would help her now and if not…she thought of life with Clive. It would never work. She knew what she'd do, it was the only answer. There was nothing left now except Martin.

'Hello Stella? Are you still there?' She sounded so distracted, he thought. Desperate. He hoped he could help.

'Yes, I'm here, I'm fine, Martin. I'll meet you just before eleven at Sara's Coffee Shop in the High Street. I'll just pack a few things. I'll come over on the next bus and go straight to the station afterwards.

Cindy rang Stella, getting Cathy.

'Is Stella coming in today, do you know? Is she there?'

'I don't think so, Cindy. She's gone over on the bus to Lower End to meet her doctor. There's a big article in the *Daily Reader* today, all about her at the club in London she went to with Douglas. It's a bit sordid and she's upset. Clive saw it and he's cleared off. He looked dreadful when I saw him –'

'Oh no, poor Clive, he's had a dreadful time already! Martha's gone and he was kicked out to live with Stella. Where is he now, do you know?'

'I've no idea, one of his mates I suppose. Stella seemed really upset, I mean *really* upset. She threw a few things quickly in a bag, including a knife from the kitchen drawer, then left in a hurry, hardly saying goodbye. I do hope she's all right,' she added, worried.

Cindy debated. 'Well, look, don't you worry, I'll try both of them, Clive and Stella, on the mobile and see what's what. I think seriously she could be heading for a nervous breakdown, Douglas was horrible to her really and she loved him to bits. Now she must be in a right state.' She considered a moment. 'Leave it with me and I'll keep in touch.'

'Thanks Cindy, yes please, if you could. I'll keep an eye on Jeeves. Take him back with me if necessary. I'll see you later then, bye.'

* * *

The coffee shop was very busy, stuffy inside and noisy outside. Martin waited for her on the corner.

'Where do you want to sit Stella, inside or out?'

She looked round, spotting a spare table under the awning. 'Outside, I'll sit over there. Could I have just a regular coffee please?'

'Sure; save a seat and I'll go and fetch them, bit of a queue, but I won't be long.'

She pulled out her mobile and called the hotel.

'Here we go then,' Martin was back, 'a regular for you.' He placed the large cup and saucer down in front of Stella, 'and an espresso for me. Now then,' he said cheerfully, 'what's the problem with the paper?'

Stella regarded him. 'You haven't seen it yet then?'

'I haven't bought a copy, no. I don't normally get the *Daily Reader*, what does it say then?'

She looked down at her hands, then up again, staring into the middle distance. 'Everything; it says everything, photos as well. All about the weekend I spent at the club, the Sirens Club. In complete detail, it spells out all that happened.'

She rubbed her eyes. 'My life's finished here, Martin, totally finished. I need to start all over again.' She looked at him.

'I just don't know how I'm going to do it, whether it's even worth the effort really; what do *you* think?'

Martin sipped his coffee. A small girl patted a dog hitched up outside the coffee shop before her mother pulled her away; he remembered when his daughter was that age.

'What do I think? Of course it is, Stella! There's only tomorrow; you've got to keep going, no good looking back.'

Sighing he looked at her and smiled, taking her hand. She looked so desolate and unhappy. She'd had a rough time really. Nothing ever seemed to go right for her for long.

'I've got to make a new start too I think; it's not working out for me either. It's just a matter of courage and finding the impetus.'

He was very fond of her. She was beautiful and needed some good luck for a change – something would come along, he was sure of it.

'We're pretty much in the same boat then, would you say?'

She enjoyed the feeling of her hand in his. He was warm, understanding and affectionate. They might even be able to start a new life together.

'Pretty much, I think, possibly,' he agreed, 'at a crossroads anyway. So,' he said, changing the subject, 'where are you off to then, I see you have your bag all ready.'

Stella stroked his hand with her thumb, feeling a little better. Perhaps everything would be all right after all.

'I've called my friends at the Fish and Fly Hotel at Aldbury; Mick's keeping a room for me there for a couple of nights, they've got a fishing competition on I think.'

She decided to take a chance.

'Would you like to come down there? I can stay for a few days. They'll always find room for me. It's ever so pretty, right in the middle of the countryside, beautiful and peaceful; I love it.'

Martin smiled again, wistfully. 'It sounds wonderful, just what I need really, some peace and quiet away from it all. Well, you never know. I might take you up on your offer, I'm sure it would be great. You're a very special person, Stella, you just need someone to look after you and tell you that – and they will one day, you wait and see. Anyway' he said, finishing his espresso, 'keep in touch won't you?' He looked at his watch. 'Better make a move, I've got to see the solicitor this afternoon and I need to sort some papers out.'

Stella finished her cooled coffee. 'Are you definitely leaving then? Home I mean?'

'I think so, it's what Linda wants. It's all a bit of a nightmare really, the upheaval of it all. Your plan sounds wonderful, I'm sure it'll be lovely there. Are you going now?'

'Fairly soon, my room's ready after four o'clock, but I can sit in their gardens and wait. It's beautiful, you'll love it.'

'I'm sure I shall. Keep me posted.' He rose, waited for her to collect her handbag and small case together and put his arms around her. 'Look after yourself, promise me. I'll see you soon.'

See me soon! He's going to come and be with me!

'I will Martin, I will, and I'll see you soon, then!'

'That's right; think positive, it's the only way. Have a great time, don't worry about the papers, it'll be someone else tomorrow, you'll see.'

She was smiling now, so much happier than when he'd first seen her. *The break will do her good*, he thought, it sounded great, but now he had to get on with sorting his own problems out. He waved once more as she headed towards the station then headed back to his car.

51

Stella eased her way out of the Victorian booking hall at Aldbury Mill. It was very warm, just a few white clouds hardly moving. The train had been quite full with anglers. She was glad she knew Mick and Trina and could have her usual room. They were good friends.

The hotel wasn't far from the station, just over a mile and a half. On previous visits she'd walked it, but the sun was beating down and she felt tired, so looked for a taxi. Eventually, once the crowd had dispersed a bit, she found one. Staring from the windows as they drove along, she wondered suddenly if this would be the last time she'd see all this lovely scenery…it was a sobering thought, but no, Doctor Carroll had seemed quite keen to join her there, it would all work out. She wouldn't need to use the knife. It was there just in case. Would it be fair on Mick and Trina if she did? She'd give Martin another call later to see if he *was* coming and if he *wasn't*, then…

'Not in the competition then, or are you?' The driver broke into her dream.

'No, I don't fish, but I like coming here, the scenery's lovely at this time of year I think, well, any time of year really, I –'

'If this sunshine continues it'll be perfect. Supposed to be changing next week, a ridge of low pressure coming so they say; rain, but then my missus always reckons weathermen tell lies and I'm inclined to agree with her….'

Droning cheerfully on regardless, not waiting for any response, made Stella glad. She settled back in her seat.

The desk was busy on her arrival. Mick saw her and took her bag.

'Travelling light are we, Stella?' Smiling, he carried it up the stairs to her room. 'Trina's very busy with the competitors, but I'm sure she'll give you a call later. If you want dinner tonight I'd suggest you come down early, maybe six o'clock?' He opened the door and put the bag on her bed. 'The bar will be packed, but they'll be out all day during the competition so it won't be too noisy then.'

'Thanks Mick, I'll come down at half past five and have a drink then. I'll eat as soon as you have the food ready!'

He grinned. Stella enjoyed her food.

'That's fine, we'll see you later. I know Rosemary's looking forward to seeing you too. I'll let you get on now, see you later!'

'Thanks see you later.'

She looked out of the window at the lawn sloping down towards the river, behind a bank of beautiful chestnut trees. The sun was shimmering, the heat rising from the terrace directly below her. Sitting on her bed she opened her bag, removing the few clothes she'd brought, plus her laptop. If he *was* going to join her, they'd go off and begin a new life, possessions a minor detail at first. He'd talked about leaving home so that was something. A faint glimmer of hope! She tipped her bag up, emptying the last bits and pieces. Out fell the knife from her kitchen. Its handle was pine. It was lethal. The number of times she'd nicked her finger on its blade by accident! Chopping an onion once, she'd nearly taken the top of her finger off, the cut was so deep.

She stared at it, slightly afraid now. She knew *why* she'd packed it – if she wasn't going to be with Doctor Carroll then life wasn't worth living. After everything she'd been through, if happiness wasn't going to come her way now then that was it. She felt calm then, it was easy really, either she'd be with Doctor Carroll or she'd be dead – simple. After tidying everything away she put her laptop on the desk and booted it up. Looking in her music library, she found it: *I'm getting sentimental over you*. If she needed a reminder of just how bad things had been, how low she'd sunk, there it was. It was very suitable.

Going down for dinner at half past five, she saw Trina with their daughter, Fleur.

'Hi Stella, good to see you again, bit busy I'm afraid! Mick's in the bar if you want a drink. We'll try and catch up later. You could come with me when I take her to nursery in the morning if you like.' She looked at Fleur, pulling at her skirt, 'Little miss! What do you think you're doing, hey?' she bent and held her daughter's hand, then turned with a look of slight confusion, 'There's no one with you then? I thought Mick had said something about your doctor coming, but he might have been wrong, he thought he'd misheard.'

Stella was cheerful. 'Thanks Trina, I'll go and get a drink. No, he didn't mishear me, just not at the moment. I'm going to call him later. He's got a few things to sort out, then he should be coming, his name's Martin.'

By the time she got back to her room it was too late to call him. She didn't think she'd sleep very well, but as soon as her head hit the pillow she was away.

The morning light seeping through the curtains woke her. For a moment she had to think where she was. On the bedside table was her mobile, all charged up. She didn't feel very hungry, Rosemary had left three packets of ginger biscuits on her tea tray – that would do.

She called reception. It was Rosemary there.

'Hello, Stella, don't worry, I'm taking Fleur to nursery this morning. Trina will see you later. Did you have a good night? Are you sure you wouldn't like me to bring something up for you?' Fleur was whining in the background…it sounded urgent. 'Sorry, Stella love, I've got to go, Fleur wants something. I'll see you later. I'll be calling into Aldbury on my way back from dropping her off, but should be back by around eleven, I'll see you then. Are you *sure* you won't have something brought up?'

Stella was positive. 'No thanks, I'm quite sure. See you later...' *Possibly.*

She'd have tea and biscuits first. She checked her watch, it was half past eight. At nine she'd call Martin. Suddenly there was a disturbance and she looked out of the window. The anglers were chatting and laughing. They'd got huge green umbrellas, boxes and rods...so much tackle and gubbins to carry. What *was* the attraction of sitting for hours dangling a rod with a fiddly small feather on the end, she wondered.

The kettle was boiling, she checked her watch again – time was dragging. No messages on her mobile. The time on that read the same as her watch. Her stomach felt sore and tense. He *must* come. Should she have explained how to get there? He'd said he'd be in touch. Did that mean he'd *certainly* be coming? *Something* had to go right....

It was nine o'clock. Her palms were sweating and her thumb shook. She pressed 'call' and watched 'calling Martin' with a little green arrow...

'Hi, Martin Carroll...Hello Stella how are you? Have you settled in?'

She tried to sound bright.

'Hello, Martin. I'm at the hotel, yes, and it's lovely. What time do you think you'll get here?'

A pause: she could hear him breathing.

'Stella, I'm not coming to the hotel. That's in your imagination.' She held her breath. 'Look, I'm sorry how things turned out for you, you *know* I am. I referred you to Emma for counselling and you know I've got feelings for you, but it's not going to happen the way you want it to. It's *never* going to happen that way.'

She lay back on the bed and stared at the ceiling. So, this was it. Now she wanted to end the call, didn't want to hear his voice.

They were all the same, men. All of them: all bastards, with the possible exception of Clive....

'Hello, Stella? Are you still there?' he asked anxiously.

What do you care? '...yes, I'm still here, sorry to call you Martin, bye.'

He tried to reassure her.

'You'll be transferred to another doctor's list. You'll be okay, Stella. Stella?' She'd gone.

Placing the phone on the bedside table, she closed the curtains then went to the bathroom and turned on the taps. If she was going to slash her wrists, it was better done in the bath. Less mess for whoever found her, Rosemary probably. Should she leave a note? No, it'd get back to the surgery soon enough what she'd done. Just get on with it. As the bath filled she booted up her laptop again and found the tune. Twist the knife one last time.

She heard the intro, then pulling her nightdress off she slowly shuffled a foxtrot, imagining Douglas holding her. Quietly, she continued the painful dance: her dance of death.

Seeing her reflection in the mirror, naked, hair tousled, eyes wide and tears rolling down her cheeks, made her stop. The hot water pipes were roaring; she went into the bathroom, turning off the taps, and then went to fetch the knife and laptop, *keep playing it, over and over...*

Sitting up in the bath, she clicked 'play again' and then made the first cut: straight down the vein on her wrist, vertically. It didn't hurt; how amazing! When she'd cut her finger she remembered, chopping that onion, she'd nearly hit the roof. With a kind of fascination now, she watched the blood flow, dispersing into the bathwater in spidery lines. She cut again, just above it this time, switching hands to cut the other side. Still no pain and yet it was deep and sliced. The water was deep red. Carefully wiping her hand, she hit 'play again' once more...the soulful trombone continued.

Trina listened and looked up; something from the big band era, a trombone solo. Stella's room, she thought. Oh well, as long as she's happy, a bit repetitive though, that must be the tenth time. Ah, it's stopped. Fed up I expect, same old tune. So now what; she waited…nothing. The phone rang.

'Hello, Fish and Fly Hotel? Yes I should think so, the twenty fourth you say, just one moment…' She checked the computer screen. 'Yes we have that available; three nights? Certainly, can I take a name and address plus a contact telephone number please? Thank you, Mr. Snell, we'll send you a letter of confirmation and see you on the twenty fourth, thank you for calling….yes I can give you a non-smoking room, that's not a problem, goodbye.'

She entered the details on the screen, then looked over the desk and through the glass panelled doors at the sun streaming in. They looked a bit smeary. She'd have a word with Rosemary…still silence. She couldn't understand it, but something wasn't right. She spotted Ruby, who was on her way to open up the beauty salon.

'You couldn't take the desk for a moment could you, Ruby? I just want to pop upstairs a minute, I won't be long.'

At the top, she swung through the fire door and knocked. No reply.

'Stella, it's Trina, are you all right in there?'

No reply. She hesitated; perhaps she was in the bath or something. She knocked again more loudly, still no reply. Feeling in her pocket for the pass-key, she deliberated, then slipped it in and turned the lock.

The room was empty but the bathroom door was open and a laptop on the floor. No wonder she could hear the music…

'RUBY…No! Oh my God, *RUBY!!!!!* Call an ambulance; NOW, *immediately it's an emergency! QUICKLY; HURRY!!'*

Struggling, she hauled Stella up from the bright red water and tried to hold her, but she was too slippery and heavy, and slid down again. Gently she patted her cheek then lifted an eyelid, at a loss to know *what* to do. Stupid, *stupid* girl; whatever had caused this? Seeing the laptop she tapped the pad and the tune returned. She watched. Stella's eyelids twitched a solitary tear, then nothing. Reaching forwards and grappling for the plug, she heard footsteps as the fire door opened.

'DON'T COME IN Ruby! Stay outside!'

'It's Mick, darling, what's the matter? Ruby's just called an ambulance, oh my GOD!'

He pulled the plug, the water gurgling out. They heard wailing sirens and the crunch of tyres on the gravel. Ruby was directing them upstairs. A flash of green uniforms through the crack in the door and they were there. As the ambulance departed, sirens and lights blaring, Rosemary returned, dodging it as it haired up the drive.

She rushed in. 'What the hell was *that* all about? Who is it?'

Mick was helping Trina, who was dizzy, her head between her knees.

'It was Stella, she tried to kill herself. They've taken her to the infirmary I think, at Chawlton, the Jago Wing. She's alive, just. Can you get the phone for me? Thanks.'

52

Cindy had tried calling Stella without success so rang Clive. He sounded flat.

'Yeah?'

'Clive, where are you? I can't get hold of Stella. Cathy said she left yesterday for a hotel, packing a kitchen knife, very distracted. We're all a bit worried.' There was no sound, just him breathing.

'I know all about the newspaper, and I'm sure she's not exactly your favourite person at the moment, but she might do something silly –'

'Do something *silly?* Ha! Well *that's* rich, I must say. Sillier than her current behaviour you mean? So what do you want *me* to do about it then?' he snorted, 'she hasn't listened to me so far, what makes you so sure she'd listen to me now, or *anyone* with any sense come to that?'

Cindy saw his point and sympathised, but if *anyone* could get through to Stella, *he* could, before it was too late.

'Clive, I know where you're coming from and maybe we're overreacting; she was going to meet her doctor first apparently.'

'Oh yes, the good Doctor Carroll.' His tone was scathing. 'More than likely another of her paramours, there can't be *many* men left who haven't had a bit of Stella Maitland at one time or another!'

Cindy winced and held the phone away from her ear.

'Well as far as *I'm* concerned, she can stew in her own juice – no pun intended,' He was quieter now, but emphatic, '*Cindy,* you can be sure that wherever Stella is right now, *some* man will be making her wet and I've had just about enough. I loved her with everything I had and all she did was throw it back in my face. Well now she can go and do the proverbial, I've *had* it –'

'Clive, please; I can understand why you're bitter, but I think underneath everything she did really have feelings for you, you know, she really did.' She changed tack. 'Where are you staying, anyway?'

'I'm at my mate Bill's, but it's not very comfortable. I'm on the sofa as he's got some other blokes staying here as well, over from Cyprus.'

'Well in that case, why don't you stay at Stella's? She's not there, you might as well use her bed and –'

Clive was quick. 'Yeah, now that's a good idea, why not! Every other man has.' He paused and Cindy wondered if he was still there, but he was thinking. 'Yeah okay, I'll be right over. Cathy will've left it all clean and tidy. I'll collect my stuff together, give Bill a call or leave him a note and be right over. Thanks Cindy, I'll see you later.'

Cindy gave Cathy the news.

'He sounded a bit pissed-off, and I can't blame him. He's collecting his stuff and going straight round; he might even like to have Jeeves back, I don't know….'

Cathy was certain. 'No, I'll keep Jeeves, poor thing doesn't know if he's coming or going, Clive'll want to be on his own. The phone rang as I left this morning, I'd popped back to fetch some more of Jeeves's things and had my hands full. I think the answer-phone was on, Clive can pick up any messages.'

* * *

Stella looked at the three other beds opposite: one was empty, one had an old lady in it looking like a shrivelled walnut and the third was occupied by a mousy-haired thin woman fast asleep and snoring, her mouth wide open. The place smelled of the disinfectant used in public lavatories, and was hot and airless. Her wrists were bandaged tightly, to halfway up her arms and felt very sore. Her throat was parched and her head ached.

She had no idea what the time was, there was no clock that she could see. She looked down at her faded blue and yellow hospital gown, next to her was a locker. She tried to sit up and have a better look but felt sick and dizzy, so she flopped back on to the pillow to wait for something...anything. She thought about the rose on her bedside table and the note from Clive: 'I love you'. He had *really* loved her, had been patient and kind to her all this time. Never wanting anything back from her except some love in return and what had she done? She lay crying sadly. The old lady opposite stared vacantly at her, chewing her gums, miles away.

* * *

Clive opened the door and caught the answer-phone light flashing by the telephone. It was a message from Emma Calvert: could Stella call her to make another appointment when convenient. A second message was empty, just the telephone number. That was from this morning – just before he'd arrived, he realised. He played it again; it wasn't a code he recognised. Out of interest he dialled it and waited.

'Hello, Fish and Fly Hotel, can I help you?'

Clive was taken aback a bit. It must be where Stella had gone. Why were they phoning here when she was there?

'Oh hello, ah, Clive Seaward here, a friend of Stella's, I think she's staying with you, not to worry, I was just trying her messages that's all, I –'

The voice became anxious.

'Did you say Stella? Stella Maitland? Please, stay there. Don't go. Hang on a minute I must fetch Mick or Trina. Don't go.'

The receiver went down with a clatter. What on earth had happened?

'Hello, is that Clive Seaward did you say? This is Trina here, Trina Boutwood from the Fish and Fly. Stella was rushed to hospital this morning. She tried to kill herself and very nearly succeeded. She's at the Chawlton Royal Infirmary, in the Jago wing, the psychiatric wing. We were trying to track someone down and called her home number by mistake. We're not sure *who* to call. Her mobile was in her bag and went to the hospital with her. We'd go and see her but we're so busy here with this angling competition. Could you go and see her, or tell someone about it? I think she'd said something to Mick about her doctor coming, but no one has yet.'

Shaken, Clive was decisive.

'I'll go, that's no problem, don't worry, I'll give them a call at the hospital and see what the position is. Thank you, don't worry.'

Searching wildly for the telephone directory he found it, under a pile of unopened letters and papers. He dialled the hospital, reaching the Jago Wing eventually and spoke to a nurse.

'Hello, I'm Clive Seaward. I'm calling about Stella Maitland. I'm not a relative, but a close friend. Is it possible to speak to her at all, can you tell me what the position is?'

'Stella's here in Parker Ward and doing quite well. We have her under sedation but I can let you speak to her if you wish?'

'Yes please, could you? Thanks.' He could feel his heart thumping.

The nurse wheeled the telephone through to the ward and plugged the jack in the socket above the bed.

'Call for you, Stella, Clive Seaward. Here you are...' She handed over the receiver.

'Hello? Clive?' She felt so dizzy and confused. She listened. There was nothing so she tried again. 'Hello Clive, is that you?'

He swallowed hard. 'Hello Stella, you silly girl, what *have* you been up to?'

She smiled, he didn't sound cross any more.

'Clive, Clive, I want to see you please!'

'I'm coming to see you right now, as soon as I can get there. Just forget everything and concentrate on getting better for me, will you? Don't worry about anything else, just get better for me, that's a good girl and remember I love you.'

Stella gripped the phone. 'I love you too, Clive!'

'Hmm, *really* this time?'

'Yes, really! Thank you *so* much for the little note and the rose. I'll see you soon, lots of love.'

'Lots of love Stella, I'll see you soon!'

Clive hung up with a big grin. Everything was all right after all. Dashing upstairs he found the note and rose where he'd left it. He picked up a pen adding: 'To Stella, my sweet rose', put the note in his pocket and carried the flower in his hand. He nipped downstairs again, climbed into the car, placing the rose on the passenger seat and started the engine.

The hospital was on the outskirts of Chawlton, some miles outside Dreighton, and smaller than the General, without an accident and emergency department, but with an on-site psychiatric unit. An obvious choice, he supposed, for Stella. He wondered how bad she was. How long she'd have to stay there. It was a bit of a trek, but worth it if it was going to help her and bring her back to him. About half a mile before you got there, was a notorious bit of road: straight enough to get a bit of speed up, but not quite long enough to sustain it safely. The limit was forty there, but without any cameras, it was hardly ever heeded. About halfway along it, sticking to forty, he was startled to see a flash of red shooting towards him on the wrong side if the road. The car had overtaken a Volvo which was doing a sedate thirty-five or less. Clive hit the brakes hard. Then the horn and flashed his lights.

Three hours later, Stella was still waiting. How long it would take him to reach her? Surely he'd have made it by now? Each time the doors opened she looked up, hoping, but was disappointed. At four o'clock she pressed her buzzer. It was a different nurse, busy, with no time to go running around after patients' visitors who hadn't shown up, *especially when the patient had brought their confinement there upon themselves,* making that view clear; then she saw the nurse who'd brought her the telephone and called her. The first nurse trotted off, rolling her eyes.

'Please,' Stella began, 'you kindly brought me the telephone this morning, but the caller hasn't come and I'm very worried. He promised he'd be here as soon as he could. I've got his mobile number, but can't reach or use my phone. Clive Seaward, do you remember? I told him I was here, but he may've got muddled and gone to the accident and emergency at Dreighton General by mistake, is there any way you could find out for me? I don't want to be a nuisance, but I know he'd be coming if he said he was.'

The nurse gently squeezed her shoulder.

'Don't worry my lovey. I'll see what I can do. I'll be back in a moment, don't get upset we'll get it sorted. Let's just have a look at your chart.' She removed the board from the foot of the bed and opened the medication sheet, checking her fob-watch. 'It's time for some medication, it hasn't been marked you've received it. I'll get that sorted and try and track your friend down, all right my sweet? I won't be long.' She smiled, removing the sheet of paper.

Stella smiled, she seemed nice. She wished she could reach the box of tissues on her locker, her nose was running. Clive would help her. She'd soon be out of here with his help. She shut her eyes, relaxing now, and dozed. The sound of the curtain being pulled round her bed and hushed voices woke her. She looked for Clive but he wasn't there. Just the same nurse and a man she hadn't seen before, an ID tag hanging round his neck on a ribbon.

She felt nervous; he was holding a syringe. The nurse appeared worried and sat on her bed. She took the tips of Stella's fingers gently. Something was wrong.

'What's happened,' she asked, agitated, 'where's Clive?'

'I called the General and spoke to the sister in the accident and emergency.' She was calm. 'They were very busy, but I've got some news for you.' She glanced up at the man standing the other side of the bed, poised with the syringe, his face bland. 'They were dealing with an RTA, a road traffic accident. There'd been a collision on the Chawlton Straight, three vehicles were involved and one of them was driven by your friend Mr. Seaward.' The doctor sat down on the bed, close to Stella as the nurse continued. 'The driver of a Volvo survived with injuries, but there were two fatalities.' She took a breath and squeezed Stella's fingertips, 'one of them unfortunately being your friend Clive. I'm so sorry, my sweetheart, *so* sorry, dear.'

'No! *No Noooooo!*'

Stella opened her mouth, trying to get her breath, choked, then tried again. The doctor lifted the sleeve of her gown, wiped a quick swab and injected her vein smoothly and swiftly. He nodded to the nurse before leaving, swishing the curtain closed behind him.

Stella flopped back, trying to focus on the nurse's face, but everything was fuzzy and numb, her arms weren't sore and nothing hurt at all. Too much champagne, was it? Her thoughts were all jumbled. She didn't know where she was, didn't care really.

Waiting until Stella had closed her eyes and was breathing regularly; the nurse marked the chart, checked her watch and left quietly, keeping the curtain pulled.

Epilogue

James Colshall slowed a little, indicated left, and then pulled sharply in to the lay-by exactly a quarter of a mile after the blue sign and stopped. He'd studied the rather sketchy map, printed at a wonky angle on the reverse side of the letter from Emma and was now stuck. After taking him twice round the same roundabout, so, it seemed, was his SatNav. He'd call the number on it, a mobile. He prayed it wouldn't be voicemail. He was fed up. It wasn't.

'Oh hi, yes, it's James. Look, I'm in a lay-by on the A362 and I can't seem to find the right exit on the Chawlton roundabout to bring me to Bickleigh House – is that you Emma?' Suddenly wondering if the person on the other end of the line was wondering who *he* was.

'Hi James, yes it's me. Oh dear, sorry! It can be a bit confusing! (*She could say that again*). Actually, it's the third exit with the local sign to Knaresborough you need. After a quarter of a mile or so there's a sign to Sutton Cranfield, follow that, then just after a small bridge you'll see a large sign on your left saying Bickleigh House and a drive between two brick pillars. Turn in there, over the cattle grid and on for about half a mile and you'll see the House. Turn round from where you are now heading back to the roundabout and it's only another fifteen minutes or so. I'll look out for you in the reception area; you'll just be in time for lunch.

'Great, thanks! I could certainly do with some! I left London at seven this morning, grabbed a quick coffee at some Services and haven't eaten a thing since. See you soon, oh and just one last thing how *is* Stella today?'

'Not bad; she's been writing something all morning, repeating it over and over. A friend of hers Clive Seaward, I mentioned him to you in our discussions I think, he died in a car accident and it really upset her, just as she was making some real progress. I think, *hope,* your visit's going to cheer her up a bit. See you soon, 'bye!'

James slipped the phone back in his pocket and hoped the same thing.

* * *

He'd known Emma since Med. School and although they'd dated and enjoyed each other's company, there was never that extra ingredient '*x*' which might have persuaded him to propose marriage. Now at fifty-four, rich and single, he had time *and* money to invest in whatever project took his fancy, and initially (after receiving the notes on Stella from Emma) that's what she'd been: a project. Now he was more and more involved, keen for it to be on a more personal level. He'd cope with any ethical problems later. Hearing of the death of someone who'd obviously meant a very great deal to her would have been another set-back. He very much hoped *some* of that pain he could alleviate. Anyway, he was nearly there now, a quick lunch with Emma and catch up, and then he'd go and see her.

* * *

'There's still so much we *don't* know yet, but heaps of TLC and then she'll be fine I'm sure.' She beamed at him. She wore a trim black trouser suit and her shining hair in a ponytail clip with fronds bouncing as she spoke. 'I'm so glad you've come today! Do you want pudding or a coffee, or shall we be getting along? Have you arranged anywhere to stay tonight?' she asked,' I take it you won't be driving back to London after the visit.'

He shook his head. 'No I won't, I found a bed and breakfast

place on the 'net, in Sutton Cranfield: Mill House. It looked quite nice. I'm staying three nights so I'll be able to follow up the visits for a couple of days, providing all goes well that is.'

Emma was convinced. 'Oh I'm sure it will. That's great! I know where you are, it's very comfortable, ideal in fact.' They walked down a carpeted corridor. 'She's just along here. I'll pop in first, make sure everything's okay, then introduce you and leave you to it. While you're with her I'll nip back to the office and fetch the flowers and fruit, then you can give them to her, does that sound all right?'

James agreed, nodding, 'Yes absolutely, after you!'

'Stella Maitland' was printed on a small card within a brass surround, attached to the door. Emma knocked twice and entered. Stella was sitting in an arm chair by the window, looking out at the azure blue sky and turned as Emma walked in, her face blank.

She was brisk but kind. 'Hello Stella! I have your visitor. I'll bring him in, if that's all right and you can show him what you've been writing about, have a chat together. Are you feeling up to it?'

Stella nodded. Nothing was real anymore and one visit was much like another. She just wanted to write; get her ordeals out of her system. Whatever this visitor wanted, he'd be interested in her writing or he wouldn't, it didn't really matter. She ran her fingers through her hair and attempted a smile, as Emma ushered him in. First impressions were reassuring. He was neither handsome nor plain, but somewhere in between, approachable. He was dressed well, she noticed, a very smart suit and just a hint of aftershave that wasn't too powerful. His eyes were kind and honest. His smile travelled up to meet them and remained there, sincere. He was speaking gently but firmly, with a kind voice.

'Stella, my name's James. I've come to visit you to see how you are. I know a bit about you from Emma. She told me you've been writing something today, would you let me see what it is? Please? Will you let me? I'd like to see what you've put. Can you show it to me?'

Stella reached for the writing pad sitting on the coffee table next to her. It was lined and covered with her untidy scrawl. She passed it over and he began to read:

'Will you be staying with us do you think Rose? You will never, you couldn't ever be replaced'

Rose reflected, it wasn't so long ago but it seemed as if an age had passed. To smell the scent of pines; a tin of Waitrose sardines in olive oil (it had to be olive oil, not sunflower oil) – hearing the tune 'I'm getting sentimental over you.' Rose smiled, sighed.

'I don't know. The funeral's tomorrow; let me get through that, then we'll see; I'll be in touch, I just don't know, sorry.'

Michelle Collette Dubois smiled. She knew 'Rose'. 'Rose' would be back: she needed the sex; she would be hurt again; emotionally involved again. Suffer once more the vagaries' of men's fertile, carnal imaginations and enjoy it all over again. Revel in the naughtiness, the badness, the defilement of it. Another man, anxious for the Rose Membership, promising those with the means 'everything possible': the ultimate in sexual satisfaction (and could deliver) would entice 'Rose' once more and she would be unable to resist the thrill of being completely, physically and emotionally owned, desired above all others. An old family phrase sprung into her mind: 'That was a close one, Daddy!' – It certainly had been but no, Rose would return, given a few months, as good if not better. Madam Dubois let the door close and picked up the telephone: 'Je Ne Sais Quoi' can I help you?' NO! NO! NO! NO!'

James read the 'no's down to the bottom of the page and lifted the sheet. More 'no's on the next page too. He looked at Stella, perplexed. She returned his stare with a level gaze.

James spoke quietly. 'Who's "Rose" Stella?"

Replying, her voice was weak. 'Me; I'm Rose, no, *was* Rose!'

James ventured a little further.

'Okay, so who's "Madam Dubois" then?'

Frowning slightly, irritated, she continued. 'Madam Dubois is me as well: I'm Rose *and* Madam Dubois. I *was!*' she corrected, 'But not now! That's all over now. But I don't know how to go on or what to do next. Who are you exactly? Do you work here?'

'My name's James Colshall. My mother–'

She didn't let him get any further. 'I know who your *mother* is! She lived with *Douglas Spencer!*' Spitting the name out, 'What do you want with *me*? Why've you come? To have a good gawp? Like some sort of freak'!

She was furious. He sat back in his chair, both serious and concerned.

'No, Stella, I haven't come to gawp at you,' his tone was quiet but not patronising, 'you're not a freak. I've been following your progress with Emma. She told me about you without knowing, initially, that I was involved in a roundabout way, by being my mother's son.' He smiled in irony. 'I'm sure that right now, the *last* thing you want to hear is a man telling you that they *care* about you? Your trust has run out and I can't blame you. But if you can try just a little, to accept me being here, listening to you, I'd be happy.'

He paused a while, the anger was draining from her features. He drew his bottom lip between his teeth, wondering. 'It may seem a silly question, because obviously it'd be better if you were well and not here at all, but is it comfortable here for you? Do you have everything you feel you need at the moment? Is there anything, perhaps, you haven't got here that you'd *like*?'

Stella thought about this. Her face crumpled and tears rolled down her cheeks. Swallowing, she composed herself and spoke very quietly. So quietly he had to lean forward to hear.

'My dog, my dog Jeeves; I miss him.'

James took a chance and softly held her hand. She didn't resist.

'Well, if I told you that he's fine, that I could take you to see him, would you like that?'

For a minute, Stella thought she was dreaming. That it must be the tablets.

'Where is he?'

Holding her hand, stroking it, he spoke very gently.

'He's been staying with your cleaner, Cathy, they're coming over tomorrow. I'll go and meet them and we'll come and see you, all of us, Jeeves, Cathy and me, how about it? Would that be good? Maybe go for a short walk in the grounds? I think Jeeves would like that. And to see you – I think he'd like that very much.'

* * *

Emma collected Stella's cardigan.

'I think you might need this, it's fresher than yesterday. James has just called. They'll be here any minute. Let's go down and wait for them, yeah?'

Slipping the cardigan on, Stella followed Emma.

'I feel a bit nervous now, just a bit.'

She took her arm. 'You *will* feel a bit anxious, maybe, but it'll pass. Out we go!'

She waited, looking. In the distance, across the grass, a little shape was getting bigger, running towards her, his signature ears flapping in the wind. Following behind she saw two figures, James and Cathy. Sinking to her knees, she called her dog. Jeeves was ecstatic; licking, yapping and wagging his tail. James grinned.

'I think he's quite pleased to see you, don't you?'

Stella fought him off gently, stroking his ears, and then held his wagging tail.

'I had a tiger by the tail, James, and I couldn't let go. I daren't let go!'

He pulled her to her feet. 'Up you come, one thing at a time, Stella, one *day* at a time, okay? And you can let go of the tiger. Here,' offering it again, 'how about my thumb? Hold that instead. Do you want to?'

Stella looked into the eyes of this kind man; *this quite attractive man, now she came to think about it.*

'Yes, yes I *do*. Can I *keep* holding it?'

He pulled a face. 'Ooh, I should think so! I'd say there's a fairly good chance, but right now, I don't know about you lot,' looking at Emma and Cathy, 'but I could murder a cup of tea! Let's find this accommodation and Cathy can put the kettle on.'

Reaching down to Jeeves, he gave him a pat, and then looked at Stella.

'Come on! Race you back! Last one has the cracked mug!'

They took off towards the house across the damp grass, autumn was approaching.

Cathy turned to Emma. 'I think she's going to be all right now, don't you?'

Emma smiled. 'I reckon so, James is a good man. She deserves him and he'll always be there for her. Yeah, I think she'll be just fine. Come on though, it's now either you or me for the cracked mug!'

Cathy hung back. 'Maybe just let them have a few minutes together?'

'OK, good plan, let's walk. But now I think they'll have all the time in the world.